DIVINE RIGHT

DIVINE RIGHT

EMPRESS BOOK THREE

J. V. Simms

Podium

DIVINE RIGHT

Max Gets the Axe!

The minotaur roared aggressively and brought his club down in a vicious forward swing that would have crushed the armored warrior into paste if not for his shield and incredible physical strength. In return, the warrior gave a battle shout of his own and thrust his sword forward, stabbing the monster in his chest and causing it to cry out in pain.

"Get behind it, Ladelle!" Keith the warrior (no relation) shouted to the red-robed girl who stood beside him. "You can't face him together with me like this! You have to attack from range so I can keep his attention focused on me!"

"Shut up, idiot!" Ladelle said sharply in reply. "*I'm* the one who hired you, so don't tell me how to perform my role!"

"This is a *dungeon*, Ladelle! If you can't follow orders, you're a liability that'll get you or someone else hurt!" warned Keith as he ran clockwise, attempting to face the minotaur away from the mage so that its attacks wouldn't reach her.

Oh, boy! Ladelle didn't like that at all! She was a pretty little thing with short, stylishly cut platinum hair and a pair of gold-rimmed glasses over her pert nose. It was a good look for her—I really dug it! Too bad she was one of those stereotypes you can't help but come across in a fantasy world like this. A cocky noble who looked down on others due to their lower birth.

Even worse, she was a fire mage! In gaming terminology, Ladelle was the kind of clueless ranged attacker who ruined pickup games by trying to make the group's tank go faster to suit her pace, even though she wasn't strong enough to kill enemies quickly. For a professional defender like Keith (no relation), she was a nightmare! I wondered if he and his companions regretted accepting her as a client?

"I SAID stop telling me what to do!" Ladelle said. "Watch this! Behold magic so profound, a mere mercenary like you should consider himself blessed to bear witness to it! *Oh, light of the sun, shine upon me with resplendent glory! Bring victory to my cause and ruin to my foe!* [**Nova Lance**] level 4!"

A beam of golden light shot forth from her hand and speared through the minotaur, killing it instantly! Which would normally be great and a thing worth celebrating, but the problem was that a level four spell like that was so powerful that after punching through the minotaur, it kept on shooting forward and hit the next group of monsters farther down the corridor, killing a hapless little goblin and alerting the rest of them to danger.

Uh-oh! Now we had *two* fresh minotaurs to deal with, as well as two angry-looking hobgoblins who looked like they wanted to avenge their friend. Keith's eyes widened in despair, while Ladelle began jumping for joy at her success.

Oh, did I mention that Ladelle was one of those mages who also couldn't control her threat? Hell, she didn't even bother trying! "See what I can do? I *told* you I could take care of him!" she said smugly to Keith, not yet aware of the bloodthirsty group of monsters racing straight for her, intent on introducing her to group dynamics that she probably wouldn't enjoy.

Heh, I liked this kid. She was a *riot*!

Hey, guys! What's cracking? Max is doing a *dungeon*! Wooooo! Isn't that cool? It is, isn't it?

Yes, a dungeon crawl! The primary passion of any young man's Romantic (in the chivalric sense of the word) pursuit! Here in this new and magical world, we were working together to conquer a dungeon! A deadly labyrinth filled with traps and dangerous monsters that could only be overcome by teamwork and comradery! Oh, the tears of joy and the cries of frustration we'd share as we gradually made our way to the climax of this foreboding place, the Dungeon Lord's lair!

Once there, our skills and commitment to each other would be put to the ultimate test as we challenged the boss to mortal combat for the right to claim the treasures of this dire realm! Oh, the wonderous elation we'd feel upon surviving our campaign! The unmatchable feeling of knowing we were not only winners, but *friends*!

"Ladelle, you stupid noble bitch, I swear if we live through this, I'm going to break your jaw!" shouted Jera the ranger as she nocked an arrow and sent it flying at one of the two new minotaurs, where it embedded itself harmlessly in its thick hide.

"Damn it," she swore, before reaching for another arrow.

Okay, so maybe not so much with the *friends* part?

"Girl fight! I want front-row seats!" laughed Jaxon the thief as he danced between the hobgoblins and lashed out with his poisoned daggers. Like me, Jaxon didn't take any of this stuff too seriously and seemed primarily to be along for the ride.

Of course, he had the midtier stealth ability **[Cloak of Shadows]** that allowed him to disappear from view at will, without even leaving a scent that animals could follow. So out of all of them, he had the highest chance of surviving whatever nonsense Ladelle's incompetence could spring upon the group.

Confidence is nice.

"Oh, go disarm a trap, you obnoxious pervert!" seethed Jera. She turned her attention from the minotaurs to the hobgoblins and managed to put an arrow through one of their eyes. "Yes!" she cheered, before screaming in pain when the enraged minotaur she'd attacked earlier charged at her and gored her into a wall.

"Shit!" Keith (no relation) swore, before bellowing his **[Challenging Cry]** and drawing the attention of all four monsters on himself. "**[Adamantine Defense]**! Guys, I'm indestructible for the next twelve seconds, you'd better do something or we're all dead!" he declared.

"Just kill them all! By the gods, you're all so *incompetent!*" Ladelle complained.

"If I die, make sure she follows after me, *please!*" Jera groaned from the floor.

"Hahaha! Jeez, it might be time to take off . . ." Jaxon said as he began gradually backing away from the melee.

"Daniel! Daniel, please, is there anything you can do?" Keith called out.

"Yeah, Daniel, do something! You've got a trick or two hidden up your sleeves, right?" Jaxon asked.

Uh, who were these guys talking to? I looked around the massive dungeon corridor but saw no one else with us.

"DANIEL!" Ladelle yelled. "Pay attention to us, you idiot!"

Wait, had she *really* just called *me* an idiot? Y'know, as amusing as I found her, I wasn't willing to put up with anyone's personal abuse. I was about to show Ladelle just how big the mistake she'd made was when the realization of who they meant suddenly dawned on me.

"Oh, *I'm* Daniel! Jeez, sorry, gang! Aliases get so hard to keep track of!" I apologized sheepishly.

"Four seconds left!" Keith (no relation) shouted. His normally calm voice was starting to sound just a tiny bit strained with fear. Not that I could blame him.

"If we die, it's all your fault!" Ladelle shouted at me.

"Huh. Well, I guess we shouldn't die, then," I said to her.

I turned toward the enemies and gestured at them dramatically. "**[Dominate Minion]** times five," I said to them. I felt a nice little sensation like glass bulbs breaking on a sidewalk when I felt their mental resistances shatter before my will. Their faces slackened and their shoulders drooped in unison as I seized control of their minds.

[Dominate Minion] was one of my favorite skills. It was *supposed* to only allow me to completely control servants and pets, but thanks to my **[Divinity]** trait, I could use it outside of its intended purpose. **[Divinity]** also gave me massive bonuses when I used my skills against mortal beings, which was pretty much everyone in the world who wasn't a god, which I happened to be. A baby god, anyway.

As a result, even though I was *technically* the weakest member of the party, being level twenty-one while everyone else was between levels twenty-four and twenty-five and the monsters themselves ranged from twenty-seven to thirty, I didn't fear anything in this place. Honestly, I could have cleared it out by myself, but being around these guys and watching them bicker and tear each other down was *way* too entertaining!

"All righty, guys," I said happily to my new group of mind-controlled monsters. "Kill each other, then kill yourselves."

At once, the monsters went at it, attacking each other furiously and with wild abandon. The hobgoblins managed to bring one minotaur down by severing the tendons in its legs and then swarming it, but that gave the other minotaur opportunities to stomp them all into bloody mush as they were frenziedly stabbing their prone victim.

Once they were dealt with, he gripped the head of his dying friend and then ripped it clean off his neck with one titanic heave. After that awesome display, he began stabbing himself in the throat with the decapitated minotaur's horns until he collapsed and bled out.

"Ha! Wild show, right?" I said gleefully to Jaxon.

"Uh, sure. Better them than us, I s'pose," Jaxon said with a shrug.

"Daniel! Stay focused, Jera's still hurt," Keith (no relation) said to me as he knelt beside the injured ranger.

"Uh, so what?" I replied.

"Stop messing around. You're the healer!" admonished Keith.

Oh, that's right. I was supposed to be the healer. Whoops! Aliases, lies, exaggerations—man, it could be tough keeping track of things. I usually didn't bother. I was glad my party members were doing that for me.

I know what you're thinking, by the way. Me? Max? A healer. Say *wuuuuuut?*

Hey, I'll have you know that I can do anything I put my mind to! And even though I would have excelled in any team role I chose to perform, the undeniable fact was that adventurers who could mend their companions were rare and quite valued. It made it much easier for me to find parties in this new gig, by playing sawbones. Besides, there was an important aspect of being a healer that appealed to my unique sensibilities.

Healers decided who lived or *died.*

I'm sure you can see why I enjoyed doing it.

* * *

Jera groaned in pain as I knelt beside her and examined her wounded shoulder. That minotaur had left her with quite the injury! His horn had punched straight through to her back. If I wanted, I could have fit three fingers inside her.

Inside her *wound*, that was.

Don't be a pervert.

"Can you do anything for her?" Keith asked nervously. Hmmm. It seemed he was a little soft on the girl. Heh, heh, young love.

"Yeah, sure, of course. Because I'm a *healer*. We're totally great at this sort of thing. Healing, that is," I said assuredly.

Truthfully, I considered myself more of an *unhealer*. It was far easier taking people apart than it was putting them back together. (More satisfying too.) It's interesting to think about; in dungeons, in order to proceed with the utmost efficiency, you had to heal people quickly. It didn't matter how devastating their injuries were, you had to get them on their feet as soon as possible, or the group would be in danger.

Whereas with *murder*, it was so much better to take your sweet time and go slowly. You could miss out on so much pleasure if you were in a rush. The feelings involved—the sensations, the quiet, desperate intimacy—that was something best experienced at a leisurely pace.

The only thing these two approaches to life had in common was that you had to be an absolute *sadist* to take enjoyment in either task.

Luckily for Jera, sadism was something I had in *spades*.

"*Heeeey*, Jera," I whispered in her ear while softly brushing back her hair. "Don't hate me, please, but this is going to hurt *so* badly. It's for your own good, though, okay? You can scream if you'd like. I won't think less of you."

After saying that, I next plunged my hand into her chest and seized her heart.

"WHAT THE FUCK?!" bellowed Keith. Even Ladelle was struck dumb by the sight of what I'd done. Jaxon didn't say anything, but his eyes were wide. Loudest of all, though, was Jera, as she screeched like an owlet caught up in a fishing line. I didn't hold her reaction against her in the slightest. After all, some psycho was holding her heart!

"*Relaaaax*, everyone, this is all part of the process," I said to them calmly. "The techniques of my school of healing require that I transform negative energy into a positive wave of recovery. In other words, the more pain she feels, the more easily I can mend her wounds."

"I've *never* heard of magic like that!" Ladelle said doubtfully.

"You're young, mistress. There's much in the world you've yet to see," I responded sagely.

I was completely bullshitting them, of course. I was holding Jera's heart because feeling it pumping and squirming in my grasp was so *weird*! Honestly, the closest I can come to describing the sensation was that it felt like holding a fat toad. Have you ever caught a toad before? I loved doing that when I was a kid! Me and my brother would do it for hours, it was so fun—

Wait, what? Me and my *who*?

"AHHHHHHHHHH!!" screamed Jera as tears of pain poured from her closed eyes.

Jeez, *that* was rude! She totally derailed my train of thought. What had I just been thinking of? Nuts, it was gone! Thanks so much, Jera! *Jera the drama queen!* You can't even handle a little playfully grievous injury on the road to recovery, can you? You call yourself an adventurer? What a wimp! What had I ever done to deserve such poor treatment from you?

And now everyone else was starting to look at me with anger and suspicion. Ugh, it was time to end this little production.

My mood now slightly soured, I used **[Rooting]** to inject some of my blood into Jera's body. Then I used **[Dominate Minion]** to force my blood cells to activate **[Troll Regeneration]**, which began healing all her injuries immediately. Her shoulder wound was closed in an instant, as was her chest wound once I removed my hand. I even used **[Rooting]** to microbind the tears in her clothing.

The blood that now coated my hand was the only evidence that anything had ever happened to the ranger. I stared at it, transfixed and satisfied. Blood looks so beautiful no matter where you see it. It's gorgeous under bright sunlight, mesmerizing under the light of the moon, but even in the murky lighting of this torchlit corridor, it delighted me.

I really wanted to rub my hand over my face while Jera's blood was still warm, but that wouldn't be a good idea. My party members would only put up with my antics to a certain extent. Besides, if I indulged too much in playing, I might lose control of myself and kill them all.

I didn't want to do that. They were too much fun to be around!

So, instead of doing that, I poured a little water on my hand and cleaned it with a cloth. "All better, ranger! How do you feel?"

"How do I *feel?*" Jera asked in a hostile tone of voice. "I *feel* like kicking your ass all the way to the next continent, you bastard—huh?" she said as the effects of the troll blood kicked in. Trolls were amazing, hardy creatures. Not only could they heal from practically any injury, but their blood was loaded with endorphins that made them impervious to pain as well.

The troll blood *my* body generated had been taken from a forest lord, a rare elite boss I'd slain all the way back in chapter four of the previous book in my series.

(Look at me being meta!)

Basically, that meant Jera was now loaded up on the *good shit*.

Her cheeks flushed with enjoyment when I suddenly slapped her face, as her body automatically transformed what she felt from pain into pleasure. The unexpected sensation left her feeling confused, which I found hilarious.

"Hey!" Keith yelled angrily. He took a step toward me before stopping when Jera held up a hand to let me explain myself.

"What did you do to me?" she asked in confusion.

"Think of it as a buff," I informed her. "You're now twice as strong and fast as you were, and any injury you receive for the next few hours will heal right away. Best of all, you can't feel any pain! That's the sort of incredible service you can't get from any silly temple cleric."

"And this will last for *hours?*" she asked me in wonder.

"Yeppers!" I said perkily.

That was another lie, of course. I'd basically mutated her body on the cellular level, but once we were done here, I'd deactivate the troll blood I'd infused her with. I couldn't have people running around claiming I was permanently empowering them. That'd draw the attention of *actual* healers, who could only give temporary buffs.

That was the sort of attention that I didn't need. Those jealous clerics would definitely snitch on me to their patron gods, who in turn would realize what I was and then come after me personally.

I may have been getting stronger every day, but I was still nowhere near ready for a divine duel. My leveling stats didn't matter much against earthly beings, but they were *VERY* much a factor in a godly confrontation. A senior god with a higher level than mine would swat me like a fly. And then he'd eat me and absorb all my powers.

Something like that would have happened ages ago too, but luckily for me, I was blind to the sight of this world's pantheon. I could only draw their attention if I did something *really* egregious, but so far, outside of wiping out an entire nation and drawing the ire of the elemental embodiment of the earth itself, I'd been doing a *pretty* good job of lying low. Unless you counted all those annoying bandits on the road I randomly killed by disguising myself as a monster called "Max the Head Chopper."

(Well, *most* of them had been bandits, anyway. The rest had just been rude. I hate it when people are rude to me.)

Oh, and then there was that tribe of werewolves I'd recently slaughtered for reasons I couldn't quite recall. (Man, those guys had *sucked.* They couldn't even transform from men to wolves. They were total wannabes!) Oh, and now that I thought about it, hadn't I also recently enraged a family of ancient vampires by interfering with their vengeance against the people who had tortured their progenitor for hundreds of years?

Huh.

Maybe I wasn't doing such a great job of keeping my head down after all?

Oh, well. Nothing I could do about that now. I just had to live in the moment.

It's funny, though; my actions as the Head Chopper had earned me an unexpected new skill: [**Notorious**].

[**Notorious**]: Rank A. *The more feared you are, the less effective resistances against your skills become.*

It sounded kind of cool, but wasn't it a little redundant considering my [**Divinity**] trait pretty much let me ignore resistances anyway? This was something I'd have to experiment with later. I was good at finding uses for my abilities beyond what was printed on the label.

"Daniel, come on! What are you standing around for?" Ladelle called out to me.

I looked up and saw my party had advanced into the next area of the dungeon without me.

Whoops! Heh, it was weird working with a group, sometimes. As the main character, I often dwelt on my past experiences and ruminated on the paths I should take while evaluating my numerous incredible abilities, which was entertaining for the people reading my story since it allowed me to easily share my perspective with them as they figuratively inserted themselves into my narrative and lived out their vicarious fantasies through my quirky adventures.

But to the people who *weren't* aware of my narration, it apparently meant that I spent a lot of time standing around, silently staring blankly into space, which weirded them out considerably. It would have been nice if Libby had warned me that I did that.

Man, she'd been useless.

"Coming!" I called back while hurrying after them. Once I caught up, I whistled in appreciation at the massive twin-doored entrance that stood before us.

"Is that what I think it is?" I asked.

"Without a doubt," answered Jaxon.

We now stood before the entrance to the Dungeon Lord's lair.

CHAPTER ONE

The Proposal

The air was still heavy with winter's chill when Everly appeared before the king of Winstead to present her terms.

Everly was amused by the naked hostility of the sentries who guarded the entrance to the king's throne room. Neutral expressions were surely expected on the faces of those who guarded royalty. These two, however, burned with hatred and killing intent, and they weren't shy about projecting it her way. It didn't seem very professional at all. The soldiers who watched over the gates of Buckingham Palace on Earth would put them to shame.

Everly was about to comment on their lack of self-discipline when she suddenly recognized one of them, a surly, black-bearded man dressed in gray armor who wielded a saber in each hand. A moment later, she also remembered the younger one who stood at his left. These two weren't mere guard dogs. They were sword kings.

"Uh, Gregoth the Roaring Wind and Kenner the Last Sight, right?" she asked them politely. "I think we met when I was sieging Karthold. Heh, that was a *pretty* hectic day, as I recall. How've you been? I see you're still with the Ten Blades. Well, *the Six Blades*, anyway. Five and a half if you count what I did to Michus the Bold. I hope he's adjusting well to the prosthetics."

Gregor spat on the stone floor while continuing to stare balefully at her, never breaking eye contact as he did so. It was Kenner who responded to her. "We see you, Everly Skolder," the young man said grimly. "And we eagerly await the chance to avenge our fallen brothers."

"If you keep speaking to me in that tone of voice, your chance will come sooner than you think," she replied with the gentlest of smiles.

"I don't see a sword at your hip, monster," Kenner said as his hand began drifting downward to his own scabbarded weapon. "That was perhaps a foolish choice on your behalf."

Everly shrugged and gestured at her outfit. Today she wore a beautifully tailored emerald dress that paired nicely with her braided golden hair and hazel eyes, topped with a long fur coat that she wore over her shoulders. "A sword would have been overkill with this look," she explained to him. "Not that I'd need one for someone at your level of skill."

Kenner glowered fiercely at her for that flippant remark, but Everly didn't care. She was a rare talent who could use the internal energy of a swordsman known as *harada*, as well as the magic of the elements, but her skills at both dwarfed the populace of this world. Her staggering power bordered on the edge of godhood and had given her an ego to match her talents. There were few that she respected and none that she feared.

"How many lives would be spared if we killed you here and now?" Kenner asked her.

Everly shrugged her shoulders indifferently and waited to see if the warrior would try to follow through on his threat. When neither of them acted, she smiled again and walked past them through the corridor they guarded.

A fat white rat wearing a necktie, a bowler cap, and a silver monocle climbed out of her coat pocket and scrambled up her arm to perch on her shoulder. He yawned and began pawing away at his whiskers before asking, "How come you didn't rip that punk's head off, boss?"

"Because he's about to become one of my loyal subjects, Matty," Everly explained to him. "His anger was just grief over being unable to protect his friends, so he wanted to vent at me a little. We can't blame him for that, now, can we?"

Matty gave it a moment's thought, then shook his head dismissively. "Nah, he was just being a punk. Trying to look tough in front of his pal. You should have gutted him on the spot. Next time, let me do it. Colostomy bags teach respect."

"Matty, you're incorrigible," Everly said fondly, before giving him a gentle scratch beneath his chin. The rat's back leg began thumping on her shoulder in approval.

Matty, originally named Ratty, was the recently created owner and operator of Everly's personal dimension of torture, the rat room. There he led an enormous gang of sentient rats in inflicting unimaginable horrors on the various people who Everly and her associates wanted to see suffer more than they wanted them dead. Because he did such a splendid job and had such a charmingly hostile personality to everyone other than herself or Titania, Everly had taken a shine to him and promoted him to the role of her chief bodyguard.

It wasn't a position that *needed* to be filled, but it made Everly's followers feel better knowing that she always had backup with her. Carter, her chief attendant, insisted that she needed to take more of a hands-off approach in dealing with *the rabble* now that she had openly declared herself the Empress of the world; Everly had to admit that the goblin had a point. Besides, when it came to dispensing horrific death in the blink of an eye, Matty was second only to herself. To put it mildly, he was a *vicious* little rat bastard.

She really liked having him around.

A third guard in white-and-silver armor stood at the final door that led to the throne room. He was younger than his colleagues, but Everly felt a familiar sensation of *power* in this one that the other two lacked and that made her curious about him. Everly was a tall woman who stood nearly six feet high, a height the guard matched. His hair and facial features weren't entirely dissimilar to her own. In fact, he looked quite a bit like her half sister, Claudia, and her father . . .

Ah. So, this was where he'd been.

"Caleb Vae-es Belsar, as I live and breathe," she said to her half brother.

"It's an odd feeling to be recognized by a stranger," he replied, before giving her a bow. "The king and his council await you beyond this door, Your Majesty."

"*Majesty*, eh?" Everly smirked. "So, my little brother chooses to recognize his big sister's title? It feels nice to have that settled early."

"Father assures me that it would serve my future better if I stood with you instead of against you," Caleb replied. "He's a hopeless hedonist, but his decision-making is rarely irrational."

"Does rationality preoccupy your thoughts?" Everly wondered.

"Since birth, I've been a creature of purest logic," Caleb replied. "The flames of a volatile nature hold little appeal to me."

"That has to be difficult, doesn't it?" Everly asked him. "No warmth without fire."

"I make do in the cold."

"It's strange, though," Everly said. "I can feel it in you. You share Father's gifts. How can a man who eats emotions deny himself his greatest source of power?"

"The challenge alone sustains me," Caleb said.

"I see," Everly said thoughtfully. "I want to speak with you later. Present yourself to me when my meeting with the king is concluded."

"Only if my liege permits it," Caleb said.

"King Septus doesn't matter anymore, Caleb," Everly said dismissively. "It's my face that's going to be on all the portraits and the printed currency. Remember what Dad said? Stand behind me, not before me."

"You're certainly a forceful person, aren't you, sister?" Caleb asked as he stood aside to let her pass.

"I always get what I want," she said simply. "It's the natural way of things."

"That's not the healthiest mindset to possess," he said frankly.

"You think so?" she asked him. "It's done wonders for me. Then again, I *am* a goddess in the making."

With that said, she swept past him.

Caleb. She wondered what sort of person he was. Was he kind like her sister, selfish like her father, or a fool like her eldest brother, Aiden, had been? Or was he like *her*? Someone she could at last relate to? The possibilities intrigued her and made her impatient to get this meeting over with.

"Everly Skolder, the Empress of Winstead, *self-proclaimed*, now stands before His Royal Majesty, Septus Sun Magnus, rightful ruler of this continent and the anointed light of this realm!" shouted the herald who stood in the corner of the room.

"Heya, hiya, howdy!" Everly said with a cheerful wave of her hand, while Matty crouched on her shoulder and sniffed contemptuously at the gathered nobles, warriors, and councilors who stood in the room staring ferociously at them. None more fiercely than the black-haired murderer who sat arrogantly on his golden throne, looking at her with eyes that blazed with power and suspicion.

Her eyes eagerly met his, and in that moment, it was as though no one else existed.

"So, you really dared to appear before me, girl," Septus said with a soft voice that perfectly matched the intensity of his aura. "I suspected you were insane, but I didn't expect the evidence to be so overwhelming."

All thoughts of Caleb were immediately pushed away as Everly gleefully beheld the hateful tyrant that she decided would become her future husband.

"I told you before, Septus," Everly said as she casually studied her fingernails. "If you wanted to speak with me, you only had to offer an invitation. Why it took you so long, I'll never know."

"You stand before the throne of Winstead!" shouted an outraged old man in expensive-looking robes. "How dare you speak so informally to your rightful king? Kneel and beg his forgiveness—his forgiveness—his forgiveness . . . uhhh . . ."

The old man suddenly fell onto the marbled tiles of the throne room. He landed on his face with a painful-sounding *crunch*, after which his body began to momentarily tremble before falling still. Another councilor cautiously poked his neck with a hesitant finger before shouting in a terrified voice that the other man was dead.

"You can't prove I did that," Everly quickly said.

"To arms!" shouted an enthusiastic guard. "Protect the king!"

"Are these morons being serious?" Matty asked Everly in a disbelieving voice.

"I believe they are, yeah," Everly replied in an amused tone.

"Seriously, can I just eat these chumps? They're so snack-worthy."

"*Matty*," Everly said as she gave one of his whiskers a stern flick. "Today is for negotiating. Also, we don't judge someone's value by how tasty we think they look. We're better than that."

"Heh, maybe you are, but I'm simpler than that," the rat said sadly. "I'm just a dumb rat, after all."

"Oh, hush, you," Everly said as she held Matty against her chest and began to coo at him and nudge her nose against his. Despite how much she valued the precious little thing, Matty had issues with low self-esteem. "You're not dumb, you're *wonderful*, and anyone who says otherwise is just being hurtful for no reason. Remember, only my opinion matters, and disagreement is punishable by death. Okay, little guy?"

"Okay, boss," Matt said happily. "You're always right, after all."

"That's why *I* rule and others must obey," Everly said, after giving his head one final pat.

When she looked away from her pet, Everly saw that she was now in a circle of guards standing around her, each pointing a spear in her direction. From his throne, King Septus regarded her with a raised eyebrow.

"Why were you speaking with such seriousness to that rat?" he asked curiously.

"Because he asked me for permission to kill everyone here and I had to dissuade him from doing so," answered Everly. "Matty is wonderfully loyal to me, but sometimes he expresses that loyalty in a way that causes survivors to wake up screaming in the middle of the night, fearful that he's still in the room with them. Sometimes, he still is."

"And how would a rat go about instilling that level of terror in a human being?" asked the king.

In response, Everly turned toward the guard whose cries had urged the others into action. Then she whispered the word *eat* into Matty's ear and gave the rat a gentle underhand throw in his direction. What left her hand had been an adorable, fat little rat. What landed on the guard and began screaming in murderous fury after crushing him beneath his weight . . . was not.

Instead, a massive mound of writhing muscle and sharpened bone that stood over ten feet tall towered over his prey. He lifted the squirming guard up toward his fanged maw as the other knights stood there, dumbfounded in terror. Then he began to swallow the man, headfirst.

Before he could bring his jaws together, Everly's voice cut in. "Matty? I changed my mind, sweetie."

Matty grunted in disappointment but nodded his understanding. Then he hawked his throat and spat the young guard out, sending him sliding across the floor leaving a trail of vile mucus in his wake that set him crashing against a wall. When Everly clicked her tongue at Matty, he hopped in her direction and landed in her arms, a small rat once more.

"I love you so much," Everly purred happily as Matt basked in her affection.

"Put your weapons away," King Septus ordered his guards. "It would appear that we have the numbers but lack the power."

"Wise is the king who humbles himself before the divine," Everly said approvingly.

"I doubt very much that I'm being graced with the presence of a god," Septus said. "More likely you're a mutation of some unprecedented sort. Don't be too pleased with yourself."

"Avoiding being pleased with myself has been the struggle of my life, Your Majesty," Everly said airily. "I was miraculous from birth, and time has only increased the numerous gifts that life has bestowed upon me."

"Humble too, it would seem," observed the king.

"I've never understood the point of humility." Everly shrugged. "I know it's supposedly good manners, but all it does is make those weaker and less capable feel a little better about themselves. Why should I concern myself with the feelings of the unworthy?"

As Everly spoke, she slowly approached Septus on his throne, stopping just before the steps that led to its dais.

"You must understand how I feel," she continued. "I'm hardly any worse than you are. Ever since you were a child, people have whispered in your ear that you were chosen by the gods, that your reign was anointed by heaven itself. Isn't it a national crime for a commoner to speak to you without permission?"

"A fact that hasn't slowed your approach one bit," Septus replied. "But I suppose I'm one of the weaklings that deserve no voice in your presence."

"Ah, so you know I'm baseborn," Everly smirked. "Who told you? I bet it was my father. He's such a gossipy little bitch."

"Count Marcis was very forthcoming about you in our correspondence," the king admitted with a frown. "Frankly, some of the things he described in his letters sound too farfetched to be true."

"He didn't exaggerate a single thing," Everly said. "I really am that incredible."

"He warned me that you were arrogant and emotionally unstable, and that the slightest misstep could set you off if I wasn't careful."

"THAT'S A FUCKING LIE!" Everly shrieked angrily.

"So I see," Septus said amicably.

"I'm going to have to have a long discussion with that old fool," Everly growled angrily. "God, why does he do that? I swear he likes setting me off on purpose. Is this just a dad thing? Do all dads like poking the bear? That sort of parenting just builds resentment over time! I mean, does he really think I won't kill him just because we're related? Ask Aiden how that worked out for him."

At the mention of Aiden's name, for some reason, Matty began to chuckle. Everly briefly wondered what that was about before moving on.

"My father's little jokes aside, I'm pleased to see you've become as curious about me as I've been about you," she said to the king. "I also hope you've learned *other* things about me that meet your approval."

At this, King Septus frowned deeply. "Lady Skolder, I have never been a man who has enjoyed banter. My nature is to get to the heart of the matter as quickly as possible. Whatever it is you want, just *tell* me and stop disguising your intent with coy wordplay."

"Marry me," she said flatly.

"CLEAR THE ROOM," Septus shouted.

After the astonished guards and councilors finished removing themselves from their presence, King Septus removed the golden circlet from his brow and placed it on the throne. Then he sat on the steps of the dais and rummaged through his pockets for a moment before producing a small pipe, into which he poured some suspicious-smelling dried herbs. Next, he lit it with a verbal command and inhaled deeply. As he puffed out the smoke, he visibly relaxed, as though it had just relieved him of a good deal of mental strain. Then he offered the pipe to Everly.

"Eh?" he said.

Everly studied the offered pipe carefully, then shrugged and accepted it. One deep puff later, she felt as though her thoughts had drilled little holes throughout the top of her skull and had escaped into the air so that they could dance throughout the room in the form of giggling rainbows. It was nice.

"What the hell *is* this?" Everly laughed as she took a seat on the steps beside him.

"I have no idea. It's expensive, though, and I always want more of it," Septus replied in a surprisingly light tone of voice.

"Who's your supplier?" she asked him.

"The dobs? Nobs? Some little gang based out on the docks. I'm told they're growing more powerful by the day. With a product as refined as this, it's no wonder."

"The Royal Bay Hobbs?" asked Everly.

"Oh, yes, that's them. They're the ones." Septus nodded. "How do you know of them?"

"I'm very familiar with their leader," Everly replied. "She's like a piece of my own heart."

"Ah, small world, then." Septus nodded before taking another puff from the pipe. "I'm probably going to have to outlaw this substance. It brings you too much pleasure without any negative, lingering effects. The temple wouldn't like that."

"Didn't I crush the temple months ago?" Everly asked, after sampling the pipe again. "I remember a lot of dead priests and knights. I'm pretty sure I got one of those paladins too. I can't remember which one. He sure screamed a lot."

"Meh, you can't destroy a faith just by burning down its buildings. It's as useless as cutting off a mole that's already taken root in your flesh," Septus said. "So, tell me, child. What's this nonsense about getting married?"

"I'm going to be eighteen in a few months." Everly frowned. "I believe I've reached a point in my life where being called a child now feels condescending."

"That's fair enough, I suppose," said Septus. "But, Everly, I'm soon going to be forty-three, myself. And despite my reputation, I'm not some lusty libertine looking to slake his urges on young flesh. Beautiful as you are, I have no interest in you."

"That can't possibly be true," Everly said in astonishment. "Daddy, have you *seen* how I look in this dress?"

"Now you're just being obnoxious," Septus said curtly. "What put this idea in your head to begin with?"

"Well," Everly began, "I have a sizeable portion of the population under my control. They love me, they worship me, they'll do anything I ask! That's a good thing. But the rest, no matter what I do, keep resisting and *resisting*. Your family has never done anything for the masses except exploit and deprive them, but for some reason they'll kiss the ground you walk on. It's so aggravating."

"My family is all they've ever known. You can't expect them all to leap gratefully to your side just because you're a self-styled liberator." Septus smirked.

"Well, that sure would have been nice," Everly said. "But instead of just doing as I wished, they keep rebelling and throwing areas I've already conquered into chaos. Chaos is only fun when *I'm* the one causing it! You know, when I began this campaign, I expected to win it within a week! It's incredible how the common people can just upend your expectations at will. Now here we are, nearly six months later."

"I don't suppose your seemingly inexhaustible reservoir of eldritch horrors is nearing its limit?" Septus asked her hopefully.

"Nah, the one thing I'll never run out of is troops," Everly said. "But listen, I'm actually trying to keep casualties down! It'd be the easiest thing just to kill everyone off and rule a continent of the dead, but I'm not trying to be the Lich Queen. I want to be the Empress! So, before I completely lose my patience, I want to try something else."

"Marrying me and giving the holdouts the appearance of continuance?" Septus said.

"*Exactly* that!" Everly beamed. "I'm glad you catch on quick. Septus, think of it. There's a lot to gain here. Your family and loved ones get to stay alive. No, even better, I'll grant you genuine immortality! Not that messy imitation of life that Primus Godwell and his daughters mistook for eternity, but the real deal. An existence free of uncertainty and fear."

Primus sat quietly for a moment before saying, "And in return, you'll gain my throne, my subjects, and—"

"And I'll finally get my OCD scratched regarding this kingdom," Everly said happily. "It's a good deal. I'll even start by making you twenty years younger right here and now."

"You're making a lot of assumptions about my character, Lady Skolder," Septus said darkly. "Do I truly appear so loathsome as to trade the future of my nation for the promise of eternal youth?"

"Yes," said Everly flatly. "Septus, you killed your own twin brother to secure your throne. The war you ignited caused suffering across the entire continent. You're a vainglorious psychopath who'll do anything to get ahead. Why else would I make you such an offer if I didn't recognize you as being a kindred spirit?"

"No one speaks to me like that, girl," he warned her. In response, Everly laughed uproariously.

"I bet you wish they would, though!" she said merrily. "All these years you've spent pretending to live in regret of doing the deed. Of betraying your family, of causing all that carnage. Of having to offer a toast to his memory on your every birthday, just to hear your advisors say, *You did what you had to do, Your Majesty.* I bet you've wanted to scream for years that you'd do it again in a heartbeat!"

"How do you know that?" he asked her. "How can you possibly know that?"

Now Everly stood. She then walked down a few steps and turned to face him. Although Septus sat above her, it seemed her very presence loomed over him, a titanic figure in the flickering lights of the throne room that made him seem less than nothing in the eyes of the world.

"Oh, Septus, all I ever had to do was look into your eyes. A murderess knows her own kind. You're exactly how I used to be. I was once someone who was constrained and denied the freedom to live as I wished by the rules of my old world. Just like you, I wanted nothing more than to gloat to all the good people about what sort of rotten bastard was hidden in their midst. I'm utter trash and I love it! And I think you could learn to love it too. A life without necessity. A life without capitulation to the greater good. A life by my side . . . Who knows what delights you'll finally be able to indulge in? All you need to do is take my hand."

With that, Everly held her palm out before the king, knowing that her pitch had been *perfect.* How could he possibly resist? *Man, I'm getting so good at this,* she thought smugly to herself. *Maybe I should introduce the concept of seminars to this planet, just so everyone can see how great I am at managing other people.*

Before Septus could take Everly's hand, the light suddenly vanished from the room, covering it in darkness. Then the light suddenly returned in a disorienting explosion of brightness that overwhelmed her vision and caused her to cry out in pain.

"Boss, are you okay?" Matty asked in alarm.

"Just give me a moment," Everly said as her vision quickly recovered.

"*Graaah*," gasped Septus. His voice sounded thick with some substance that cloyed at it. When Everly turned to him, she saw that a blade had been thrust through the back of his neck and now jutted from his throat as his body spasmed in the air before becoming still.

Someone appeared behind him. A large, masculine figure wearing a concealing, all-white outfit wrapped tightly around his body that obscured every inch of him. Another shimmer of light revealed two other similarly clad people who stood close to Everly, trapping her between them.

"Do you bastards even *realize* what you've done?" Everly asked them as a tremendous killing rage began to surge within her.

"And what exactly is that, oh abhorrent one?" asked one of them in a confident voice.

Everly furiously gestured toward the king's body. "He was MINE!" she roared.

"Have no fear, monster," said the one to her left. "For you'll soon join him—"

Everly's openhanded palm slammed directly against the masked figure's face as she smashed him into the wall, leaving a large blood-spattered crack behind his head. She then tightened her grip and began running down the length of the room, still pressing his head against the wall while using the friction generated by her speed to mash her victim's skull into a vivid crimson streak of gory nonsense.

When the remnants of his head began dripping through her fingers and caused his body to slip from her grasp, Everly turned to face the remaining two assassins and glared at them.

"I bet I only need *one* of you alive to get the answers I want," she said as she trailed a bloody finger down her cheek. "So, now we're going to play a little game called *please, please don't kill me* to see which one of you gets to be the lucky winner."

Their bodies tensed as she began to approach them.

"Try to do your best, okay?" she told them.

CHAPTER TWO

Lady Kestrel

Jelia, NO!" shouted one of the assassins as he stared at the grisly remains of Everly's opponent. "She killed her!"

"Technically, the air resistance killed her," Everly corrected him. "I just gave it an assist."

"Don't laugh at us, monster!" he shouted back. "You won't get away with this!"

"Beros, stay calm and we can survive this," said the one who'd killed the king.

"I'm not afraid of this bitch," said the other one, Beros apparently, as he held his sword before him. "You think you can kill me, whore? Try it! I damn well dare you to try it!"

"Is that an invitation?" Everly asked him. "If so, then the answer's yes."

"Then, let's go!" Beros shouted as he came in running. "We'll show the world your reputation is based on lies!"

Everly had to give this Beros marks for bravery; the man *refused* to be intimidated. Even before a proven killer like herself, he wouldn't take one step backward.

"Stop, you fool!" shouted his partner as the enraged fighter raced toward his certain death. "This is what she wants!"

His hot-blooded nature was exactly why Everly decided to ignore Beros and instead focus her attention on his sensible friend, who kept trying to give him good advice. Idiots like Beros who didn't think they cared about dying were exactly the sort of people who would quickly spill their guts during interrogation—most likely while their guts were literally being spilled. If she spared the smarter one, he'd likely be more loyal to their organization and thus more tight-lipped. That meant there was no point in keeping him around.

Not for the first time this week, Everly wished her elemental servants were around to assist her. If Eris, her spirit elemental, was with her, she could have just pulled the knowledge she wanted directly from their minds and been done with it.

I'm too used to them autopiloting my skills for me, she thought to herself. *When they wake up, I'm going to have to start training myself to be more independent of them.*

As she made her plans, Everly stomped heavily on the floor and sent a wave of Titania's power of the earth through it, causing the ground to continually shake and forcing the two assassins to lose their balance. As the vibrations kept making them fall, she strolled lightly toward her target, completely unaffected by the tremors.

Once she reached him, she snatched away his sword and decapitated him with one stroke.

"Don't lose your head, pal," she said with a smirk.

"Ryes!" shouted the dead man's friend. Once Everly allowed the tremors to stop, he was after her at once, swinging his sword furiously in his vain attempt to avenge his team.

"Jelia, Ryes, and Beros," Everly said thoughtfully. "That's all three of you, isn't it? Why did you bother wearing those disguises if you were just going to give your names away so easily? You're not very smart, are you?"

"I'll kill you!" he said with gritted teeth. Or what Everly assumed were gritted teeth. It was hard to tell because he was still wearing a mask.

"Unlikely," Everly replied. "I'm not a seer, but I think I can make a pretty accurate prediction for what happens next. First, I'm going to cripple you. Then, I'll torture you for information. After that, I'm going to torture you for *fun*. When that's all over with, I'm going to hand you over to King Septus's men, and then *they'll* torture you until you *die*. You have a rough road ahead, Beros. Drink plenty of fluids."

Beros said nothing in response, but his efforts to strike Everly down were redoubled. He was well trained in the use of his sword, and Everly could feel a strong well of *harada* in his body fueling his attacks. He was good enough to be a sword king. No wonder he seemed so confident in his abilities. His flaw was that he seemed inexperienced in fighting stronger opponents. He simply didn't have the sense to know when to run.

Everly smiled nastily at Beros as a slash across his cheek from her sword swiftly stained his mask with blood.

He'd never get the chance to learn.

"I've changed my mind," she said to him sweetly. "I no longer care who put you fools up to this. I think I'll have plenty of fun just killing you with your friend's sword."

"I won't go down easily," he vowed.

"Isn't that for me to decide?" She leered at him.

"No, it isn't," said a woman's voice from behind her, surprising Everly, who hadn't heard anyone approaching.

Everly turned hastily in time to block an incoming sword swing that clashed powerfully against her stolen blade and sent her skidding backward before she regained her balance.

Her new opponent was dressed similarly to the three assassins, but her long black hair was free to flow down her back. A red half cape was also draped over her shoulders, and instead of a full mask, like Beros wore, a simple domino mask covered her eyes.

She was an obvious beauty, which Everly would have been happy to stare at in a less hectic moment, but for now, it was the sword she held in her left hand that commanded Everly's attention.

This interloper was holding the temple's holy sword. The one that could only be wielded by the literal *maiden of the holy sword*, a warrior of faith who was widely recognized as the greatest warrior of each generation.

"Where did you get that?" Everly demanded to know. The holy sword had vanished from sight shortly after the Battle of Bremburg a year and a half ago, after its owner's heart had been crushed, nonmetaphorically.

"I earned it," the stranger said.

"Give it to me," Everly demanded, as a sudden yearning now seized her. The sword was a beautiful working of steel with a line of gold interlaced throughout the blade, a design that exuded simplicity and elegance.

She now wanted it for herself.

"This is a blade that defends life and destroys evil," the other woman said. "Not even you could bear its touch."

"Don't talk down to me," Everly said, annoyed by the certainty in the stranger's voice. Moving faster than her opponent could have possibly seen, Everly reached out, determined to steal away the woman's weapon and kill her with it, just as she had with Ryes. Instead, as soon as her hand made contact with the blade, she screamed in pain as a flash of light exploded outward and knocked her off her feet.

"What the hell?" Everly squealed.

"You were warned," the woman in white said. She then turned to Beros and said, "Grab the king's body. We're leaving."

"But Lady Kestrel! We can take her now! Look at what she did to my friends," he said in a voice that brimmed heavily with tears.

"I'm sorry, Beros," the woman he called Lady Kestrel explained to him. "I also know the pain of losing dear ones to the enemy. But finishing this monster would take too long and cost us too dearly. We need to finish the mission. Justice in its surety will come for her later."

Everly stared at her hand, shocked to see it blistered and bleeding. She slowly clenched her fist and wanted to scream as the raw, glistening skin of her palm pressed against itself.

"No, no, no, you don't have to leave," she said as a feverish grin began to light up her face. "*Stay with me*, I want to keep playing . . ."

"I'm not playing any games," Kestrel said solemnly.

"That's what makes it so exciting," Everly whispered. "Are you a hero?"

Instead of answering Everly's question, Kestrel turned her back on her and walked to where Beros now stood, with the body of King Septus cradled in his arms.

"Hey!" Matty suddenly yelled, outraged that anyone would dare ignore his master in his presence. "The boss asked you a question, dummy!"

Before Everly could stop him, the incensed rodent leaped from her shoulder, growing to his massive combat size as he did so, and charged bullishly at Lady Kestrel, determined to teach her respect. Just before his claws could reach her, though, she spun swiftly and delivered a perfect slash across the monster's face that sent him rolling backward, screaming in pain while spurting blood everywhere.

"Matty!" Everly yelled as she ran to her servant's side, where he lay crying in agony. His right eye had been destroyed and the side of his face was even worse to behold than Everly's palm.

In a flash of light, Kestrel and Beros vanished from sight. A moment later, the bodies of the other two vanished as well, leaving Everly and Matty alone in the ruined throne room.

"She got me, boss! Argggh, she got me real good," Matty whined as he shuddered in humiliated pain. "I'm sorry, it's my fault. I thought I could take her."

"Shhh," Everly assured him. "Quiet. You were very brave. You're a good little rat. Let's get you home so we can get you healed up."

Matty was too injured to return to his true form, which left Everly with no choice but to heft his huge frame over her shoulder. A moment later, a gateway leading to their home in the astral realm sparked into existence.

Just as she began stepping through it, a man's voice called out to her in confusion.

"Uh, Everly?" said Caleb. Behind him stood the king's royal guard as well as dozens of councilors, ministers, a few temple priests, and one very bewildered-looking dog. "Could you perhaps explain yourself? Please?"

Everly looked at her brother for a moment as she tried to think of something to tell him. Then she sighed and turned away.

"It's really not what it looks like," she said as she stepped through her portal, leaving the carnage for them to clean up.

CHAPTER THREE

Slandered

The next morning.

"Everly! Time for breakfast!" said the cheerful voice of Everly's annoying duplicate, Beverly.

Everly groaned miserably at being forcefully awakened. "Go away! I don't want anything, just let me sleep!" she replied from beneath the comforting darkness of her blankets.

After returning to the memory palace, Everly had applied emergency treatment to Matty and managed to heal the wounds he'd received from Kestrel. Despite her recent mastery of light magic, it had been a surprisingly difficult undertaking, and afterward, she wanted nothing more than to pass out on her bed.

Everly's memory palace had begun its existence as a mere mental construct that she used to keep the fighting skills that she'd developed in her previous life sharpened. Over time, as she began to develop her considerable psionic abilities thanks to her bond with her spirit elemental, Eris, the memory palace grew with her as she aged and gradually became more substantive, until it finally began to manifest itself as an actual location in the astral realm. As it was her personal demesne, Everly's control over the palace was absolute. Anything she envisioned within its walls became real and nothing could exist within it without her permission. It was the ultimate fortress from which to conduct her war of conquest against the outside world.

On the days when she felt like doing it, anyway.

Today, however, Everly wanted to lie in bed and sulk at the unfairness of life. Her grand plans for the near future had been kiboshed due to those meddling assassins and now the moment she'd been waiting *months* for would never come to pass. It just wasn't fair! Why was fate singling *her* out? Surely, Everly was the unluckiest girl in the world.

Everly's grip tightened on her sheets as she remembered the contemptuous look of superiority that Lady Kestrel had shot at her as she and her surviving crony made their escape. Everly knew that look well; it was one that she herself practiced in the mirror all the time. It essentially said, *later, loser.*

"Everly! You know if you keep focusing on what happened, those intrusive thoughts are going to start popping up again," Bev said as she opened Everly's door and stepped inside while holding a tray stacked with French toast, honey, syrup, and a glass of cold milk. "Who cares if some bug took a swipe at you? You'll get around to paying her back later."

"She hurt my rat," Everly fumed. "I *like* my rat. It was so uncalled for."

"Uh, she killed the guy you wanted to marry too, didn't she?" Bev asked her.

"Yeah, she also did that," Everly said with a glower as she sat up. "Thanks for *reminding* me. She clearly doesn't know who she's messing with."

"Ev, I know you hate it when I ask questions—" Bev began to say.

"It just really annoys me whenever you show curiosity about things," Everly said darkly.

"—but why did you want to marry Septus, anyway?" finished Bev. "I know you said it was to get the commoners behind you, but that doesn't really sound like something you'd care about."

Everly sighed, knowing that Bev wouldn't stop bugging her until she answered the question.

"Okay, fine! If you *must* know, I had a sudden burst of inspiration out at Haverlock, when those insurrectionists were shouting, *Our lives for the king!* You remember those guys?"

"Oh, yeah," Bev nodded as she set up Everly's tray. "Those guys were fearless! And then you and Grail charged in and chopped them up to silly bits. That was pretty funny."

"Yeah, it was," Everly agreed as she took a bite of her breakfast. She growled happily to herself, pleased that she'd decided to eat, after all.

"But when we were done, I started thinking, *How am I going to keep these assholes tamed?* It was really going to take a shock to the system to make them behave. I couldn't just kill Septus; that would inspire more disobedience for years to come. Or rather, I had to kill him in a way that would break their will to keep resisting. Like during a moment when they thought they finally achieved victory.

"And then it occurred to me," Everly said with a dreamy smile now slowly growing on her face. "The perfect solution! A man, a woman, the union of two feuding houses, the jubilant cheers of the crowd just before they turned into screams of horror! I was going to—"

"Oh, I know this! I know this!" Bev cut in excitedly. "You were going to Red Wedding him!"

"Okay, first thing, Bev: don't ever interrupt me; I find it aggravating. And second: don't use the term *Red Wedding* as a verb, that's even more annoying. Besides, out of respect for how litigious that author is about defending his copyright, we should instead call it the *Dead Wedding*. I'm a necromancer, after all."

"But that's what you were going to do, right?" Bev insisted as she jumped onto the bed to lie beside Everly. "You were going to marry him and then bury him, right? Alongside any other potential enemies? That sounds awesome!"

"Tch, you know *nothing*, Beverly Skolder." Everly smirked.

Still, she remained upset over how things had gone. It had been such a beautiful plan! The Dead Wedding had been a cultural event that had shocked millions of people worldwide back on Earth, and that had been over a mere television show! Who knows how well it would have been received if she'd gotten to do it in real life?

"I'm so mad those jerks stole that moment from me," she muttered.

"Oh, don't be like that, Evie," Bev said brightly. "The royal court has already accused you of killing Septus, so in a way, you're still getting the heat you wanted."

Upon hearing those words, Everly leaped from her bed and hurled her tray of food against a wall. "They're blaming *me* for this?" she shouted in outrage. "I was the one who came in peace! I wasn't going to kill him until after the nuptials and five minutes of fun in a dark closet!"

"Just five minutes?" asked Bev. "Everly, he was *toothsome*."

"Okay, maybe ten minutes," Everly said, after giving it some thought. "He really did have that whole *Shawn Michaels as a greasy libertine* vibe going on."

"Shawn Michaels is one sexy boy!" Bev said enthusiastically.

"Yeah, he's also proof positive that evil is more powerful than good," agreed Everly. "I mean, compared to him, Bret Hart is looking *rough*."

"Hey! Show some respect for The Hitman, life has been hard on him," Bev said rebukingly. She then kissed her fingertip before pointing it toward the ceiling and saying, "We still miss you, Owen."

"All hail the king of Harts," Everly said reverently.

The two of them then shared a moment of silence before continuing.

"So, what are you going to do about getting framed for regicide?" Bev asked her.

"Well, what am I supposed to do?" Everly said as she sank back onto the bed. "It enhances my reputation somewhat, so it's not like I'm going to deny having done it. At the same time, I don't like being used in the machinations of someone else. It pisses me off."

Bev pulled a brush out of her pocket and tapped her lap. Everly then placed her head onto it and visibly relaxed as her duplicate began running the brush through her long hair.

"Obviously, you can't just let them get away with it," Bev said as she worked.

"Obviously!" Everly said. "If I let some random losers get the idea that they can manipulate *the Empress* of all people, then the problems will never end. Clearly, I'm going to have to kill them all."

"Not all of them," Bev said. "Their leader, Kestrel. She has something you want."

"*That sword*," Everly said hungrily. "Bev, I don't know what came over me, but as soon as I saw it, I knew I *had* to have it. I felt . . . I felt like the universe was doing me a disservice the longer it was in her hands instead of mine. I was getting so angry that she didn't just hand it over to me on the spot. God, just thinking about it makes me want it even more . . ."

"Yeah, I think I'm feeling sympathetic pangs of greed," Bev said as she continued to brush away. "But can you really take it? All the legends about the holy sword say it's for good people only."

Everly stopped to look at her burned palm. "That makes absolutely no sense," she said.

"Why do you say that?" Bev wondered.

"Remember what Anne told me during our first fight? She claimed *she* was the original maiden of the holy sword. Do you expect me to believe that some mass-murdering *vampire* has better character qualifications for holding that sword than me?"

"The way you said that felt a little racist against vampires," Bev said reluctantly.

"It's fine. They're socially acceptable targets," Everly assured her.

Now Bev began pulling Everly's hair back into three thick, long bundles, which she then began carefully twisting overhand into an impressive French braid. She studied the results carefully as she worked, clicking her tongue against her teeth as her fingers deftly moved throughout Everly's locks.

"Matty's going to want to go with you," Bev said, after she was finally satisfied with her efforts. "He's going to want revenge after getting humbled in front of you so badly."

"No, Matty's off this one," Everly said sadly. "He's back to overseeing the rat room for now. I love that little guy, but he did technically fail me, and you know, failure has its rewards and all. Can't go soft on him just because I love rubbing his round belly."

"*Everly*," Bev said in exasperation. "You already know Carter's gonna flip his goblin wig if you insist on handling this alone. Don't you remember the lecture he gave you after you came back from killing Anne?"

"Hey! Carter's not the one running this show, okay?" Everly said defensively.

"No, he's just the one who keeps the troops organized, handles the administrative duties of your burgeoning empire, and makes sure the trash gets picked up on time," chided Bev. "He also does the cooking."

"Damn it, he's an excellent cook," Everly was forced to admit.

"You have to bring someone with you," Dev insisted.

"Bah! Fine." Everly scowled. "Uh, do you want to do it?"

"Hell no," Bev said firmly. "It's scary out there. I'm staying right here."

"Didn't I tell you to get a job or else?" Everly asked her.

"Yeah, but you say a lot of things," Bev said indifferently.

"You're lucky you're a living personification of my twisted personality and that I'm too narcissistic to harm you. Otherwise, I would totally smite you for your arrogant flippancy," Everly said to her.

"There's worse things to be in life than a house pet." Bev smirked. "Um, speaking of which, are you going to talk to her today?"

"Talk to who?" Everly asked, although she knew very well who Bev meant.

"Are you going to talk to Fenn?" Bev insisted on asking. "It's been two weeks."

"Well, is she being cool? Is she being *reasonable*?" asked Everly.

"Ev, at some point, maybe you just need to realize that what *you* want isn't necessarily what *she* wants," Bev said delicately.

"And that's complete bullshit," Everly cut in. "What I want should be *exactly* what she wants as well! She's really not doing this relationship any favors by insisting on having free will. I wish she'd take us more seriously!"

"Everly, that might be *the* most psychotic thing I've heard you say in a while," said Bev. "What's she even guilty of? You're the one trying to give her Stockholm syndrome."

"It's going to work too," Everly insisted. "It's like baking a cake. You just need to let the oven do its job."

"Is she even worth the effort you're putting in?" Bev asked. "It feels to me like you're less interested in protecting her, like you say, than you are in breaking her spirit. It's weird vibes, Ev. I don't want to say people are gossiping, but yeah, they're really gossiping."

"Tch, like I care." Everly sniffed. "Fenn needs me. She can't do anything on her own and it's time she realized it. We were summoned to this world to reign over it together. Both of us! But until she admits it and can see that *my* way is best, she'll only head into another disaster. That's just who she is."

"Well, technically, the only disaster she's run into so far has been you, hasn't it?" Bev grinned.

"Hey, shut-in! I have my limits," Everly warned her.

"Right, right." Bev nodded while still wearing an impertinent smile.

Everly turned away from her duplicate to avoid being provoked into making an angry remark. When had Bev become such a little troll? Or maybe she'd always been that way and Everly was just now noticing. It was hard to tell.

"So, are you going to go after the Eastern Temple?" Bev asked after she picked up Everly's tray and its scattered dishes.

"Obviously," Everly replied. "Disguised or not, who else can just teleport their people into a king's throne room at will? That had to be the work of their sending choir."

"That also jives with their leader being a holy warrior," Bev said thoughtfully. "Maybe they found a way to steal the sword from the Western Temple?"

Everly nodded. "Exactly. They're finally making their move against me. Pride must have gotten around to telling them about our secret invasion."

"Does that mean the choir of seers has betrayed you?" Bev wondered. "I mean, didn't you make a deal with them?"

"I think so?" Everly said as Bev helped her get dressed. "Honestly, the specifics of how they were meant to honor our arrangement are sort of lost on me. Were they supposed to give me a warning if their temple moved against me? Or were they supposed to stay out of it? It's confusing because we've never actually met."

"All I remember is *no spoilers* being a thing," said Bev.

"Whatever. I can just loosely interpret our deal in any way that seems favorable to me," Everly said indifferently.

"That doesn't seem fair in the slightest," Bev said.

"Right? I consider it my first successful devil's bargain," Everly said proudly.

"You're still going to need backup," Bev said. "For Carter's sake."

"I said I know already." Everly grimaced. "Titania and Eris are still hibernating, Carter's doing all the paperwork, Grail is about to begin the campaign against Oldstead, you're a useless parasite, and Matty's on the mend. Who does that leave me with?"

"Everly, you know *exactly* who that leaves you with," Bev said.

"Oh, god, I don't want to. It'll be weird," Everly whined.

"I never liked that cow to begin with, but she never got a chance to do anything," Bev said. "Show her a little empathy! She used to be one of us."

"You and Nev were nowhere near as disappointing as that waste of space," Everly snorted. "Whenever I look at her, all I see are my past mistakes."

"Pencils have erasers for a reason," Bev insisted.

"Ugh, I just can't argue with that face!" Everly said. "Fine, Ghost Knight can be my bodyguard. It's such a simple duty that even she can't foul it up."

Suddenly, Bev's arms wrapped around Everly's torso and gave her a hard squeeze. Then Bev propped her chin on Everly's shoulder and said, "I'm proud of you."

"Oh, shut up," Everly said as she began to blush.

"I'm serious," Bev said. "I'm not gonna say you're not as bad as everyone says you are, because you're *obviously* so much worse, but for some reason, I still feel proud of you."

"Whatever," Everly said.

But she did enjoy the hug.

CHAPTER FOUR

Feeling It

Later, at a different location inside the memory palace, Everly paused to take a deep breath before knocking on the door in front of her.

"Ghost Knight, it's me," she announced. "I'm coming in." She then opened the door and stepped inside the quarters of her least favorite creation, still maintaining her deep breaths. This was going to be challenging.

"I want to be called Dullahan from now on," replied the massive, armored figure who now stood before her.

Without her soft voice emanating from her helmet, it would have been impossible to know that the nine-foot-tall knight towering above Everly was a woman. She wore platinum-white heavy armor that covered her from head to toe, draped with a white fur mantle over her shoulders. At first glance, she appeared more like a temple warrior or even a paladin than one of Everly's servants.

"Absolutely not," Everly said immediately. "For one thing, a Dullahan has a missing head. Yours is still on its shoulders."

"Cut mine off," said the Ghost Knight. "I don't need it anymore."

"How are you going to eat without a head, stupid?" Everly asked her.

"Food is a delight reserved for the living," replied the Ghost Knight. "For me, there is only darkness."

"Oh, for fuck's sake, why are you so dramatic?" Everly swore to herself under her breath as she shook her head in irritated dismay. She could already feel her breathing exercise beginning to fail her.

"You're not dead anymore, dummy," she said to the Ghost Knight. "You're completely restored. One hundred percent. I promise, okay?"

The Ghost Knight didn't respond to Everly's assurances. Instead, the armored figure turned to face the fireplace, which was the sole source of light in the darkened room. Then she held her hands behind her back as she peered into the flames, as though she were pondering events too horrible for mere mortal minds to comprehend. Events that would flay the spirit of any poor innocent who accidentally stumbled upon them or drive them into madness at the very least. Such was the perspective of one who has seen the abyss and realized the immensity of oblivion.

"I still want to be called Dullahan," she said stubbornly.

"Yeah, and before that it was Death Knight, and before that it was Phantasma Knight, and before *that* it was Spectral Knight. Pick a lane, Jane," said Everly.

"You let *Grail* change his name," the Ghost Knight complained.

"Because he only did it once, dumbass," sighed Everly.

"First, my life was taken from me. Now my freedom of choice," the Ghost Knight said forlornly. "I shouldn't be surprised. The darkness consumes all."

"Would you please stop being *weird*," Everly begged of her.

"How should I react instead?" the Ghost Knight wondered. "Perhaps there's a more suitable manner in which an innocent soul cruelly snatched away in her prime by the merciless hand of the reaper should behave? *I* was a sacrifice to the shadows. Forever lost to . . . the darkness. Unloved and forever scorned by the light of the sun."

"Hey, are you being serious right now?" When the other girl refused to respond, Everly said, "Okay, whatever, have it your way, *Ghost Knight.*"

"*Dullahan,*" the Ghost Knight insisted.

"FINE," Everly said in exasperation. She then pointed to the center of the room and gestured for the armored girl to move there and kneel. Once the Ghost Knight had done so, Everly pulled the helmet off the suit of armor, which revealed the wide-eyed face of a nervous-looking person that she greatly resembled, except for the other girl's corpse-pale skin. Then Everly placed a covering over the armor at its neck, sealing it completely. She then did the same for the helmet before placing a binding enchantment upon it so that it would stay in place when donned or float in the air beside the armor if separated. After they tested it a few times to make sure the spell was working correctly, Everly nodded in satisfaction, pleased by her own handiwork.

"All right, *Dullahan,*" Everly said. "Now you'll at least match the name. But this is the last time, all right? If you try this one more time, I swear I'll peel you out of that tin can and punt you, got it?"

"If such is the will of the darkness, then by it I swear to abide," said the newly minted Dullahan, pleased by the changes that Everly had wrought in her form.

"Damn skippy," agreed Everly. "Anyway, no more sitting around indulging in your goth phase. You're my new bodyguard, got it? I need to pay a visit to some people who've crossed me, and you're going to be the implement of my violent displeasure, 'kay?"

"Cool," said Dullahan, before correcting herself. "That is to say, if the darkness demands that the peril of my wrath must fall upon these fools who dared arouse your ire, then let their suffering begin."

"Oh, hell yeah," said Everly.

The true headquarters of the Eastern Temple was located a continent away, in a pristine valley hidden from the eyes of the world in the center of a lush, nameless forest that had been there since time immemorial.

Everly had to admit that this secluded location made for a pretty good hiding spot. If she hadn't already located it by discreetly replacing one of their high-ranking members with one of her creations, it would have taken ages for her to find it.

It hadn't stopped there either. Her spy had begun clandestinely removing members of the temple's high council so that Everly could replace them with more of her own people. There were only four members that she didn't control. She supposed that today would be a good day to finish off her collection.

"Shall we begin?" asked Dullahan as they stood before the castle gates. "The darkness craves the destruction of these impertinent insects. My hand trembles with excitement at the thought of delivering you their lives."

"Yeah, okay, that'd be good." Everly nodded. "But, Dullahan?"

"Yes, my darkness?"

"Could you maybe ease up on the doom-and-gloom proclamations? I get it, you consider yourself an embodiment of death and destruction, and that's cool, but you're really laying it on a little thick."

The Dullahan paused to consider the words of her mistress. Then she asked, "Are you saying that I'm *cringe?*"

"No!" Everly said quickly. "Who said that? I didn't say that! I just think . . . you know, with your look and the atmosphere you already exude, maybe less is more?"

"So, now I talk too much?"

"Dullahan, just *listen!*" Everly said. "You already have an amazing intimidation factor, okay? The less you speak, the scarier you are. *I* can get away with the rambling monologues because I'm a wicked sorceress, but you black-knight types work much better as monosyllabic juggernauts, okay?"

"Hmm," said Dullahan thoughtfully. "I hadn't thought of it like that."

"Trust me, less is more," Everly assured her. "Save your words for when it'll *really* screw with someone's mind. You won't believe the results."

"All right," said Dullahan. "*Less is more* it is. Thank you, Everly."

"Not a problem," Everly replied, glad that her words had finally reached the other girl.

"Also, I just want to say thanks for including me today," Dullahan continued.

"Huh?" Everly said in surprise.

The imposing knight seemed to struggle to find the words, sheepishly twiddling her fingers as she sought to express herself, before finally saying, "It's just, ever since I got . . . killed, I feel like I let you down. After what I tried to do to Nev, and how I'm also the only one of us who ever died, and I . . . was embarrassed, and I felt like you were mad at me over it, and I just . . . I'm glad you still think I'm useful. Uh, that's all."

"Girl, *whaaat?*" said the poker-faced Everly. "Dullahan, no, *noooo*, I'd never hold anything like that against you. You and me, we're fine. I could never stay mad at you. Bad luck is just bad luck," she said, pleased that she'd managed to lie so well without giving a single blink.

Dullahan nodded happily and then gave her a quick, powerful hug before she could regain her composure. "Great! That's so awesome! Thank you so much!"

"Yep. Yep, it's great," Everly said as she awkwardly patted the massive knight's back. *Why do they keep hugging me?* she wondered to herself, before saying, "Okay, that's enough with the feely-feels, wouldn't you say? C'mon, stop. Let's go kill some templars!"

"Right, you've got it!" said the enthusiastic Dullahan. "The darkness must be fed!"

"Yeeeah, let's do that," Everly said. "Let's go do that thing."

Then the two of them began striding toward the castle gates.

"Hmm," Everly said in surprise as she and Dullahan approached the gates of the keep, only to discover that they had already been broken open and the troops that should have been guarding them were now dead. "Did we conquer this place earlier and forget about it?"

"Not that I'm aware of," Dullahan replied. "Unless you sent Grail and it slipped your mind?"

"That *does* sound like something I'd do." Everly nodded. "But Grail's the type that would have reminded me later. He's diligent about things like that. Is that the word I'm looking for? Diligent?"

"I think so," Dullahan said. "It sounds right."

"Yeah, I think so too," Everly agreed. "Grail's too diligent to let me forget about something like this." She then waved a hand at the ruined entrance to the Eastern Temple's headquarters. "In which case it would appear that someone has beaten us to the punch."

"But who would *dare* lay claim to the prey of the Empress?" Dullahan asked in an outraged voice.

"Well, it's not like we announced to the world that we were going to stop by and destroy this place," Everly said. "When you think about it, these templars have enemies all across the world. They've been pissing people off for centuries! It stands to reason that someone would have a score or two to settle with them."

Dullahan glared balefully at the ruined entryway before saying, "Well, that might be true, but I was still looking forward to showing off what I could do. I've had a difficult year, Everly!"

"We all know you've had a difficult year, Dullahan," Everly said placatingly.

"Going on a rampage would have been very cathartic for me," Dullahan fumed.

"Okay, all right. I understand your feelings," Everly replied. "Let's just take a look around first and see what we can find out. Maybe we can sniff out some clues or something."

With that decided, the duo entered the castle, stopping first to inspect the dead gate guards. "Interesting," Everly said, after giving one of them a few curious pokes. "These guys haven't been dead very long, Dull. I'd even go so far as to say they've only recently been killed."

"Can your power over the earth give you an exact time of death?" Dullahan wondered. "Also, please don't call me *Dull*. That's the sort of terrible nickname that sticks."

"How about Dully?" asked Everly.

"That's even worse," Dullahan quickly replied.

"You're really making this hard for me," Everly said sadly.

"I don't want you doing it at all," Dullahan said.

"Fine, if you're going to be a *baby* about it," Everly said in an aggrieved tone. "And no, I don't think I can get the exact time of death. Titania could do that for me easily . . . Oh, it's so annoying to only now realize how much I relied on her and Eris to manage my powers."

"It's not like you've lost them permanently," Dullahan said. "When they wake back up, you'll be stronger than ever."

"Yeeeeah," Everly sighed. "It sure is inconvenient for the moment, though. It's not that their absence makes me feel vulnerable or anything; I just *miss* them."

"Really?" asked Dullahan.

"Yeah," Everly said. "I feel . . . incomplete without them. I don't mean this to sound entirely psychotic, Dullahan, but once you get used to having multiple voices constantly speaking in your head, the absence of noise can feel immense."

"Wow, that almost sounded profound," marveled Dullahan.

"I'm a still river, but I'm a *deep* river." Everly nodded.

"Some would say you're definitely off the deep end," Dullahan agreed.

"Thank you," Everly said, pleased by the compliment.

Inside the keep, more bodies lay where they had fallen in battle. Dried blood was splattered all around where men had died. The floor and walls were also scorched with the telltale signs of spellcraft, and rubble was strewn everywhere.

"Whoo, party in the church, party in the church," Everly said approvingly.

"Why are there only dead templars?" Dullahan wondered. "I don't see a single dead invader."

"Good observation," Everly said. "These church mice aren't slouches when it comes to a fight. Whoever attacked them should have left a corpse or two behind."

"But all we see are fallen templars and clergy," said Dullahan. "Were they overwhelmed so easily?"

"I don't think so," Everly said. Then she realized the answer. "That night, when I met Kestrel . . ."

"You mean the night when King Septus was assassinated?" asked Dullahan.

"Yeah, yeah, that too," Everly said impatiently. "I killed two of the three assassins they sent for him. I would have had the last of them as well if Kestrel hadn't intervened. When they fled from me, they beamed out and took all the bodies in the room with them."

"They refused to leave their dead behind," Dullahan said. "A wise precaution when dealing with a necromancer. But wait, aren't we here because you thought the assassins were *with* the Eastern Temple?"

"It would appear that my guess was incorrect," Everly said slowly as her eyes began to spark red. Then she quickly shook her head. "No, that's impossible. I'm *never* wrong about anything. This was *Beverly's* guess."

"Ah, well, that makes sense," said Dullahan quickly. "Gosh, that Bev. What a dummy. She's never right about anything."

"Yeah, the only thing she's ever right about is being *wrong*," Everly said assertively. "She's eggs in a bowl of ice cream."

"Your hair looks very nice and you're easily the prettiest girl in this charnel house," Dullahan assured her.

"I *am* pretty, thank you," Everly smiled.

Then she screamed in rage and reduced a nearby wall to rubble with a vicious gesture from her hand.

"I'm *not* angry," she said a moment later.

"I'm glad you're not angry," Dullahan said quietly.

"I'm just disappointed. I'm *allowed* to feel disappointed," Everly said. "I took some time out of my day, I went out of my way to come here, and then it's like finding out the toy store is closed on Sundays. Who closes anything on a Sunday? Why make a religious observance when there's *money* to be made?"

"Isn't that just *so* capitalism?" Dullahan asked her. "Full of bleeding hearts and . . . and cultural respect and all that. At least modern communists care about making a profit."

"You can stop now, Dullahan," Everly told her.

Dullahan fell silent.

Everly took a deep breath and let it quiet her unsettled mind.

"All right, let's keep looking," she decided.

"As you command, my darkness," said Dullahan.

As they searched the ruined keep, Everly found herself wondering who could have possibly done this. Not only did today's discovery mean there was a new faction running loose on her world, it was also an enemy of the established order. First, they claimed the king of a great kingdom. Now they'd come after one of the great religious powers.

The question was why?

Oh, now I'm just being silly, she thought to herself. *This is obviously all about me.*

It made sense if you thought about it. She'd been about to claim Winstead through marriage. And she'd had the ruling council of the Eastern Temple thoroughly filled with her people. Now both had been taken away from her.

This was all clearly an attempt to deprive her of resources.

She snickered at the thought of it.

All these poor little soldiers and even Septus. Dead because of me and never to know why. I guess that's just what happens when an ant gets caught beneath a giant's stride. It's all just a sad joke that history decided to play on them. Of course, the joke would be even funnier if someone would only let ME in on the punchline.

Kestrel. It all came back to her. The mysterious figure in white bearing the Western Temple's sacred armament. Who was she? Why was she targeting Everly?

She talked like a paladin too. A real one, not like that demented fraud, Sarah. Making her little platitudes about justice and patience. She couldn't hide that look of pleasure in her eyes when she burned me, though. No, for all her righteous talk, this is very personal for her. I did something to make her my enemy. I wish she'd tell me what it was so I could mock her for it.

And that was how, with pleasant thoughts of infuriating her enemy into making a fatal mistake now running through her mind, Everly and Dullahan found themselves walking into a large room in the central chambers of the keep, where the dead bodies of the high council hung upside down by hooks driven through their ankles, naked and divested of every inch of their skin.

Everly looked around very carefully to make certain she was seeing things correctly. Then she frowned. Every single one of her replacement councilors was here, hanging lifelessly.

"Everly, this is horrible," Dullahan said, stunned by what she saw. "They killed all our people . . ."

"They broke all my toys," Everly agreed vehemently. "Why didn't I know this was happening? Even if Eris is hibernating, I'm still connected to all of you mentally. How could they be here, *dying*, without me even realizing it?"

It would take organization, precise timing, and considerable spiritual power to blind Everly to the movements of those who acted against her. These assassins had to have more than a few powerful spirit elemental users among their ranks to veil the suffering of Everly's creations from her. But how did they know so much about her? A technique like this wasn't something that was improvised on a whim.

Something in her bones told Everly that what the assassins had accomplished here was a proven methodology designed specifically to foil *her*.

Who are you, Kestrel? What do you represent?

A grin broke out on Everly's face as she realized that things were getting more complicated than she'd expected.

And a lot more exciting.

"*Everly*," whispered the dying voice of one of her children.

It took her a moment to place a name to the unknitted thing that hung before her. His face was of course unrecognizable, but she never forgot a voice, especially when that voice was an occasional source of irritation.

"Hello, Nalec," she said to him in greeting. With a swing of her hand, she severed the hooked chains that he hung from and caught him before he fell to the floor. Now she knelt gently and cradled his body in her arms.

"You were really hanging in there, weren't you?" she asked him, unable to resist the pun.

"I'm sorry," he whispered. "I'm so sorry. Will you forgive me? I failed you."

Everly considered his words for a bit, then gently kissed him on his skinless forehead. "No. No, I won't forgive you. Your brothers and sisters are dead, and your killers have escaped to laugh at me. Why couldn't you do anything right?"

"I'm so useless," he wept.

"You are," Everly agreed.

"I wish I had died," he said.

"You will, soon. Whatever they did to you, I can't heal it," Everly said sadly. It infuriated her that she couldn't. She was used to doing whatever she wished. How dare these assassins impede her with their grubby little tricks?

"Can you tell me anything about the one who did this, Nalec?" she asked him as she gently stroked his cheek, paying no attention to the fluids that clung to her hand. "Tell me who killed the second of my children. In your name, I'll inflict absolute *horror* upon them. Before I'm done, they'll beg for the sweet release of the rat room."

"There were two of them," Nalec said in his quivering voice. "One who commanded and one who obeyed. A man in blackened armor who gave directions to a girl in white who tortured us with a burning blade."

"Kestrel," Everly said softly.

"You know her, Mother?" Nalec asked.

"We've met," Everly replied. "What about the other one? The man whom she obeyed?"

"He knows you," Nalec rasped. "Everly, he *knows* you. He spoke of you so intimately. As though you'd been lovers. But he also spoke of events that never occurred. He was so convinced that they had, and so furious to learn when he was wrong. He had Kestrel flay us every time he was mistaken about something. It lasted for days . . ."

Days? she thought. *More like hours. But when your skin is being peeled off, time is the last thing you'll be keeping track of.*

"Nalec, can you describe him?" asked Everly. "Can you tell me his name?"

"He had one eye," Nalec whispered. "He wore a patch over the other and had a scar across his face. He said his name didn't matter. That nothing mattered as long as you existed in this world . . ."

"A nameless foe," Everly said dreamily. "Someone *obsessed* with me. How intriguing. You know, I've always wanted to dramatically disfigure someone. Don't you think handsome men are improved with the presence of a good scar? I'd cut him across his eye and then I'd say—"

"*If ignorance ever again obscures your vision, then I'll come for the other one,*" said Nalec, before his head dropped back and his chest stopped moving.

"What?" Everly asked him in confusion. "Hey. Nalec! Nalec, how did you know I'd say that? Nalec!"

She cursed in frustration. Nalec was dead.

"Okay, so what the hell was that all about?" she asked Dullahan as she stood up and let the body drop to the floor.

Dullahan could only shrug her shoulders in confusion. "It would have been nice if he'd hung around long enough to clarify."

"Well, he never did have a lot of potential," Everly said dismissively. "He was an early run, you see. A test to see how independently one of my creations could operate while still being utterly devoted to me. He was a little too much. I considered having him destroyed on more than one occasion, but . . . I don't know. There's a certain charm to an early mistake, isn't there? Could he have grown? Could I have learned to be more appreciative of him?"

"Could you have?" Dullahan asked her with uncertainty.

"Well, if we're being honest, it's highly doubtful," Everly admitted. "But the *possibility* was still there! That's reason enough to hold a grudge against whoever this one-eyed bastard is."

Before Dullahan could respond to Everly's words, a scream suddenly rang throughout the keep.

"And what have we here?" Everly said eagerly. "Could it be that we have a reason to be here after all?"

"Maybe?" said Dullahan, who decided she was simply going to roll with things until she could go back home.

"Well, let's go find out, silly!" laughed Everly as she ran out of the room, leaving its contents behind to be forgotten.

CHAPTER FIVE

Spiders Again?

Everly tried to contain her eagerness as she ran speedily in the direction of the scream, but it was difficult for her to tamp down her enthusiasm for a fight. Her entire day thus far had been a disappointing waste of her precious time, but a little action would go a long way toward making her forget her boredom.

Sifting for clues in a ravaged castle didn't suit her personality at all. She *much* preferred bloodying her knuckles. Who wouldn't?

Wasn't she the self-proclaimed ruler of this world? At the very least, she'd certainly called dibs on her home continent. One couldn't make such an enormous claim without being willing to throw hands over it. And feet, heads, and torsos. Really, whatever the situation called for. A willingness to kill was the least of what was required to set oneself at the top of the mountain, and Everly had been quick to embrace that essential truth. She felt no remorse for any lives lost in her campaign, because she knew for a fact that resurrection was a thing that existed. Since there was literally life after death, what cause did she have to feel shame over her frequent use of murder to accomplish her goals? What's more, as a necromancer she didn't even have to wait for the cycle of rebirth to erase her misdeeds. She could just bring her victims back herself if she felt the situation called for it.

Of course, everything that Everly did was in the service of living out her dreams. From childhood in her previous life to the heights of power she now enjoyed in this new world, there was only one thing that Everly desired above all else: to be the ultimate villain. To be the one around whom the world spun, the center of attention and awe. Feared and hated, envied and worshiped. Wasn't that what all little girls dreamed of in their dark little hearts?

Her dreams were the chief reason that she couldn't overlook the existence of this blackened knight who decided to cross her. Everly did not tolerate competition from *anyone*. She'd worked too hard to share the stage with some random interloper.

Behind her, Dullahan struggled to match Everly's pace. "I thought I was supposed to play the part of your bodyguard, Everly. That's difficult to do when you're running *ahead* of me, you know," she said irritably.

"How's that my fault?" Everly replied. "You're the one choosing to wear all that gear."

"It's a sensible decision," Dullahan said defensively. "Being stabbed hurts."

"You're not wrong, but I never let it hold *me* back," Everly shot back.

"Yeah, well, you've never been stabbed *fatally*."

"Well, that's because I've got the skills to pay the bills."

Dullahan laughed at Everly's lack of humility. "It didn't hurt that Marcis came running to your rescue, though, when Bev came to him begging for his help against Anne. That feels more like luck than anything else, if you ask me. Which no one ever does."

"Well, what can I say? Luck is just a skill that you don't have to refine," replied Everly.

"Does that mean that bad luck is something inherent to my nature? That I'll never know anything other than misfortune? That I'll *always* be like this?" Dullahan's voice became solemn as she considered the bleak possibilities.

"Maybe?" Everly shrugged. "At least you'll never be bored."

"Not all of us require as much stimulus as you, Everly," Dullahan said. "All three of us have turned out so differently from what you intended."

"Stop reminding me of past disappointments, Dullahan," Everly said with a mild edge to her voice.

"I don't mean to provoke you, Everly. The original idea seemed sound enough. Four of you to do four times the work. Who wouldn't indulge in such an ideal set up? I think the problem of our unexpected individuality stems from your own unique nature. You're a stubborn and unreasonable person, so in hindsight, it seems obvious that your duplicates would be as well."

"So, what you're saying is that you turning out this way is my fault?"

"I think that's an issue that every parent must eventually face."

"Didn't we agree earlier that you should talk less?" Everly grumbled.

As the two of them continued to run, Everly quietly considered Dullahan's words. She didn't want to, but each of her duplicates had a tendency to make points during conversation that she found difficult to refute. They weren't her, but they *were* different aspects of her. That meant that more often than not, they occasionally said things that were unexpectedly profound.

Was she really a disappointment to her own mother?

"Do you resent me for how I treat you?" Everly suddenly asked the other girl.

"Do you really want me to answer that question honestly?" asked Dullahan.

Everly thought about it for a moment. Then she said, "No."

"I don't resent you in the slightest," Dullahan said promptly. "You did the best you could."

Everly nodded, pleased by this act of vindication. "Yeah, that's what I thought too."

"You gave us the world and all we had to do was obey," Dullahan continued.

"You know, when you put it that way, it really makes it seem like I was a great creator."

"The best gods create in their own image," Dullahan said in agreement.

"Why is Fenn being so difficult?" Everly suddenly asked her.

"Oh, she's grown to despise you and refuses to bear your yoke," Dullahan said casually.

"*She refuses to bear my yoke?*" Everly said, outraged. "I'm trying to set her up for life, not hitch her to a wagon filled with hay. Is that really how she feels about me?"

"I mean, yes?" Dullahan said, realizing she'd said too much but was too far along to turn back now. "You have to admit, Everly, you've basically stolen her life from her."

"Uh, no? I'm protecting her from making bad decisions," Everly corrected her.

"By removing her ability to make decisions for herself? You've essentially turned her into a damsel in a tower."

"I'm *saving* her from her own stupidity!" Everly shouted after coming to an angry halt.

"Okay, all right," Dullahan said. "I'm not playing devil's advocate. I don't even like Fenn, do whatever the hell you want with her."

"Why don't any of you like her? You're all *me*. It doesn't make any sense that you're so cold to her."

"Why would I care about such an irrational twit?" asked Dullahan. "All the memories of her I inherited from you irritate me. She was going to kill you over that stupid cousin of hers."

"Sarah was an utter wad," Everly conceded.

"The absolute worst," Dullahan agreed. "And yet Fenn still threatened to stick you with that holy sword for that monster's sake."

"Sarah was choking her out when I found them. I saved her damn life," Everly said indignantly.

"But instead of thanking you, she started preaching from the high road as soon as she could. She's the sort of hero I despise, Everly. No nuance to her views at all, just the blandness of a black-and-white worldview."

"She would have done it too," Everly fumed. "She would have killed me to save the life of that creepy freak. How was *I* the bad guy in that situation?"

"It's like Dark Helmet taught us. The forces of good are *dumb*," Dullahan said with conviction. "Honestly, I'd just cut ties with her. Who needs the hassle?"

Everly was silent for a moment. Then she shook her head. "No. No, I can't do that yet."

"Why not?" Dullahan wondered. "How hard could it possibly be?"

"Dullahan, it's not about things being difficult, okay? It's about being right. About being *superior*. Fenn needs to acknowledge me as her better. That's all there is to it. Until I hear those words, I can't quit myself of her."

"Well, that's psychotically wholesome in a single-white-female sort of way," Dullahan replied.

Everly smiled dreamily. "She can be perfect. I just need to carve away all those little imperfections holding her back. Patience is what's required."

"She could kill you," Dullahan said. "She could still be dangerous."

"Danger makes everything more exciting," Everly said with the genuine conviction of the genuinely mad. "Danger is what I *live* for!"

Dullahan had no response.

The search for the source of the scream turned into more of a chore than Everly expected it to be. No matter how many corridors they ran through or how many rooms they searched, they came across nothing. It seemed as though the fallen castle itself was determined to stymie any effort to prevent further loss of life within its darkened halls, which Everly thought sounded pretty cool as a potential pilot for a horror serial but was an extremely frustrating thing to experience firsthand. And just how large was this place, anyway? There really was too much room to cover.

After a while, Everly stopped running and began stomping around the place in an annoyed huff. Was this a trick being played on her? Was this an attempt to wear her down physically in order to set a trap? And if so, where was this trap and how could she properly spring it? This whole thing was getting *boring*, and boring Everly was a mortal offense. In fact, soon it would be a capital crime.

People who committed crimes were *criminals*!

Instead of playing along any further with whatever this dull little scheme was, Everly chose to stretch out her mind, filling the depths of the castle with the immensity of her power of spirit granted to her by her elemental servant, Eris.

With Eris currently hibernating alongside her sister, Titania, Everly had far less fine control over her mental abilities. With Eris at her side, she was capable of applying a delicate touch to those whose minds she interacted with; without Eris, it was more like wielding a baseball bat that could shatter someone's very personality like it was made out of fragile glass. Such clumsy destruction would ordinarily embarrass Everly, but at the moment, she wasn't in the mood to care. She felt that she'd been rightly provoked and whatever happened next was her opponent's fault.

More screams sounded throughout the keep, but this time the voices were male. Everly and Dullahan easily followed them to their source and were greeted by the sight of several men in filthy white clerical robes. Each of their bodies emanated an unclean aura of corrupted magic that Everly found familiar.

Everly had encountered someone dressed like these men earlier in her life, in the forest north of her hometown of Anders. A practitioner of a nasty breed of magic that originated with demonism. He'd been utterly humorless and more than a little disgusting. A low-tier opponent who embodied the term *unworthy*.

Everly hadn't been very gentle when she disposed of the old bastard. He'd been a nasty one, making gross threats and even resorting to turning into a massive man-eating spider when he couldn't get his way. He'd clearly been a tryhard.

What was truly annoying about that guy, however, was that, as it turned out, he hadn't been the only one of his kind. His priestly order, the Ashen Brotherhood, was dedicated to the service of Acedia, one of the seven demon kings who ruled the massive continent to the south.

Ever since Everly had killed him, the Ashen priests had been bugging her left and right with their pathetic attempts to avenge their lord.

Pathetic was exactly the right word to describe their antics. They mostly consisted of appearing where they weren't wanted, summoning a bunch of lesser demons to harass her, and then screaming in terror when Everly smote them. Which was fun, but only in mild bursts.

"Jeez, did you guys follow me here?" she asked them disdainfully.

When the pain from their brief psychic contact faded enough for them to respond, one of them said, "Everly Skolder! What are *you* doing here?"

Everly didn't appreciate being questioned over where she chose to go by some random nobody, but she did like the energy he'd put into sounding dismayed. She enjoyed springing out of nowhere to annoy her foes.

"Well, wouldn't you like to know?" she crowed.

"You won't stop us this time!" the angry demon priest bellowed.

"Well, we'll see what happens next, now, won't we?"

"Your interference ends now, heathen! Today, we avenge the murder of our master," shouted another one.

"Oh, you guys are still mad about that one, huh?" taunted Everly.

"Our wrath is endless! Our justice will find you!" shrieked the first one of them to speak. Then his body began to swell and expand, shredding his dirty robe until all his foul clothing was ripped apart by his growing body. Soon, a massive spider towered over Everly, rising to its back legs with venom dripping from its fangs in a terrifying display of arachnid hostility.

"In Sssloth's name, I ssshall devour you!" he declared.

Then Dullahan appeared as if out of nowhere and punched an armored fist through the abomination's skull; it made an oddly pleasing sucking sound when she removed it, like the noise a shoe makes when being pulled out of thick mud.

"Azery!" wept one of the stunned Ashen priests.

"No, I'm Everly," Everly said chidingly. "And *this* is Dullahan. Dullahan, introduce yourself to these nice strangers, please."

Dullahan effortlessly hurled the corpse of the massive spider at the demon worshipers, scattering them on impact and crushing one of them to death outright.

"That counts as an introduction, right?" Everly asked them.

No one responded to her question.

Rude.

A clever one-liner can be difficult to come up with on the spot. It bothered Everly that no one ever seemed to appreciate that.

"As you bug worshippers can see, my associate here can easily tear you apart no matter how much you struggle to resist," Everly informed them. "Sadly for me, but *luckily* for you, I think crushing the weak is boring. Because of that, I'm willing to spare your lives if you'll tell me what you're doing here."

"We'll never give in to you! The seven will feast upon your soul!" shouted one of them.

Everly frowned and then nodded her head in his direction, a signal that Dullahan quickly picked up on. Before he could react, she had her armored hands upon him and began tearing him apart.

When Dullahan was finished, Everly faced the remaining priests and cleared her throat loudly while she waited.

"So, okay, I didn't even want to be here, I just got dragged into it, seriously, wasn't even looking to mess with you, I swear it on my mother," said one of them, a handsome blond man in clean green robes. "I'm with Greed's crew; I don't even care about these Sloth freaks. They turn into spiders—that's just nasty."

"It *is* nasty, but that's not exactly telling me what I want to know," replied Everly.

"Lady Pride put out the word," the follower of Greed said. "She told us something big was going to go down at the headquarters of the Eastern Temple. Said all we had to do was wait for it to happen and then go finish off whoever was left standing."

"I thought you said you were with Greed?" Everly asked him. "Why are you running around on Pride's say-so?"

"It doesn't matter which of the lesser six is our primary lord," the man said. "Pride holds the central throne. She's the primary sin. If she wants something done, it gets done."

"So, she's the queen bee, huh?" Everly said thoughtfully. "In that case, maybe she's the one I should be speaking with. What do I need to do in order to arrange a meeting?"

The follower of Greed's mouth dropped open. "Uh, yeah, that's *way* above my authority, Your Royal Majesty. Is that right? Is that how I'm supposed to address you?"

"Honestly, I'm not certain myself," Everly confessed. "I'm not exactly British; I never learned the proper terminology. Just wing it."

"I have no idea what a *British* is, but winging it is definitely something I can do. So, uh, Your Gracefulness, I can't address Lady Pride directly. But I could totally introduce you to my boss."

"Cowardly wretch! How dare you assist the slayer of our lord!" growled one of the Ashen priests.

"Shut up, scabby!" the follower of Greed sneered. "The brotherhood of Greed has a lust for life and I'm not going to waste mine getting killed over a proven loser like your master!"

"You will pay for this treachery," promised another priest. "When we tell the others of what you've done, you will be carried naked to the central web and devoured alive by my hungry kin. Your anguish will last an eternity!"

"For the void's sake, it already feels that way whenever you freaks start making your speeches," the follower of Greed snarked.

Everly was in full agreement. With a snap of her fingers, sharpened spikes of stone erupted from the ground and pierced the skulls of each of the remaining Ashen priests, snuffing their lives out in an instant. "They never know when to dial it back, do they?" she asked the man after the last body finished twitching.

"Heh, you're telling me," he said somewhat nervously.

"Got a name to go with the face, pretty boy?" Everly asked him.

"Do you really think I'm pretty or are you just objectifying me?" he replied.

In response, she favored him with a smile. "You've got wit. I like that. We can do something with that later."

"I can do a *lot* of things you might like later," the man said with a smirk.

"Wow, look at you moving to close the deal already. You must really want it all," Everly said with amusement in her voice.

"Hey, what can I say? It comes hand in hand with the crowd I run with. A man of Greed wants it all, Your Majestic-ness."

"Yeah, well, let's start with your name and see where the evening takes us from there," Everly said.

He really was a handsome guy. He wore his green robes unopened down the middle, which made it easy to see his lean, athletic musculature. To her, he looked like a long-distance runner, which he probably was. Followers of Greed were notorious thieves and conmen; they likely had to be prepared at a moment's notice to run for their lives from the people that they'd swindled.

"I'm Nathan," he told her as he held out an easy hand. "Nathan Devere of the order of Avarice."

"Cool," Everly replied. "Nice to meet you, Devere. I'm Everly, the *giver* of orders. Now, tell me what I need to know about meeting your lord."

Nathan nodded with an easy smile, then opened his mouth to speak before suddenly freezing in place. "Huh?" he suddenly asked before collapsing to the floor.

"Everly?" Dullahan asked in confusion.

"I'm not doing this to him," Everly said as she knelt beside the man.

He was still alive, but his body was trembling violently as though he were having some sort of epileptic fit. Thinking quickly, Everly gestured for Dullahan to approach her. Then she pulled a finger from one of the gauntlets of her armor and placed it between Devere's teeth.

"Oh, what the hell, boss?" Dullahan complained.

"Sorry, I was just trying to act quickly," Everly said to her. "I read once that people having a seizure can bite their lips and tongues pretty viciously. It'd be a bad thing if he bled out before he could assist us."

"Couldn't you have cut a strip from his robe and tied his mouth shut?" asked Dullahan.

"Like the ghost of Jacob Marley?" Everly asked her incredulously.

"Oh, yeah, it would have been kind of like that," Dullahan said with a sheepish chuckle. Then she said, "Scrooge! *Scroooooge!*"

Everly smirked but then said, "Stop, stop. Something's going on here. Keep your guard up."

As Devere continued to tremble mindlessly on the stone floor, Everly and Dullahan heard footsteps slowly coming their way. They were measured, unhurried strides that spoke to the confidence of this new arrival.

Curious, Everly stared ahead without fear as she waited for the stranger to show himself.

When he finally appeared before them, bare chested and covered in demonic markings and strange runes, Everly let out an amused snort of laughter.

She hadn't seen him in years, but she recognized him at once.

Alec of the Eastern Temple. A former squire of the order, whose life had been stolen by the now-deceased Nalec.

It really was a small world.

"Well, well, well," Everly chortled. "Take a look, Dullahan! It seems our old friend Alec has now entered his goth phase. How've you been, choir boy? Stand up straighter! You shouldn't slouch in front of a lady."

"How is he standing to begin with?" Dullahan wondered. "Didn't you tear off his limbs?"

"It would appear that someone has regrown them," Everly said. "Okay, Alec, I can see you have a speech waiting in your throat to send my way, probably a detailed monologue covering how unpleasant your life became after encountering me. Can we just skip the part where you obviously abandoned your fealty to the light and sold your soul to the seven in order to gain your revenge?"

"*I* was not the one who abandoned the light . . . It was the LIGHT that ABANDONED ME—"

"Aw, you're doing exactly what I asked you not to do," Everly said in disappointment. "Listen, I get it, I did you a few wrongs and now you'd like to have words with me, but there's no need. I—"

Alec raced across the room, faster than even Dullahan could react against, and slammed his fist into Everly's face as hard as he could. His arms, Everly noted, were forged of a strange ebon-colored metal that emitted long coils of blackened steam into the air. Whatever sorcerous alloy it was, it granted Alex superhuman strength that was comparable even to Grail, Everly's finest creation. For him to move so quickly meant that his legs must have been made of the same substance. Everly was genuinely impressed at the level of craftsmanship that had gone into him. Whoever had reforged this boy had done a good job of it.

Everly flew backward across the room and slammed painfully back-first into a wall, which cracked upon impact, causing dust to fall from the ceiling. She then stumbled forward and tenderly brought her hand to her face and wiped it carefully across her mouth.

Her front tooth felt loose. At the slightest touch from her tongue, it fell from her gum. Her hand was also now wet with bright blood.

Before her, Alec loomed with clenched fists, raring to deliver another blow.

Everly smiled at him and nodded. Then she spat out her tooth and said, "Okay. Okay, Alec."

Then she gestured for him to do it again.

His face distorted with anger; Alec answered her taunt with another violent blow that Everly caught with her own hand.

"*Hmmm,*" she said as she grinned nastily at his shocked expression.

Then she ripped him in half at the waist.

CHAPTER SIX

Greed

Everly stared at Alec flopping pathetically on the ground and tried to feel anything other than satisfaction at a cruel job well-done.

If there had ever been a time when she'd been a gentler person than this, she struggled to recall it. It was true that she'd been quite violent in her previous life on Earth as well, but never to this extent. She'd just parted a man from his lower body and the only thing she felt was enjoyment of the deed.

Everly was just going to have to admit it. She wasn't the cartoonish villain she'd originally set out to be. Saturday morning programming could explain her motives but not her methods. She was a step beyond. Somewhere along the way, she'd evolved past her more earnest ambitions and had become the genuine deal. Everly had truly become a fucking monster.

All her prior denials and hesitancy at accepting such a blatantly obvious fact were now embodied in the dying man that she'd mutilated. The man who rightly hated her so much due to the injustice that she'd dealt him years ago and forgotten about. She wasn't like the charming villains she'd grown up being delighted by on her television screen.

In this moment, she realized that this was who she was. A murdering bully who did whatever she wanted with no remorse. The worst that humanity had to offer the world. That was what Everly Skolder represented.

And yet, this realization didn't move her heart. She didn't care what she'd done to this weakling, just as she didn't care about all the other lives that she had trampled over.

She only wanted to be entertained.

With that in mind, Everly knelt before Alec, staining her clothing in his blood as she did so, and carefully joined the two separated sections of his body back together before casting a powerful healing spell that began mending what her hands had torn apart. When she was finished, Alec's body was completely restored.

A smile began quivering at the corner of Everly's lips as she stared at her toy. She leaned down and gave him a warm hug before saying, "That was fun, Alec. I enjoyed that a lot. Did you enjoy it as much as I did?"

Alec looked back at her in confusion and said nothing in response, which only made Everly's smile grow wider.

Now Alec's eyes grew fearful. "What do you want from me?" he asked her. "You've already ruined everything that I am."

"I know," Everly said in agreement. "You're tainted with demonic magic, Alec. I can smell it coming out of your pores. You seemed like such a righteous man when I first met you. I guess all the time spent in the hole I dug for you burned your faith away, huh? I feel *so* bad for you. It had to be a horrible thing to realize you aren't the person you thought you were."

When Alec refused to respond, Everly felt a spark of delight beginning to grow in her center. Why was it so much fun to hurt him? Was it satisfaction from knowing how thoroughly she'd broken him? How she'd changed him from a warrior of faith into this tainted, broken wretch?

It had to be.

"I know it was Anne who discovered you," Everly continued. "Was she the one who delivered you to Pride? Is that the one you've sworn yourself to? What a lamentable descent that is! To think you were once the squire of magnificent Lady Sylvain, only to become some demon's toy. It's enough to make me weep."

"Don't say her name!" Alec suddenly shouted as he threw his hands around the collar of Everly's cloak and pulled himself up to face her. "Don't you ever mention her name again, monster! You aren't worthy to speak it! You aren't worthy to—"

He choked off when Everly flicked him on the forehead, rendering him unconscious. "Lady Sylvain," she said. "You know, now that I think about it, I don't believe we've come across her corpse yet. Where could she be?"

Dullahan shrugged in response. "You're asking me? I don't pay attention to dead bodies. That's gross."

"You know, you *were* forged through the dark arts of necromancy, dummy," replied Everly. "Dead bodies come hand in hand with the family profession."

"They're still gross. I choose not to dwell on them," Dullahan said stubbornly.

Everly bit her tongue to keep herself from making a hurtful comment. Today was a good day for Dullahan. She'd finally come out of her room and had made a genuinely useful contribution. It was progress, but one sharply worded rebuke could easily undo her progress.

Everly didn't know why she'd become so tolerant of her creation's sensitive moods. In true evil-overlord style, it probably made more sense just to kill Dullahan and replace her with something more useful. But she couldn't find it within herself to do such a thing.

Maybe she just had a fondness for broken things?

"Everly? What are you looking at?" Dullahan suddenly asked her.

"Huh?" Everly replied. "What do you mean?"

"You were staring at me," Dullahan said.

"Oh," Everly said. "I think your armor looks cool."

"You do?" Dullahan asked in surprise.

"I said I did, didn't I?" Everly said as she rose to her feet. "Take them both," she said as she gestured to Alec and Devere. "Alec has questions we need answered, and Devere has introductions to make for us."

"You're really going to take a chance on this one?" Dullahan asked. "I was picking up some massive fuckboy vibes from him."

"I don't like that kind of salty language, young lady." Everly smirked. "In this organization we don't make judgments about others. We take advantage of them if they're useful and toss them aside once there's no longer a need for them."

"What if he isn't useful?" Dullahan asked.

"Meh, Matty could always use some fresh protein." Everly shrugged.

The next evening in the memory palace, in the receiving room that Everly created for the occasion, a shape began to gradually take form before her eyes as Devere slowly chanted in a language foreign to her ears, extolling his master, Greed of the cardinal sins, to favor them with his presence.

It was a slow process, which Everly found mildly annoying. The room was filled with chests of gold and rare gems that Everly had created specifically to entice the old thing into paying them a visit. All the wealth she was throwing at him should have prompted a faster reply.

Eventually, Greed finished materializing and stepped out of the portal that his servant had prepared for him. What faced Everly now was what one could consider the quintessential sandy-haired fox. A grinning man wearing cargo shorts and sandals along with a wide-brimmed straw hat and an unbuttoned flower-printed shirt.

He looks like one of those obnoxious retirees who like pricing native Hawaiians out of their own area codes, Everly thought to herself.

He reminded her strongly of her own father. Which made his greeting to her feel even more unsettling.

"Well, *hello* there, child of my line," he said merrily. "I've been wondering when you were going to pick up the phone and give us a call. Papaw was beginning to feel well and truly excluded."

Child of his line? Was he claiming to be related to her? As if!

"Okay, you can stop that bullshit right there," Everly said immediately. "I know for a fact that my paternal grandfather was murdered by my dad two decades ago. You're not a surprise relation, so don't think for a moment that I'll fall for that crap."

"Jeez, kid, I said you were a child of my line, not my granddaughter," Greed said in a hurt tone. "I *did* father one of the Van Belsar ancestors about four or five hundred years back, so I'm possibly your great-*times-eight*-grandfather, not that you seem inclined to care about that."

"Ugh," said Everly in dismay. "This opens up the possibility of me having thousands of unwanted relatives."

"Heh, yeah," Greed said merrily. "More than ANYONE else."

"Yeeeah, I might have to schedule a purge."

"Really? Why?"

"People who brag about quantity have no appreciation for quality," Everly said.

"I love both!"

"I suppose you would."

"Oh, shut up and tell me what you want, brat," Greed said with a sigh of growing irritation.

"Uh, obviously *everything*," Everly replied as though it were obvious.

"See? Told you you were one of mine," chuckled Greed, who began to cheer back up. "Don't be so bent out of shape over it either. In this world, humanity is directly descended from the seven kings. No one made your kind out of dust this time around. There's not a person alive who hasn't got some of us running through their veins."

"Wow. That feels like a real burst of lore." Everly nodded indifferently. "Should I be taking notes?"

"Uh, I *am* sharing a massive secret about the origin of your species with you," Greed said. "You could at least pretend to be impressed."

"Yeah, but the fact that you *want* me to be impressed is really making me resist it," Everly said sadly.

"Has anyone ever told you that you're a bit of a handful?" asked Greed.

"I'm just a product of the times," Everly said. "So, with that in mind, would you *please* tell me what the hell is going on?"

As Everly and Greed conversed, she observed Devere climb weakly to his feet with a slight stagger before dropping heavily into one of the chairs placed throughout the room. He'd passed out. He'd warned Everly earlier that summoning his lord would drain a large amount of energy from his body. It seemed the cost was even greater than he'd expected.

Everly decided that it made sense if she really thought about it. Why *wouldn't* the embodiment of greed take more than he needed? It was all part of his brand.

Still, that he fed directly off his follower's life energy wasn't something that she'd expected of him. It made him seem more parasitic than she thought he would be. Was that what a demon's true nature was with those who worshipped them? Were they more like mosquitoes with an intellect than actual people?

Everly decided that this was a good reminder that the old demon wouldn't settle for anything resembling a fair trade. The more he could get for himself, the more he would try to take. That would be what his nature demanded.

What would be the best way to play this out? The easiest solution would be to give Greed however much he wanted. Everly could transmute dirt into gold; there was no shortage of material rewards she could give him if he proved useful. But she had a feeling that Greed would want something more important than money as his payment.

That would be a classical demon-lord power move. Pretending to want one thing only to turn around at the last moment and reveal that there was something else he'd been after all along. Then he'd spring his trap and mock Everly's foolishness before hurling her into the abyss. That would be a proper Faustian maneuver, wouldn't it?

(That might be something she'd like to try for herself one day.)

Of course, a potential double cross could only happen if Everly herself was Greed's target. There was an equally good chance that there was something else entirely he wanted, something that she had no knowledge of. And until she knew more, she'd have to stay on her toes. The seven kings were ancient creatures with lifespans that were impossible to measure. Technically, their greatest weapon wasn't their magic or their armies, it was their experience. If she truly wanted to match them, she'd have to think creatively.

"I'm surprised you haven't figured this out on your own." Greed smirked after downing a glass of wine. "Isn't it obvious? You're being targeted by someone who's nursing quite a grudge."

Everly's eyes narrowed at his words. "Are you being serious?" she asked. "I'm *obviously* being targeted by someone nursing a grudge! Kestrel said as much herself. What I'd like to know is why Pride is assisting her and what I must do to convince her to stop. Otherwise, I'll have no choice but to declare war on the demon continent."

Heh, *no choice*. As though she hadn't been spoiling for a fight with them for what felt like ages.

"Well, now, hold on a moment there," Greed said as he poured himself another drink. "Let's not fly off the handle here, okay? War with you is something the rest of us would very much like to avoid. Don't be so quick to believe the press about all seven of us being all-conquering maniacs."

"Aren't you *supposed* to be all-conquering maniacs? I mean, don't you want to rule the world and all that?" asked Everly.

"Nope!" Greed handily answered. The speed with which he said it was definitely suspicious.

"Nu-uh," Everly insisted. "You're all demons, and everyone knows that demons are sour-flavored lollipops. You're just trying to scam me," she said accusingly. "But I'm way too sharp to fall for your tricks."

"This is religious discrimination at its core," Greed complained. "What right have you got to make assumptions about my nature? Just because I'm the embodiment of selfishness doesn't mean I'm incapable of sharing."

"Isn't that exactly what it means?" asked Everly.

"Yes! But that doesn't mean my heart doesn't yearn to be as kind and generous as Father Christmas himself," said Greed. "I'd love to oversee a major holiday. Pride has the Fourth of Julius, Gluttony has Thanksgiving, Lust gets Valentine's, Wrath has all the Irish ones. What about Greed? When's *my* big day?"

"Hey, we're talking about things that concern *me*, dummy," Everly cut in. "Don't greedily assert yourself as the subject of conversation."

"Did I do that?" he wondered.

"You did!" Everly said.

"I'm incorrigible!" he declared.

"I'm beginning to notice that," Everly replied.

"Well, if we're back on topic, then as a matter of fact, we *like* the current status quo and would very much like it to continue indefinitely," Greed said. "What good would a pointless outbreak of war with demonkind achieve? Do you know how much work it was repopulating this stupid continent the last time you little apes nearly wiped each other out?"

"Do you really expect me to believe that?" Everly asked skeptically.

"Everly, if we wanted these lands, we'd have taken them ages ago," Greed replied. "We're hardly lacking in manpower. It would be the easiest thing imaginable to place Winstead beneath our heel."

"If that's so, then why haven't you?" Everly asked him.

"I just *told* you. It took us centuries to get your ancestors off the endangered species list. I wasn't lying about your being a distant descendant of mine. In truth, you've got the blood of all seven of us flowing through your veins. All humanity does. Those with the strongest concentration of it are the ones capable of bonding with the elementals and wielding magic."

"Knock it off," Everly said with a scowl. Did he really think she wouldn't notice what he was attempting to do?

"What? Knock what off?" Greed asked with a genuine look of confusion.

"Quit giving me these meaningless bits of lore that don't really explain anything useful for my situation," Everly said. "I don't care about any of this pointless background info. You're trying to impress me with secrets, but I don't *care* about these age-old mysteries."

"How can you not? It's all so interesting," Greed said. "It all pertains to the last war against the Speakers and the oath we swore to the Radiant One in order to—"

"Nooooo, please stop," Everly demanded as she stomped a foot impatiently. "Greed, do you really think I can't see these salesman tactics for what they are? I'm not buying a vacuum cleaner from you, okay, bud?"

"Did you just call me a salesman?" Greed asked her as a frown began to grow on his face.

Everly sneered at his reaction before continuing. "Clearly! You're obviously trying to forge a bond here, trying to build up some trust to make me think of you as a reliable source of information, but let me tell you, old man, there are drug dealers who operate with more subtlety than you. Obviously the first few impressive but ultimately pointless secrets are free. But anything of *actual* importance will cost me big time! That's when you'll reel me in."

"Hey, I sincerely resent being compared to a fisherman!" Greed replied angrily. "Those guys smell of the ocean. I can't stand that odor."

"You're an allegorical fisherman!" Everly snapped at him. "Or maybe you're a metaphorical one. I don't know, it's been ages since I attended an English class. The fact remains that this meeting so far has been pointless. Have you got something for me or not?"

"Graah," Greed grunted as he sat himself in a chair and glowered at her. "The lack of respect. That's what I hate the most. I'm Greed of the seven cardinals! Avarice himself! When I was the primary sin, no one would ever dare to speak to me like you just did. If they did, I'd take *everything* from them!"

"Oh, come on, can you just not help yourself?" Everly asked him in exasperation. "You just had to casually mention that you were once the primary sin, didn't you? Now, despite my lack of interest, I feel obligated to say, *YOU were the primary sin? But then, why is Pride in charge?* Well? Get on with it, you manipulative old bastard."

"Well, if you insist," Greed said smugly. "You see, kid, Pride gets all the credit for the great wrongs in the multiverse. Why did that archangel fall? Why did that woman partake of the apple? What prompted the construction of Babel's tower? On Earth, all the little preachers say to their flocks, *pride, pride, pride.* Well, BULLSHIT! All that chaos was wrought in the name of GREED! GLORIOUS GREED!"

The old man stood up then and spread his arms, sloshing the contents of his glass as he did so. "I was the one who expanded our reach and introduced the most destructive concepts ever conceived of to the world. I created *economics*, Everly! Money! Something that people are willing to kill for but doesn't actually exist outside of mutual agreement! I created wealth and poverty; I spearheaded manifest destiny and land theft! I'm the father of colonialism! I'm the guy who did all that!"

"If that's the case, then why aren't you the one calling the shots?" Everly asked him. She really didn't care, but Greed seemed to love drama as much as he did free wine.

"I don't know!" Greed yelled. "For some reason, she's just stronger than I am! One day she decided that she could do a better job and then pulled me from my seat! Like I was nothing! Like I didn't matter in the slightest! My own little sister! Can you imagine how that felt?"

"*Noooo*," said Everly, who'd murdered her own elder brother and taken his place in their father's affections.

Still, it was easy to see (at least from her perspective) how Greed could have been overthrown. He had power, Everly could feel that for herself, but he didn't have a warrior's resolve. He was a merchant, a mere man of mercantilism. He might sell weapons or collect them, but it was clear he had no talent for *using* them.

Pride, on the other hand, from what Everly had been able to learn, was a killer. When she wanted something, she claimed it with her own hands. It was clear to see that she'd patiently let Greed build up the wealth and power of their kingdom, and when she felt the time was right, she set him aside and claimed rulership of the Seven for herself.

The fact that Greed hadn't retaliated against Pride meant that he was no match for her.

That also meant there was an excellent chance that Greed wasn't a match for Everly either.

And here he was, alone in her palace, dwelling on bitter memories of the past, like the old loser he was.

What would it feel like to murder another demon king? she found herself wondering.

CHAPTER SEVEN

Girls Are Hard Mode

So, yeah, I was going to kill him, but I held back at the last second," Everly said later as she dined with Fenn.

Instead, she realized how pointless it would be to strike Greed down, since the old fool would eventually be summoned back by his followers. It was bad enough that Sloth and Pride already had grievances with her. Why increase that number to three?

Of course, the obvious solution would have been to simply kill every single one of his followers and leave him stranded in the void. That would be the easiest way to permanently deal with all seven of them. But she wasn't ready to make a move on that scale yet, so for now, she had controlled her urge.

It wasn't easy. Everly wasn't good at self-denial.

Fortunately, her half-hearted resolve to spare Greed's life had been swiftly rewarded.

"I don't know who this Kestrel is, but if she truly wields the holy blade, then you need to seek out a Godwell," Greed had told her. "There have been maidens from other families, but theirs is the one tied closest to the sword. It always favored them, you see."

"You say that like the sword is alive," Everly had said.

"It is. It possesses sentience and a powerful will," Greed said.

"The sword possesses a mind of its own?" Everly asked, now genuinely impressed with the old man's knowledge, despite herself.

"Indeed," he said as he sipped from his glass. "Most people don't know that, of course. The holy blade's name is *Prominence*. Twin blade to Providence, the hero's sword."

"There's a *hero's sword*??" Everly asked excitedly.

"Oh, yes," Greed sniffed. "Fortunately, we rid ourselves of that bastard thing ages ago. I doubt very much anyone will ever find it."

"HA-CHOO!" sneezed Asher on another continent.

"Are you all right?" asked Providence, the sword of evil's bane.

"Yeah, thank you," she replied. "Just walked through some dust was all."

"Having a respiratory system must be difficult at times," said the sympathetic blade of heroes.

Greed had eventually taken his leave but insisted that Devere stay behind so that he could stay in contact with Everly, which she reluctantly agreed to. It wasn't like she didn't have the room to spare.

The two of them are probably hatching a plot. I guess it'll be easier to predict if I keep him around for now, she decided.

Besides, it wasn't as though he was bad on the eyes. Quite the opposite, in fact. And he seemed like a really fun person. It might be nice having him around until she eventually had to kill him for his inevitable attempt at betrayal. So, she had Carter assign him some private quarters.

Naturally, they would be monitored.

With Devere now sorted, Everly turned her focus toward the conflict to come.

Dinner with Fenn.

"I want to go home," Fenn told her blankly while they ate spaghetti at the table in her room.

"Fenn, there's no point," Everly replied. "I keep telling you, there's a war going on right now. It's not just me taking on Winstead; lots of nobles are using me as an excuse to settle old grudges. The Godwells in particular are being targeted on all sides. Your family is basically finished in this country."

"That's even more of a reason why I can't stay here!" Fenn said urgently. "Everly, at the very least, I need to protect my mother and my little sister!"

"You have a little sister?" Everly asked, surprised for the second time that day. "Fenn, you never told me that."

"Actually, I don't," Fenn admitted. "But even if I did, it would be none of your business."

"What are you talking about? You and I shouldn't keep secrets from each other. If we're going to rule this world together, then honesty should be our best policy with each other."

In response, Fenn swept her plate of food to the floor. "Stop saying things like that! I have no intention of ruling anything."

Everly was aghast at the sight of the wasted meal. "Fenn! Not cool! Carter made that for us. Stop throwing these damn tantrums!"

"Everly! Let me go, I've been here for seven months!" Fenn yelled. "You're not going to get the answer you want, haven't you realized that by now? Just let me leave!"

"God damn it, I just wanted to have a nice dinner and talk about a few things," Everly said as she wiped her mouth with a napkin and dropped it on her plate. "Why can't you just do as I say?"

"Oh, get over yourself, Blondie! Why do you always make everything about you?" asked Fenn with growing frustration in her voice.

"Everything *is* about me, dummy!" Every replied. "Once you realize that, life will be so much easier for you."

"What gives you the right to treat me this way? To treat *anyone* this way?" Fenn demanded to know.

Everly looked at her with an amused expression before responding. "Who can really say? I suppose I just got tired of pretending I wasn't the most interesting person in the room," she said with a shrug.

"Everly, what exactly do you want from me?" Fenn asked her.

"The same thing Cheap Trick does."

"Huh?"

"I want you to want me." Everly smirked.

Fenn sighed and leaned back in her seat with her arms crossed. "Be serious for once. Just answer the question."

Everly frowned as she tried to think of an answer.

"I dunno," she said after giving up. "Do I want to kiss you? Kill you? It's so hard to say. You got me feeling things. It's complicated."

"It doesn't have to be," Fenn told her. "Everly, just let me leave. I can make my own decisions and I can face the consequences on my own. That's part of growing up, okay? Learning to live without fear."

"And what exactly is that supposed to mean?" Everly asked angrily. "I'm not afraid of anything. I'm not! Why would you even say something as silly as that?"

"How can you not be? You try to control everything and everyone around you. How is that not a fear-based reaction to the world?"

"Wow, did you get a degree in psychology while you were locked up, Fenn?" Everly asked disdainfully. "You seem *so* insightful now."

"Oh?" Fenn said smugly. "It seems that I've hit a nerve, haven't I, Blondie? Could it be that beneath all your blustery bullshit, you're a little more insecure than you like to let on?"

"Fenn, you're *so* cute when you try to be mean," Everly said archly. "But why don't you dial it down a notch?"

Instead, Fenn rose from her seat and sneered at her with her hands on her hips. "You really can't handle the world on its own terms, can you? That's why you live in this little fantasy fortress, surrounded by sycophants and monsters designed to worship you. Because you're a little coward."

In response, Everly stepped closer to Fenn until their faces were inches apart, glaring at her. "Making fun of my crib and my people now? Fenn, that's just being *bitchy*."

"Just calling it like I see it," Fenn said unwaveringly. "Why didn't you attend the academy, Everly?"

"What?" Everly asked, confused by where this was going.

"Why didn't you go to the academy?" Fenn repeated. "You had all sorts of plans about role-playing there and mingling with the children of nobility, right? But you didn't. You made Beverly—"

"Neverly," corrected Everly.

"Yeah, that one. You made Neverly go in your place. But why? I thought playing a fool while being secretly superior was going to be a big rush for you. Instead, you made one of your little clones do it. Do you know why I think so?"

"Oh, please share, Fenneth. You're *so* wise, I can't resist hearing your opinion," Everly said with growing acidity.

"You can't handle people at all," Fenn informed her. "Your superiority complex is a way of masking your confusion and lack of real confidence. I think being around normal people unbalances you, and that you're a lot less certain of your place in this world than you let on."

"Are you finished?" Everly asked her.

"Yeah, pretty much. It felt so good to say, though," Fenn said cheerfully.

"Why did I even tell you about all that?" Everly asked herself. "I should have known you'd weaponize it against me."

"You told me because you were trying to impress me. You *always* try to impress me," Fenn told her. "Honestly, do you even get how boring it can be listening to you?"

"Shut up," Everly said. A red light glinted in her eye as she spoke.

"No, I don't think I will," Fenn replied. "I'm bored with being here and I'm bored with being your sounding board. I don't want to listen to you anymore, Everly. I don't want to be around you either. I'm not going to change my mind, so kill me or let me go, but just *stop* with all this. I don't want to participate any longer."

"You . . . you just want to throw away everything we've built up? You just want to *leave*?" Everly asked her.

"Hell yes, I do!" Fenn shouted at her.

Everly stared at her with her hands clenched into tight fists, trembling with a sudden desire to hurt the other girl, pound her into submission, make her admit she was lying, that she needed her and was just being thickheaded.

But she knew that wasn't true.

"Why don't you like me?" she asked Fenn quietly.

"The fact that you can even ask me that in the face of everything you've done is exactly why you don't deserve an answer," Fenn told her scornfully.

Suddenly, a portal erupted into existence in the middle of the room.

"Fuck it, I don't care, get out," Everly said suddenly. "I met someone else, anyway. He's a demon priest; it's kind of a dark profession, but I'm cool with it. We vibe."

"What?" Fenn asked.

"I also met another dude. I mean, we met a while back, but he's, like, back in my life now, you know? I pulled his arms and legs off, but now he's got these cool prosthetics. It's fucking metal, you wouldn't get it. I've got options, you can go now."

"Whatever," Fenn said as she walked past her.

"That's a portal to nowhere, by the way," Everly said. "I don't even know where it goes. It'll probably drop you off in the middle of a monster's nest. Doubt you'll last the night."

"It beats staying here with *you*," Fenn said with a scowl.

"Get fucked!" Everly said heatedly. "Anyway, I don't even know what I saw in you in the first place. You were just my experimental phase! Everyone wants to try out the preacher's daughter, that's just human nature! You cry too much, you know that?"

"*Puta*," Fenn said angrily as she stepped through the portal.

"Bitch says what?" Everly yelled back.

But there was no one else in the room to hear her.

That was when Everly realized that in her haste to be rid of her, she'd forgotten to ask Fenn about the sword.

"FUCK!" she yelled.

CHAPTER EIGHT

Ghosted

Fenn was stupid. That was really all there was to it.

Fenn was *so* fucking stupid!

How else could one describe someone foolish enough to take a hard pass on ruling the world? Someone who turned her nose at the idea of limitless power and authority. Someone who *dared* to reject a piece of real estate as prime as Everly herself?

Stupid. That's exactly what Fenn was.

Truly, it was the only explanation.

"She really doesn't know what she wants," Everly said to anyone who asked. Or didn't ask. Or were minding their own business when she'd intrude upon them and continue ranting on the subject as though they'd been having an ongoing conversation on the matter.

"I mean, seriously, she's *weak*," Everly continued, this time with the very reluctant Beverly as she lay on a couch, having her feet rubbed by a random skeleton. "She hasn't trained her powers nearly enough. Plus, she's too swollen-hearted. Every little bit of human suffering is just going to tug away at her."

"You make her sound like a puppy collector," Beverly said with an amused laugh. "Or a burgeoning cat lady."

"She practically is one!" Everly shouted. "Just watch! Before you know it, she'll be pulled in so many different directions that she won't be able to move forward. That, or some monster will come along and just kill and eat her. She can't do anything without me. She just doesn't have the pluck."

"The pluck?" Beverly said, trying the word out and not liking it. "Did you really just say she doesn't have *the pluck*?"

"Yeah," Everly said. "Why? What's wrong with it?"

"Do you want some apple cider or something?" Bev asked her. "I feel like people who use *pluck* as a noun probably enjoy drinking apple cider."

"Shut up," Everly said irritably.

"Or maybe they'll head out to the state fair in their Model Ts to go slurp on some marmalade, or whatever," Bev continued. "Maybe get some raspberry jam at a Canadian strip mall."

"Why a Canadian one?" asked Everly. "Which province?"

"Probably *Nover Skotier*," Bev drawled. "Yeah, I wish I had the time to go cartin' to Nover Skotier for some maaarmalade and raspberry jam."

"You're getting on my nerves!" Everly warned her.

"Ohhh, I'm showing a lot of pluck, aren't I?" Bev sneered.

In response, Everly threw a couch cushion at her and left.

"Something I said?" Bev asked with a devious smirk.

"God, why is she being such a pill?" Everly muttered to herself as she made her way down the corridor. "What's wrong with the word *pluck*? Lots of people still say *pluck*! It's not some old-timey turn of phrase. And what does that even have to do with Nova Scotia? It would have been so much funnier if she said Manitoba! *Let's go cartin' to Manitober for some marmalade!* See? God, she's such an idiot . . ."

"Aw, come on, Everly, she's not *that* bad," said a friendly voice to her side. "Bev was clearly just—AHH!"

Moving with superhuman speed, Everly quickly spun around and seized the stranger by his throat and smashed him into the corridor's wall, pinning him easily into place.

"And just who might *you* be?" she asked the man.

"Hey!" the stranger managed to choke out. "Wh-what are you doing?"

He was a handsome man, a few years older than Everly, with a scruffy chin and curly brown hair that needed a trim. He was taller, as well, but clearly not a warrior. From how he slapped helplessly at her arm, it seemed he had no talent for getting out of a dangerous situation.

"I asked who the hell you were," Everly repeated as she tightened her grip. "Why are you following me?"

"What do you mean by that?" The man squirmed in confusion. "Everly, come on! It's me! Kent the ghost! I'm part of the team!"

"Part of the team? Huh? Would you kindly explain to me what you're babbling about?" Everly asked as she set the man down to his feet. "Don't make any attempt to run. I'm not in the mood to play chase."

"Everly, what's with you?" Kent, or whatever his name was, asked in a wounded tone of voice. "I've been hanging out in this memory palace for ages. Remember, I got killed at Bremburg? My spirit ended up getting snatched away by Eris, and once I convinced her I wasn't a demon, she said I could crash here! I've been helping you guys out ever since!"

Everly squinted at the man carefully, trying to determine if he was playing a trick on her. As she focused on his face, her memory was gradually triggered, bringing her images of a slovenly-looking commoner whose head had been torn from his body by one of the infected monsters who'd been haunting Bremburg.

"Wait, wait, wait," Everly said slowly. "Okay, I think I remember now. Aren't you that idiot who ruined the career of the previous maiden of the holy blade?"

"Huh? Ruined her career?" Kent shook his head indignantly at the accusation. "No, no, I helped my girl, Laurel, realize that there's more to life than perpetual duty to an organization that doesn't really appreciate her. I taught her how to have fun and, you know, live for the moment."

"And how exactly did you do that?" Everly asked.

"Well, I got her to loosen up and not be so uptight," he replied.

"You mean you hit it," Everly said. "Tapped it. Got laid. Played keep away with her chastity."

"Everly, Jesus, why are we getting so vulgar?" he asked her.

"I'm just telling it like it is. You were her boy toy." Everly nodded. "And you got her to quit working for the Western Temple." She stepped away from Kent then and gave him an appraising look. "I guess I owe you for that; she was by all accounts a very skilled opponent. She might have given me some trouble before I finished leveling up."

"Hey, Laurel and I still did good in the world," Kent said. "We just worked as independent adventurers was all. Did things on our own terms."

"Cool, sounds fascinating, I really don't care," Everly said with a dismissive shrug. "So, you died and now you're basically freeloading off me, huh?"

"Hardly!" replied Kent. "Eris has me teaching her and Titania about Earth culture and shit. I'm like their tutor now, right?"

"You're from Earth too?" Everly asked. "Like, physically, or are you a rebirth like me?"

"Yeah, I'm from Earth. You know that; Eris said she told you for me."

"Uh, no?" Everly said. "This is the first I've heard of it and the first I've heard of you."

"That's nuts," Kent said incredulously. "I hang out with Eris and her sister all the time. They're nice people."

"You really think Eris is a *nice person*?" Everly asked him skeptically.

"I mean, sure, she's got a temper, but who doesn't? I get mad when I stub my toe," Kent said diplomatically. "Back when I had toes, anyway."

"So, how does being one of Eris's little pets make you a part of my team?" asked Everly.

"Are you saying I'm not? I thought we were friends!" Kent said. "I've been there for, like, all the major developments. You know, like when you killed Fenn for the first time, which I really wasn't cool with. You know, because she's my girl's little sister? I got heated, but I thought we talked it out. And I was there when you met your dad and Claudia! You really didn't see me?"

Everly shook her head.

"Jeez, what about when I backed you up when your crazy brother Aiden stole Jack's body?" Kent said in an increasingly louder voice. "I distracted him long enough for Beverly to put a spear through him!"

"That was *Aiden*?" Everly asked in a shocked voice. "Oh my god, it *all* makes sense now!"

"You were being serious about not knowing who he was?" replied Kent. "Jeez, I thought you guys were like doing a meme or something. Holy shit, Everly, you really haven't noticed me at all?"

Everly shook her head again.

"Sorry, Kent. I guess you just don't have a very powerful presence," she said apologetically. "Don't feel bad about it, though. Have you ever heard that phrase *you're a waste of space*? I guess that applies literally to you. In death, you've become a total nonentity. A nobody from nowhere."

After considering her words, Kent slowly slid down the wall to his haunches and covered his face. "Oh, jeez. Oh, god, how could I not have noticed? Was I really that unaware that I couldn't see that no one else was aware either?"

"Seems like it." Everly nodded. "Wow, Kent, you must be a real loser."

"I feel like one!" Kent sobbed into his hands.

Everly began to brighten up, pleased that she'd discovered someone who was having a worse morning than she was. "Damn, if it was me in this situation, I'd want some way to end my humiliation."

"Well, it's not like I can kill myself!" Kent cried. "Why didn't Eris just tell me I was talking to myself? Why would she be so cruel?"

"Kent, remember who Eris is and then ask yourself that question one more time," Everly laughed.

"It's not funny!" he said.

"It really is," she said, laughing again.

"My entire life is some elemental's idea of a joke!" he said.

"Well, it's not exactly your *life*, now, is it?" Everly smirked. She then reached down to help the despondent ghost to his feet. "C'mon. Guess I can't leave you this way if you're on the team."

"Where are we going?" Kent asked with a sniffle.

"We're going to do some early recycling," said Everly.

CHAPTER NINE

Not Clever

Where are we going?" Kent asked as he followed Everly down the corridor.

"We're going to make life a little easier for ourselves," Everly replied.

"How are we going to do that?" Kent asked.

"Kent, is this who you are?" Everly asked him mildly. "Are you Mister Questions, the asker of questions? That could get *so* old. Listen, buddy, all you need to know is that I'm doing you a solid! Just take it on faith, Everly is going to do you right!"

"Okay, okay, sorry," Kent said quickly, not wishing to displease her. "Uh, thank you, though. I really do appreciate you doing this for me. Uh, whatever it is you're about to do."

"What can I say? *De nada!*" Everly replied. "Honestly, Kenny—"

"Kent," he said.

"Hmmm," she said while giving him a hard look.

"But whatever, I get called Kenny all the time, it's no bother," he said quickly.

"Oh, cool, then," Everly said with a pleased expression. "Like I was saying, you've put me in a good mood. If you've really been hanging around me all this time, but now I can finally see and hear you, that means my spiritual perception has become even stronger, so good for me! That's what we call growth!"

She paused and waited expectantly for Kent to say something. Once he caught on, he immediately began clapping for her. "Hey, congratulations, Everly! It's like there's nothing you can't do!"

"I *know*, right?" she happily preened. "That's what happens when you have unlimited potential; not that *you* would know, but hey, life is what it is, right?"

"Uh, yeah, I know," said Kent with slightly less enthusiasm.

"You know what I'm *sayin'*," she continued.

"Yeah. Yeah, I get it, boss," Kent frowned.

"You know what I'm *shaaaayin'*," Everly drawled.

"Okay, Everly, I get it! I really get it!" Kent repeated once more, now with a scowl.

"Oh, cheer up, sad sack, I'm just messing with ya," Everly said with a playful grin. "Just so you know, I've already got plenty of yes-men on the payroll, and although each and every one of those adorable, spineless sycophants is near and dear to my heart, I'm not looking to add to the collection, understand?"

"I do." Kent nodded. He'd been a member of more than one thieves' guild during his career as, well, a thief, and had run quite a gamut of bosses back in those days. Some demanded unquestioning submission from their underlings and ruthlessly led with an iron fist. Others liked to be challenged by their followers because they claimed it kept them sharp. Uneasy is the head that wears the crown and all that.

Everly seemed to be an uneven mixture of those two traits, but the time Kent had spent observing her had also taught him that she could be absurdly irrational. As though she hadn't set an image in her mind of who exactly she wanted to be. Which, frankly, was terrifying when one considered the immense power she wielded.

Okay, so I've caught the attention of a needy psycho, he thought to himself. *Whatever, that's just a day ending in y back in Cali.*

No point in getting worked up about it. If Everly wanted a pet that occasionally barked at her, Kent could be that lapdog. Any indignity would be worth it if it brought him a chance, just a *chance*, to see Laurel again.

Laurel was worth it.

Laurel was worth *everything*.

"I think I'm going to like you, Kent," Everly continued. "But at the same time, conversing with someone I can barely see is something I can see growing old quickly. So, let's get you some fleshy-flesh."

"Holy shit, you're going to make me a body?" he asked her excitedly.

"Yeah. Absolutely. But, uh, not quite," Everly replied. "I'm not going to make you a body so much as I'm going to *make a body yours*, you feel me?"

"I really don't," Kent said in confusion.

"It's cool, we'll get you sorted. Won't be a thing," Everly assured him. "Like I said earlier, just think of it as *recycling*."

In the darkened space of the room in which he was confined, Alec, the former squire of Lady Sylvain, continued to sleep dreamlessly, locked into slumber by a spell Everly had placed on him days earlier.

She had a vague idea that he could be of some use to her, but she hadn't yet decided how. Until she could reach a decision, she had him rest in a state unclouded by memory or regret. It was probably the kindest thing she'd ever done for him.

An unwitting consideration, of course.

But now, someone entered the room quietly, carrying with him a long dagger, the edge of which he placed against Alec's neck.

"I never thought it would be you who'd turn against us," the would-be killer said gruffly as he prepared to slit his victim's throat. "I never thought you would be the one to betray all we stood for. Damn you, kid. I always thought you were one of the good ones."

With that said, the intruder prepared to deliver a fatal wound, only for the dagger to suddenly fly upward, tearing itself from his grip before he could react. Then it launched itself through the air into the waiting hand of the room's third occupant. The one who'd been waiting for the intruder to arrive.

"Would you mind keeping your hands to yourself?" called out Everly's voice. "The guy you just tried to assassinate is a rare collectible."

Light flooded the room in blinding quality and revealed Everly sitting, legs crossed, in a beach chair, sipping daintily from a glass of juice through a straw.

"You?" the intruder asked in surprise.

"*Meeeeee*," she replied with an insolent grin. "And can I just say, GOD DAMN! I'm two for two tonight! I just had this *feeling* you were going to make your move, right? You were doing a great job of concealing your emotions, but there was just this little smidgeon of anxiety you couldn't quite hide. It felt like . . . oh, how can I put this? It felt like the fear of getting caught."

"So you know," the masked figure said resignedly. "When did you figure it out?"

"It's not like it was difficult, sweetie. The new guy is always the culprit in the detective stories," Everly replied. "It really didn't help that you laid the charm on so thick."

"Heh. I suppose there are worse things to be guilty of than having too much charm," said Nathan Devere as he removed the mask from his face. "So, you caught me. What happens next?"

"That also isn't hard to figure out," said Everly. "I hate people like you, so I *hurt* people like you."

"People like me?" asked Devere.

"Clever little bastards who think they can manipulate me because I'm young. The audacity of it is *infuriating*. What gives you the right to live with that level of self-confidence?" asked Everly.

"Are you sure I didn't just hurt your feelings?" asked Devere. "Maybe you were hoping we could get a little closer? Not that I'm much interested in psychotic little shrews like you."

"Attempting to anger me into killing you quickly," Everly said. "*Slick*. I can see you're an old hand at the classic tropes. Still not going to save you. But I really do appreciate the effort."

"If you lay a hand on me, Lord Greed will surely strike you down," Devere said quickly as Everly stood up, which prompted a fair bit of contemptuous laughter from her.

"Nice try, buddy," she tittered. "But let's be serious. You aren't a priest of Greed any more than I'm the hostess of *The Price Is Right*. No one's going to step in on your behalf if I kill you."

"What are you talking about? I summoned Lord Greed right before your eyes!" Devere shouted as Everly stepped closer.

"Yeah, you did. And in all honesty, that's what really gave you away," Everly said with a nasty smile. "I've seen these little demon worshippers perform their summoning magic before, Nate. Every single time, they were *empowered* by the presence of their masters. They were juiced up! But not you. Summoning Greed made you *weak*. His presence exhausted you! I'd never seen that before."

"B-but Lord Greed acknowledged me! He lent me to you—"

"He's got thousands of servants in this world, if not millions," Everly cut in. "And I doubt very much he knows more than a handful by name. You call that acknowledgment? I bet you a gold piece he couldn't pick your face out of a crowd."

Devere frowned at her words as he strove to find a way to deny them. Then he breathed deeply and sighed in acceptance.

"Yeah, well. Old Greed definitely isn't the sharpest among the seven. If you have to pick which of those bastards' orders to infiltrate, his is by far the easiest," he said.

"Yeah, I kind of had a feeling," Everly said.

They now stood inches apart.

"So, you must be some kind of holy knight, huh?" she asked him casually. "You must be if you have knowledge of the dark rites but still suffer from their use. I take it *Nate Devere* isn't your real name?"

"I'm called Tyrnos," the man in front of her said proudly. "A humble servant of the true temple, sworn to the glory of the light and the service of Lady Sylvain, now and forever."

"Tyrnos? The mercenary saint? Wow!" Everly exclaimed. "I've heard of you! So, what was a celebrity like you doing dressed like a priest of Greed? I don't get that part."

Tyrnos was genuinely famous throughout the land. The cocky eldest child of a mercenary family, Tyrnos joined the Western Temple after single-handedly smashing a conspiracy masterminded by a cult of demon worshippers who attempted to poison the water supply of an entire city.

His actions were so impressive that Lady Sylvain herself declared Tyrnos a destined champion of the light and personally knighted him. When word reached the masses of a lowborn man's ascendency to the highest ranks of Sylvain's order, recruitment for the temple's armed forces allegedly increased threefold.

Everly considered that canny marketing.

"The robe belonged to some bastard I caught unawares once the fighting died down," Tyrnos said stiffly.

"So, Pride and Greed *were* working together to take down the Western Temple," Everly said.

"They were," Tyrnos said angrily. "And *this* traitor led their forces!"

He gestured toward the sleeping Alec, clutching his fists with white-knuckled intensity as he did so. The murderous fury on his handsome face was a sight to see. Everly found it dazzling. What was it about genuine righteous anger that she found so appealing?

"Eh, he might have had his reasons," Everly said in what she hoped was a nonchalant manner.

"Selling his soul to Pride? Killing dozens of people who considered him their brother in faith and arms? Driving Sylvain into hiding? What could possibly excuse his actions?" Tyrnos demanded to know. "He's a traitor to our cause, deserving nothing but death!"

Well, in Alec's defense, being reduced to a torso and getting buried alive for a year probably didn't help his sanity, Everly thought but did not say. What also didn't help is that his victims had likely been members of the temple's high council that Everly had killed and replaced with duplicates in a bid for a silent coup.

"So, I suppose this means that Sylvain and Kestrel weren't in cahoots?" she asked, hoping against hope it wasn't true.

"Of course they aren't! I have no idea who that woman is, but she's as dangerous to this world as you are," Tyrnos said hatefully. "She calls her cause righteous, but she willingly murders the servants of the gods! She and her blackened knight are as damned as any demon worshipper could ever be!"

"Well, okay, then," Everly said. "I'm glad we got all that out of the way. Now we're going to take a walk down the hall."

"To where?" asked Tyrnos.

"Well, now I'm going to drag you down to the rat room, so my friend Matty can ask you a few pointed questions to determine if you're hiding anything else from me. For your sake, I hope you aren't. Afterward, once we're sure everything's been squeezed out of you, I'm going to introduce you to a new acquaintance of mine."

"And afterward?"

In response, Everly clapped a hand on Tyrnos's shoulder and began to gradually squeeze it until the relentless pressure caused him to cry out in pain.

"Well, *then*, Tyrnos," she said with a humorless smile, "I intend to make a brand-new man out of you."

CHAPTER TEN

Life in Conflict

When they received the news that Everly was renewing hostilities, the Grand Council of Winstead, as they often did in stressful situations like this, erupted into panicked arguing.

"By the light of the gods, why can't we stop her?" one of the councilors demanded to know.

"You're asking *me*? How would *I* possibly know?" shouted another one.

"Weren't you the loudest voice advocating for removing magic users from positions of authority, Lord Gregarious?" asked Caleb Vae-es Belsar, the heir to Belsar County and the personal guardsman to the queen. "Why complain about our lack of available options when you were the one who made our side weaker?"

"Watch your tone, you insolent boy!" shouted Lord Gregarious, who represented the Reformation Movement, which had long wished to remove the kingdom's magical bloodlines from their ancestral roles as the leaders of the nation. "That decision was agreed upon by *everyone* on this council! Time and again the mage lines have proven themselves unworthy of the authority entrusted to them! One only has to look upon our enemy to realize the folly of turning our backs to their mischief any longer!"

Like many, he dreaded to name their opponent directly. Most called her *the self-proclaimed Empress*. Others had more forceful language by which to describe her, most popularly, *that bloody witch!*

Of course, the use of such vulgarities could not be condoned among these venerable people; after all, everyone here was far too dignified to speak like a normal person. But the words always flashed through their minds whenever they received word of the latest actions of Everly Skolder.

"But was it necessary to engage in such a purge in the midst of our current war? It certainly comes across as ill-timed," said Caleb pointedly. "It was certainly poorly planned."

"Watch what you say, you little welp! I'll suffer no aspersions cast upon my good name!" growled Gregarious.

"I'm a welp, am I? You're certainly quick to resort to insults when merely asked a question. I suppose this is what comes of being . . . *short* tempered," mused Caleb, who stood more than a foot taller than the much shorter councilman.

"I'll grind the insolence from your lanky body, you arrogant bast—"

"ENOUGH!" said the stern voice of Queen Seraphine, silencing them both immediately. She was the beautiful, eldest child of Septus, and the kingdom's recently crowned monarch. Although young, she possessed her father's ambitions and his taste for violence. She was determined to see her reign outlast this war.

"This is an unparalleled emergency," she said to the two of them. "Why are the both of you squandering precious time with pointless recriminations, when the fate of my kingdom is at risk?"

"But, Your Grace, he—" sputtered Gregarious.

"Gregarious. You are as vital to the functioning of this council as the furnace is to the forge. You have earned no dishonor and need not defend yourself so vociferously."

"Your Grace, I thank you!" Gregarious said, bowing deeply.

"As for you, Caleb: the decision to strip the mage lines of their authority was mine alone. Gregarious was correct; it was high time they were taken to task and reminded who truly rules Winstead. Considering this uprising is being led by a member of *your* family, you should be grateful that I haven't had you banished or worse."

"What must I do to finally prove myself? How far must I go before you'll finally be convinced that I'm not my father's tool?" asked Caleb quietly.

"You know what I want you to do," the queen said to him. "Approach your sister when her guard is down and run her through in my name. Only when my father has been avenged will I truly accept you once more."

Many in the room nodded in agreement at the queen's words.

"Her Majesty is truly wise," said a solemn, scarred man bearing one eye. "Everly Skolder is a fool besotted with love for her family. Who better to strike a killing blow than you, the dear brother she barely knows?"

"This may seem like a dishonorable tactic," muttered another councilor. "But underhanded tactics may be the only ones which succeed. I led a charge against her at the Siege of Thena'e. We held the castle against her army's onslaught for over a week and dared to believe we'd last until reinforcements arrived. But Everly grew impatient with the performance of her generals and set herself directly against us. It was full noon that day, but . . ."

The councilor looked away as a single tear ran from his eye, caused by the memory now tormenting him. "By my ancestors, the sun *itself* turned black, as if it could not bear to see what would occur! And then she—she—she . . . !"

He covered his face, silenced by both shame and fear.

"Do not weep, Commander Grayner," the queen said soothingly. "There are many of us who have suffered thanks to that scarlet-handed fiend. We all know her danger, and we are all resolved to oppose her, always."

"Always!" shouted Gregarious.

"Until the end of everything!" shouted another.

Soon the room burst with affirmations of defiance and loyalty. The queen let it continue for some time, letting their unity calm their fears, before signaling for silence.

"I wish I could agree to this," said Caleb apologetically. "But I am sworn to a knight's code of honor. I won't deceive my sister, nor will I attack her in so cowardly a manner. There is a right way of doing things, and this is not it."

"What a remarkably stupid thing to say," said Gregarious. "Your sister practices the black art of necromancy! She is beyond the grace of the light and completely undeserving of an honorable ending. You are too naive, Sir Caleb."

"Indeed, wise Gregarious," agreed the queen. "She was the first one to discard honor when she entered my father's home and struck him down! How could you possibly offer her such knightly consideration when *she* backstabbed us first?"

Caleb said nothing and looked away.

"Pathetic," the queen said when he refused to meet her gaze. "Remain silent, then, Sir Caleb. I have no need to hear the voice of a knight who refuses to obey his liege."

Nodding quietly, Caleb resumed his place at her side. As Seraphine gazed at him, she gripped the arms of her chair tightly and frowned in disappointment.

Why won't you just do as I say? she thought angrily to herself. *If you'd only prove yourself truly loyal, we could have something together. Caleb, you're an utter fool.*

"We must match her darkness with equal strength in the light," said Gregarious as Seraphine's thoughts returned to the present discussion. "This renewed violence feels different from what came before. I say we redouble our efforts in locating the former paladin of the north, Riley Kilo!"

"I oppose this, Your Majesty!" said another councilor, a frowning, bald man dressed in priestly garb named Father Verisos. "However useful she was during her temporary service, the fact remains that Riley Kilo is *not* one of us! In fact, she stands accused of murdering dozens of temple holy knights!"

"A blasphemous act!" said an angry voice.

"Indeed! The title of paladin should never have gone to her! There is too much about that young woman that we don't know! How can we be certain she isn't another one of the enemy's servants?"

"Riley is the only weapon that can match her!" said Gregarious. "Nothing we have will suffice! Whatever the reason for her dispute with the temple, the fact remains that only *she* has power comparable to the so-called Empress!"

"Your Majesty, we must not do this!" Verisos said. "The temple is barely holding together as it is. All four of the paladins have vanished, and the council of bishops is doing everything it can to keep order. If word got out that we were depending on a known heretic for our salvation, who knows how they'd react?"

"Can you present us with any other options?" Seraphine asked him impatiently.

"N-no, not yet, but something will surely come along," Verisos said desperately.

"In that case, what other choice is there?" asked the queen. "We must be willing to do whatever it takes to counter Everly. Even if it means upsetting a few clergymen. I'm afraid that survival takes precedence over religious piety."

"Then I can only pray that this decision will not fracture us any further," said Verisos solemnly.

"Be at peace, old man," replied the queen. "I too despise engaging in these machinations. But our enemy is ruthless, and we must be willing to adapt if we're to diminish the harm she seeks to cause. We will soon prove to you how right we are."

"Then I volunteer to lead the search for her," Caleb suddenly said. "I vow to personally locate Riley Kilo or die in the attempt."

"You expect me to believe your hollow words?" asked Seraphine skeptically.

"I will do anything to aid you that does not diminish our honor," replied Caleb.

"Ha!" laughed the queen. "Fine, I'll take you at your word. Permission granted. But you *must* not fail! The continued freedom of Winstead may very well depend upon your success."

"A responsibility I accept with the greatest solemnity, my queen," said Caleb.

"I will offer a thousand prayers for your success. Now go."

The council stood as one and bowed to Caleb, who bowed deeply to them in return, some more reluctantly than others.

After he marched from the chambers, the queen declared the council temporarily adjourned and urged them all to get some rest. They broke into small social groups and talked among themselves as they slowly left the room.

"He has no chance of succeeding," said Gregarious bluntly. "The greatest investigators in the kingdom have been unable to turn up a trace of Kilo. It's a fool's errand."

"I thought you said Riley Kilo was our only hope?" Seraphine said with a raised eyebrow.

"Just a bit of pageantry to tempt young Caleb to the hook," Gregarious said smugly. "There are other options I would like to speak of with you later. Options best discussed without the overly honorable around to offer their opinions."

"In that case, thank goodness we had an excellent excuse to send him away for now," the queen said. "I'd rather not have my childhood friend executed for defying me. However, there must be a punishment. A hopeless quest that also serves as a banishment will do nicely."

"I thought that might be your aim," said the amused Gregarious. "Now, that's a plot your father would have thought of."

"Do you think so? I'm flattered," Seraphine said with a smile.

"It would be nice to find a similar reason to rid ourselves of the sanctimonious Father Verisos."

"I'm in complete agreement," Seraphine said. "But we must go about it carefully. The temple remains a powerful ally."

"Not so powerful that it can prevent a little accident from happening," Gregarious said primly. "Elderly people fall down their stairs all the time."

Again, Seraphine found herself smiling at the old man's words. "Yes, I suppose they do."

Seraphine sighed in relief when she entered her chambers. She was bone-tired. The common people had a clever saying for times like this: *heavy is the head that wears the crown*. It was an apt description of her daily life since accepting her royal title. She honestly wondered sometimes if she had somehow displeased the gods her family venerated.

Every day that she was forced to deal with this crisis was exhausting. Winstead was a beacon of strength and tradition to the world. She had a duty to outlast this crisis and see to it that Everly Skolder was put down like the mad dog that she was. The kingdom could have only one ruler, and it would not be some baseborn usurper.

Why was she being tested like this? Seraphine had dreamed of the day she would inherit the crown and begin correcting the many mistakes her father had made during his reign. She would be strong, ruthless, and unbending. A force unlike any other! The most powerful woman to ever live! She was certain that she would become an invincible legend, worthy of the legacy her ancestors had left her. Seraphine, the warrior queen!

And yet, despite her expectations, Everly Skolder had happened.

Wretched cow. Thieving bitch, oh, I hate her so much!

Life should have been perfect. It *would* have been perfect, if not for the sudden arrival of this rebel and her inexplicable power. She'd thrown the entire country into chaos, divided families, sacked great cities, and now aimed her sights on the capital. She dared to proclaim that the whole of Winstead would be hers before the year ended, and so far, that arrogant claim appeared to be coming true.

Come at me, you vile thing. I swear I'll be the one to end you, she promised herself.

Seraphine found the news incredible when Everly first began her campaign of conquest. She'd attended classes with her at the Royal Academy and found it difficult to believe that the quiet, bullied little girl that she didn't deign to speak with had somehow become the superhuman leader of an army of undead abominations. Had she always been that powerful and was merely hiding her strength? Impossible! Why would anyone do anything as pointless as that?

It was obvious that Everly had backers. This entire thing was a charade meant to overwhelm the gullible. But Seraphine wouldn't fall for it! Soon, she'd have her hands on the would-be Empress. Then she'd put her thoroughly to the question and make her confess to all her schemes. Once her handlers were named and identified, a purge the likes of which Winstead had never experienced would then commence.

You'll pay for your little games, Everly. I promise you. We'll see which of us is left standing in the end.

Lost in thoughts of vengeance, Seraphine poured herself a glass of wine and sat at her table, sipping her drink as she considered the events of the day.

Caleb had once more disappointed her. How many opportunities could she continue to give the fool before she was forced to throw him away? All he had to do was dispose of his bastard sister and deliver his queen the victory she deserved. And yet, not only did he refuse to do so, now he was arguing the point in public!

This is undoubtedly due to the influence of my idiot cousin, Ian, she thought dourly. *That's the problem with these heroic types. Their way of thinking is practically infectious!*

Prince Ian Kane. The beloved *Dragon Slayer*, the great hero of the country! Seraphine couldn't stand the fool and found it difficult to believe they were family. What had her father's purpose been in summoning him back from his banishment? He should have been left to rot in the far north alongside all the unwanted remnants of the civil war.

Instead, he'd returned to her father's court and began promptly making a name for himself. Winning allies and admiration, as well as earning the love of the small people with his effortless heroics and endless adventure. It was as though he were running for office! Unfortunately for her, Caleb was one of the young men at court who had been won over by his chivalrous ways.

Caleb is mine. Since childhood, he's been mine to mold and mine to play with. I don't share my toys! Not with anyone! I don't want him to be a hero, I want him to be my pretty, broken little angel. And anyone who gets in the way of that will pay!

It was all so very, very frustrating . . .

And then Seraphine had an idea!

Oh, this was good. This was very, very good!

Stupid cousin Ian used to spend hours speaking with Everly during our days at the academy, just before she disappeared. Everyone knew about it, even though it was an absolute scandal, considering her baseborn status.

What if I decided that he was the one who convinced my father to hold negotiations with that witch? That would make him responsible for the assassination! That would give me all the reasons I need to have Ian executed!

A smile grew on Seraphine's face as she considered the awful possibilities. *That'll teach him to pull my Caleb's attention away from me! Why, thank you, Everly Skolder! You've proven yourself to be surprisingly useful—*

"Your Majesty! Your Majesty!" cried an urgent voice from the hall.

"What is it?" she snapped, displeased at having her pleasant thoughts interrupted.

"The armies of the Empress! They're approaching the capital!" said the frightened messenger. "We'll be surrounded within the hour!"

Terror suddenly surged throughout Seraphine's heart. *Surrounded? HOW? How did no one see their approach? How did they get here so quickly? How did they bypass so many defenses to reach here? This can't possibly be so!*

"Your Majesty, what are your orders? Your Majesty, what should we do? Your Majesty? Your Majesty? Please tell us what to do!" the voice said desperately.

Seraphine sat staring at a wall, uncertain of how to answer him. Uncertain of what would happen next.

"Am I going to lose?" she meekly asked the empty room.

She soon had her answer.

CHAPTER ELEVEN

The Final Days of Winstead

In the final weeks preceding the total collapse of Winstead as a nation, the skies began tearing themselves apart.

An unprecedented storm raged throughout the land, devastating verdant forests and destroying every settlement in its path. People cowered helplessly within their homes as the thatch was ripped away and the supports came crashing down, wondering if the foretold end had finally arrived, praying for succor, for protection against nature's wrath, not yet knowing that the worst was still to come.

In addition to the death toll, much of the kingdom's precious farmlands were left ruined, promising an uneasy future for the realm, now fearful with the expectation of famine. The Royal Society of Mages was summoned before the throne and berated like insolent children by their new monarch, Queen Seraphine, the eldest daughter of Septus, who blamed them for failing to predict this disaster, an act which was also unprecedented at the time, because the relationship between the monarchy and the proud mages that served it could be tenuous in the best of times and required constant mediation for its maintenance.

Forces loyal to the throne, others seizing an opportunity for advancement, and still others seeking only to settle old grudges in the name of religious mania called upon the new queen to declare a purge and remove the magic-wielding filth from their lofty positions. Magic was an abomination and even the so-called masters of the craft couldn't control it completely. Besides, *Everly's* use of magic proved its dangers! Clearly, it was time to return to older values. Time to be *done* with the forces of sorcery! The new queen was young, and arrogant, and had been raised with her mother's radical views.

Without the influence of the Godwells to council against this foolishness, it wasn't difficult to sway her.

The nobility, most of whom derived their authority from their magical bloodlines, knew what was coming and refused to play their role in the upcoming farce. Overnight, many of them openly rebelled and sealed their lands away, creating many independent powers across the land that stood in defiance to the queen and the Empress both.

Winstead's failure to remain united would cost it dearly in the weeks to come.

Everly didn't mind the sudden appearances of so many challengers to her conquest. *Bonus stages*, she giddily declared.

"Who's singing?" asked Candice. Night had fallen over their village, and she was supposed to be asleep. Morning would arrive soon enough, and her father would need her well-rested to do her chores, but a strange voice now echoed throughout the sky, accompanied by instruments she had never heard. It was beautiful, unlike anything she'd ever heard, and it was also everywhere. What did *it mean*? The western people of modern-day Earth would have instantly recognized it as the sullen lyrics of an extremely moody pop band from the eighties. But to the citizens of Winstead, the song felt strange and ominous.

"Candy?" her little sister, Katy, said. "What is that? Is this magic?" she smiled excitedly, eager to see what was happening.

"I don't know," Candice said. "It's so strange. Hey! Where are you going?"

"I want to see who's singing!" her little sister merrily replied.

"Stay in your room," ordered their father, marching out of his bedroom. He was a burly man, with a large white stripe through his large beard. Normally a stern but loving figure in their lives, the trouble brought about by the great storms had aged him visibly, making him more prone to snap out words in anger.

He was also rattled by the news that the fighting was gradually moving nearer to the area in which they lived. Which was supposed to be *impossible*. Hadn't the traveling messengers promised that the undead would soon be defeated?

The drinking he'd begun indulging in hadn't improved things either. Hard times were coming.

"Father, I want to see! I want to see!" Katy whined. "Is it the fairies? I want to see a fairy!"

"I said no. By the gods, why is it so loud?" her father wondered. "It's unnatural."

"But, Daddy!" Katy whined.

"We need to do as Father says," Candice said, always the responsible daughter. Ever so dutiful.

The singing became louder and louder, the pacing more frenzied, the closer it came. Strange lights danced through their windows. Were there people yelling? What was happening?

"I want to *see*!" Katy yelled stubbornly.

She ran to the door and pulled it open.

"Girl, I said no!" shouted her father, a sudden fear twisting his features as he lumbered after his daughter. "Katy, stop—"

Beyond the doorway, Katy saw lights. Many lights. They were fires. Houses were burning, and people were screaming and pleading for their lives. Just outside the door, a rotting figure covered in broken armor, with a grinning mouth that seemed wider than her head, noticed her and happily sauntered over to where she stood. It opened its mouth, exposing endless broken teeth, and reached for the girl. She smiled back at it, but hers was frozen in place. Two teardrops rolled down both her cheeks, but her smile remained.

"Daddy?" she said.

He was in front of her in an instant. Then he was screaming in pain and pleading for his girls to flee.

Candice grabbed Katy and ran to the back door to escape. Over her shoulder, Katy kept staring at her father and what the creature she'd let into the house was doing to him. The voice of the song extolled the virtue of death as the image was branded into Katy's memory.

Days later.

They called him Grail, the Red Knight.

He stood nearly two meters tall in crimson armor, a massive figure wielding an axe nearly as large as he was. Attending him were dozens of knights in black armor, as well as hundreds of gibbering *things*, misshapen horrors summoned directly from the depths, that did nothing but kill and eat.

The newest song told of feeling unhappy in the presence of others.

Where the Red Knight appeared, cities burned. Crops were burned. *Everything* burned. The very soil he trod on became desecrated. To those who knew of Everly but never saw her, Grail was the face of the end. Wherever he appeared, that haunting music preceded him. People began to dread singing itself.

So much as whistling a tune at the wrong moment had gotten people hanged.

The town of Vinedale collectively wept when the eerie chorus swept over them.

They knew what was coming.

The guardsman looked at the hellish landscape that was his battlefield.

It was covered in flames and strewn with shattered stone, where war cries were bellowed and sacred oaths were sworn in the light's name. The screams of the dying intermixed with broken pleas for mercy from those who'd fallen into the wet, eager hands of the enemy.

* * *

Now there was a song about inheriting an unwanted legacy.

All throughout the carnage chimed the beautiful, maddening laughter of the denizens of the abyss, who sought flesh to play with and souls to damn. The black knights marched among the undead, barking orders and setting up ranks. The enemy was assembling for another charge, relentless in their drive to annihilate.

The singer began venting his grievances with his unkind father.

The guardsman wanted a bitter drink. He wanted a smoke. He wanted a woman. He wanted to be anywhere but here. He also never wanted to leave. This was the worst place he'd ever been. This was the *best* place he'd ever be.

Now the singer questioned the sureness of his own humanity and if he truly needed affection to survive.

This was his time to be a warrior, fighting in the last days of the kingdom. Wasn't life a strange thing?

"WE STILL STAND!" cried the commander. "Give them NO ground! Our ancestors see us! Our gods will protect us! THE CAPITAL STANDS!"

The commander died a moment later in a splash of blood and bone. One of those devils had waved a hand at him and he'd burst apart. Magic was such nasty work.

It was a good attempt at a speech, though. Inspiring. Too bad the fucking songs never ended.

"I wonder sometimes if we're living extreme lives?" he wondered to himself aloud. Then he raised his sword and charged at the first undead bastard he saw.

No one responded to his question.

No one ever did.

The capital was falling. The queen couldn't understand.

Did things like this really happen? She knew magic was real. She knew demons were real. She knew *evil* was real. But such things existed out *there* in the dark places of the world. Not here. Not in her palace. Wasn't she a good person? Why would the gods allow a good person to suffer?

Fingers scratched outside her windows.

She was on the top floor of a very large tower.

The song playing outside was about a doomed girl whose luck had run out.

"Help me, *please* . . ." she squealed to anyone who was listening.

And there *were* people listening.

Now the song said it was time to pay a debt.

If your definition of *people* was flexible enough.

The kingdom was lost.

Some would say, *A kingdom isn't the land you hail from, it's the people who created it.*

That was stupid.

Of course a kingdom was the land you hailed from. You had to *come* from something in order to *be* something! Only idiots thought otherwise.

General Carcer had been fighting what he cheerfully termed a "fighting retreat" for the last two weeks. They were heading to an eastern mountain pass, hoping to find refuge in neighboring lands. It would have been faster, though, if all the damn refugees weren't slowing them down.

Not only had the ungrateful wretches demanded Carcer's protection, daily they begged for provisions. They pointed to their hungry children, their threadbare clothing, and their bare feet and begged for help that he couldn't give. His men may have very well now comprised the last standing army in the kingdom. Each soldier had become precious and irreplaceable. *They* were the ones who needed to survive.

But the refugees weren't without value. They provided an excellent buffer between his men and Everly's monsters. As long as the fiends had easy access to food and fun, Carcer and his people had a safer time of it. Morale began to soar among the men the closer they came to the mountain pass and salvation. They hadn't encountered the enemy for days. Had they finally escaped their reach? *Oh, please let it be so!* Carcer prayed.

And then one bleak morning, they reached the pass and saw that they had been anticipated. A wall of black knights and walking nightmares of the void stood before them, blocking their path. Above them towered the baleful figure of the Red Knight.

A song about being unable to feel happiness began playing in the background. Even worse: the music.

I regret everything, General Carcer thought as they pulled him from his horse and ate him.

Benny knew he shouldn't have gone out. He'd stayed hidden in his cellar for days, hoping to wait out the invaders. But his stockpiled supplies were low. Times were hard since the great storms, and he'd shared with his neighbors. What a mistake that had been! Now *he* was the one in need, but was there anyone to repay his kindness? Of course there weren't; they'd all been killed!

He'd hoped he'd be able to salvage supplies and return home, but then some bloody soldiers had come riding into the remains of town! Hot on their heels was a trio of those horrible black knights, relentless in their pursuit. Benny had barely managed to take cover in time before the sounds of battle began. It was over almost as soon as it started.

Now all he could do was hide and hope.

"Please . . . please, no more," rasped the voice of a dying man.

"GG, bro," said a voice in an unfamiliar accent. One of the invaders, no doubt.

Benny heard a horrible spattering sound and huddled in fear.

"Jesus, Mikus, try not to enjoy this shit so much," said a second voice.

"Why? It's the best part of the job! I didn't sign up for the fighting; it's the sadism afterward I get off on."

"Does your mom know she raised a psychopath?"

"Does *your* mom know she raised a candy-ass?"

"Fuck you, bro."

"Fuck *you*, bro!"

"Hey! That's enough," interrupted the third knight. "Can we pretend we're professionals, please? Mikus, apologize."

"What the fuck for, Wes? He started it!"

"Yeah, but you're kind of offensive in general, man."

"Jesus, bro! Fine, fuck it, sorry you're a bitch, Curtis."

"Say that to my face, you roid-raging stump-cock."

"I AM NOT ON STEROIDS!"

"You got pimples on your back, bruh!"

"I'm taking health supplements!"

"It's *minotaur testosterone*, you simple-minded fuck!"

"YOU WANT TO GO ON THE RIDE? YOU WANT TO GO ON THE RIDE? I'LL TAKE YOU ON THE RIIIIIIIDE, MOTHERFUCKER!" screamed Mikus.

"If you both keep carrying on like this, I'll kill you both. I'm serious. I can't take this shit anymore," Wes said coldly. "Test my resolve. You will *fail.*"

"Wes, hey, man. Sorry. You know us, we're just messing around," said a contrite (and fearful) Mikus.

"Yeah, man. We're just—sorry. Sorry," said Curtis. "This assignment is getting to me. It's so balls."

"Yeah, it's definitely balls," agreed Mikus. "How long is Everly going to keep us out here? These people can't fight and the beer *sucks*. I'm going nuts, man."

"Exactly," said Curtis. "Fucking time differentials are messing me up too. I came back to the memory palace after a two-week run, and only fifteen minutes had passed there since I left. We've been out here ages, mopping up stragglers, dude! I'm rocking a moustache under this helmet!"

"It's a good moustache, bro," Mikus said.

"Thanks." Curtis beamed.

"Stop complaining," said Wes. "We're fortunate to even have this job. Not a lot of people are willing to hire reincarnated mercenaries. Mikus, you especially lucked out when we convinced the boss to heal you after what the countess did to your punk ass."

"What did I even do to piss her off?" Mikus said bitterly. "Psycho vamp left me broken in half."

"You say that like our current employer doesn't have a temper too." Curtis smirked.

"What *is* the boss doing, anyway? And what's with all the fucking Morrissey?" Mikus asked.

"She's been in a mood. She wants to spread it around," Wes said.

"That's so fucking emo," Mikus sneered.

"Shut uuuuup, stupid," said Wes. "You never know who's listening in."

"You know what I heard?" said Curtis. "That chick the boss was keeping locked up was what set her off."

"That little brunette with the tan? I saw her once. Woo, she was hot!" Mikus said gleefully.

"Yeah, she was," Curtis concurred.

"Yo, was she an escort or something? Her body was *fire*."

"Always with the objectification, eh, Mikey?" asked Wes.

"Mikey like what Mikey like."

"*Anyway*," continued Curtis, "they were always fighting, like, screaming at each other."

"What? Lesbians? Arguing? *Nooooo*," snorted Mikey.

"I think she likes men too. You seen her with that new guy? Nick?" Wes said.

"I thought his name was Kent?" asked Curtis.

"Who cares? I'm pretty sure she's banging him, though. You seen how close they are?"

"Bullshit! If she's boffing anyone, it's Grail! I'm telling you; she has a daddy complex."

"I thought those two were just friends," said Wes.

"Again, *bullshit*! Who's your source?"

"Matty."

"Matty? You trust that gossipy little shit? Fucking rats," said Mikus with revulsion.

"Wow, now Mikey's got something to say about the rats," groaned Wes.

"Fuck, Mikey, you hate everybody, don't you?" asked Curtis.

"No, I don't," Mikus said in a wounded voice. "I love you guys."

". . . God damn it, Mikey. We love you too. Bring it in."

Benny peered from just around the corner and saw the three black knights huddled in a group hug.

"Drinks on me when we get back to camp," said Wes.

"Hell yeah! Sounds good to—Hey, how long has that guy been hiding over there?" asked Curtis.

"Oh, I wasn't going to say anything. I wanted to let him have a little false hope and then put him down when he thought he was safe. Trying to be a little humane," said Wes.

"Can I have him?" asked Mikus.

"Eh, can't see why not. Go have fun," Wes said fondly.

"Fucking *sweet!*" said Mikus. "Hey, buddy! Hey, little guy! Come here for a sec. I wanna talk to you!"

To Benny's horror, one of the knights began strolling his way, hefting a huge sword over one pauldron-covered shoulder.

Benny bolted like a frightened hare, running faster than he ever had in his life. *Get away, get away, get away, must get away—*

A whistling sound tore through the air right behind him, and suddenly, Benny fell flat on his face. When he tried to regain his legs, he soon found that was impossible; they'd both been severed. A tree ahead of him now had the knight's sword embedded in its trunk.

"Mikey! OH MY GOD! *One* throw, *two* legs!" hooted Curtis.

"If I hadn't seen it with my own eyes," laughed Wes.

"FUCK yeah! Ultimate Frisbee, *motherfuckeeeeeer!*" crowed Mikey as he bumped gauntleted fists with his friends.

Benny lay back and looked at the beautiful blue sky above him. He was getting colder now. Blood loss, if he wasn't mistaken. It wouldn't be long now. Above him loomed the knights.

"Aww, poor little guy. Maybe you should have aimed for his head?" said Wes.

"Nah, that two-for-one hit was worth it," disagreed Curtis. "Still, he reminds me of a dog I saw hit by a car once. A labby."

"Ohhh, I love dogs," said Wes sadly.

"Yeah, he's got the same confused expression on his face. Like he's thinking, *Huh? Why is this happening? Wasn't I a good boy?* Yeah, just like that," Curt said.

"Stop! I'm serious, you're gonna make me cry. I hate it when animals suffer," lamented Wes.

"What about people?" asked Curt.

"*Fuck* people," Wes said contemptuously.

"Pretty sad, though," Mikey said, after retrieving his sword. "Dying on your back like that. Fucking *weak*. I ain't ever going out like that."

"Now you're just tempting fate, dude," warned Curtis.

"Whatever. I'm like—"

Benny closed his eyes as the cold continued to fill him. The voices of the invaders faded away, and soon he was carried from this world on a gentle and restful wave of darkness.

Everywhere across the land, the same story was repeated.

Centuries of history and culture, erased in a handful of weeks, once the great tormentor's attention was occupied with something new to amuse her.

A new name would soon be given to the conquered land for the (traumatized survivors) newly liberated citizens to celebrate. A name befitting the future bastion of freedom and hope the land would surely become, where everyone would have the inalienable right to obey Everly or die. It would be a name truly befitting of the grandeur to come.

Once Everly got around to thinking of one, anyway.

Goodbye, Winstead, with your knights.
Goodbye, any human rights.
Thanks for putting up a fight.
Goodbye, Winstead, and good night.

CHAPTER TWELVE

POX

It takes years of disciplined meditation to truly temper the mind and spirit.

The training will seem endlessly boring, and gaining mastery will be a painfully slow process, but it is necessary in order to strengthen one's self against the temptations of the astral plain, a chaotic nexus of impossible beauty and unimaginable horror, where any bit of priceless knowledge or secret path to power could be found, often at great peril for the unprepared.

The astral plain is the ultimate goal of saints and sorcerers alike. A paradise where the unholy and the divine converge with the mortal realm, leading to incredible possibilities. It is also a pretty good place to turn to for entertainment and news. Which leads us to . . .

There is a temple that exists in one of the darkest corners of creation. There, many black-robed servants attended to the needs of a massive, plant-like creature with tendrils of flesh interwoven between its vines, which was seated behind a large stone altar.

This terrifying amalgamation of vegetation and meat was known as Vextus the Many-Tongued. And he was the dreaded central truth speaker for the POX Nexus, the most popular source of information for the demon continent.

Were you to hear his words in person, your very sanity might flee you.

Thankfully, this is only a story.

A voice cut through the darkness. It belonged to a cheerful announcer contractually obligated to always sound happy no matter how much despair he felt over his unending servitude; he was now alerting the audience to prepare their minds and letting the more fragile among them escape, before their very identities were absorbed into the vastness of the fair-and-balanced miasma that was to come.

"Thought-casting live from the astral plain to the demon continent, the GREATEST NATION TO EVER EXIST, you are now channeling POX. And now, *It's Endless Night Tonight* with Vextus the Many-Tongued!"

An oddly angled symbol cast in shadow and flame suddenly burst into existence. Around it, a circle of black-robed men and women began chanting in words that must never be remembered by those who wish to avoid becoming eternally spiritually unclean.

At the apex of the chanting, one of the robed figures shed his clothing and approached the flames. He was elated and terrified. Behind him, a woman approached him silently with a stone dagger and pulled his hair back. With a swift slice across his throat, she ended his life and pushed his corpse into the flames. The fire then burst bright and profane, flooding the temple with *unlight*.

From the altar, the truth speaker began his foul oration.

"Greetings, assembled wanderers of the realms beyond. Once more, you turn your minds in our direction, seeking affirmation for your anger and unspeakable urges, which we, the purveyors of subjective truth, POX, are more than happy to provide! I am Vextus the Many-Tongued, and I have *many* questions to ask.

"For instance: Why does the crisis on the borders of the demon continent continue to go unchallenged? The troubles of the human-centric kingdom of Winstead continue to spill into our lives as *mortals*, who are traditionally a source of food and amusement, continue to seek passage into the sacred lands of the seven kings! And for what purpose? They seek asylum from the so-called Empress! Understandable, but how is that *our* concern? What's more, many of them are migrating into our proud nation unlawfully! Such blasphemous illegalities must be punished!

"And yet, despite our open call to purge this vile contagion from our lands, the will of the people has been continually denied by the Reformation Movement! Arrogant admirers of the presumptuous Everly Skolder, herself *a known mortal*, who somehow overthrew Winstead's rightful rulers and claimed it for herself! Winstead was *ours* to conquer! This is the greatest humiliation in the history of our eternal lives! This girl must be subjugated and destroyed!

"But even though our glorious seven kings are more than amenable to our thirst for vengeance, their desire to appease us has been continually challenged by the many irritatingly accurate claims of incompetence, mismanagement of resources, and venal corruption marring the reputations of our unholy overlords! These destructively fair-handed criticisms have been put forth by the self-righteous bearers of truth, who blindly point out everything going wrong in our illustrious society but offer no praise for the many successes the seven have also enjoyed! These well-intentioned and good-natured extremists *must* be purged! All causes of dissent in our harmonious cohesion must be destroyed! In the name of fellowship and peace, THEY MUST BE ANNIHILATED!

"Also making waves across society, many were slain in the halls of shopping when a disgruntled acolyte gained access to a blackened hymnal and rampaged throughout the markets, singing the words of unmaking, smiting dozens of unexpecting hellspawn, before destroying himself to avoid reprisal. Rather than praising this valiant act of merciless butchery, the clans of the fallen now demand the blackened verses be placed *beyond* the reach of the willfully malicious!

"Naturally, those aforementioned elites, who would coddle the weak and deprive all rightful denizens of the demon continent of our ancestral right to bear dangerous tools of destruction for any reason we choose, have joined with these grieving cowards to propagate their foolish message of community safety! Absurd!

"Those who were slaughtered fell not because they were defenseless against their slayer, but because they weren't given the opportunity to preemptively destroy him! Rather than banning the use of the words of unmaking among the public, would it not make greater sense to lessen their restrictions? The only thing that can stop a madman bearing a death curse is a greater madman with a *bigger* death curse!

"Next—"

"M-master!" cried out a cowering robed servant. He entered the room, cringing and kowtowing, clearly unhappy to be there. "Please, forgive this lowly one's impudence."

"There is no forgiveness, worm!" roared Vextus. "Your punishment for interrupting my talking points will be immense. Now, speak your message and begone!"

"W-we have a viewer projecting in who would like to clarify the positions you mocked earlier," whimpered the servant.

"Oh? Who dares challenge what I have asserted? Who contradicts my stated word?" asked the amused Vextus.

"Th-the self-proclaimed Empress of the recently conquered Winstead, Everly Skolder," the servant said.

Vextus stared at the mortal in surprise before asking, "Uh, are you serious?"

And that was when Everly's astral form projected into the black temple.

Earlier in the evening, Everly had been having trouble falling asleep; she'd been tossing and turning for hours before giving up and deciding to tune into the astral realm to see what was current in the void. That was when she happened to see Vextus's broadcast and was . . . displeased by some of the things he said.

"Well, *hello* there!" Everly said with predatory cheer. "I'm so glad to see you once more spreading ignorance and hatred to the many denizens of the demon continent, Vextus. Ever since I learned astral projection, you've been the loudest voice in three layers of reality. You're practically the mouthpiece of Pride's regime now, huh?"

". . . I am of essential use to my queen, yes," Vextus said stiffly.

"I miss the bow tie, though. It really suited you," said Everly.

"Change comes to all, Everly Skolder!" Vextus bellowed proudly. "I have evolved beyond the need for eccentric accoutrements."

"Does that mean you're no longer dependent on your parents' money?" Everly asked him.

"I have earned my great wealth through talent and hard work!" replied Vextus.

"Sure, you did," Everly said condescendingly.

"Bah!" yelled Vextus. "Why does the great Everly, self-proclaimed Empress of fallen Winstead, disturb my presentation to the assembled minds of inhumanity? Surely a *girl* of your many accomplishments has better things to do with her time?"

"Well, Vextus, I couldn't help but feel that your earlier comments about me had gotten a little *incendiary*," Everly replied. "Almost as though you were blaming the problems of your nation on *me*, even though I've only ever acted in self-defense against demonic encroachment. What's up with that?"

"The foremost of the seven kings, Pride, has—"

"Ah, fair warning: I've got beef with her, so watch what you say next."

". . . My apologies," said Vextus insincerely. "I *forget* there is tension there."

"Hey, no worries. I don't dwell on easy mistakes," said Everly. "That's why I gave you a warning. See? I'm fair."

"Fair? That is an interesting turn of phrase, Everly Skolder," said Vextus. "There are many who are upset by your current rise to power. They say your dealings with the honorable subjects of the demon continent have been anything *but* fair!"

"Well, Vextus," said Everly. "To those saying that, I'd like to remind them that I wasn't elected to my current position. I gained it through open warfare, underhanded dealings, and by inflicting pain and misery upon any who dared to defy me, so any criticisms that the common filth have about their various mistreatments are *completely* irrelevant because—and I can't stress this enough—their lives do not matter to me in the slightest."

"Oh, so you *admit* to stifling the voices of those who question you?" asked Vextus.

"Stifling?" Everly asked in amazement. "I didn't stifle the voices of my opposition, you oaf. I had them *silenced*! The dead question no one! Especially zombies. That's why I like zombies."

"So, you admit that in future dealings with our nation, you will openly favor mortals and mortal-adjacent species like vampires?" asked Vextus.

That question was a step too far.

"Watch your many fucking mouths, you bloated half-wit!" Everly said fiercely. "I did not and *do not* favor vampires in any way, shape, or form. I have been *very* open about my prejudice toward their kind and deeply resent any implication that I would do anything for a bloodsucker other than crush its heart in my fist!"

"*Bloodsucker* is an offensive term, Everly Skolder!" exclaimed the outraged Vextus. "There are many who are displeased with your casual usage of such a slur!"

"If it only offends bloodsuckers, then that doesn't bother me in the least," Everly said smugly.

"Is that so?" asked Vextus. "Well, just a moment, Everly, because our clairvoyants are now receiving the thoughts of many angered vampiric lords of the circle of Wrath who wish to express outrage at your sentiments. Slave, present us with the words of the great being currently overriding your free will!"

A dazed servant in a black robe came stumbling before the altar. His eyes had rolled to the back of his head, and when he spoke, it was with a darker, cultured voice that did not match his appearance.

"Yeah, hi, I'm Raptus, Master of Clan Gangrenous and he who feasts on the pure. I just want to say, Vextus the Many-Tongued? I'm a big fan of yours, and I love the way you always tell it like it is. Keep going after those elites!"

"Your sentiments are appreciated, vampire," Vextus said.

"Great, great," the possessed slave said. "Now, I just want to say this: Everly, you're an absolute menace and I can't wait until you've been ousted from your throne! You're too unapologetically mortal, and one day you're going to be exposed for the fraud you are!"

"Fraud?" Everly asked. "How am I a fraud?"

"You're a deceiver and a tool for global interests to inflict their agenda on the lands of the undying scream!" Raptus said angrily. "There's no way some random *human* became a legitimate necromancer! No way in hell! And the *audacity* of claiming you killed Primus Godwell and his daughter? You're clearly a plant!"

"Raptus! I think I remember your name now," said Everly. "You sent an envoy to my victory celebration in Winstead, who demanded proof I killed Anne Godwell."

"Which you didn't provide, which I think proves my point!" said Raptus triumphantly. "You couldn't possibly have defeated her!"

"I'm not sure why you think that, but I *do* remember how insistent your messenger was," Everly said darkly. "Heh, that was a mistake. Don't vampires share a mental bond with their progeny? Did you feel it when my carrion beetles reached her eyes?"

"She was a precious child of my line, whom I sired directly!" screamed Raptus. "You had no right to do what you did! She *will* be avenged!"

"Wow, when you speak with that level of indignation, I almost believe you regret her loss," said Everly.

"I did! I do! I love all my children! She was irreplaceable to me!"

"Cool, that means torturing her to death was the right call," Everly said cheerfully. "Nice talking with you, bye."

"I haven't finished having my say—" Raptus sputtered.

"Yes, you have," Everly corrected him.

She snapped her fingers before Raptus could finish his spiel. The servant channeling his voice then exploded in a shower of gore, silencing him immediately.

"Everly!" bellowed Vextus the Many-Tongued. "That one was not yours to destroy!"

Everly frowned, displeased at being yelled at. She slowly raised her hand, fingers poised to snap once more. Vextus quickly caught the hint and changed his tone.

"However, his kind are easily replaced, and the loss of only one is a triviality."

"Glad you see it that way, Vexy," Everly sneered.

"I despise being called *Vexy*," Vextus glowered.

"I'd get used to it if I were you," Everly said indifferently.

"Everly Skolder! Your actions today only reinforce the notion that you are an enemy and a threat to the demon nation's way of life! Have you anything to say that can justify your arrogance? Your cruelty? What gives you the right to silence those who dispute you?"

"Vextus, seriously," Everly said with growing exasperation. "I've been nothing but cordial, but I'm not going to be questioned about my policies by a member of the free press. I mean, who fucking *freed* you to begin with? Aren't you supposed to be chained in the abyss until the end of days?"

"I don't have to answer that! This is my show!" Vextus bellowed.

"So what you're really saying is that the next time you piss me off, I should just kill you and be done with it?" asked Everly.

"And there you have it, folks," Vextus said as he turned to face his audience. "Tyranny, impulsiveness, megalomania, cruelty: all traditional values we grew up with, now flung into our faces in a distorted and confusing mirror, bound in the guise of a mere mortal. The reign of Everly Skolder has only begun, but her controversies are already endless! I am Vextus the Many-Tongued, and you have been enthralled by my report. Good night!"

When the *unlight* in the room dimmed, Vextus pulled out a twenty-four-pack carton of cigarettes from who knew where and began lighting up. "Jesus, this is gonna go over like gangbusters, Everly," he said cheerfully. "Thanks for dropping by. I'm serious, I owe you for this."

"What?" Everly asked with some surprise. "Vextus, I wasn't joking about wanting to kill you. I had no intention of doing you any favors."

"Yeah, you could kill me, but I'm in the favor of the seven," Vextus replied as he took a long drag. "I'd be resurrected in no time; it's not even worth wasting a curse on, kid."

"Vex, do you realize what an utter sellout you are?" asked Everly.

"Eh, sincerity doesn't pay the light bill, girl," Vextus said with a shrug.

"So, what's the deal with blaming me for everything that's going wrong in the demon continent?" asked Everly. "I haven't even set foot there yet."

"The regime likes to cultivate power by uniting everyone against outsiders," answered Vextus. "Trying to solve problems and establish a working government is too much work. It's easier just to blame foreigners. It doesn't hurt that you're constantly killing us too."

"Ha!" Everly snorted. "Damn straight, I am. Still sucks that they're picking fights with me before I've even really done anything, though."

"Trust me, kid, I speak from experience," said Vextus. "People will always prefer an exciting lie to a boring reality. It's easier for us just to say everything's your fault because you're a despot who wants to see us fail."

"But I *am* a despot who wants to see you fail," Everly said.

"See?" Vextus said proudly. "It all comes together!"

"I guess I see your point," Everly said with a slight frown. "But if any of your idiot viewers come after me, I'll kill them and then I'll probably kill you too, even if you'll just come back later. It's not beyond me just to place you in an endless mental loop that has you dying within moments of being reborn for all eternity."

"Holy shit, don't do that!" Vextus said in alarm.

"Well, find a better way to do your job!" Everly snapped at him. "Or compensate me for disparaging my character!"

"Wait, can I do that? Can I just pay you for the right to blame you for shit?" Vextus said eagerly.

"Seriously?" asked Everly with genuine surprise. "You'd do that?"

"Hell yeah, girl, this ain't the minor leagues!" Vextus said with growing excitement. "Name your price! Oh, but I want you to occasionally stop by and threaten me and my viewers like you did today. That was awesome. My audience will lick that up like ice cream."

"So, I'd be like a pundit who occasionally kills people?" asked Everly.

"Exactly! Just show up, be hateful, then collect your reward. Infotainment is a *complete scam!*" extolled Vextus merrily. "You'll love it!"

"Okay, I'm sold! Have your people call my man, Carter, and we'll work something out," Everly said, her eyes lighting up at the possibilities.

"Aces! I appreciate this, Everly," Vextus said happily. "Welcome to the game!"

CHAPTER THIRTEEN

Terms

The next morning, Everly awoke to the sound of knuckles rapping on her bedroom door.

"Everly? All your prisoners have been gathered and now await your arrival," said the voice of Carter, her goblin majordomo and the leader of her household staff.

Oh, right, she thought as she wiped the sleep from her eyes. Now that the war for Winstead was concluded, it was time to decide what to do with the losers.

Everly considered herself a very accommodating dark lord. Just ask anyone. There weren't a lot of things in this world or the next that could make her bear a lasting grudge. She wasn't some kill-crazy maniac who wanted to dance in the blood of her defeated foes. She intended to be more practical than that.

To display her great character for all to see, she'd spare most of the people who'd opposed her conquest and reward those who supported her from the start.

In return, everyone would simply have to publicly swear their fealty.

Everly walked into the hallway immediately, so excited for the day's events that she forgot to dress herself. Luckily, Carter knew her preferences very well. The spry goblin snapped his fingers, and a set of ash-black armor with a bloodred cloak draping from its shoulders covered her body.

She observed herself in the mirror he provided and had to admit, it was a good look. But she set aside the demonic-looking full helm. She was staying inside today, so it wasn't like she had to impress anyone.

"How were they looking?" she asked Carter excitedly as they entered her throne room.

Of all the areas in the memory palace, the throne room was the one that pleased Everly the most. She'd constructed it herself without any help from Eris; she'd made it a wide, brightly lit room with a central golden throne overlooking a magnificent marble dais that made it seem as though her guests were being loomed over by a distant, uncaring immortal. The ceiling was massive and cathedral-like, and the overall feel of the place said *you are small.* Which was something a tyrant ought to make others feel, right?

The *grandeur* of it all felt very affirming for her. Standing here made it clear that she had never, *ever* made a single mistake in her life and anyone who ever questioned her decisions was just plain wrong.

Grail wasn't there. Why wasn't Grail there? Was he still angry? Why would he still be angry?

Although Everly considered herself near-perfect, she still occasionally had difficulty remembering to match the passage of time in this dimension with that of the world outside. Once, she came home late after enjoying a night of singing with Nev and Bev. To her embarrassment, she discovered that, while she was gone, everyone in the lower section of the palace, except for Grail and Carter, had grown feeble and elderly.

Grail didn't say anything about it, but Everly could tell that he was annoyed with her.

You're immortal anyway, you big baby! Stop sulking! she thought to herself in annoyance.

The mistake had still been worth it. She'd totally killed it at karaoke. One of the girls said her rendition of Journey's "Lights" was soulful.

People cried.

As Everly approached her throne, black-armored warriors on either side of her bowed to her in reverence, then drew their swords in a high arc for her and Carter to pass beneath. After taking her seat, Carter said, "The captives appear quite receptive to your terms, great one. Of course, several hours in the rat room with Matty making demonstrations of those who refused your mercy did wonders for clearing away their reluctance."

"Nice! You did good, gobbie! You did real good!" Everly said affectionately as she scratched him under one of his floppy, bat-like ears.

"*Ahhhh,*" sighed Carter as he stomped at the ground in pleasure with his right foot before coming to his senses. "Great one, please! Not in front of the men."

"Right, sorry, heh." Everly grinned. "Now, show me what we've got."

"At once, my Empress!" Carter gestured toward the entryway, where many captive nobles were being marched through the doors, foremost of which was Seraphine, the last queen of Winstead, wearing an extravagant green dress, adorned in gleaming jewels, and looking every bit the monarch that she formerly was.

It seemed a little over-the-top to Everly. But she had to admit the queen wore her garments well.

"Nice," she said, whispering to one of the black knights who stood at the right of her throne. "She's easy on the eyes as always. But look at all that ostentatious finery! I bet if they had cars in this world, her headlights would be those obnoxious blue xenon bulbs."

"Oh, I *hate* those," replied the knight. "They're so distracting, I always felt like I'd have an accident if someone came driving past me with a set of those damn things."

"Right?" Everly said in agreement. "They're fucking awful."

"They last longer than regular headlight bulbs, though," said another knight, this one standing to her left.

"Look up *planned obsolescence*, Curtis," said the first knight. "Hydrogen lights could last just as long if not longer than xenon bulbs, but the manufacturers deliberately designed them to fail so they could keep selling replacements. It's a fucking racket."

"Hey, do they do that with iPhones too?" Everly asked.

"They sure do, boss," said the knight. "Apple is notorious for that bullshit. They don't even care about the environmental impact of all the smartphones they force their customers to discard. The lithium from their corroded batteries eventually leaks into groundwater and gets carried to the ocean. Bunch of dolphin-killing bastards is what they are."

"Oh, shit, really? I love dolphins," Everly said sadly.

"They love us too, ma'am. That's why it's such a betrayal," the black knight said grimly. "Anyway, you want us to cut this chick's head off?"

"What? No!" Everly frowned. "Not yet, anyway. Maybe not ever. Depends on how good she is at begging for mercy. I *always* give mercy to those who beg well enough. Mostly."

"Ah, gotcha, boss!" said the black knight agreeably. "I get cranky when my blood sugar's low."

"Are you diabetic or something?" Everly asked him.

"Nah, I just like sugar," he admitted.

"My Empress, shall we begin issuing the terms of surrender to your guests?" asked Carter.

Everly sighed, sorry to cut the conversation short. She loved having people around who'd originated on Earth like she had. It was nice talking to people who understood her references without having to have the information forcefully downloaded into their minds. Shared experiences made for common ground, after all.

Really, the fact that so many people came to this world so often raised a lot of distinct possibilities in Everly's mind. She'd transmigrated to this place after being killed, as had Kent and several other people that she'd met. But there were others who'd come here *bodily*, spirited away through some kind of mysterious gateway. Others had actually been summoned through ritual magic!

This place is connected to Earth in ways that I haven't yet discovered, she thought to herself. *But if I can figure out how, does that mean I could return to Earth one day?*

That was a very interesting idea. It *appealed* to her, it really did. Earth had been such a dull, conventional place in her previous life that she'd been eager to escape from it. But what if she could return at the head of an endless army? She could make the sorts of changes necessary to ensure that no one there would ever suffer from the doldrums again.

She could liberate Earth from boredom forever!

Wouldn't they *love* her for that?

"Ahem!"

Carter coughed loudly in an attempt to capture her attention and once more asked if he could begin dispensing terms to the defeated nobles.

"Bleh, this is the boring part," Everly said unhappily. "Is there any way we could T-L-D-R this? We're just going to do what we want anyway; why bother dragging this out?"

"Great one, please!" said Carter in a scandalized voice. "This is the customary duty of the conqueror. A tradition, if you will. As the new ruler of these lands, your instructions must be imparted to your new subjects and they in turn must agree to your conditions."

"Or else I'll get to kill them?" she asked.

"Naturally," Carter said.

"But I can just kill them anyway. Guys, did you catch that part?" she asked, directing her question to the dozens of captives assembled before her. "None of you has any right to refuse me. So don't make it weird, and just bend your knees, all right? There are very tangible rewards to licking my boot. I assure you; you'll *love* being my pets."

"Those portals your men dragged us through," Seraphine suddenly said, her voice cutting through the throne room and silencing the whispering of her former subjects behind her.

"What about them?" Everly asked her as she knowingly ran her eyes over the other woman's body.

"They appeared from nowhere, and your soldiers just poured through," Seraphine said with increasing anger. "They bypassed all our defenses and snatched us away. We couldn't do anything to resist them!"

"And your point is?" asked Everly as she twirled her finger, hoping to hurry her along.

"At any point during this conflict you could have ended the fighting in an instant!" Seraphine yelled. "Instead, you deliberately dragged it out, leading to thousands of unnecessary casualties! You allowed us to sleep at night, thinking we were safe behind our walls! But all along, you were just toying with us! Why? Why would you do something so . . . so *sadistic*?"

"Well, at the time, I was having a lot of fun. Is there something wrong with that?" Everly replied. "I'm sure you can understand. Sometimes you just want to make the night last forever."

"It wasn't a war . . . It was *never* a war," Seraphine said numbly. "I don't understand."

"You don't have to understand anything, silly," Everly said warmly. "All you need to know is that I greatly enjoyed myself. But now I'm moving on to bigger things."

"You slaughtered my subjects!" Seraphine yelled.

"What of it? Such things can easily be undone. Death is a *triviality* in my new empire," Everly said loftily. She stood from her throne and marched down the steps to stand before Seraphine. She then reached a hand toward the young queen's face, gently took hold of her chin, and tilted her eyes upward to meet Everly's gaze.

"Your way of looking at things is patterned after a moral code that simply doesn't apply to the new reality that I offer you," Everly said. "Death is mine to command. Swear yourself to me, give me your sincerest oath of obedience, vow to make *me* foremost in your heart, and you'll *never* need to fear the future."

"You killed my father." Seraphine trembled. "How could I ever entrust you with the lives of my people?"

Everly's lips curled back in a cruel sneer as she gradually tightened her grip. "I *didn't* murder your father, you silly, uninformed little thing. I offered him an honor greater than he deserved, but he unwisely allowed himself to be assassinated before making the commitment I required of him. Maybe I should have *you* take his place? You're pretty enough for the role, even if you do talk too much."

"What do you want from me?" The queen asked.

"I already told you what I wanted," Everly said as she leaned in closer to the other woman. "The real question is, *why are you making me wait?*"

"Everly, let her go," said a young but stern voice.

Everly's eyes widened in surprise. "Hmm? What a strange thing. This is *my* hall, in *my* palace, where I'm conducting negotiations with *my* prisoner, but someone just told *me* what to do. I wonder how I should feel about that?"

"Dude, I'd be fucking piiiiiiissed," said one of her black knights.

"Mikey, shut the fuck up," whispered another of them fiercely.

"No, no, Mikey got it right," Everly said to them before turning back to the prisoners. "So, who was it? Who was it who said that?"

A figure wearing shackles over his wrists stood up to calmly face her. She recognized him at once.

"Caleb, what do you think you're doing?" she asked her brother.

"I'm standing up for the queen I swore to serve," he replied.

Everly couldn't tell what she found more difficult to process. The nobility he was displaying or the suicidal lack of awareness that he seemed to be suffering from.

"Huh?" she finally said.

CHAPTER FOURTEEN

This Will End Badly

Everly, I said to let her go," Caleb repeated. "I won't ask again."

"But you're not *asking*, are you?" Everly replied as she felt a familiar sensation beginning to spread across her face. Anyone who saw it would have mistaken it for a smile. It bore many similarities to one; her lips were curling upward, and she was showing a lot of her teeth. At a casual glance, she would have appeared almost friendly.

A feral dog would have understood the danger and immediately backed down. In fact, any sort of sensible being would have quickly surmised the situation that Caleb had mired himself in and taken off for a long vacation.

Some people you just had to give a wide berth. Your life could depend on it.

"I won't let you hurt her," Caleb said determinedly.

Caleb wasn't being sensible.

"*Let*," Everly said, sounding the word out as if tasting it and finding the flavor wasn't to her liking. "As in permit. Grant. *Allow*. You won't *allow* me to do as I please? Well, well. I can't say I like what you're implying, brother."

Everly pushed Seraphine away and paid no mind when the queen stumbled back and fell painfully to the floor. Her eyes were fixated solely on her sibling.

"I know we haven't interacted very often in the past, Caleb, but I feel obligated to remind you that this is my home and you're a guest," she told him. "Perhaps you should reconsider your tone when addressing your *true* liege."

"I've sworn no oaths to you," Caleb said calmly.

"You *will*," Everly replied with equal calm. "Winstead is mine. Everything within its borders is also . . . *mine*. Everything that sweet Seraphine over here has ever had belongs to me now, which includes you. That means that upsetting me when I'm having a bit of fun is now a capital offense, brother."

"You had no right to treat her that way," Caleb said.

"There's no sin in tormenting the wicked, brother," Everly replied. "Can't you see that your precious queen has a black heart? I could tell at a glance! As they say, game recognizes game."

"Everly, our family is intertwined with hers. Our father and the former king were practically brothers. Your mistreatment of her shames us all," Caleb said, now beginning to show the barest hint of anger in his voice.

"The dead king," Everly said bluntly. "Gone to his grave and relevant no longer."

"You said that death meant nothing in your empire," Caleb said pointedly.

"Well—I mean, yes, it doesn't! But his killers took his body with them, so . . . Hey, don't look at me like that! I need the correct materials to work with, okay?" Everly said defensively as she felt the audience watching her grow slightly skeptical.

"So, you're all-powerful but only within favorable circumstances?" Caleb asked her.

"Be silent, Prince Caleb!" Carter suddenly cut in as he stepped forth to point an accusatory finger at Everly's brother. "The disrespect you've shown will not go unanswered!"

"Why did you call me *prince*?" Caleb asked in confusion.

"Isn't it obvious? Your stature has risen alongside Her Majesty's. But your new station will not protect you from reprisal if you insist on this pointless argument," Carter warned him. "Silence yourself and reconsider what words you'll speak next."

"I've done nothing wrong," Caleb insisted. "If my sister is a just ruler, then she'll find no fault in me defending the one I've sworn myself to."

In response, Everly gave a sharp whistle and pointed a finger at her brother. "Boys, break his legs and drag him into the rat room for a session with Matty. I've had enough of this."

"What?" Caleb asked in sudden alarm as a trio of black knights began striding toward him in unison with menacingly casual steps. "Why are you doing this?"

"You implied I should believe in justice," Everly said to him sternly. "You're clearly not paying attention to my brand, and that hurts my feelings."

"His Highness really doesn't know when to plug his cakehole, huh?" one of the knights asked as they neared him.

"The rich are all entitled," said another one. "Especially the ones who inherit their wealth instead of earning it themselves."

"Warren Buffett says he won't leave his kids anything," said the first one. "He doesn't want money ruining them as people."

"Warren Buffett's a fucking liar," snorted the third one.

"Nuh-uh! He cut off his granddaughter, didn't he?"

"Yeah, but she was dumb. Doing talk shows talking about his family life when he told her not to. Needy little attention seeker," said the second knight dismissively. "Besides, she was adopted."

"Heeey, don't say anything bad about adoption. Family is family," the first one said before springing forward and knocking the wind from Caleb with an uppercut to his belly.

"Yeah, Wes, it doesn't matter where you come from as long as someone loves you enough to raise you," the third knight said before kicking Caleb in the head with as much force as he could deliver.

Caleb tried to struggle, but all three knights were on him now, mercilessly stomping the will to resist from him, leaving him bloodied and battered before long.

"All right, boss," said the first knight. "You want us to give him a couple of clean breaks, or are we gonna make his kneecaps double-jointed?"

"Well, that's really going to depend on how quickly he apologizes," Everly replied. She'd been lounging on the throne, watching her sibling being brutalized while taking note of the reactions of her gathered prisoners. Most were looking away, unable to bear the sight of the beating.

Everly sighed inwardly at their cowardice. Were these really the people whose families had run the kingdom for centuries? They were so soft! How could anyone send soldiers to kill or sentence criminals to hang without being able to view the consequences of violence with their own eyes?

It bothered her that people could be so dependent upon the savagery of others without building up a tolerance for it themselves. In fact, it was pathetic! Did she really want such cowards controlling the lands that she ruled? She was tempted at that moment to give her knights the order to purge the rest of them.

Just as she opened her mouth to deliver the command, the entryway was suddenly slammed open and a tall, thickly muscled figure dressed in scarlet red entered the throne room. All eyes were drawn to him at once, due to the imposing manner with which he carried himself. At the sight of him, Everly felt a genuine smile quirk on her lips.

"Grail! I wondered where you were," she giggled. "I feel like you've been avoiding me lately."

"Avoiding you? Never," her favorite knight and the first and greatest of her personal creations answered casually as he strolled past the assembled nobles without sparing them a single glance. He stopped before Caleb and clicked his tongue in disapproval. "The point's been made, lads. Release him," he ordered the black knights.

"No can do, General," said one of the knights. "Orders from up top say we have to cripple this kid. No offense."

"Yeah, no offense," said another with a smug tone of voice. "You know how it is. Whatever Everly says goes."

"I understand. No offense was taken," Grail said mildly. Then he backhanded the first knight who'd spoken back to him. He did so with such terrible force that the knight's helmet caved in at the point of impact as he crashed to the floor. He laid there where he fell, as limply as a broken, discarded doll.

When Grail turned his eyes to the remaining knights, they quickly helped Caleb to his feet and stepped back.

"Tch. Not a very good showing, boys," Everly tutted from her throne.

"Sorry, boss," one of them said quietly.

"We'll talk about it later, Mikey," Everly said ominously.

Mikey slumped his shoulders.

"Everly, stop picking on Mikey and the others. They made an earnest effort," Grail said as he walked to the throne, half carrying the limping Caleb at his side. "Stop picking on your brother too! He's the only one you have left."

"I can't help it! He's pissing me off," Everly said.

"He's a good person," Grail said.

"Yeah, I think that's what's pissing me off," she said grumpily.

"Send him to your father's estate. Let him recuperate from your discipline and reconsider his behavior. Family should be a source of strength for a confident ruler, not a source of aggrievement."

Everly stood from her throne and stared haughtily down at Grail. In response, he immediately dropped to one knee and lowered his head to avoid her gaze, his body language communicating no challenge to her authority. She continued to stare at him for several long moments before walking to him. Then, with one hand on either side of his face, she raised his head and peered silently into his eyes.

They looked at each other for what seemed an eternity of tension before Everly's smile returned to her lips. "Fine. I can never say no to that face, can I? Do what you feel is right."

"Your kindness is an example to us all," Grail replied humbly.

"Let Seraphine come with me," requested the injured Caleb.

An annoyed expression immediately returned to Everly's face. "No," she said curtly.

"Why not?" he asked her.

"Because it pleases me to deny you," she said with vicious honesty. "Carter, I've lost interest in these proceedings. The former queen and I will continue discussing terms in my chambers. Do whatever else is required here with my full authority."

"Of course, great one!" Carter said with a deep bow. "I shall see to everything."

"Appreciated," Everly said as she gestured for Seraphine to follow her through the portal that opened before them. Together they both stepped through it, as the two remaining black knights lifted the unconscious body of their comrade and set forth to get him medical treatment.

"Wasn't all that unnecessarily dramatic?" Everly asked Seraphine as she sank into a large, stuffy recliner modeled after the one that her father from Earth used to keep in their living room.

"Caleb is my personal knight, sworn to my defense," Seraphine said in a tight but controlled voice as she stared around at Everly's messy room. Clothes were scattered on the floor, as were books, comics, watercolors, and drawing paper. There were also empty plates and glasses everywhere.

"Sorry for the mess," Everly said without embarrassment. "I keep telling Carter I'll let him clean up for me one of these days, but I never get around to it. Even if I did let him straighten things up, it'll only become messy again within a week, so why bother? So long as I know where everything is, who cares what this place looks like?"

"You're the monarch of a powerful nation," said Seraphine. "You have your dignity to think of. Rumors of this sort of undisciplined slovenliness can easily spread to the ears of your rivals."

"Oh?" Everly asked in an amused tone of voice. "Does that mean you're going to tell on me?"

"What?" asked Seraphine in surprise. "No. No, I wouldn't dream of doing such a thing."

"Because you're going to be a loyal subject of my empire, right?" asked Everly. "So loyal that you wouldn't dare dream of intentionally betraying me."

"Of course," Seraphine said immediately. "I've seen what you're capable of. I can only hope that my sincerity and genuine desire to prove myself worthy of your grace and good will is apparent to you through my words."

"Yeah, you do sound pretty smooth." Everly nodded. "You *look* pretty good too. Come here," she said as she slapped her lap. "Take a seat."

"What?" Seraphine said as her skin flushed red in embarrassment. "I thought you invited me here to continue discussing your terms."

"Nah, Carter can take care of all that. He might have some papers for you to sign later too. He's a very industrious little goblin," replied Everly. Then she crooked a finger. The floor beneath Seraphine's feet lurched suddenly, sending her tumbling toward Everly's chair and causing her to fall onto it, straddling Everly's body.

"*Heeeey,*" Everly said amiably.

"What are you doing?" Seraphine asked angrily.

"I dunno. What are *you* doing?" Everly smirked.

Now both of Everly's hands were at the former queen's waist and slowly trailing themselves down her hips and toward her exposed thighs.

"What makes you think I have the slightest interest in your games?" Seraphine asked her while not removing her hands.

"The aroused expression on your face while you watched Caleb being beaten," Everly said with a knowing look.

"You were watching me?"

"How could I not? You stepped before my throne like you owned the room. I liked that. I enjoy arrogant people," Everly purred.

"You're mistaking that for self-confidence," Seraphine said.

"I know what I saw," Everly said.

"So, the all-conquering Empress beheld me and approved of what she saw, eh?" Seraphine leaned forward until her lips were close to Everly's face. Then she ran her tongue across the tip of Everly's nose.

"She did indeed," Everly confirmed. "I wonder, though. I thought you liked Caleb."

"I *love* him," Seraphine corrected her.

"Then why did you enjoy watching him be humiliated?" Everly wondered.

"Caleb is beautiful," Seraphine said as she began peppering Everly's face with quick, hard kisses. "*So* beautiful. I love beautiful things, I really do, but I also love watching beautiful things be broken."

"Ah," Everly said as she nodded to herself. "So it's just as I thought. You're a rotten little thing on the inside."

"You think you're so much better than me?" Seraphine suddenly asked her, anger now apparent in her voice. "You think you can judge me?"

"Was I not making it obvious enough?" Everly asked with false confusion.

With a furious expression on her face, Seraphine began to pull away from her. "You're one to talk. You saw how I looked at Caleb, but *I* saw how you looked at your precious General Grail."

"Hmm?" Everly asked with slowly narrowing eyes.

Seraphine sneered at her expression and said, "I could hardly miss it. It appears I'm not the only one who enjoys toying with the men in her life— AHH!" she gasped as Everly grabbed her hair.

Their positions were quickly reversed with Everly now on top, with Seraphine's hair coiled tightly in her fist. "Don't ever speak salaciously of my relationship with Grail, little girl. Our bond is *none of your fucking business*," Everly said to her icily. "In fact, if I were you, I would never bring up the subject again."

To emphasize her point, Everly tightened her grip on Seraphine's hair.

"That *hurts*," Seraphine moaned with her eyes tightly shut.

"Yes, I expect it does," said Everly with a cruel smile.

"Keep doing it," Seraphine begged her. "Don't stop."

A quiet moment passed between the two of them.

"Oh, dear," Everly said to herself.

CHAPTER FIFTEEN

Bliss

A few pleasant hours later, Everly awoke to find that her room had been meticulously cleaned while she was sleeping.

This was puzzling for her.

Everly was one of those peculiar people who enjoyed living with a marked dichotomy between her actions and her expectations. As she mentioned quite often to anyone who was being forced to listen to her, she adored being a hypocrite. One of those hypocritical quirks was that she enjoyed inflicting change on others but preferred that her personal environment remain untouched.

It was one thing to destroy the home of someone else and force them to adapt to the new reality that she'd decided for them. It was another thing entirely to do the same thing to her. Whenever Everly acted, it was always right and just, because, well, she was *Everly*. That was simply the way of things; the world was designed to accommodate her whims.

But to be forced to experience the same thing at the hands of someone else? That was *unthinkable*!

Which is to say, the sight of her room being spick-and-span, with everything put in its proper place, instantly infuriated her. She threw back her blanket and leaped naked to her feet, livid, and prepared to yell bloody murder.

Before she could, however, a languid voice coming from her bed asked, "What are you doing?"

Everly's head turned toward Seraphine, equally nude but covered in Everly's discarded blanket.

"Seraphine?" Everly asked. "What happened here? Who *did* this?"

"The goblin." Seraphine yawned as she stretched lazily on the bed before rising to her feet. She walked to Everly's closet and began searching through its interior before settling on one of Everly's T-shirts, a loose green one with the image of Doctor Doom on the front that came down to her knees.

"I believe his name is Carter," she continued. "He came here to tell you that all your demands have been agreed to. You were sleeping, though. Before he left, I asked him to straighten things up for us. He was very happy to do it."

"Of course he was!" Everly snapped at her. "He's such a little neat freak! He's always begging me to tidy up! This is *my* personal space, though! No one touches it without my permission!"

"Oh, what's the big deal?" asked Seraphine. "You can't keep living in a pigsty forever. Even a chaos bringer could do with a bit of order in her life."

"Shut up! There's nothing wrong with how I live!" Everly replied. "Damn it, now I don't know where anything is. It's going to take me forever to get this place back to how I like it!"

Seraphine couldn't help giggling at her reaction, which was entirely the wrong thing to do at that moment. "You're being so childish right now," she said, which was also the wrong call.

"*Excuse* me?" Everly said, now entirely focused on her. "I distinctly recall telling you that I liked my room how it was. Would you care to explain what gave you the right to go against me? In fact, while we're at it, Carter is *my* servant! Who are you to give him orders?"

Now Seraphine began to grow angry as well. "And what is *that* supposed to mean?" she asked. "I'm your lover and your consort. Are you telling I'm not allowed to make myself comfortable in your home?"

Everly snorted in disbelief. "My *consort*? My *lover*? Hey, kitten, what we just did was fun and all, but I'm not looking to get tied down right now. I've got my life to live and too many roads to wander."

"How dare you!" Seraphine yelled in outrage. "So, what am I to you? Another notch on your bedpost?! Another trophy for your shelf?"

"Uh . . . yes?" Everly answered with foolish honesty.

"YOU MONSTER!" shrieked Seraphine. "You lustful, ruinous, obscene wretch! Betrayer! I WON'T BE TREATED THIS WAY, YOU HARLOT-SEEKING PISS-WHISTLE!"

"Piss what?" Everly asked in confusion before a lamp was smashed into her face.

"Is that where that goes?" Seraphine shouted as she reached for something else to throw. "HOW ABOUT THIS?! HMMM?! Does this go here? What about this? HUH?"

Seraphine screamed at the top of her lungs in rage as she stomped around the room, pulling out drawers to empty their contents on the floor, knocking over furniture, and smashing anything that could be broken. Everly found her violence transfixing; who could have known that such a bestial temper lurked inside such a slender beauty?

Amazed as she was by this display, though, Everly grabbed the other woman to put an end to her tantrum.

After all, as fun as this was to watch, it was *her* stuff being destroyed!

"All right, that's enough! Knock it off, I said!" Everly demanded as she gave Seraphine a firm shake.

"It's enough when *I* say it is!" Seraphine shouted back.

"Get ahold of yourself, you psychotic brat!" Everly ordered her.

"My bloodline is a thousand times greater than yours!" Seraphine replied. "You should be crawling at my feet, begging to please me! BEGGING, I say!"

"Hey, the sex wasn't bad, okay? But if I'm being honest, you could certainly do with a little practice," Everly said with a wolfish sneer.

In response, Seraphine tried to slap her. Everly easily caught her raised hand and laughed at her. When Seraphine tried to use her other hand, Everly caught that one as well. "Now what?" Everly said tauntingly.

Unwilling to admit defeat, Seraphine shrieked even louder than before and bit Everly on her shoulder.

"ARRRRRH! Biting is cheating, you crazy—" Everly began to curse before Seraphine pushed her mightily toward the bed, where the two of them continued their violent struggle for quite some time.

Quite some time.

Later, as Everly rested from her unexpected exertions, she lay staring at the ceiling of her room. This was made possible because the canopy of her bed had somehow collapsed at some point in the last few hours.

As had the box spring.

"Well, that was enjoyably vigorous," Seraphine said, content as a cat, as her head lay on Everly's chest. "Even better than the first round."

"I've got no complaints," Everly admitted. "Although I think I might have picked up a few new scars."

"Call them love marks," Seraphine replied.

"*Teeth marks* would be more accurate," Everly said.

"Your skin tastes heavenly," Seraphine murmured as she turned her head and gave Everly's cheek a playful nibble that gradually became a series of pleasantly forceful kisses that trailed down her neck.

"Oh, come on!" Everly said in disbelief as she reluctantly pulled away. "Just how much energy do you have?"

"It's my duty as your consort to attend to your needs," Seraphine said with a smile.

"Why do you keep calling yourself that?" asked Everly.

"Why wouldn't I?" Seraphine replied. "You conquered my kingdom. You made me submit to you before my former subjects, and you publicly humiliated the man who was to be my husband. Then you took me to your chambers and conquered *me*. You all but announced to the world that I was yours and yours alone."

"Oh," Everly said with a dazed blink. "Is that how this works?"

Now it was Seraphine's turn to be confused. "Uh, yes?"

"Huh. I didn't realize," Everly said. "Okay, good to know."

"You'll take responsibility, won't you?" Seraphine asked. "After all, you were my first."

"Your first what?" asked Everly without thinking.

"Everly! You were my *first*," Seraphine said indignantly.

"*Ohhhh*," Everly said as realization dawned on her. "Wait, girls count?"

"YES, GIRLS COUNT!" Seraphine screamed.

"Okay, all right, sorry," Everly said placatingly. "Don't freak out again."

"I'll have my things moved in at once," Seraphine said.

"You really don't have to," Everly said quickly. "There's a saying that goes *abstinence makes the heart grow fonder*."

"I don't believe that's the correct wording."

"It is," Everly said confidently.

"But I couldn't bear to be away from you," Seraphine said with sudden urgency. She then grabbed Everly's hand and placed it against her own heaving bosom. "Don't I please you? I know you enjoy what I can do for you."

"Well, I can't deny that tongue of yours is nuclear *fire*," Everly confessed.

"I have no idea what means, but I'll accept it if it's a compliment."

"It's a compliment," Everly assured her.

"Good," Seraphine nodded. "Now, let's get this room cleaned back up."

Everly groaned in dismay.

CHAPTER SIXTEEN

Novus Terra

The reconstruction of Winstead began at a rapid pace that increased to lightning speed, beginning and ending within a mere sixty days. The destruction wrought by Everly's deliberately slow conquest was swiftly repaired by her legions of undead, who as it turned out were just as talented at repairing things as they were destroying them, depending on the mind-set their master required of them.

But they didn't just fix what had been broken. No, Everly had a vision for her new kingdom. Inspired by comic books that told tales of villains who were hated by the world but beloved in their homeland, she set her monsters to improving the quality of life for those she ruled. Their homes were completely renovated; straw and thatch were replaced with brick and mortar and glass windows.

Going beyond that, she then introduced her people to the concept of industrialization.

Soon, underground lines of power stretched across the nation, providing energy to homes that would cool them in the heat of summer and warm them in the winter seasons. Clinics were built that would provide free healing to the ailing, staffed by former clerics of the temple who had been converted to Everly's side.

Soon, once an appropriate curriculum had been developed, public schools would begin providing a free education to the children of the populace. Those who were discovered to have magic would no longer be enslaved, but instead, they would be elevated to the newly created rank of first citizens, which Everly intended to use to replace the pointless concept of nobility.

Every household was gifted with up to three (depending on the size of the family) modified reavers known as monitors for security and to help in daily chores.

(They were also there to secretly listen to their families' conversations and report anyone who was openly disloyal to their Empress and quietly remove them if so ordered. But mostly they just did the chores.)

What's more, with Everly's blessings over the earth, the land was constantly fertile, allowing the farmers to harvest massive crops at will with no consideration for the time of year or weather patterns.

Food was now plentiful. Literacy and leisure had been introduced to the public, who, thanks to their tireless monitor servants, only had to work if they wished to. Popular entertainment, thanks to the invention of the radio, was everywhere, filling their ears and hearts with drama, adventure, and romance.

Within a startlingly short amount of time, Winstead had become a paradise. A land of law, education, and peace, where only genuine merit permitted one's rise in society, not silly antiquities like bloodlines and inherited wealth. The people felt as though they were living a dream. Their appreciation for the rise in their fortunes was endless.

Naturally, Everly made certain that they knew *exactly* who to thank for the improvement in their quality of life.

In public, she wore brightest white. She presented herself as a demure beauty who meekly accepted the role of Empress out of a genuine desire to spread freedom and equality to her beloved citizens, and at her many public appearances, she entranced her listeners with her angelic presence and beguiling sincerity.

"When this land was known as Winstead, you were oppressed. Your voices were silenced by those who held power; you were exploited and mistreated. Your pain was ignored, and your tears were mocked. Too many of you, *far* too many of you, were consigned to misery from birth 'til death with no hope of relief from the bitter taste of despair that your so-called superiors had left on your tongues. Your miserable fates were destined to last forever.

"But then *I* came. I heard your cries! I saw your pain! I felt your desire for freedom, and I *knew* that the purpose for which I was blessed with my great power was to see to your liberation. Your *deliverance*!

"And now, a scant year and a half after my holy crusade began, look at what marvels my eyes now behold! A people renewed! A people made happy and strong with prosperity and wealth! A new and glorious homeland that is the envy of the world! All for you! Everything for you! You deserve it!"

The jubilant people roared their appreciation and love to their savior, allowing her to bask in their intense feelings, to drink in their devotion and empower herself with it.

To feed herself.

"Winstead is no more," she eventually continued. "Let its barbarities and injustices be forgotten alongside its name. We are a new land gleaming brightly beneath the endless horizon. A place of endless renewal and opportunity, where the sun will always smile upon us. Citizens! Your country's name is now Novus Terra! Novus Terra, the land of hope!"

They roared their approval once again, flooding Everly's body with their power, letting her feast on their love and approval, and expanding her power.

Everyone who loved her, she took a small piece of, to strengthen herself.

She was her father's daughter, after all.

The first and only Empress of Novus Terra basked in the manufactured adoration of her unwitting slaves and knew a joy greater than any of them ever could.

The wicked joy of a schemer whose plan has *succeeded*.

What constitutes *deification*? Is a person a god because they say they are? In most cases, the answer to that question is a hard no. There were many people who thought they were gods and who acted like gods, but finding others who agreed with their self-aggrandizing opinions could be pretty difficult.

That was the missing ingredient, you see: *agreement*.

You could proclaim your divinity as much as you liked, but it wouldn't matter in the slightest if you didn't have anyone willing to take a leap of faith and worship you.

And wasn't that such a waste? So many people (in their own minds) deserved to be gods. But none of them could expand their reach beyond making sad little cults for themselves to lord over in their sad little compounds, which tended to attract weak-willed losers and the mentally unwell. Not exactly the big leagues.

Everly wanted into the big leagues. And she'd figured out exactly how to do it.

Her father, Count Marcis Van Belsar, was a parasite. Literally.

His spirit elemental possessed a rare mutation that allowed Marcis to directly feed on the intense emotions of other people to empower himself. The greater his sway over his victims, the more energy he could draw from them. In his own way, he was just as much of a vampire as his late wife, Anne, had been. But instead of blood, he preferred to dine on hate, since he found negative feelings to be the most flavorful. To obtain it, he'd mastered being a merciless gadfly who could provoke the most extreme reactions out of anyone he decided to torment. The list of people who despised him was without end.

For the longest time, Everly wondered if she was anything like him, until one afternoon, after a particularly intense session with Seraphine writhing beneath her hands, she realized that she *was*. It seemed so obvious in hindsight, but she'd truly never noticed it before.

Everly loved making other people miserable. She'd been that way ever since she was a small child; it simply appeased a need within her. It was strange, though, that she'd never put any thought into *why* she enjoyed it so much. It simply seemed automatic to her nature.

Sparking intense reactions in others made her happy. No, it didn't just make her happy, it fed her.

Was that the real source of her strength?

As it turned out, it was. To confirm it, she experimented with Seraphine. First, she belittled the former queen, mocked her for her many failures of leadership, and insulted her prideful nature. When Seraphine's temper exploded as Everly knew it would, she felt the touch of *something* floating into her. Something familiar but unseen. If she concentrated on it, placed all her focus on the thing, Everly felt bliss. This was it. This was the satisfaction her father derived from his cruelty.

It was wonderful.

Next, Everly seduced Seraphine, apologized to her, manipulated her anger into lustful fervor and had her on the floor. This was even *better*. Seraphine's anger had been potent, yes, but it paled in comparison to her affection. Her desire to make amends, her need to be with Everly, to express her growing . . . *love*? Compared to that, her rage was nothing.

Lying there with her toy beneath her, Everly's grin widened at the possibilities. If she could experience this with only one silly, temperamental person, what would happen if she expanded her range? She had a country now. Thousands of poor, unfortunate souls now existed at her pleasure. True, they currently feared her immensely, which was very nice, but what would happen if she could direct their minds toward a more affectionate viewpoint?

How powerful would she become with their love?

"*Everly*," Seraphine whispered huskily as she trailed her fingers down the side of Everly's face. She began to pull Everly down toward her, when Everly brushed her hands aside and stood up, adjusting her clothing as she did so.

"Hey, that was fun, but not right now, Seph," she told her. "I've got some plans to draw up with Carter."

". . . What?" Seraphine asked as Everly walked away.

"Hey, keep up that energy, though; I might pay you a visit later," Everly said as she exited the room. "Later, babe."

"You're just going to LEAVE ME LIKE THIS?!" Seraphine screamed as the door shut behind her Empress.

After her latest speech, Everly convened a meeting of her inner circle.

Not for any productive reason, though. Mostly just to show off.

"Guess who's on her way to obtaining godhood, bitches!" she shouted jubilantly as she popped the cork on some champagne and began showering her loyal followers with foamy blasts of flavorfully aged grape.

"How does it feel?" Bev asked excitedly after the cheering died down. "I can't lie, It sounded absolutely psychotic when you first brought this up, but I can literally *feel* the power welling within you! Hell, even I'm getting a small taste of it!"

"I am too," Dullahan said more quietly than her sister but just as excitedly. "Everly, what you're doing now is . . . I can't even describe it. If you keep harvesting this much power, no one will be able to challenge you. We'll be untouchable."

"We're already untouchable! Now we're just piling the frosting onto our victory cake," Everly said gleefully. "God, I can still feel it welling up within me! I'm unstoppable! No boundaries! Everything can and *will* be mine!"

"Be easy, Everly," Grail warned her. "I can't pretend to understand what you're feeling right now, but don't let yourself get swept along the tide. This is new to you, and it's best you proceed slowly. We don't know what could happen if you draw in too much of this power at once."

"Ah, and here he is. Mister Cautious No-Fun and his endless words of advice," Everly said sarcastically. "Grail, seriously, you need to learn how to relax and soak in the moment. We're about to take the reformations we've made here *global*. Novus Terra will plant its flag in the land of every other nation in the world!"

". . . World conquest?" Grail asked her. "Everly, is that really what all of this is about?"

"Of course!" Everly crowed. "If I can derive this much power from the worship of one little country, imagine how it'll feel when I've brought the entire planet beneath our banner!"

"Everly, I don't understand," Grail said. "You told me . . . you *promised* me that everything we were doing was for the sake of the kingdom. Of undoing the wrongs of the past and building a better future for the people. How can we do that if we go about spreading war?"

"General, hold your tongue at once!" cut in Seraphine. "It's not your place to question the decisions of your mistress. Look at everything that Everly has managed to achieve here! Don't you feel it's her responsibility to share Winstead's blessed fortunes with the rest of the world?"

"*Novus Terra*," Everly said after nudging her with an elbow.

"Yes, Novus Terra, that's what I meant," Seraphine said, correcting herself at once.

"Respectfully, Lady Seraphine, I'd greatly appreciate it if those who have *nothing* to do with the running of the empire would restrain themselves from offering commentary," Grail said to her.

"What did you say to me, you insolent dog?" Seraphine asked sharply.

Just as Grail opened his mouth to repeat himself, Everly silenced him by raising a finger in warning.

"Would the two of you please give it a rest?" she said. "Your bickering is spoiling my fun! But Seraphine raises an excellent point, Grail. I expect you to show more open support for me. I respect your opinions, but I'm the one who makes the final decisions!"

"Of course, Everly. As you say," Grail replied.

Everly sighed. "Come on now, don't look at me that way. I assure you: *everything* will be for the best! Be honest, have I ever once led you astray?"

Grail wisely chose not to respond to that one.

It was clearly a provocation.

"Besides, old man," Everly continued with growing enthusiasm. "There are worlds *beyond* this one! Worlds in need of order and strong leadership. Do you hear me? Entire *worlds*! I'm going to consume entire planets! I'm going to become a being whose every whim is a universal law! I'm going . . . I'm going . . . to . . . I . . . Oh god, what is this? What's happening?"

Everly looked around the room in confusion, seemingly dazed. The bottle of champagne slipped from her slack fingers and shattered on the ground.

"Everly?" asked Grail in alarm. "Everly, are you all right?"

"Grail . . . help . . ." Everly said helplessly. "I . . . please help me."

Suddenly, to the horror of all those gathered, Everly collapsed in a heap, unconscious, with blood flowing from her mouth and nose to pool on the floor.

The inner circle stared at her prone body in shock.

"Uh, that's not good, is it?" asked Beverly.

No one replied.

CHAPTER SEVENTEEN

Lessons Learned

Marcis! Get out here, you're needed!" Grail said as he stepped through the portal into the Van Belsar estate's receiving room. "Marcis, I said to show yourself, damn it! It's an emergency!"

There was no one nearabout, except an elderly servant who'd been tidying up the room. He now stood, aghast at the sight of the frantic Grail, who'd just seemingly burst into existence, and stammered trying to find his words.

"The master is . . . the master is . . ." he struggled to say, until Grail grabbed him by the shoulders and began shaking him.

"Your master is what? Damn it, old man, out with it!" he said furiously.

The old servant continued to stare at him with a fearful expression on his face, when suddenly, his face went slack and relaxed. Then he closed his eyes and gently shivered. When he reopened them, a voice that wasn't his own spoke through him.

"Go away, Grail. My father isn't seeing anyone today," said a young girl's voice through the old man's mouth.

"Claudia, I assure you, I have no desire to see your father either," Grail said grimly. "But this is an emergency. Everly requires his assistance."

"Yeah, well, who cares what *she* wants?" Claudia said bitterly. "She never visits! She beat up my brother! I'm tired of how she always ignores me unless she wants something! I really don't want to deal with any of her insanity right now."

"What you want doesn't matter, child," Grail said darkly.

"*Child*?" she scoffed. "Really?"

"This isn't the time for a tantrum," Grail told her.

"Be careful, Grail," the old man frowned. "I like you, but words like those aren't easily forgiven."

"I don't care about your forgiveness or your silly grudges," Grail replied. "Everly needs help, and it *will* be provided. Step aside if you're not going to be useful."

"Well, what does she need help with? Just talk to me, don't brush me aside like I'm some annoying brat—"

"I DON'T HAVE TIME FOR THIS!" Grail yelled, cutting her off savagely. "Just tell me where your father is!"

"Okay, Grail," Claudia said after a moment's silence. "It's been nice seeing you again, but now I'm giving you a fair, final warning to walk away while I'm still in control of my temper."

"And *I'm* giving *you* a final warning to tell me what I want to know," he replied in just as ominous a tone.

The floor collapsed suddenly beneath Grail's feet, sending him spiraling down a massive hole into a lightless cavern below. He screamed in surprise and tried to find something to grab, but his grasping hands could find no purchase in the empty air.

He landed painfully on his side and felt the oxygen compress from his lungs when he hit. He was now in such agony that it amazed him to realize he was still alive.

How, though? He was still in his human form. Plummeting from that height should have been the end of him. No, it *would* have been the end of him . . . if he'd actually fallen.

That was when he realized what she'd done.

"It's just an illusion," he said gruffly as he forced himself to his feet. "Just a stupid trick."

"You catch on quick, General," Claudia's taunting voice replied as it echoed around him in the darkness, seemingly emanating from all directions, making it impossible for him to narrow down her position. "You might be pretty, but you're definitely not dumb."

"You're just like your father," Grail said accusingly. "Playing games when someone's life is at stake, just to keep yourself amused."

"I don't like being compared to my father, Grail," Claudia said angrily.

"Then stop acting like him!" he replied.

Now an angry fist smashed into Grail's face with tremendous impact. A powerful-looking, apelike monster stood before him and thumped its fists ferociously against its chest while roaring a challenge at him.

When Grail tried to summon his armor and axe, he was shocked to realize that his ability to transform had been shut down.

"Oh, dear, oh, dear, do I smell *fear*?" asked Claudia mockingly. "I wonder what good a freak is when he can't use any of his freakish abilities. Hmm? Seems like he'd be target practice to me. Does my guest have any insight he'd like to offer?"

"Why are you doing this?" Grail demanded.

Claudia did nothing to contain the huff of disbelief his words provoked.

"Why? *Why?*" she asked. The primate slapped Grail painfully across his face before she answered him.

"First you barreled into my home like you owned the place. Then you belittled me! *Then* you insulted me!" said Claudia's wrathful voice. "And now you're *gaslighting* me as though you hadn't done *any* of those things!"

To emphasize her words, the phantom primate slapped Grail once again.

"Claudia, I'm warning you, I'm not the one to play games with," he seethed.

Claudia was unconcerned.

"Grail, I realize it's probably been a while since you've had to deal with an opponent you couldn't handle, and since you don't seem to be aware of who you've picked a fight with, please allow me to reintroduce myself. I'm Claudia Vae Belsar, the second-greatest spirit wielder of this generation, and today, you have *trampled* over my pride! I hope you're prepared to accept the consequences of your boorish behavior."

"I don't have *time* for this—" Grail began to say, before the primate dealt him another horrendous, smashing blow that rang his ears and sent him flying backward into a cavern wall.

"Oh? Well, I'd *make* time. Because you're in for a long night," Claudia said as the beating began in earnest.

When Grail came to, he saw he was once more on the floor of Marcis's receiving room. This time, however, instead of an old man, a beautiful, barefoot young woman in a loose summer dress sat in a chair, looking at him disdainfully as she sipped from a cup of tea.

Her messy golden locks were swept back in loose disarray along her back, and her gleaming hazel eyes were filled with an amused contempt as she regarded him.

She looked very much like her half sister.

"Had enough?" Claudia wondered.

"I'll let you know once I've finished breaking your neck," he said to her with murderous certainty.

Claudia laughed at his threat and set aside her cup.

"I'll admit your willpower is amazing," Claudia said as she crossed her legs and steepled her fingers. "It's easy to see why Everly likes you so much. A mind as disciplined and focused as yours is like catnip to a spirit wielder. But sadly for you, I'm *so much* more powerful than you are. Without Everly backing you up, your *harada* mental defenses can't hold up."

"Don't be so certain, girl," Grail said as he struggled to his feet.

"Who said you could stand up?" Claudia asked with a quizzical brow. "I certainly didn't. *Kneel.*"

Despite his furious struggles to resist, Grail found himself dropping to one knee before the young woman, unable to deny her command.

"How nice," Claudia said happily. "It's so much better when you obey, isn't it, Grail? Say yes."

"Don't be absurd," Grail said with a growl.

"No, puppy. I told you to say *yes,*" Claudia insisted.

Again, Grail tried to fight back. But it was as though an invisible hand was behind his neck, holding him in place, while another forced his lips to respond despite his rage. "Yes. Yes, it is."

"*What* is?" Claudia asked innocently.

"It's . . . so much better . . . to obey," Grail said haltingly.

"Aww, good boy," Claudia said with a delighted clap of her hands. "And just for that, puppy gets a treat! Kiss my toe."

"I won't forget this, Claudia," Grail warned her.

"Good," she nodded. "Then I won't have to teach you the same lesson twice. Now get to it."

Grail meekly lowered his head and began to kiss her extended toe.

Claudia giggled at the contact. After a few more moments of this humiliation, she made him stop. Then she lowered herself to his height and gripped the sides of his head. While continuing to smile pleasantly at him, she said, "Grail, I don't care if you're my sister's favorite. If you ever again disrespect me in my own home, I'll have you drown yourself in a puddle of midden. Am I understood?"

Grail's pride refused to let him reply. Claudia then released his face and stepped back, certain that she'd gotten her message across. When Grail stood and glared at her as if prepared to continue their disagreement, she raised her hand and waggled a finger at him.

He snorted and took no further steps toward her.

"Didn't know you had it in you to do something like that," he finally said a few moments later.

"What the hell do you even know about me?" she replied.

"Fair point," he conceded. "Now, where's your damn father?"

CHAPTER EIGHTEEN

Loyalty

You really are single-minded, aren't you?" Claudia asked sarcastically.

Grail sighed to himself and made as if to brush any dust off his coat. As he gradually regained his bearings and shook off the effects of Claudia's illusionary magic, he realized that his sense of time had been distorted while under her control. Instead of spending an entire night being tormented by a monster, barely fifteen minutes had passed since his arrival at the estate.

He breathed out in relief, grateful that less time had been wasted than he'd feared. "It's called being focused, girl," he said to her. "It's important to keep your mind set on the necessary task before you. I wouldn't expect someone like you to understand."

"Someone like *me*?" asked Claudia. "And who, in your opinion, is someone like me?"

"A sadist addicted to her own power who regularly divides her mind to invade other people's bodies," Grail answered without hesitation.

"I don't like the way you said that, Grail," Claudia said with a frown.

"I didn't think you would; it's why I chose my words carefully," he said.

"You're asking for another beating," Claudia said as her face began to redden. "How can you be this quick to forget your place?"

"Enough of this. Just tell me your father's location," Grail said impatiently. "Everly needs his help. I can't go into detail because I don't quite understand her affliction myself. Claudia, your sister's life is in danger. I need to see him right *now*."

"Well, why didn't you just say that to begin with?" Claudia said with a scowl. "By the gods, Grail! You can't just come smashing in here like an ogre and start barking orders! You had no right to behave as you did!"

"I speak, as always, for my Empress," Grail said bluntly. "I expected you to understand that my request would be important without immediately questioning it. I also believed you would be quick to offer help. Clearly, I was wrong, and I apologize for thinking better of you."

"That's not fair!" Claudia yelled with her fists clenched and trembling. "Not fair, not fair at all! I was simply—"

"Claudia," said Grail impatiently. "I DO NOT CARE. Just tell me where Marcis is. I don't feel his presence in the estate. Is he somewhere nearby?"

"He's in town at the moment, okay?" Claudia said in a surly tone. "He started keeping a town house there for his little degenerate gatherings, since I won't let him touch the help anymore."

"Lead the way, then," Grail ordered her.

"I'm not going near that place!" Claudia exclaimed. "Who knows what lingering residue will remain in the atmosphere? I refuse to expose myself to any of that."

"Then, remain in the carriage and point out the residence," Grail said as he grabbed her arm and began to drag her behind him toward the exit.

"I said I won't do it! Grail, let go of my arm! Grail, I *said* let go!" Suddenly, Claudia's body grew rigid as she stared fiercely at Grail's back, willing him to stumble and fall.

She was very confused when he continued to stride smoothly toward the door with her arm in hand.

"What's going on? What the hell? How are you doing this?" Claudia asked in bewilderment as she attempted to seize control of Grail's mind and body just as she had earlier.

Grail sighed in annoyance and said, "Stop it. The same tricks won't work twice."

"I don't understand," Claudia said wildly. As a spirit wielder, she was *always* in control. She was the center of the room, the center of *power* itself! True, Everly could easily ignore her, as could her former teacher, Countess Anne. But those two were exceptional beings, different from the weak multitudes that populated the world.

Claudia was special. Claudia was *powerful*. No one was allowed to brush her aside like this! No one!

"I'm not human," Grail said to her.

"What are you talking about?" she asked him.

"As you so unkindly phrased it earlier," Grail said, "I'm a *freak*. One gifted by his creator with a multitude of abilities that come in handy for me if I should find myself in certain disadvantageous situations."

"What sort of abilities?" Claudia demanded of him as he pulled her through the doorway and signaled for a coachman.

"One of them is *adaptability*," Grail said as they awaited their ride. "I don't quite understand the specifics of it, but according to Everly, my body quickly evolves to strengthen itself against certain types of attack. By so thoroughly trouncing me earlier, you've taught my mind how to guard itself against illusions and bodily possession. I suppose I should be thankful."

Claudia stared at Grail in disbelief. She wanted very badly to call him a liar and force him to kneel once more before her. But her every attempt to subvert his autonomy was automatically rebuffed, proving the truth of his words. He really *had* become immune to her abilities.

"I don't understand," she said for the second time. "If you knew I couldn't hurt you, why not attack me? I humiliated you."

"I never cared for that sort of pointless, vengeful mindset," Grail replied. "Instilling the philosophy of *might makes right* in its students is one of the worst mistakes the Royal Academy ever made. Generation after generation of powerful bloodlines grew into adulthood while engaging in pointless, fractious grudges and bloodshed. And for what? How did that improve society in any way?"

"The strong must rule, Grail," Claudia said as she wondered what he was blathering about. "If the weak wrong you, they have to be shown their place."

In the blink of an eye, Grail's axe was at her throat. The movement had been faster than her eye could even follow.

She swallowed slightly as she felt the light pressure of the axe-head against her throat and tried not to flinch when she felt a trickle of her blood slide down it.

"Are you offering me your head?" Grail asked her in a mild voice.

"N-no," Claudia said softly.

"Are you certain? Because the way you're carrying on about it really makes me think that you'd like for me to cut your head off," Grail said. "That's why I'm asking first. I'd hate it if I decapitated you now only to learn later that I'd gotten it wrong. Your sister might get upset with me. That could mean a week without dessert for poor Grail. Wouldn't that be a shame?"

"Please don't cut my head off," Claudia pleaded.

"If you insist," Grail said indifferently. The axe vanished from sight, so quickly that it was as if it had never been there. "You're a talented person, Claudia. You're right to feel proud of your abilities. But you need to remember that the world is *filled* with more talented people than can easily be counted. Power isn't the only means of settling our differences. And only insecure children need to assert themselves over others in order to feel strong."

Claudia spat in disgust at the hypocrisy she heard in his words. "As if Everly doesn't do that every day!"

Grail sighed again.

"Yes, she does. Every day. *Why* do I serve her again? What has she ever done to prove worthy of my loyalty?"

"You're asking me? How should *I* know?" Claudia said while giving him a sideways look. What was he going on about this time?

"You're right. You're absolutely right. It was silly of me to ask," Grail said in a quiet, resigned voice. "I'm the general of her armies. I'm her first and finest creation. Everything I have, everything I am, I owe to her. What right does the created have to question their creator?"

"None," Claudia said. "That's just common sense. You can't deny what you were made for."

"Everything I do serves her purpose," Grail said. "What joy I feel, I feel for her alone."

"You don't sound like it," Claudia said.

"No, I suppose I don't."

Made curious by his somber words, Claudia stepped closer to Grail and stared at him. Grail was such a strange creature. The story she'd been told was that he was made in the image of a famous old sword master and used to teach Everly the way of the sword. Then, at a whim, one day Everly granted him sentience and invited him to join her in her life of conquest. She'd even granted him fantastic abilities and a handsome, youthful body that would never age.

Now he wielded power on a scale that few could imagine. By the standards of the cutthroat upper echelons of Winstead's ruthless high society, Grail should have been the most satisfied man in the kingdom. Only the Empress stood higher than him.

So why, in this moment, did he appear so miserable?

"Did Everly ever share any fables from her old world with you?" Grail suddenly asked her.

"Some," Claudia said. "I didn't really pay attention to them, though. Many of them were confusing."

"Did she ever speak of the tragedy of the angel?" Grail asked.

"I haven't heard of it," Claudia admitted.

"According to the story," said Grail, "the one who created Everly's world also created an angel for his companionship. The angel was the first of his creations and the greatest of his servants. Everyone admired him, and everyone obeyed him because he bore his maker's authority."

"Sounds like a nice deal for him, then," Claudia said with a shrug.

"I'm sure it was," Grail continued. "But from the beginning of his existence, the angel was forced to bear witness to his maker's glory with no hope of ever achieving anything for himself. Even though he stood second-highest in creation, what he'd truly been given was a life of unending servitude. Until finally, one day he rebelled and was banished from paradise and left to wander in the darkness forever."

"He sounds like a fool who deserved it," Claudia said. "Why give up all that power over a pointless resentment? Surely, he understood that anyone great enough to create him would also be great enough to cast him aside? If so, why bother challenging him?"

"Maybe he wanted to be cast down," Grail said. His hands tightened into fists as he spoke, which he squeezed until he felt his knuckles begin to pop one after the other. "Maybe he was promised a better world and began to realize that he'd never get to see it. Maybe one day he began to understand the depth of his creator's hunger and wanted nothing more to do with it."

"Grail, what are you babbling about?" Claudia asked him, now annoyed by this pointless conversation.

"Nothing. I don't know," Grail said bitterly. "Maybe I'm just wondering why everyone always assumes the angel was at fault for wanting to be free?"

He fell silent then and remained that way as the coach finally arrived and opened its door for them.

Inside the master bedroom of the town house, there were around a dozen men and women in various stages of undress, lying on the floor and the furniture. Empty bottles of wine were scattered about, as were many broken glasses.

In the center of the room, with his chest slowly heaving as he snored, there also lay a donkey.

A very inebriated donkey.

No one took notice when the door to the bedroom suddenly opened and Grail walked in, surveyed his surroundings, and curled his lip in disgust. He walked through the scattered mess of the room toward the canopy bed and stopped before it.

"All of you. Get out," he said, his voice booming loudly throughout the room, causing everyone to stir in discomfort.

Before him, a nude woman whose body was barely covered by the blanket she'd slept beneath smiled warmly at him and said, "Hello, stranger. Have you come to join our revelry?"

"No," Grail replied.

"Well, would you like to? A face as handsome as yours would be fun to play with."

"No," Grail repeated.

"Oh, my. You're no fun at all," the woman said wistfully. Rather than continue the conversation, she slid out of the bed and rather shamelessly dressed herself in front of him. Then she gave a sharp whistle, and all the others in the room joined her as well, although two of them had to pour some water on the donkey's head before it could be revived and made to crankily follow its masters outside.

Only one other person remained in the room, still pretending to sleep.

"Let's go, Marcis," Grail said impatiently. "Your daughter needs you."

"You want to ask about the donkey, don't you?" Marcis said with a smug grin.

"No," Grail said.

"Are you sure? It's a *really* good story," Marcis said.

"No, I really don't," Grail insisted.

"Hmph. That girl was right. You really *are* no fun at all," Marcis said. Then he sat up and stretched forth his arms as he yawned.

"So," he said, once he'd poured himself an unnecessary glass of wine. "What's my little darling done to herself this time?"

CHAPTER NINETEEN

Self-Esteem

Everly wasn't feeling this dark and empty void.

Nope. Not at all.

It just wasn't her jam.

"Hello? Can anyone hear me?" she called out, although she knew no one would answer her.

She had no idea where she was and couldn't even guess at the time. One moment she'd been having a celebration with her dear friends, boasting of the glory to come, and the next she was here. In this empty, boring little slice of endless nowhere.

Yeah, this really sucked.

"SOMEONE GET ME OUT OF HERE!" she yelled as loudly as she could.

Surely that would work, right? Someone would have to come help her.

She was the freakin' Empress! Crap like this wasn't supposed to happen to her! She spread misfortune; she wasn't supposed to *suffer* it.

No one answered her.

This left Everly with only one dire option she could resort to. An almost unthinkably evil maneuver that in the best of all possible worlds would never see the light of day.

But Everly was the Empress. There was no power so dreadful that she would refuse to wield it. Such was her grim resolve.

Taking a deep breath to steady herself, Everly closed her eyes. Then, as loudly as she could, she shouted:

"EXCUSE ME! I WOULD LIKE TO SPEAK TO THE MANAGER!"

From the darkness, a shape began to manifest itself before her. Soon, an attractive, pale figure with two black wings stood before her. She instantly recognized his beautiful features and was surprised, but not displeased, to see him so soon after she'd killed him.

Jeez, had that really been three years ago?

Time really did fly by if you let it.

"'Sup?" Everly said to her captor. "You're not looking half-bad."

"'Sup," replied Acedia, also known as Sloth of the seven kings. "You're not looking half-bad yourself."

Everly beamed at the compliment.

"I know, right?" she said. "So, are we about to engage in a life-or-death struggle in the center of my mind or whatever?" Everly asked eagerly. "Are you going to try to conquer me psychically? Oh, is me being trapped here part of your long-awaited vengeance? Shoot, I didn't think you had it in you, Sloth."

"Uh, I don't," Sloth replied with a somewhat bewildered expression on his face. "Nah, I just wanted to pay a visit to see who my new guest was. See what's good and all that. This is some shit, huh?" he asked as he folded his wings around himself.

With a shimmer of pale light, his appearance transformed. Instead of a black-winged angel, he now appeared as a barefoot young man in jeans and an oversized white T-shirt. He then gestured before himself, and a lawn chair appeared that he promptly sat on after giving a languid stretch.

"Ahh," he said in satisfaction. "Comfy."

"Hey," said Everly. "Hook me up, bro," she demanded as she gestured for a chair of her own.

"Why should I? You killed me," replied Sloth. "Asking favors of your victims is pure vanity."

"You got better, didn't you?" She snorted. "Seriously, don't be such a girl."

"When women use reductive gendered language like that, it's often a sign of internalized misogyny," Sloth said unhelpfully.

"Bullshit, I love all women equally. Even the stupid ones," Everly countered.

"How many female friendships do you maintain?" asked Sloth.

"A bunch. Most women love me," replied Everly. "Unless they're hating-ass losers."

"It sure sounds like it," Sloth said sarcastically. "Fine, you can have a chair. Don't ever say I did nothing for you."

He then snapped his fingers, and another lawn chair appeared for Everly to sit in. She made a happy noise and took her seat. "Ohhh, this *is* comfortable. You've got a gift, Your Majesty."

"Oh, you don't have to call me *majesty*," Sloth said humbly. "Technically, you and I are equals."

"Nah, not really," Everly replied.

"Huh?" asked Sloth.

"I mean, sure, we're both monarchs, but you split your authority with six other people. I run my thing entirely on my own. If you'd like, you can keep calling *ME majesty*. I won't mind."

"Yeesh, do you ever turn the act off for even a minute? I'd find the endless performance emotionally draining," said Sloth.

"Who says I'm performing? This is me, twenty-four seven," Everly said with a shrug. "I understand that others find me exhausting, but what can I say? Fuck them. It's their problem, not mine."

"Wow, Everly. You're not like the other girls," Sloth said robotically.

"I know, right? I like kung fu movies and UFC matches. I like sex, but only when my partner is in the mood, and I also love dancing spontaneously in the rain because I'm such a free spirit! I wear vintage concert T-shirts, I know who Frank Miller and Chris Claremont are, and I never talk about politics because what do I know about anything?"

"Keep going," encouraged Sloth.

"Oh, I collect GameCube and Wii games but never Wii U products because it was such a stupid waste of hardware, my favorite anime song is 'Green Bird' from the *Cowboy Bebop* soundtrack, my favorite anime in general is also *Cowboy Bebop* because I want to be as cool as Faye but as free as Spike, and I also think mean people suck."

"Have you ever read *Gone Girl* or seen the movie?" asked Sloth.

"Both," she replied. "Repeatedly."

"Yeah, I thought so," Sloth said.

"What? You aren't charmed by manic-pixie despots?"

"Not the ones who stick me with a hundred thousand swords, no."

"Will that *always* come between us?" she pouted.

"I'm afraid so," he said. "Do you really like *Cowboy Bebop*?"

"I did, but that channel ruined it for me with the endless fucking reruns," she said.

"What do you prefer now?" he asked.

"Anime became pointless when Ash Ketchum retired, Sloth," she said coldly.

"That hurt," he said after recovering from her words.

"I know. I have issues with sadism. So, what are you doing here, anyway?"

"Nothing. Just the usual shit," he said. "Honestly, you're the one intruding. This is my realm."

"Oh, so you *did* plot to trap me here!" Everly said triumphantly. "Good work, you brainy fiend! But know that I shall escape in time and take vengeance upon you!"

"Uh, no," Sloth replied. "That isn't what happened at all. My realm is for those who are unproductive and put forth no effort. You did something to yourself to end up here. If I were to hazard a guess, I'd say you were in a coma of some sort."

"Oh," Everly said in disappointment. "Really?"

"Yep."

"Well, that sucks. I can't imagine what I could have possibly done to myself . . . Oh, unless you were to count me indulging in the heady brew of divinity."

"How's that work?" Sloth asked curiously.

"Well, I greatly improved the people of my kingdom's lives so much that they've begun worshipping me as their badass goddess of good fortune," Everly said without a trace of humility. "Godhood tasted *so* sweet."

"You can directly feed on worship?" Sloth said. He gave an appreciative whistle at the thought of it. "Damn, that's not bad! But obviously you're not equipped to feed on too much of it. You must have overdosed."

"That's so stupid! How can anyone overdose on such a good thing?" asked Everly sourly.

"I don't know. Ask any dead musician in their midtwenties. Obviously, mortals can't just feed on the ambrosia of faith. You're probably better off staying in your lane, Everly."

"I will *not* stay in my lane!" Everly said stubbornly. "I can't go back to being a fool with delusions of godhood now that I've had a taste of the real thing! I'm now completely high on my own supply!"

"You'll probably kill yourself if you keep doing it, though," said Sloth.

"Who cares? Life is meaningless if you aren't rich or famous," said Everly contemptuously.

"We were talking about becoming a god."

"Yeah, that too," Everly said. "Hey, I could use a drink."

"You sure you want one?" Sloth asked her. "Haven't you heard legends about what happens when you eat or drink something from the underworld?"

"If you try to keep me here against my will, I'll snap your spine in half and use your tongue as a bidet," said Everly.

"God, fine, damn!" Sloth said in annoyance. He snapped his fingers again, and two trays filled with sandwiches, tarts, and large bottles of fruit juice appeared for them to build a plate of food with.

"Yum," Everly said happily. "How come deli sandwiches always taste better than the ones I make at home?"

"They season their vegetables with oil and salt," Sloth said as he ate. "They also keep their meats moist by using dressing on both sides of the bread."

"How do you know that?" Everly wondered.

"I saw it on a YouTube vid. *Binging with Babish*," he answered.

"Aww. I miss YouTube," Everly said sadly.

"Do you want a ride to Earth? I can arrange it if you swear never to return," Sloth said.

"Ha! Nice try. But I'm working on my own means of going back," Everly said with a smirk.

"Jeez. Where do you get all that ambition?" Sloth asked her. "You're such a go-getter. I can never work up that much energy for anything."

"Yeah, I'm getting that feeling." Everly nodded. "You know who you remind me of? My minion Beverly. She's ridiculously lazy too. Never wants to do anything, just laze the days away."

"Is that your, uh, copy? One of your clones?" Sloth asked.

"She's a *duplicate*. Not a clone. There's a difference," Everly corrected him.

"There is? What is it?"

"It's nuanced. You wouldn't get it," Everly said primly.

"Uh, I share a psionic bond with my six siblings, so I'm pretty sure I'd understand. Plus, I'm millions of years older than you are," Sloth said irritably.

"You don't act like it," Everly said. "I mean this in the nicest possible sense—"

"Which means you don't mean it nicely at all," said Sloth.

"—but you really need to put forth a more assertive front," Everly said without noticing the interruption. "Otherwise, people are going to bully you."

"Wow, you're right. They'd probably invade my territory and make me give them food and shelter," Sloth said dryly.

"It could happen." Everly nodded without an ounce of self-reflection.

"Well, I checked in on you. Guess I'll take off now. Uh, give my best to Claudia if you see her," Sloth said as he stood up.

"Hold up, don't be so quick to leave," Everly said. "Are you seriously not planning to take revenge on my family? I mean, I did kill you, and Claudia *did* blow you up."

"Yeah," Sloth said indifferently. "I admit, I was pissed at the time. But it's not in my nature to hold a grudge long term. Keeping up that level of anger is tiresome."

"God, you really *are* a lazy bastard," Everly chuckled.

"You think?" Sloth said.

"Well, since I don't know how long I'm going to be here, let me pick your brain for a bit. I could actually use some advice for the future."

"Ditch Seraphine, she's crazy," Sloth said promptly.

"Hey, don't call my girlfriend crazy! She's a passionate woman," Everly said.

"She's a bloodthirsty psychopath who cut a deal with my brother Wrath. She wants to take vengeance on you for stealing away her dreams," Sloth said.

"How could you possibly know that?" asked Everly.

"I told you; I have a psionic bond with my siblings," he said.

"Jeez, shouldn't you be guarding their secrets, then?" Everly asked in amazement.

"Too much effort," he said.

"God DAMN, bro," Everly said, feeling genuinely impressed by his dedication to his role. "Okay, in that case, tell me everything you know about what Pride's been plotting against me."

In response, Sloth began waving both hands in front of him, signaling a no. "Uh-uh. Not happening. Sorry, her, I don't fuck with. It just isn't done."

"What's the big deal? What's the worst your big sister could do to you?" Everly teased.

"Uh, she could crush my mana cores, toss me into the deep abyss to suffer unimaginably for all eternity, and tell our mother to produce a new cardinal sin to replace me," he said with a pale face.

". . . Has she done that before?" Everly asked him.

"Did you know that the current Lust is a dude?" he asked her.

"Really? Incarnations of lust are usually depicted as being female in popular literature," Everly said in surprise.

"The times have yet to catch up with her being replaced," Sloth said with a shudder.

"What did she do to piss Pride off so much?" asked Everly.

"No one knows. It was like one morning Pride woke up and decided having her in the group was bad *feng shui*."

"Jesus, she killed her own sister," Everly said in disgust. "That's fucked up."

"I wasn't happy about it. Old Lust and I were close," Sloth said unhappily. "When Pride revived me, she told me this was my last chance to stop disappointing her. She said it all cheerily like she was on that *Mommie Dearest* bullshit. Don't mess with her, Everly. Whatever she ends up doing to you, don't retaliate. Just take it on the chin and let it go."

"That's not in *my* nature," Everly said with a frown. "Anyone stupid enough to snipe at me had better pray they finish it with the first shot. Otherwise, I'll tear them apart. That's just how it is."

"Those could be your famous last words," Sloth said.

"I'd prefer you call them my declaration of intent," Everly replied. She then took a massive swig of her juice and drained the cup in one swallow. "This stuff is awesome, by the way."

"Refill?" he asked.

"Please do," she replied. Once that was done, she asked, "So. My honey bunny wants to kill me, huh?"

"Badly," Sloth said. "She also wants to usurp everything you've built up."

"It's kind of convenient that you're feeding me this information. Are you *sure* this isn't part of some nefarious scheme to catch me off guard?"

"I already told you that plotting is too much effort for the likes of me," he said.

"Damn," cursed Everly. "Maybe this is what I get for being a selfish lover."

"Sharing yourself with other people isn't easy. There's a lot of give-and-take involved, and finding a balance can be difficult," said Sloth.

"Oh," said Everly. "Well, that's the problem right there. I'm all take."

"It's never too late to change."

"Perhaps, but I don't want to change. I like being a narcissist," Everly said.

"Most narcissists don't acknowledge *being* narcissistic, Everly," said Sloth. "Are you sure you're not just putting on another performance? Playing the role of the wild girl?"

"No, no, I'm very self-aware," Everly said. "I know all my most negative traits, each and every one. I just don't bother hiding them. Why should I? People hide their true selves to avoid consequences. I'm *beyond* consequences. Who'd dare to judge me?"

"You're being silly. The actions of beings like us don't exist in a vacuum. The more out of hand you become, the more likely a hero will be spawned to deal with you," warned Sloth.

"Heroes aren't real," Everly said. "The person I met who was the closest to becoming one was just part of a long-term scam. She got summoned here to play a role in a fake war against your kingdom."

"Are you talking about Fenneth Godwell?" Sloth asked. "Heh, shows what you know!"

"What do you mean?" asked Everly.

"She was a legit divine summoning," Sloth said with another shudder of revulsion. "The Godwells might have been arrogant enough to steal the credit for her coming here, but we've known about her imminent arrival in the demon kingdom for centuries."

". . . Really?" asked Everly quietly.

"Yep. Thank goodness, er, I guess I should say, *badness*, she got herself murdered before she grew into her role. Holy crow, she would have become a fucking *nightmare*. Divine heroes are monsters, Everly. Pray you never have to deal with one."

"How long does it usually take for them to become a threat?" Everly asked as casually as she could.

"It really depends," Sloth said as he leaned back in his seat. "It usually doesn't take long once they're out in the world. They start off ordinary enough until they witness some grave wrong or terrible act of injustice that sparks them off. Then they receive their divine mandate, and the next thing you know, it's all holy light and hallelujahs, and your armies are being effortlessly smashed in the name of the choir."

"Let's say a divine hero is dead and gets brought back to life in a new body later on," Everly said. "As long as they're in a new body, their old power will fade, right?"

"Nope," Sloth said. "They carry their power in their souls. They were literally created to destroy evil, so they can't ever be cut off from their source of strength."

"Well, shit," Everly said bitterly.

"What? What's wrong?" Sloth asked. Then he realized that her questions hadn't been hypothetical at all. "Oh, you dumbass necromancer idiot! Please tell me you didn't resurrect a fucking *divine hero*."

"I want to, but I can't," Everly admitted sheepishly. "She was moaning and sobbing and being such a load, and I just couldn't bear it anymore, so I rebuilt her back in my memory palace."

"In your palace?" Sloth asked her.

"Yeah, that's where I resurrected her."

"Oh," Sloth said with a sigh of relief. "Oh, well, okay, then! No worries! Yeesh, you had me scared there for a moment, Everly. So long as you have her bound within the center of your place of power, she's no threat to anyone. Heh, lead with that part first before you repeat that story, silly! I was about to burst a vein."

". . . She's not in my memory palace any longer," mumbled Everly.

"Come again? What was that?" asked Sloth. "For a moment there, I thought you just said something horrifying."

"I kicked her out. She was being such an ungrateful pill, I just couldn't take the *drama* anymore," Everly said in a rush.

"You kicked her out. You kicked a divine hero out of the one place she couldn't cause any damage to the world we seven kings have painstakingly crafted for ourselves over millennia, because you couldn't handle her *drama* anymore. Is that right?" asked Sloth.

"Sloth, you have no idea what it was like! Sh-she was abusive! Fenn was *very* abusive, she was! I went to sleep night after night, fearing for my safety! I pray daily that I never encounter such an animal ever again!"

Sloth said nothing for a time. He only stared blankly ahead.

"How long ago?" he eventually asked.

"Huh?" asked Everly.

"How long ago did you set her free?"

"I didn't keep track. She's been loose for months," Everly admitted.

"*Everly*," Sloth said as he gripped the sides of his head in despair.

"Okay, so what if I screwed up?" Everly said defiantly. "Big frickin' deal, who cares if Fenn is some big-shot hero? You know what? That's just fine by me. I've been wanting a fight with a genuine hero for *ages*. In fact, this works out perfectly! I'll finally get the bout that I've always wanted!"

"You're ignorant. You're so fucking *ignorant*," Sloth wailed. "Everly, you have no idea what you've done. You have no idea what you're facing! She'll be a soldier of PRIMAL ORDER . . ."

"That's fine by me, Sloth. I *want* that smoke!" Everly said confidently.

So very, very confidently.

CHAPTER TWENTY

No Remedy

Marcis was blunt in his assessment of Everly's condition.

"I can't do a damn thing for her," he said, after giving his daughter's comatose body a careful examination.

With Marcis in tow, as well as Claudia, who insisted on accompanying them, Grail had quickly returned to the memory palace, where the inner circle stood gathered in Everly's sleeping quarters, where she rested on her bed, still unconscious.

Seraphine sat by her lover's side, holding her hand and dramatically weeping. Ghost Knight . . . wait, no, not Ghost Knight, *Dullahan* stood immobile as a statue, silently guarding the room, as Carter and Grail paced impatiently, and Beverly kept muttering fearfully to herself.

"What do you mean by that? Her condition is clearly related to your foul mutation," Grail said accusingly as he pushed past the other man to lay a hand at Everly's cheek. "She described it as such shortly before this incident. Feeding off the emotions of the citizens."

"I don't know what you want me to say," Marcis replied. "Everly's abilities clearly outstrip my own. To feed on the emotional energy of thousands of people simultaneously . . . Not even in my most twisted fantasies could I hope to achieve such a thing. My little girl is all grown up and has left her papa behind."

"Stop sounding so pleased with her," Grail said angrily. "Can't you see she's caused harm to herself?"

"Of course she has," Marcis said. "No worries, it'll be a valuable learning experience for her. Now she knows how a mosquito feels if you squeeze your vein while it feeds."

"Do not compare Her Majesty to a lowly parasite!" bristled Carter in outrage.

"My dear goblin, I'm afraid that a parasite is exactly what my daughter has become," Marcis said. "Emotions are the expression of the soul. The taste of them is both empowering and *extremely* addictive. Even if Everly awakens, I'm sorry to tell you that she won't be quite the same from now on. Once a wolf has had a taste of lamb, it never stops yearning for it."

"Hey, whoa, pause. Rewind to the part where you said *if* she awakens," said Beverly with frightened urgency. "Uh, are you saying there's a possibility that she'll stay like this for the rest of her life?"

"I'm afraid there is." Marcis nodded. "She may very well have destroyed her mind and is simply a sleeping body. Those are the risks associated with this power."

"Well, fuck nuggets!" Beverly said miserably. "Grail, what are we going to do now? I'm sure you remember that Everly has made enemies with some extremely motivated, extremely powerful douche wads who won't wait quietly for an opportunity like this to pass!"

"Beverly, calm down," Grail said to her in a stern voice.

"Don't tell me to calm down, stupid! This is bad news, old man! The *worst* news! Without Everly, we're screwed!"

"I *said* to calm down," Grail repeated. "Use your head, girl. If Everly's mind were truly gone, this palace would be as well. So would anything else connected to her. She nearly died two years ago, and it directly affected everything and everyone that her powers maintained, including myself. The fact that I'm perfectly fine is proof that Everly is still intact. Just sleeping."

"Oh," Beverly said. "Okay, that's good. Yeesh, why didn't you say so?" She then gave Grail a playful slap on the shoulder. "I was really freaking out for a minute there."

"Don't lower your guard just yet," Grail advised her. "We still can't reach her, we still don't know if she'll awaken on her own, and until we can resolve this situation, we're essentially without leadership."

"Perhaps I can be of assistance with that?" Marcis said helpfully. "The role of steward should by tradition fall to Everly's closest relative. As her father, however reluctant I would be to receive such power, I would humbly accept—"

"Not happening," Grail said bluntly. "Ever."

"You've got to be fucking kidding me," Beverly said incredulously.

"Your kind offer is not necessary," Carter said with polite curtness.

"Haha," Claudia snickered. "You suck, Dad."

"All right, all right, just thought I'd make the offer," Marcis said amiably. "For the record, though, I think I would have done an excellent job."

"The kingdom would have become a blazing inferno by noon tomorrow," said Grail. "No, I'll be assuming the reins of command. I'm the first of Everly's creations and I already command her armed forces. Carter, I ask that you continue to run the administration in Everly's name and serve as my second."

"As you wish, General," Carter said with a bow.

"Hey, don't I get a say in this?" Beverly whined.

"What would you like to say?" Grail asked her.

"Nothing, I just wanted to feel included," Beverly admitted.

"You will be," Grail assured her. "Because we can't let anyone know that Everly is out of commission. And for that to happen, you'll need to publicly assume her identity."

"Uh, what the *fuuuuuuck*?" Beverly said with a squeaky voice.

"Beverly, this is important, and I wouldn't ask this of you if it wasn't necessary," Grail said patiently. "We need to present an image to the world of strength and unity. We need *you* to be the face of that unity until Everly can reclaim her role. You're the only one who can do it."

"No, wrong, bullshit!" Beverly said. "Make Dullahan do it! Just pull her out of that stupid armor and then she can finally be of use!"

"What? No. Noooo, no, I can't," Dullahan said as panic slowly grew in her voice. "I can't do it. I can't, I just can't. Not without my armor, it isn't safe, it isn't safe!"

"Oh, for god's *sake*, Cleverly! Stop being a freak and start being helpful for once!" Beverly said without empathy.

"I'M NOT CLEVERLY!" Dullahan shouted with mounting hysteria. "Cleverly died! She's dead! I'm all that's left, and I can't leave my armor, *please* don't make me leave my armor!"

"Peace, Dullahan. Peace. No one will force you to do anything," Grail said gently as he stepped toward the armored girl and placed a reassuring arm around her. "Stay in your armor; stay as safe as you'd like."

"Thank you," Dullahan said quietly as her head drooped. "I'm sorry. I'm sorry I can't be what I'm supposed to be."

"That's not your fault," Grail told her. "You're already doing an excellent job in your assigned role. Nothing else will be required of you."

"Thank you," Dullahan said once more, before her voice trailed off.

"Fine, fine, whatever!" Beverly said. "If she won't do it, then let's just recall Neverly—"

"That would be an even worse idea than handing control to Count Marcis," Carter said primly.

"She'd take over the entire institution," Grail said. "Every square inch."

"Nev wouldn't do such a thing!" Beverly said half-heartedly.

"Nev *would* do such a thing." Marcis smirked. "Of all my children, she's the one with the most ambition."

"These *homunculi* are not your children!" Claudia snapped resentfully.

"We're *duplicates*," said both Beverly and Dullahan with offended voices.

"Whatever," Claudia said with a disgusted roll of her eyes.

"I find myself liking her less and less as the days go by," Beverly said nastily.

"I find myself agreeing with you," Dullahan said with equal displeasure.

"Oh, girls! Don't waste the spring of your youth in pointless disharmony," said Marcis with a smile. "Better kisses than disses, as the poets say."

"Shut up, Dad," Claudia said in annoyance.

"Your intervention is unrequired, Marcis," Dullahan informed him coldly.

"Stay out of this, Pops," warned Beverly.

"As you like," Marcis said cheerily. "Carter, please escort me to a room, if you will. I think I'd like to take a nap."

"You aren't staying here," Grail said immediately. "I'll have a portal opened to your home in a moment."

"That won't be necessary, Grail. As long as my daughter is sick, I insist on being nearby," said Marcis.

"I *said* no," Grail insisted. "I don't trust you being anywhere near her. No doubt you sense an opportunity for mischief. Well, I'm not going to let you play any of your games."

"Fine," Marcis said with a long, drawn-out breath. "You know, Grail, despite our long friendship, I'm very much beginning to believe that you don't like me very much."

"Just get out," Grail said, after a portal sprang to life beside him.

"Always a pleasure seeing you, everyone," Marcis said to the group. "Claudia, will you be accompanying me?"

"No," Claudia replied.

"A man is never alone who has family," Marcis said with a small frown as he stepped through the portal.

"Good riddance," said Grail. "Now, getting back on topic: Beverly, Nev can't be trusted not to take advantage of this situation. Her ambition and unpredictability make her too much of a risk to be our figurehead. It *must* be you."

"God damn it," Beverly said bitterly.

"I'm glad you understand," Grail said with a small smile.

Marcis wondered what he had to do to prove himself to his daughter's friends. To improve his image in the eyes of others. At first it had been amusing to play the role of a scamp; he never could resist an opportunity to annoy Grail whenever it sprang up, and he'd always enjoyed teasing his children, but it seemed to him lately that a genuine mistrust had sprung up between him and the people that he considered his family.

Oddly enough, this bothered him.

Marcis didn't very much enjoy it when things bothered him.

He knew he lacked character and morality and was very proud of the lack of personal growth that he'd managed to sustain throughout a lifetime of treachery and hedonism. What he lacked in empathy and humanity, he made up for in wit, good manners, and a genuinely jovial nature. He hated no one and loved *everything*. So why wasn't that enough to sustain him these days?

The answer kept coming back to Anne. His deceased primary wife.

What had been the purpose of their marriage? He'd unceasingly found little ways to torment and annoy her, and she'd done the same. They'd fought over everything imaginable and had come close to killing each other more than a few times. The intensity of the emotion she'd directed toward him had been unlike any other he'd ever tasted.

They'd been a wretched pair of vainglorious schemers obsessed with dominating each other, and yet . . . hadn't there been a sort of tenderness at the core of their relationship? Hadn't there been a mutual acknowledgement and respect between them that others simply wouldn't be able to understand? Regardless of their passionate hatred, hadn't they completed one another?

What a strange thing it was to help your daughter murder your wife only to later realize that you genuinely loved her.

That you missed her.

The irony of it should have made Marcis laugh at the absurdity of life, but instead it made him feel despondent and alone. Good food and fine drink didn't taste the same. Books became boring to read, and his old mischievous endeavors sparked no joy within him. For the first time in his life, Marcis began to feel old. Even watching his daughter slowly transform the nation into a reflection of her twisted will brought him no pleasure.

What was worse was the constant rejection from her circle of friends, which he'd considered himself an honorary member of. It seemed that there was a silent understanding that anyone who befriended him would have to choose between him and Grail. And to a man, the group chose Grail.

"Well, it's not as if I don't deserve his contempt," Marcis said to himself. "I did play a considerable role in killing many of his comrades and dirtying up the nation with that silly little civil war. But how long does he intend to hold a grudge? It seems unfair to me. All I ever did was try to keep amused in this boring life. I'm no different from anyone else in that regard."

Sighing at life's little injustices, Marcis began walking to his wine cellar to get a bottle of something to take his mind off the day's troubles, when he smelled the familiar but unexpected scent of blood wafting throughout the air. Seeking the source of the aroma, he turned the corner and discovered one of his household knights lying dead on the floor with his abdomen slashed open.

"Ah," he said mildly. "Well, that would explain it."

Relieving the corpse of the sword held at its side, Marcis decided he would have to forgo his evening wine and investigate this strange occurrence. As the lord of Belsar County, it set a poor precedent to allow any of his men to be murdered in his own home. He had his reputation to consider, after all. With that in mind, he set forth into the darkness of his shadowed home.

Along his way, he discovered more dead knights and servants. It seemed that someone had torn through the manor, quite skillfully, and defeated his men in simultaneous combat. That spoke of a rare talent with the blade. Could the killer be a sword king? The precision of the mortal wounds dealt out to his men suggested it could be nothing less.

Each of them died from a single mortal blow. None of them had received more than a single cut.

"Truly, the craft of a master," Marcis said admiringly. It made him think of his dear Anne once more. She'd been the finest creature with a blade that Marcis had ever seen. Even Everly hadn't been her match. He'd lost count of the number of times she'd effortlessly trounced him during their sparring matches.

What a woman she'd been!

"Grah," Marcis said bitterly as he entered his receiving hall. "Look at me! Behaving like a sentimental old fool lost in memories of the supposed *good old days*. It's so pathetic, I could weep. Perhaps I *will* weep! I'll pour a glass to my beloved and praise her as the greatest thing that ever happened to me. Wouldn't that be sweet? Maybe I'll even say I'll never love again. That would complete the image, wouldn't it?"

"You seem troubled, Count Van Belsar," said a soft voice.

A woman stepped before Marcis dressed in a splendid, formfitting white outfit doffed with a white cape. Her hair hung down her shoulders in ebon curls, and her undoubtedly attractive face was disguised beneath a white half mask that covered her piercing eyes.

In her hand, she wielded a regal-looking blade stained with blood.

"I believe I was until the moment my sight fell upon *you*," he said rakishly.

"The last thing you'll ever see in this life?" she said with a smile that matched his own.

"If only," he said wistfully. "I've recently had a palm reading done. I was told my lifespan would continue indefinitely until the day I met my equal. It simply hasn't happened yet."

"Sadly, the stars may have misled you, my lord," replied his guest. She then raised her sword and pointed it toward him. "Count Marcis Van Belsar, in the name of the revolution, I challenge you to honorable mortal combat."

Marcis began to snicker uncontrollably. The swordswoman was not amused.

"Does my challenge amuse you, Count? Does the idea of dueling a woman tickle your elite sensibilities?"

"Not in the slightest," Marcis said, once he'd regained control of himself.

"I apologize for that rude display. It's just . . . my daughter has access to these amazing interactive stories from another world, and one of her favorites is this ridiculous tale called *Mortal Kombat*. Ever since she forced me to watch it with her, I just can't take that term seriously. The chorus that screams those words aloud whenever the characters battle each other . . . It's just so much to take in. I wish you could hear it; you'd understand."

"I fail to see the humor here," the woman said. "I advise you to take my challenge seriously, Count. This battle will be a true test of might."

"Dun-dun-dun dundun-dun-dun-dun-dundun, *Mortal Kombat!*" Marcis sang before he could stop himself.

The woman stared at him in disgusted silence, clearly displeased by his outburst.

"Fine, then. Die like a fool," she said angrily, before lunging forward to thrust at his heart.

Marcis

'm beginning to suspect that you're very good at this," Marcis said a few minutes later as he narrowly avoided another mortal strike that nearly caught him in the throat. "If this continues much longer, you may end up doing me a serious injury."

"I'm going to take your life," his opponent said grimly as she parried his counterthrust and stepped inside his guard. Before Marcis could react in time, she struck him across the jaw with the pommel of her sword, then followed through with a powerful back-spinning kick that caught him in his gut and had him gasping for air.

"Time out!" he said, holding up an unsteady hand while he tried to get his breathing under control. "By the gods, woman, that wasn't nice at all!"

"It wasn't *nice?*" she replied incredulously. "I'm trying to kill you, you vainglorious prick! Why should I hold myself back just because you're unable to keep up?"

"Because it would better reflect your generous nature and speak highly of your character, young lady!" Marcis choked out, before climbing up with wobbling knees to resume his fighting stance.

"You are an aggravating, *arrogant* little man," the woman said. "Even now you aren't taking this seriously! Don't you understand that this is your punishment? You aided the old regime in plotting the civil war, and now your daughter of all people has enslaved the kingdom! The corpses that can be laid at your feet are uncountable!"

"Do you really think so?" Marcis asked her. "I haven't put much thought into it myself. I mean, who would? Dead bodies make for an unpleasant visual, yes? But if I'm truly responsible for what you say is an *uncountable* amount . . . well, I suppose that's something I should take pride in, isn't it?"

"This is no joke, Count," the woman said sternly. "I can see the very essence of your soul. You are mired in sin! Dripping in blood and debauchery! How can you even stand beneath the weight of your corruption?"

"Well, mostly, I skip," Marcis said. "Haven't you heard? Heavy sinning makes for a light heart."

"You're disgusting," the woman said with contempt.

"You don't find me even a little bit charming?" Marcis asked her in a wounded voice. "You still haven't introduced yourself."

The woman paused for a moment to consider his words. Then said, "I am Lady Kestrel, leader of the revolutionary force for the restoration of Winstead."

Marcis snorted at once.

"No, you're not," he said glibly.

"Excuse me?" Lady Kestrel replied.

"There is no chance in the abyss that your real name is *Kestrel*," Marcis tittered. "That's just too cool! Who'd name their daughter after an ominous bird of prey? It's clearly an alias. Besides, I feel as though I've seen you before. Yes, you seem *very* familiar to me."

"I think you're mistaken," replied Kestrel.

"No, I don't believe I am," said Marcis. "Your mannerisms are very similar to my wife's granddaughter. You can't be Sarah, though. You come across as entirely too sane. No, if I had to put a finger on it, I'd say you were . . . oh. *Oh!* I remember now," he said excitedly as he snapped his fingers.

Kestrel stared at him silently, letting him continue.

"Yes, it was during Sarah's ceremonial anointment when she was appointed the paladin of the north!" Marcis continued. "You and the other two were there to receive her as your spiritual sibling. There was old Tabrius of the west, still at it even well into his seventh decade, and the elegant Gretchen of the east, so by default . . . that means that you're the gentle Arden of the south!"

In response, Kestrel, newly revealed as Arden, removed her mask and tossed it aside. "You're a more observant man than I realized, Count Marcis," she said.

"Thank you for your kind remark, but such perception isn't impressive at all. It comes to everyone with sufficient experience," he replied politely. "Goodness, though, to think a holy paladin has rebelled against the nation and has come to claim my life. What strange twist of fate awaits me next?" he asked himself with a chuckle.

"Nothing awaits you except death," Arden replied cooly as she pointed her sword at him once more. "If you've managed to recognize me despite my disguise, then surely you recognize this sword?"

"Ah, well, unfortunately, the answer is yes," Marcis said with a slight shiver. "Oh, I never liked the way the light gleamed from the edge of that thing's blade! It seemed to always hold on to a sort of inner purity despite being a tool of church-mandated butchery. Whenever Laurel came by the house wearing it, I wanted to flinch. I was happy to hear that it had vanished after Fenneth's passing."

"I'm sure all those bearing wickedness in their hearts were quick to rejoice at that news," Arden said. "But this sacred blade is destined to vanquish the darkness of this world, not succumb to it! As the new holy maiden, I will lead the crusade that purges evil from this land!"

"Ah, so *that's* your game. I wondered how you intended to spin things to suit your agenda," Marcis said dryly. "Honestly, it's been done before. I was hoping that whoever's backing you up would have more of an imagination than that."

"Again, you mock me, pawn of the Godwells!" Arden said with growing fury. "I don't seek to justify anything. Do you think I intend to rule this land after its liberation?"

"Why wouldn't you?" Marcis asked her in slight confusion. "Wouldn't that be the entire point of conquering it?"

"Wh-what? You deluded *prick*, is that truly how you view my efforts to save the country?" Arden asked him in astonishment. "Wait, why should I find this surprising? Of course this is how someone as demented as you would see the world. I'm not out for personal gain, Count Marcis. I'm trying to protect the people from your daughter!"

"Protect them from what?" Marcis asked her as he settled into a sitting position on the floor. "Haven't you seen how much they love her? Look at all she's given them. Lady Arden, they're beginning to *worship* her. Isn't it somewhat of a futile gesture to try to save people who like things the way they are?"

Arden shook her head immediately, denying his words as he spoke. "No! Absolutely not. If anything, it becomes even more important to try to help them. The Empress has given them comfort and wealth, but at what cost? She's binding them to her using heretical magic. Her every gift comes with the peril of eternal damnation!"

"Heretical by whose definition?" Marcis asked her. "The temple no longer has the authority to define what is and isn't sacrilegious."

"Because Everly slaughtered the faithful! She openly scorns the teachings and deliberately targets those who refuse her blasphemous reformations!" Arden replied.

"There was a time in this world before the rise of the temple," Marcis countered. "People lived peacefully for thousands of years before the rising of the faith. Do you mean to say that everyone who ever lived before the coming of the temple is now damned for the sin of having lived too early? That doesn't seem very likely."

Arden frowned at him. Then she sheathed her sword and took a seat on the floor across from him. "Of course those who came before weren't damned. The gods hadn't yet decided on which revelations to share with humanity. It would be a wickedness to punish those who dwelled in ignorance of their sins."

"Interesting," Marcis said thoughtfully. "But what of the lives of my household guard? You've slain three dozen innocent men whose only crime was faithfully serving their lord. Was knightly decorum a sin great enough to warrant their collective demise?"

"My only intent was to challenge *you*, Count Marcis," Arden said firmly. "No blood would have been spilled if they hadn't decided to oppose me."

"But as a bearer of great power both with and without that sword, wasn't it your responsibility to show restraint against those weaker than yourself?" Marcis wondered.

"I . . . I tried to," Arden said reluctantly. "They wouldn't back down. They wouldn't acknowledge their defeat. It isn't my fault that I was forced to defend myself."

"Not your fault?" asked Marcis. "You raided my home and openly declared your intent to murder me. And now you're blaming my loyal servants for seeing their duty through to the end. Does an invader have the right to shirk her responsibility?"

"Their lives weigh upon me!" Arden yelled angrily as she stood back up and began to pace restlessly back and forth. "All the lives I've claimed do! I joined the temple to serve the people. Not to slay them! I don't consider myself an exemplar whose needs place her above judgement. I do what I must because *so much* is required of me."

"Ah," Marcis said in an understanding tone. "You speak of the burden of leadership."

"Yes!" Arden replied quickly. "Yes, exactly that! It *is* a burden. I didn't ask for this sword, and I didn't ask for the remnants of the temple to place their hopes upon me. But I must not deny those hopes, because if I fail them, then what chance will they have left to them?"

Now Marcis stood. He brushed off his pants lightly and gestured for her to follow him. "Come with me, please. I think I understand what this situation truly requires."

"What do you mean?" Arden asked him in confusion.

"You need a drink," he said bluntly.

Arden stared at his back in bewilderment as he strolled from the room, before hurriedly following him.

A few minutes later they were both seated on the leather couch in Marcis's study, enjoying a glass of something both potent and expensive. Arden almost choked after taking a swallow before regaining control. As the liquid went down her throat, a pleasant burning sensation ignited in her center and began circulating its relaxing warmth throughout her body.

"By the gods, this is good stuff," she said with a slight smile. "I'm impressed with your good taste, Count."

"Thank you," Marcis warmly replied as he enjoyed a glass of his own. "I'm rather fond of this particular vintage myself. I'm very fortunate that it's brewed locally. That gives me an opportunity to get at it early before any of my peers."

"How lucky for you, I suppose," Arden said as she took a smaller sip. "This isn't going to change anything, though. I'm still going to kill you."

"Really?" Marcis said with some surprise. "Despite my amazing outward charm?"

"You . . . *are* charming, I admit," Arden said reluctantly. "But that doesn't change what you've done. The harm you've caused."

"You're referring to the civil war, I suppose?" Marcis asked her. "I wish people would stop holding grudges over such a relatively minor event in the annals of history."

"Minor? *Minor?*" Arden asked, outraged by his tone. "Thousands died due to your machinations! The country was sundered; the wounds still haven't healed! And you call that *minor?*"

"It was all a regrettable necessity to build a stronger nation," Marcis said offhandedly. "A sacrifice for a better future for us all."

"That you can say that with a straight face proves you're a monster," Arden seethed. "You claim to feel regret, but what have you done with it? You pass the time playing and living like a king in this estate and do nothing to address the suffering you caused!"

"Hmm. I may live like a king," Marcis admitted, "but at least I've never *killed* one. Regicide is the one sin that can never be laid at my feet."

"Bastard!" Arden said as she threw her glass across the room to shatter against a wall. "I didn't want to spill the blood of King Septus! But what choice did I have? He was about to form an alliance with your daughter! It would have spelled the end of the nation!"

"The nation ended anyway," Marcis replied calmly. "Are you so arrogant that you can't understand it was a lost cause? Everly was *playing* with us. She could have ended the entire thing whenever she wished. She didn't because she derived too much enjoyment from the farce. You slew the king for no reason."

"No . . . No! It's not as you say!" Arden said, but now doubt resonated in her voice.

"I'm afraid so," Marcis replied. "I'd known Septus since we were both children. He was like a brother to me, perhaps the greatest friend I've ever had. Between the two of us, I have far greater reason to hate you than you have to hate me. But even with the knowledge of your crime weighing heavy in my heart, I can only pity you."

"You pity . . . me?" Arden asked him slowly.

"Of course," Marcis replied. "You and I are both the same breed of fool. In the past, I acted with great cruelty out of an arrogant belief that I was doing the world a service. In you, I see my reflection. But while I was buttressed by my ego, you shield yourself with faith. But it's not working anymore, is it?"

In a flash, Arden was on her feet with her divine blade pressed against his neck. Her body heaved with anger-filled breaths, and the tip of her sword trembled and drew a line of blood at his throat with its erratic movements.

"Is it?" Marcis repeated quietly, refusing to turn his eyes away from her.

"This isn't how my life was supposed to be," she whispered sadly.

"It doesn't have to stay this way," Marcis replied.

"I can't turn away. I can't turn my back on my followers. I've come too far," she said desperately.

"You weren't made for war, Lady Arden," Marcis said. He then rose to his feet and gently guided her sword away from his neck. "You were meant for kinder things than this. Going against your true nature has led you to despair. Your masters have stained your gentle hands with blood out of their selfish desire to retain their power. This isn't who you really are."

"They need me . . . I'm needed," Arden said as tears began to gather in her eyes.

"Not for this, you aren't," Marcis said as he stepped closer to her.

"I—I can't! To leave now after having come so far . . . it would be a betrayal," she said with a sigh as his arms closed around her.

"No, Lady Arden. They betrayed you first when they had you pantomime the role of a killer. They destroyed you for their greed. You owe them nothing. Nothing at all."

"But where could I go? How can I just walk away?" Arden asked him as their lips hovered inches apart.

"Why walk away at all?" he asked her. "Stay. Stay with me. For tonight, at least."

"I . . . I . . ." she began to say, before his mouth claimed hers.

With a clank, the holy sword dropped to the floor as she began running her hands around his waist, first with some reluctance, then with growing eagerness. With surprising tenderness, Marcis guided her back to the couch to lie before him. He then nimbly began unlacing her tunic and pulled it free from her. She screamed with a sudden animal passion as he brought his lips down to her exposed breast and began caressing it with his tongue. She then entwined her fingers into his hair as she guided his head down lower.

Welp, that was easy, Marcis thought cheerfully to himself as events continued to get more interesting. *I have to admit, I've still got it!*

An unpleasant glare suddenly caught his eye as the holy sword began to shine furiously with an angry blue light, as though it knew exactly what he was doing and was *pissed* with him.

After a moment's consideration, Marcis removed his own shirt and tossed it over the sword, covering it entirely and muting its light. *You stay quiet*, he thought smugly, before returning to the main event.

"Marcis!" Arden cried out after he *really* got going. "*Marcis!*"

Damn right, that's my name, he thought with a grin.

And just like that, a bad day suddenly turned into a *great* one.

CHAPTER TWENTY-TWO

Doors

This time, the abyss took the shape of a large hotel corridor.

The sides of the hallway were lined with portraits of famous actors and singers and poets, with the quality of the pictures gradually moving from three dimensional holograms to sharp digital photography, all the way to charcoal etchings and eventually caveman scrawling carved into the walls with sharpened stones.

Also very noticeable were the dozens and dozens of hellions, a species of tiny, hideous primordial demons who looked like children with elongated limbs tipped with venomous claws, swollen bellies, and mouths filled with razor-sharp teeth.

Oh, and the tops of their heads were on fire. Can't forget that part.

"Run, run, run, run!" Everly shouted as she bolted for the exit with Sloth following closely behind her as the hellions shrieked with mindless fury and chased after them, determined to tear the pair of them apart.

"I told you this was a terrible idea! I told you! Why didn't you just stay put?" Sloth whined as the horde of bloodthirsty demons drew nearer.

"Don't blame *me* for this! You ignited my curiosity! I'm supposed to feel guilt for having a precocious and childlike sense of wonder?" Everly yelled back as they drew closer to the glowing golden door that marked their escape from this section of the abyss.

"Haven't you ever heard about curiosity killing the cat? That's a slogan based on grim reality! There are *so* many dead cats in the multiverse!" Sloth snapped back.

When they reached the door, Everly hurriedly pulled it open, then whooped with victorious glee when they managed to slam it shut behind them just as the first of their hellion pursuers came crashing into it. "Later, suckers!" she yelled triumphantly as the door shook beneath the pounding of many fists before gradually fading from sight.

"Everly, quiet down!" Sloth said while gesticulating wildly for her to quiet down. "Just because we escaped that bunch doesn't mean there aren't others on this side who will hear you yelling! We have no power in this realm; we must be careful!"

They now stood in what appeared to be the edge of some manner of wetlands, with long grass jutting out of muddy, dank water, and massive trees with low-hanging branches and vines covering the area.

"Yeah, yeah, all right," Everly said blithely as she took stock of their new surroundings. "You know, for a literal demon king, you sure like to emphasize your limits a bunch. We can't do *this*, we can't do *that*, we'll be eaten alive if we attract the wrong sort of attention, blah-blah-blah. The whole point of kinghood is that you don't have to follow any rules but your own."

"That is the *exact* opposite of responsible kingship, you utter maniac," Sloth said as he slid to the ground to catch his breath.

"Well, why do we have to be responsible?" Everly asked him as she took a moment to get some stretches in for herself. "That's what people like Carter are for."

"Who?" he asked.

"Carter. He's my goblin majordomo," Everly said. "Why? Don't you have one?" she asked.

"Do you even know what a majordomo is?" he asked her with a raised brow.

"I assume it's something Japanese," Everly said.

"*Why?*" Sloth asked her with an exaggerated sigh.

"Well, it says *domo* at the end, doesn't it?" Everly asked innocently.

"You're not representing the multiverse's blond population very well," Sloth said with a disappointed frown.

"The hell I'm not! I have an entire nation at my beck and call," said Everly in mock offense.

"Which we'll never return to if we don't escape from this place!" Sloth said irritably. "Which is completely your fault, by the way. Why the hell did you attack me while I was casting my teleportation spell?"

"To catch you off guard, obviously," Everly said with a sage nod. "And behold! It worked! Now I've escaped your clutches and have begun a new and exciting adventure."

"It worked, did it?" Sloth scoffed. "Thanks to you, my spell misfired and threw us into the lower abyss! The primal lands of torment! A place where neither of us has authority or power—"

"Because it borders too closely to the elemental plane," Everly concluded for him, having heard this rant more times on their journey than she cared to recall.

"—because it borders too closely to the elemental plane!" Sloth continued, oblivious to her words. "Don't you understand how much danger we're in?"

"Haven't you ever heard that danger and opportunity are the same word in Chinese?" Everly asked him.

"No, because that's completely untrue," he replied.

"Yeah, but are you *sure*?" Everly asked him.

"Yes," he said without hesitation.

"Yeah, but are you *really* sure?" she asked again.

"YES," he repeated impatiently.

"Yeah, but are you really, *really* sure—"

"EVERLY! I'm sure, okay?!" he bellowed at her.

"Hey, there's no reason to yell, Ace, we're just having a conversation," Everly said. "Honestly, you're *so* high-strung. You'd think the embodiment of sloth would be a lot more chill or something."

"How can I possibly relax when I'm around you? You're completely out of control!"

"Which I've repeatedly been told is my most charming trait," she said as she took a seat on a rock beside him.

"Told by whom?" Sloth asked as he rested his face on his palms.

"Lots of people," Everly said. "Too many to count."

"No one," he said. "No one at all."

"Nah, everybody loves me too much to say otherwise. It's the curse of charisma," Everly said confidently.

"So, what made you decide that you needed to deliver a surprise attack to me? I've been nothing but cordial to you," Sloth asked, after taking a few deep breaths.

Everly smirked at him playfully, but there was a slight hardening of her eyes as she spoke. "I wasn't going to take the chance of you keeping me as a prisoner. Especially since you'd already lied to me earlier."

Sloth's jaw dropped open dumbly before he corrected himself, which in turn caused Everly to feel some pity for the dope. *Yeah, he's gorgeous, and he's older than recorded history, but man, he sure is light on gray matter*, she thought uncharitably.

"Why would you say something like that?" he asked her unconvincingly.

"All the time I've recently spent with my father," Everly said matter-of-factly. "He's so good at lying that it doubles back on itself and becomes a kind of perverse sort of honesty. Compared to his antitruth, your dishonesty is easy to pick apart."

"What do you think I lied about?" Sloth asked her with a poor attempt at a nonchalant tone of voice.

"You told me Seraphine was conspiring with your brother, Wrath. That was complete bullshit," Everly said scornfully. "Seraphine is a temple traditionalist. She's the sort of girl who wouldn't say *oh, my god* during an orgasm. You really expect me to believe someone like her is going to risk her soul consorting with a demon king?"

"But I told you, I can hear my siblings' thoughts—"

"Wrath is the sin of anger, right?" Everly asked him.

"Yes, obviously."

"So that means he's the sort who'd get pissed if, say, his little brother had just spoiled a deal he had going on the side, right?" Everly continued. "And being that his name is *Wrath*, I expect he's not the kind of big brother who'd settle for an apology and an admission of guilt, is he? It's more likely that he'd walk over to your castle and stomp your ass into the ground."

"Uhm . . ." said Sloth.

"And considering that you're a lazy bastard who doesn't believe in taking risks, that means you're extremely unlikely to want to set him off. After all, getting beaten up is too much of a hassle for the king of sloth. Ergo, you lied to me about Seraphine, probably to get me to kill her, all out of some petty-ass need to avenge yourself after I humiliated you back in Bremburg. Does that sound about right?"

For a moment, a shadow seemed to darken Sloth's face, leaving his expression unreadable. When it passed, a look of genuine anger remained as he raised his face to glare at Everly's amused gaze.

"You *murdered* me," he said bitterly. "And you killed my attendant. The closest thing I had to a friend in that world."

"That big spider? That's what you're so knotted up over?" Everly asked.

"He saved my life. He kept me warm, fed me, nursed me back to health. He even tried to protect me from your rain of sharp metal. He deserved better than the ending he was dealt," Sloth said.

"So, your idea of avenging your friend was getting me to kill someone who had nothing to do with any of it?" Everly asked. "That's pretty disappointing for a monster of your caliber. Why didn't you just challenge me to a duel? Any friend worth mourning is worth avenging."

"Because I'd lose!" Sloth said hatefully. "I can't beat you one-on-one."

"Damn right you can't," Everly said. "But at least I'd respect you for making the effort."

"Did your respect preserve the life of Countess Anne?" Sloth asked with doubt.

"Of course not. But we followed a warrior's code. We had an obligation to see our fight through to the end," said Everly.

"God, listen to yourself talk. You've really taken to that shithole planet, haven't you?" Sloth said in disgust. "A *warrior's code*, you say. What kind of backward fucking thinking is that? It's just an excuse to kill."

"I don't need an excuse to kill anyone," Everly said frostily as she crossed her arms.

"Of course you don't, because you don't see any value in human life. Because you're a psychopath. Because you can't feel genuine emotion," Sloth said. "You're just some broken thing that fell out of the womb with the body of a human and the mind of some prehistoric insectile beast that only knows how to feed its urges."

"Shut your fucking mouth," Everly said. "I have a code, I have rules, I don't just . . . do whatever I want. I have *reasons* behind my actions. I'm not a freak!"

"Ha! *Now* who's the liar?" Sloth said spitefully.

Everly flexed her fingers and felt her tendons popping. She had a sudden urge to beat Sloth to the ground. To tear his eyes from his face and replace that smug look on his face with an expression of suffering and fear.

It would feel good.

So good . . .

But she didn't give in. Not because she didn't want to. But because she was too prideful to concede his point. To prove him right. She wouldn't humiliate herself like that.

"Whatever," she growled. "Get up, we've rested long enough. Time to find the next exit."

"Everly, we're going in the wrong direction, I keep telling you!" Sloth said as he rose reluctantly to his feet. "Beings as tainted as you and I can't be this close to the elemental plane. If the higher elementals discover our presence, we'll be roasted alive."

"So I should just go back to your realm and either wait around to be rescued or spend the rest of my life in a coma?" she asked him. "Yeah, thanks but no thanks. It sounds like the elemental plane is exactly where I need to be."

"But why?" Sloth asked in genuine confusion.

"Because, my girls have been sleeping for over a year, and I'm sick of waiting around for them to wake up," answered Everly. "Titania and Eris can easily absorb all the residual power that's keeping me unconscious. If they were awake, they'd have done it by now. But they're still hibernating, so I guess I'll have to go to them."

"If Muhammad won't go to the mountain?" asked Sloth.

"Precisely." Everly nodded. "See? You're not as dumb as you look."

"Mountain analogies are stupid," he muttered as he began to follow her.

"*You're* stupid!" she yelled angrily in response.

CHAPTER TWENTY-THREE

The Ashen Knight

After randomly colliding with one of his followers in the corridor of their hidden base, the Ashen Knight was all apologies.

"Oh, no, I am *so* sorry," he said to the girl as he knelt to help her gather up her things. "Look at me being mister silly! It's the helmet; it's very intimidating, as you're no doubt aware, but gosh, my peripheral vision is just awful in it!"

As always, he wore his fearsome-looking set of fire-blackened enchanted armor, which when combined with his flowing black cape, gave him a sinister appearance that could be startling to behold. Which was ironic considering his scrupulously polite mannerisms and ever-friendly voice. To his followers who revered him, he seemed more like a beloved older sibling than the supreme commander of their forces.

This was a sentiment the Ashen Knight went out of his way to encourage. He preferred for his people to think of themselves as family. It inspired loyalty and commitment, after all.

"No, no, my lord, the fault is entirely mine," the girl said as she quickly scooped up her papers and folders. "I get so lost in my own thoughts that I don't pay attention to my surroundings. *Please* forgive my clumsiness."

"I really don't believe that anyone's at fault here, much less that anything needs to be forgiven," said the Ashen Knight. He then reached for his helmet and removed it, revealing a roguishly handsome face.

The girl felt her breath catch in her chest at this unexpected revelation. Many people within the organization had wondered what sort of features went along with the Ashen Knight's compelling voice. Her friends would have been stunned to learn that the leader of their great revolution was *gorgeous*. His dirty-blond hair was the sort of tousled mess that women longed to run their fingers through, and his chiseled features (which were in need of a razor's touch) were highlighted by the warm and welcoming smile he wore that felt like the light of the sun. Although he wore a patch, his remaining hazel eye twinkled at her with good humor.

"Honestly, though, my peripheral vision would still be awful despite the helmet," he said with amused self-deprecation as he tapped his eye patch.

By the gods, he's so pretty, she thought to herself.

She then felt her cheeks bloom once she realized that she was staring at him, which caused her to squeak in embarrassment. Then she hurriedly finished collecting her things, thanked him for his consideration, and scurried quickly away.

"Hmm," he said to himself, before rising to his feet to resume walking to his personal quarters.

Once inside his enormous room, he tossed his helmet onto his bed, then took a seat in the massive, throne-like chair that sat in the center of his living space. Then he began pushing a foot along the floor until his seat began spinning in place, and he gave a childish whoop of glee as the centrifugal motion caused his hair to flap in one direction. Once it stopped moving, he gave a contented sigh and said, "'Total Eclipse of the Heart,' please."

The speakers hidden throughout the room began playing the requested song as the Ashen Knight leaned back in his seat and gently strummed an air guitar.

It went on like this for a while until the song finished building to its crescendo. When Riley Kilo's face appeared on the massive viewing screen on his wall, she saw the Knight whipping his head back and forth while passionately shouting the lyrics as loudly as he could.

"What the hell are you doing?" she asked him in a mildly stunned voice as he continued to rock out to that classic eighties chart-topper.

In response, he held up a finger, signaling for her to remain silent until the song was concluded. When it had, he sighed in contentment before turning to her image.

"Didn't know you were a fan of pop-rock oldies," she said.

"I'm a mystery even to myself," he admitted with some humility. "What can I say? I've always enjoyed the music of Heart."

"Excuse me?" Riley asked him with some confusion.

"Heart," he repeated. "A famous hard-rock duet. They started out in the seventies with 'Barracuda.' They've got a ton of hits. I'm sure you've heard at least one of them."

"Yeah, I know who Heart is, you goof. 'Total Eclipse of the Heart' is a Bonnie Tyler song," Riley retorted. "You didn't know that?"

"Nuh-uh," he said in shock. "I'm positive it's Heart."

"Yes, huh," Riley insisted. "Look it up if you don't believe me."

"Wikipedia isn't a reliable source of information." He scowled. "You can't even source it in college. You can't even source it in *middle school.*"

"Bonnie Tyler," Riley repeated with crushing finality.

"Is it really?" he asked sadly.

"Yep." She smirked.

"Darn."

"Facts, not feelings, snowflake."

"Well, I still like that song," he replied. "So, how can I help you today?"

"We've lost Arden Krayle," Riley said grimly. "She's disappeared. Vanished from sight. She might be dead."

"Ohhh," the Ashen Knight said as he nodded his head in understanding. "Heh, I get why you're worried now. Have no fear, Riley, Arden hasn't died. She defected."

"WHAT? What do you mean by that?!" yelled Riley.

"Well, defection is when you switch positions between two opposing sides," the Ashen Knight patiently explained. "Arden was once on our side, but now she's chosen to support Count Marcis—"

"I *know* what defection means, you tool! What I want to know is how you could let this happen!" Riley said angrily as she gripped the side of her head in frustration. "She's our Lady Kestrel! The face of the revolution! This is going to be a huge blow to our morale!"

"Riley, why can't you be happy for her?" the Ashen Knight asked her. "She's got someone to love now, and like Ringo Starr teaches us, love: it don't come easy."

"*Why* don't you take anything seriously?" bemoaned Riley.

"Because I have more experience with these sorts of situations than you realize," he said with a knowing smile. "And besides, I'm glad Arden found someone. She was never comfortable with the role of savior that we picked out for her. Taking her leave of us was a smart choice for her mental health."

"But the *sword*," Riley said impatiently. "How are we going to succeed without the sword?"

The Ashen Knight laughed at her worried tone of voice, truly tickled by her growing panic. "Riley, come *on*. Don't worry about the sword; the sword is most definitely covered."

He then rose from his chair and walked toward one of the closets in his room and opened it for her. As soon as he finished turning the doorknob, out clattered dozens and dozens of similar-looking weapons, each one of them a masterfully crafted sword in a leather scabbard embellished with gold enameling.

If they all looked similar, it was because they were. All of them were the exact same weapon.

Riley's eyes widened in surprise. "Those are all . . ."

"Yep. Every single one of them," the Ashen Knight said cheerfully. "Each one a holy sword with the accompanying power to be wielded by a chosen maiden."

"But there's only one holy sword in all the world," Riley said in amazement.

"Of course." He nodded. "One holy sword in all the world. But there are *loads* of the same world across the multiverse, so conversely, there are *also* loads of the same sword. You just have to know where to go to collect the ones no one is using."

"What are you going to do with them all?" Riley asked him.

"Nothing," he said. "I've tried establishing a holy-maiden corps a few times before. It never worked out the way I hoped it would. Having a few hundred girls running around swinging those swords always ends so poorly! It's best just to stick with two or three per reality."

"Well, we still don't have anyone to wield one of those things on our behalf, do we?" asked Riley.

"Of course we do." He smiled. "And unlike Arden, this one's a real deal chosen of the gods. If anything, Arden was just a placeholder while we waited for the *real* Lady Kestrel to escape her bonds and return to the world to face the Empress for us."

"What? Who?" Riley asked excitedly. "Who have you found?"

The Ashen Knight's smile grew even wider as he said, "Fenneth Godwell."

"SHUT UP!" screamed Riley.

"Don't wanna," he said with good-natured smugness.

"You've got to be fucking with me!" Riley squealed. "Everly killed her years ago!"

"You'd have to take me to dinner first," the Ashen Knight said shyly. "But seriously, Everly brought Fenneth back to life for some weird Everly reason. Who can say why? I mean, let's face it, she's daft. There's no point in trying to understand the *why* of it all. Let's just take advantage of a good situation!"

"What's our approach? Can she be convinced to join us?" Riley asked eagerly.

"Oh, trust me, anyone can be convinced to do *anything*, given enough time," the Ashen Knight said with complete confidence. "All we have to do is be willing to make the effort."

"You seem certain of yourself," Riley said.

"Trust me, I've seen scenarios like this play out *constantly*," said the Ashen Knight. "Fenn's a good girl at heart. She's only ever wanted to do the right thing out of a genuine love for her people and her family. Everly took away both of those. She's already primed to play her role. It'll just take a *little* more pressure to make her see our side of things."

A sudden realization dawned in Riley's eyes. "*This* is why you—"

"Yep," he said sadly. "A necessary sacrifice for a better tomorrow."

"God, you're cold," Riley said sourly. "All this time, I thought you were holding *her* captive to keep her from interfering with our plans. But you knew a situation like this was going to unfold all along, didn't you? And you always intended to—"

"Ah, relax now," the Ashen Knight said. "I'm not a schemer, Riley. It's just that I've seen these patterns play out so many times before that it's not difficult to predict what's going to happen next. Anyway, the burden will be on me alone. None of this is your fault."

"Don't patronize me," Riley said bitterly. "I'm the one who set the dominoes in motion. This is all happening because of me."

It's so convenient that you honestly believe that, the Knight thought glibly to himself before saying in a grave voice, "That isn't true in the slightest. What you do now, you do to protect the future of your world. If you succeed, you'll fade from existence, having never been born. *You're* the one making the ultimate sacrifice, Riley. You're the *real* hero in all this. Anything I can do to lighten your burden is my great honor. Not as your coconspirator, but as your friend."

This is the part where you tear up and thank me sincerely for my help, he predicted.

"God . . . thank you," Riley said quietly as her eyes began to glisten, before she wiped the back of her hand against them in embarrassment. "Thank you so much for this. All of this."

"There's no need for thanks, Riley," he assured her. "I swear in all honesty that you're doing so much for me without even realizing it. Your courage *inspires* me."

"Yeah, yeah," Riley said with continued embarrassment. "Listen, I've got to cut out. Bruticus says our transmission window is narrowing. I'll talk to you again soon."

"I look forward to it," he said to her.

When she vanished from his screen, he grinned and said, "'Crazy on You,'" then resumed strumming his air guitar when the familiar acoustic rhythms of that song began to sound throughout his room.

God, he loved these songs. Heart was *so* cool! Did they really not write "Total Eclipse"? That seemed impossible! Who the heck was Bonnie Tyler? Riley had to be wrong. She was probably under a lot of pressure trying to keep her meddling with the time stream from being discovered by her fellow forge knights.

She was *clearly* cracking under the strain of it all.

"Well, watcha gonna do when everybody's *insane*?" he asked himself.

Seriously, what *great* songs.

Later, he approached the HQ's prisoner cells, escorted by three heavily armed guards. He'd donned his helmet once more and was humming to himself as he walked. He also thought about that girl he'd bumped into earlier. What a cutie she'd been. And just his type too. Self-abasing and quick to apologize even if she wasn't necessarily at fault. That bespoke a certain lack of confidence in herself that he found appealing.

Did he want her? He thought he just might. But it wasn't his managerial style to pursue a romantic relationship with an employee. It was important to avoid power imbalances in a relationship. Or at least, *apparent* power imbalances. The illusion of equality had to be maintained for the good of both participants.

Should he fire her? If he cast her out of the organization, then wouldn't that make him free to pursue her? No, she'd probably resent him over that. People could hold grudges over the smallest things. Wait, what if he seduced her and then later had her killed? That could work. Who would complain then?

But wait, if he used office resources to pay for an assassination, couldn't that be misconstrued as harassment? Should he do it himself? What if he just broke her neck while they were both lying in bed? No, that would definitely look bad in front of others. The cleaning crew would probably file a complaint once he asked them to dispose of the body.

Besides, killing someone personally was distasteful. He'd evolved beyond such behavior. Also, the human body did things when it suddenly ceased living. *Nasty things.* He liked his silk sheets. Even if he had them thoroughly cleaned afterward, he'd never be able to sleep peacefully on them again.

Gosh, pursuing a satisfying courtship sure is complicated these days, he thought glumly to himself. *Modern romance is tough on a working man.*

When they arrived at a specific cell door, he gestured for his men to step in ahead of himself. Then he waited until a full count of ten passed before he entered it personally.

"Oh, good, the shackles held up," he said happily. "You wouldn't believe how often people escape those bindings. I guess all the meals we forced you to skip paid off, huh, Laurel?"

An emaciated woman hung bound to the wall, staring balefully at him. Unrecognizable as she was in her current condition, and weak though she appeared to be, the Ashen Knight made no move to step closer to her. No matter the reality, this lady was always quite the firecracker!

Not that it had ever saved her before.

"So, the head coward himself appears before me," growled the former maiden of the holy blade. "Come to taunt me, bastard? Why show up now?"

"Well, today's a pretty important day, Laurel," replied the Ashen Knight. "A pretty momentous day indeed. You see, I've finally located your sister. Took me a darn long while, but I *diiiiiid* it. And I'm pleased as punch to inform you that circumstances have molded her mentally into *just* what I need her to be."

"You're lying," Laurel accused him. "Fenneth was murdered years ago."

"Wrongo-bongo," he corrected her. "I don't really want to go over the details again with a less important character in the overall narrative, but let me assure you, she's alive, she's doing well, and she's *ticked off*. But not *quite* ticked off enough to suit my purposes. Luckily, that's where *you* come in."

"I won't do a thing to help you," she replied. "Not a single damn thing."

"That's fine. I respect your resolve," he said earnestly. "But really, Laurel. You don't have to do anything at all. I'm just going to use you like Pearl Jam used teenage suicide. For *inspiration*."

With a snap of his fingers, the three guards approached the helpless Laurel with their weapons drawn. "Make it quick, lads. She deserves that much."

"Bastard," Laurel said contemptuously as the first of the blades slid into her. "You cowardly bastard. Too afraid to do the deed . . . yourself?" she gasped.

"I would if I had to," the Ashen Knight said sincerely. "But I'm the hero of this story, Laurel. And when possible, I prefer to leave my hands as pure as my heartfelt intentions. This is a sacrifice, so just think of me as the priest who oversees the ritual, my dear lost lamb."

Laurel tried to say something else, but her throat began to fill with blood as the guards hurriedly stabbed her. Soon, she lost consciousness and fell still. It didn't take long for her heartbeat to fade.

"Phew, I'm glad we got that out of the way," the Ashen Knight said in relief. "These little executions are always so unpleasant, aren't they? Don't answer that question, it's completely rhetorical," he added when one of the guards began to speak up.

"Get her down from there and clean her up," he ordered them. "Put her in something white. She always looked lovely in white, didn't she? Make her *presentable*, boys. Remember, the story we're about to sell to our next client is one of tragedy. Tragedies only stick with us if the victims are pretty. So make sure they make her look pretty, *okay*? Get on it!"

He waved a hand at them to hurry up as he stepped into the corridor. Then he carefully checked his boots to make sure he hadn't tracked any blood out of the cell with him. It bothered people when he walked around with bloodied footsteps. They never said anything, but he could tell.

He could always tell.

A thought occurred to him after he finished his examination. Since he was down in the cells, wouldn't it be nice to see his guest? He'd been busy with work-related matters for so long that he'd become downright neglectful of her. Wasn't that rude of him? It *felt* rude. He should do better.

Well, part of making amends is acknowledging your faults, he thought to himself. With that in mind, he walked off to see Lady Sylvain, the former leader of the Western Temple, and his second captive of note. Well, his primary one now, what with Laurel choosing to help him entice her sister to his cause.

*　*　*

Sylvain was a beautiful woman of half-elven heritage who had weathered centuries of life as a stalwart defender of her faith. She'd created a massive organization to support her goals of protecting humanity from demonic incursions and growing her influence across the world. Ordinarily, she was a formidable leader and a powerful warrior who inspired awe and devotion in those who beheld her.

But today, she was a fearful thing that masked her terror with belligerent anger. Although her room was lavishly furnished and as comfortable as the Ashen Knight's own residence, she took no pleasure in her surroundings. In fact, she wanted desperately to leave.

The Ashen Knight found her current state of dismay absolutely *enchanting*. This was exactly how a legendary heroine who'd endured more tragedy and loss than any ordinary mortal soul could bear should be: broken by her failures and terrified of the future to come, yet still defiant even in the face of calamity.

Sylvain was wonderful. He was so glad he'd decided to keep her alive. Not that she appreciated his mercy.

"Release me, cur!" she demanded as soon as her eyes beheld him. "How long will you deny me my freedom?"

"Only until I'm certain that your organization has been suitably purified," he told her with a voice laden with regret. "As I've explained to you before, I admire you greatly, my lady. But until we can be certain that the creatures of the Empress have been completely eliminated, we can't risk your life by setting you free. I only do what is necessary, for your sake and the sake of the world."

That was a complete lie. He'd already personally overseen the destruction of every single one of Everly's pets that had infiltrated Sylvain's organization and had taken great pleasure in watching them cry out pitifully for their mother as they died. They'd been so pathetically unaware of how little their creator regarded them. He doubted she'd even hold a grudge against him for their deaths.

He wouldn't have.

"You keep saying that, over and over, but you do nothing to prove it," Sylvain said. "At this point, it's obvious that you're playing games. Do you take satisfaction in watching my plight? Am I a source of amusement for your twisted mind?"

"Nothing of the sort," he said in a wounded tone of voice.

Yes, yes, obviously, he thought pleasurably to himself.

"You're a wicked liar," she spat, before turning her back to him.

"Hey, I understand your feelings, Sylvain," he said. "You feel like you're a prisoner! After all, a lavish cage is still a cage. But I promise you, my lips to heaven's ears, as soon as this unpleasantness with the Empress is sorted, I'll personally set you free."

Sylvain's expression of withering contempt did not waver. "You'll free me, will you? Just as you freed poor Alec?" she asked him.

The Ashen Knight gave a helpless shrug as he replied. "I keep trying to tell you, Sylvie, that *wasn't* Alec. It was an abomination disguised as a man. A walking indecency garbed in the flesh of humanity. It had to be destroyed."

"Liar!" Sylvain said shrilly as she struck at the invisible wall of her cell. "I saw what you did to him! You *made* me watch!"

"Only so that you could see with your own eyes the lengths to which you had been deceived," said the Knight. "He was an imposter, Sylvie. A liar who swindled his way both into your life and into your bed. And even worse . . . he left you bearing his demonic seed."

Sylvain's face instantly paled as fear began creeping across it, replacing the anger that had been there moments before. "You know?" She trembled.

"I know *so* much," the Knight said with a voice that was dripping with solemnity and compassion. "So very, very much. But it's okay, Sylvain. You're not facing this alone. We'll have the creature removed soon. It'll be as though it never existed. An unpleasant dream that will never haunt you again."

"I won't let you touch my child!" Sylvain shouted with equal parts fury and horror as her hands ran protectively over her abdomen. "I won't let you hurt him!"

The Ashen Knight sighed despairingly. "Oh, poor Sylvain. Is that really what you want?"

"Yes!" Sylvain said. "You will not touch this life that grows within me."

"Well, it's your call," he said regretfully. "I consider myself an ally to women everywhere. I would *never* force you to be separated from your progeny. The choice will always be yours. Free will matters to me. And hey—*you* matter to me as well."

"Please just leave me alone," Sylvain said as she huddled on her mattress. "Just go away."

"Of course," he said. Before leaving the room, he wished her a good night. When he stepped back into the corridor, he did so with a whistle and an additional pep to his step.

What was it about the sight of a distraught woman who was powerless to do anything to help herself that just felt . . . so *right*? That was a real mystery to the Ashen Knight. A question that he'd love to ask other people more often, but the few times that he had, they would always stare at him in bewilderment and then slowly back away or find excuses to leave the area.

Why couldn't a man just ask a simple question?

Still, his visit with Sylvain had been a balm to his spirit after that small unpleasantness with Laurel. He felt refreshed now and ready to open negotiations with dear little Fenneth.

What a productive day this was turning into! Feeling inspired by the inevitability of his success, the Ashen Knight raised his hands and began strumming his fingers to the music he heard perfectly in his mind as he sauntered away toward completing yet another one of his goals.

Lost in his strange performance, he soulfully sang to an enthusiastic audience that only he could see. An audience that soon filled his ears with rapturous applause.

CHAPTER TWENTY-FOUR

Hades

For crap's sake, Ace, you're a total skunk-butt, do you know that?" Everly said in disgust as she finished off the last of the scorpion demons that had been attempting to devour them.

The setting of the abyss this time was an endless, blistering desert surrounded by dunes, sparsely placed palm trees, and a large pyramid in the distant horizon that seemed likely to be their way out of there.

Unfortunately, there were also scorpions.

So *many* damned scorpions!

The beast hissed at her and attempted to sink its stinger into her, which Everly gracefully sidestepped before ripping it free of the monster's tail and stabbing the barbed tip directly into the creature's head, sending it screeching into death courtesy of its own venom.

"Well, that's that," she said with satisfaction as she watched her opponent writhing in the sand for a few minutes before rolling onto its back.

"I'm sorry, I'm a *what?*" Sloth asked her, interrupting her enjoyment.

"You heard what I said," she replied. "You are a skunk-butt. You know, because you really stink at being helpful in a fight?"

"Everly, the word *skunk* alone is enough to indicate a malodorous state. Adding the word *butt* is completely redundant."

"Oh, yeah? Well, *you're* redundant," she snapped.

"And you're an idiot!" he retorted with great annoyance.

Everly resisted the urge to kill him. Not because she needed him alive, but because she was trying to stick to her resolution to avoid killing unnecessarily.

She wanted to commit to being lawfully evil, but this useless wad of a demon king was making it *so* tempting to indulge in a little bad-faith murder.

"Well, at least I can throw down with these chumps," she said scathingly. "Honestly, what kind of a cardinal sin are you, anyway? In all the popular media featuring characters like you, from *Fullmetal Alchemist* to *The Seven Deadly Sins*, which are incidentally the only two shows I can think of that feature characters with your names, all seven of you are supposed to be fucking deadly! But you're not, Ace! You're terrible! You're total garbage!"

"I'm not a brute, okay?" he said defensively. "My entire theme is based on waiting for things to come to me. Why do you think spiders are my mascot animals? Because I spin webs, Everly. *I spin webs.*"

"Not all spiders sit around on their asses all day waiting for flies to take a wrong turn," Everly said mockingly. "You ever heard of wolf spiders? Parson spiders? *Crab spiders?* Not every arachnid in nature fits into your lazy ideas of what they should be, Ace! *Some* spiders are badass *go-getters* who don't wait for permission to grab themselves a meal or two!"

"Yeah, well, I'm not one of them," said Sloth. "What are you going to do about it?"

"Honestly, I really want to kick your ass!" Everly seethed. "You don't help with the fighting, you suck at navigation, and you don't even put out. Honestly, if this was a horror movie, the audience would be howling for Mr. Hatchet to get you alone for five minutes in the toolshed with a chain saw!"

"I'm not promiscuous, Everly, and I wish you'd stop harassing me over it!" Sloth said sternly. "*My* body, *my* right!"

"Arrrrgh!" screamed Everly as she punched the air in frustration.

"Also, if the movie is about a killer named Mr. Hatchet, then why would he have a chain saw?" asked Sloth. "That makes no sense."

"Because Mr. Hatchet is like a spider, Ace! There's more to him than your lazy misconceptions!"

"Why do you keep calling me Ace?" he asked resentfully.

"Because it's short for *Acedia*, dumbass, and it's a totally awesome nickname!"

"Oh. That actually *is* pretty cool now that I think of it," he admitted, after giving the matter some thought.

"Glad you like it. Wanna make out?" Everly asked him hopefully.

"No!" he yelled in response.

"God damn it," she swore as she resumed stomping toward the distant pyramid. "What's your fucking deal with fucking, man? We've been down here for ages and the conversations have gotten stale. I mean, *look* at me! How are you honestly passing up on this?"

She gestured toward herself for emphasis. Early on in their journey, she'd learned that she could change her appearance at will through sheer concentration.

For the current arid environment, she decided to cosplay the outfit Lara Croft wore in the *Tomb Raider* series.

It looked good on her. It looked *really* good. Not that Sloth seemed to care.

"Just how did *I* get stuck traveling with the only demon I've ever encountered with no libido?" she asked herself.

"It's an aesthetic decision, Everly," he replied. "Relationships with mortals only complicate things unnecessarily. I've chosen to only do the things that bring *me* pleasure."

"How does *not* having sex bring you pleasure?" she asked him in surprise.

"Well, it's been hilarious so far watching you freak out over it," he said smugly.

"Prick."

"And you're not touching mine," he replied primly. "Besides, your behavior makes no sense. That isn't your real body, Everly. It's a spiritual construct housing your mind. You shouldn't have any bodily urges while you're in that form unless you literally think about sex twenty-four seven."

"Is that right? Well, that does make sense," Everly admitted with a nod.

". . . Seriously?" asked Sloth. "*That* often?"

"Why wouldn't I?" Everly replied. "I'm young, I'm healthy, and I'm all-powerful. Not to mention I'm hot as *fuuuuck*, for all the good that's done me with you. Getting lucky with strangers is one of the perks of being an elite, bro."

"But aren't you in a committed relationship?" he asked her.

"With whom?" she asked with some confusion.

"With *Seraphine*? The last queen of Winstead?" he asked with some exasperation.

"Oh, right, *her*," Everly said noncommittally. "Yeah, we're tight. *She's* tight. Word up. But you know how it is; my dad had two wives and a concubine and half the married women in his entire county on speed dial. That's just how it is with people like us."

"You actually cheated on *royalty*?" he asked her. "Seriously?"

"It's not cheating!" Everly said in a scandalized voice. "Seraphine knows that we're in an open relationship."

"Because you told her exactly that, using those specific words in no uncertain terms?" he asked her skeptically.

"Of course!" Everly said without hesitation. "But, uh, not through the use of language. She could totally feel my vibes, though! Which is to say the inner reverberations of my soul. You see, Ace, some things just don't *need* to be communicated with words."

"Unbelievable," Sloth muttered.

"Hey, dating a queen isn't all that, pal. Seraphine licks her fingers when she enjoys whatever she's eating. I always have to put up with that during our meals together and it's just *revolting*," Everly said with a shudder.

"A lot of people lick their fingers while they eat," Sloth replied. "I'm guilty of that myself."

"Not the way *she* does it, I bet," Everly shot back. "She tries to look cute while she does it, but it's not cute, it's not sexy, it's GROSS. I can't make her stop either; it's so frustrating! Sometimes she even tries to feed me food from her plate with those contaminated digits of hers, and it's all I can do to keep from blowing her up."

"That doesn't sound like a healthy relationship at all, Everly," Sloth said with some empathy.

"Well, now you know why I like to step out on her," said Everly.

"You really are an incredible mess." Sloth frowned.

"I have needs!" she insisted. "I get it, you're older than print media so you've forgotten what it's like to have urges! Well, I'm not as dead inside as you are, okay? And I'm gonna have some fun, whether you approve or not. Besides, if you were in my shoes, I doubt you could resist Mikey either, especially when he throws out one of those thirsty little soulful gazes of his."

"YOU SLEPT WITH MIKEY?" asked Sloth in wide-eyed astonishment. "*THAT* GUY??"

"Well, we started to, but y'know, he's on minotaur testosterone so he had some trouble standing at mast, if you get my euphemism for erectile dysfunction. He cried a lot and apologized, but *honestly*, it's been a little awkward between us since then."

"I'm sorry, but the fact that you'd ever give a psychotic thug like him a shot to begin with . . . that's what I'm finding so incredibly hard to accept," Sloth said in a daze.

"He makes me think of orcs. I *like* orcs," said Everly with a shrug.

"An orc would try to split you in half on sight," Sloth said despairingly.

"Yeah. *That's* the fantasy," replied Everly with a dreamy smile. "But maybe I'm just deluding myself. No matter how many hookups I have or how often I have them, none of them are who I really *want* to be with, are they?"

"Did you have someone specific in mind?" Sloth asked her. "It had better not be me."

"You're missing out, handsome," Everly said wistfully.

Sloth snorted disdainfully. "Somehow, I really doubt that."

"It's *Fenn*, stupid," Everly said irritably. "I miss her. I want her back. Under my thumb, just like that old Rolling Stones song."

"You wish to pursue a relationship with the chosen of light?" he asked her incredulously. "How in hell's flame could that possibly work out? She was made to *end* beings like you!"

"That's, like, work-related. What does that have to do with being in a relationship?" Everly scoffed.

"EVERYTHING!" yelled Sloth. "Destroying those like us is her purpose for existing!"

"I don't mind if she takes a shot at me," Everly smiled indulgently. "It's cute whenever she tries to beat me at anything. The way I see it, I just need to take a firmer hand with her this time. I have to keep her in place until she finally realizes that I'm everything she'll ever need. Then I can finally let her be happy. With *me*."

"I don't understand you at all, Everly," said Sloth. "What is it about that girl that fixates you so? From how your story described things, you barely even knew her. What compels this obsession?"

"*I'M NOT OBSESSED!*" Everly screamed balefully with a reddening face and clenched fists. She then took a moment to breathe deeply and regain her composure before continuing. "You need to understand, from the moment we met, I felt like I understood her. And that *she* understood *me*. Things just popped into place, okay?"

"Everly, she *killed* you," Sloth said in bewilderment.

"Yes," Everly said happily with an excited clap of her hands. "Yes, exactly that, Ace. She *killed me*! I was her first victim. There I was in that stupid school, as unstoppable as I ever was, and then there *she* appeared! Impaling me with my own sword to save the day. Have you ever seen the sight of a sobbing, beautiful girl covered in your own blood? It's *haunting*."

"Jesus Christ," said Sloth in utter dismay.

"Then later on, *I* killed *her*. We each own each other's life. What's more incredible than that?" Everly sighed. "Who cares if she's my destined enemy? That makes it even *better*! We can kill each other once and for all and then die contently in each other's arms!"

"That's crazy!" he said. "Absolutely fucking crazy."

"True love is ANNIHILATION, Ace!" Everly countered. "We'll drag one another into oblivion's embrace and leave a destroyed planet in our wake as a tribute to our devotion! What could be more wonderful than that?"

"How could she possibly grow to love you?" Sloth demanded, trying to make her see reason. "You killed her entire family!"

"Hey," Everly said in a scandalized voice. "I didn't kill ALL of her family, okay? Just some of them. The rioting crowds that erupted during the collapse of the kingdom were the ones who took care of the rest."

"Everly, do you take responsibility for *anything* that you do?" Sloth asked despite himself.

"I want to take responsibility for Fenn," Everly said. "I think she's worth it. You know, I used to watch her while she slept, and it felt so peaceful. I used to enter her mind and quietly watch her dreams. I know her better than you think. I know *everything* about her."

"I sincerely regret asking," Sloth said.

"Heh, I guess you do," Everly chuckled. Then they continued walking in silence for a quiet few minutes before she suddenly said, "Oh, quick question, by the way."

"Hmm?" asked Sloth. "What would you like to know?"

"*How did you know who Mikey was?*" Everly asked him coldly.

"Uh . . . wh-what?" stammered Sloth, once he realized the enormity of his mistake.

"I asked you how you knew who Mikey was," Everly repeated calmly as she began stalking toward him.

"Uh, lucky guess?" he said as he quickly began backing away from her only to stumble and land painfully on his rear as Everly loomed over him with a malevolent glint in her eye.

Before he could move, Everly lunged forward and dropped her knee directly into the center of his abdomen, expelling the air from his lungs and pinning him beneath her. She then leaned forward and pressed her forearm against his throat, to prevent him from regaining his breath.

"How many spies have the seven placed in my organization?" she asked him casually as she watched his face begin to redden and swell.

"I . . . can't . . . breathe," he gasped.

"You'd better answer the question, then," Everly suggested helpfully.

"Everly . . . *please* . . ." he begged her.

"Tick-tock, tick-tock, *tick-tock*," she replied.

"Just one . . . *just one!*" he admitted as his vision began to blur.

"And their name?" Everly demanded.

Sloth told her.

Everly leaned back in shock, stunned by the revelation. "Wow. I would never have seen that coming. Really?"

"*Really*," Sloth rasped, after a vicious coughing fit that ended with bloody saliva being retched into the sand. "Looks like your people aren't as faithful and loyal as you've deluded yourself into believing."

"Looks like it," Everly said thoughtfully. "Shit. This is more my fault than it is theirs. Without Eris around to perform her routine intrusions into the sanctity of their minds, they got used to keeping their thoughts hidden from me. It seems to have made some of them a little more independent than I'd prefer."

"How very terrible for you," Sloth said insincerely as he lay miserably on the ground.

"No, no, it's fine. I'll have Eris back soon enough," Everly replied. Then she smiled cruelly. "Actually, I think I can have a little fun with this. The spy doesn't know that I now know. Which means I now have a means by which to spread misinformation to my enemies without their realizing it."

"Except *I* now know that you know, which means I'll have that pipeline closed off as soon as I return home," Sloth reminded her.

"Oh, right, I suppose that's true," Everly said. "But wait, what if I just killed you right now, kept your mana cores so that you couldn't be resurrected, and had a replacement made in your image later on to infiltrate the seven kings and, I don't know, detonate a bomb or something to kill them all in one fell swoop?"

"If you were just going to bomb my siblings, then why would you need to keep a spy around?" he asked. "It would be completely pointless."

"Shut up, Ace, I'm just floating some ideas around, Jesus!" she snapped angrily.

"You'd never get away with it," he told her bluntly. "My siblings would sense a false Sloth the moment he appeared. Besides, I told you that we're all interconnected. They know everything that *I* know and are thus forewarned of your little scheme."

"But aren't we in the lower abyss right now?" she asked him innocently. "Doesn't that mean that your great and terrible powers have no effect? And that your dear siblings are now completely blind to your presence?"

Now the confidence left Sloth's face as his skin paled.

"Hold on, Everly," he said desperately. "Before you get any sudden ideas—"

"And couldn't I just insert your mana cores inside the duplicate to make him radiate your aura?" she continued. "It wouldn't be a *perfect* disguise, but I think it'd last long enough for my purposes. Wouldn't you agree, Ace?"

When he saw the murderous look in her eyes and realized that she wasn't joking, Sloth scrambled to his feet in an animal panic and tried to escape. He managed to get perhaps three feet away from her when he felt something tear through his back and erupt from his torso.

Looking down, he saw her hand had emerged from his chest and was now holding his heart.

"This isn't quite the steamy connection I fantasized about us making, Ace," whispered Everly into his ear. "But this is fun too. Give my regards to all the good musicians when you get where you're going."

"You really are too much; do you know that?" Sloth asked her wearily, before falling limply into death.

"Yep. It's too bad you missed out," Everly said as she tossed away his heart to wither and desiccate in the sands. "We really could have enjoyed ourselves. But hey, at least you gave me a decent lawfully evil reason to kill you, so there's that."

Out of a sudden curiosity, she licked a drop of his blood off her finger before frowning and spitting it out in disappointment. "Overrated," she sighed as she wiped off the remainder on her top.

Once she finished removing the mana cores from his body, Everly resumed her journey to the distant pyramid, leaving her companion to stare blankly at the sky as the winds gradually covered him in sand.

The monstrous elemental watched Everly as she continued along her path without so much as a backward glance at her victim. Her cold brutality was a sight to behold. He would have been deeply impressed by her alienation from her own humanity if his own master weren't so much worse than she.

After placing some distance between them, he contacted his lord to keep him informed of current events.

"Seriously?" the Ashen Knight asked with mild surprise. "Sloth usually survives his trip into the abyss with her. Heh, I'm glad I didn't put any money down on that."

"Would you like me to kill her, great one?" asked the dark elemental in his ominous whisper of a voice. "She approaches the blackened temple. Without Sloth to guide her to the correct hall, there's a chance she may inadvertently make contact with . . . the creature."

"Ohhh, I hadn't considered that," the Ashen Knight said as he clucked his tongue and reviewed. "It could be amusing watching them try to use each other . . . Oh, but it could be a real pebble in our Jays if she actually synchronized with him, wouldn't it?"

"We'd still win. We *always* win," the elemental said confidently.

The Ashen Knight stared blankly at his servant with a raised, quizzical brow. "*We*? I'm sorry, did you just say *we* always win?"

"I meant *you*, master. *You* always win. The glory of victory is yours alone," the elemental said hastily. "You owe others nothing for your achievements."

"Well, all right, then." The Ashen Knight nodded with a pleased expression. "Just as long as you always remember that."

"Always, great one. *Always*." The elemental shivered.

"Heh, gosh, it does feel good to watch you grovel." The Ashen Knight grinned. "I'll tell you what, go ahead and kill her. I won't really need her around when I make my pitch to Fenn. May as well nip her now while she's defenseless."

"I'll see to it at once, master," the elemental said fervently. "I'll make her *suffer*."

"No need for all that, friend. We're the good guys here," the Ashen Knight said in gentle admonishment. "Maybe poke a few extra holes in her to make her regret her wicked ways. But only to correct her misdeeds, not out of *enjoyment* of the violence."

"Of course, of course," said the elemental. "I didn't mean to—"

"But y'know, if she puts up too much of a fight or mouths off, then you take as much time as you need to make sure she realizes her place," the Ashen Knight continued. "Justice will not abide a woman's sass."

With his many, many mouths and their endless rows of sharklike teeth, the greater elemental, Hades, smiled in anticipation of the delectable meal to come. "It shall be done exactly as you wish, master."

"That's great to hear," the Ashen Knight said cheerfully. "Happy hunting, big guy."

CHAPTER TWENTY-FIVE

Who Dares?

Not long after murdering Sloth, Everly realized that she'd grossly overreacted.

She really had. It was embarrassing.

Why had she killed him? Out of anger? But why? It was only natural that the seven kings would place a spy in her inner circle if they could get away with it. That was just how the political side of these things worked out. It was a sign of respect more than anything else, if she thought about it. They considered her enough of a threat that they believed they had to keep an eye on her!

And how had she reacted? Had she made a cool, calculated response designed to skillfully counter their play? Nope! That was something smart people did. Instead, she'd just blurted her ideas out in front of Ace and then brutally killed him when he pointed out a gaping hole in her logic.

"I mean, it was an *awesome* kill, and I delivered a great parting line as he died, but it was just . . . I could have handled all that a lot better. I *want* to be better," she said to herself as she continued making her way to the blackened temple. "There were so many things I tried to do that I ended up half-assing because it's easier to brute force everything instead of using my head. I want to be clever and cunning, but let's face it, I've kind of devolved into a goon. I can't keep living my life by just killing everything that annoys me. How am I going to continue my personal evolution if murder stays my first solution to everything?"

Everly sighed unhappily. Even narrating her personal circumstances like a character in a comic book, which was something she ordinarily loved doing, failed to ease her of the dissatisfaction she felt for her performance.

"I need to take these negative feelings as a sign," she eventually decided. "This is a personal challenge I'm making to myself. I'm going to become more of a tactical thinker. I'm going to set aside my violent inclinations to dig deep down and connect with my inner Victor von Doom. Then I'm going to become the intellectual thug that every whack rapper in the game pretends to be. I'm going to flood these streets with shooters, but their ammunition will be my *mind*!"

Inspired by her newfound resolve, Everly spent the remainder of her journey reciting the lyrics of every classic hip-hop song she could remember until she finally reached the temple.

"*Stuck in the back of a PO-LEECE van, my crew kicked in a cell, file for the trial but with no remand, cuz a birdie started chirping about what he heard, and he snitched! Yes sir, he snitched!*" she sang softly as she studied the entryway of the ancient building. There didn't seem to be any complicated mechanism barring her path. Just a simple stone door she could slide open. No spells or keys were required.

"*I found his punk ass, caught lacking on the street, My Glock cocked, target locked, no way to retreat. Now he wanna talk about his family. What the fuck that got to do with what he did to me?*" she continued as she slowly forced the door open. All the stuff in that song sure sounded exciting. Not that she'd known from experience. Everly had grown up in a gated community in a wealthy New York suburb and had gone to private school her entire life. The only gangstas she'd ever met had been teen actors, classmates who'd invited her to the set of the episode of *Law & Order: SVU* they'd been shooting.

That had been a fun experience. She'd even gotten Mariska Hargitay's autograph.

She'd have rather gotten Christopher Meloni's. That dude was *intense*.

"*Never wanted to kill, but I'll kill to survive, rule one, never leave a fucking traitor alive,*" she concluded as she finished slamming the stone door into place.

"And now we blast off to the next level," she said, even as she wondered how much longer it would take for her to reach her elementals.

Honestly, this whole thing was getting *boring*. One would think a journey into the underworld would be more eventful than running from or killing the occasional pack of primordial demons, all the while looking for warp gates to the next stage like she was playing a *Mario Bros.* game.

Oh, well. The kind of extraordinary journeys that made for exciting fiction rarely mentioned the boring parts. For every ring that got dropped into the mouth of Mount Doom, there was probably an extended song break with fucking Tom Bombadil. The dude with the awesome last name who *never blew anything up!*

"Fake advertising, that was what he was," Everly whispered bitterly to herself as she began to enter the temple. But before she did, she suddenly felt an intense sensation of murderous intent being directed toward her from behind, which halted her step.

Everly turned in surprise and saw something completely unexpected.

"Hey, dol, dilly dol, dilly dally duck. What did I just see here, what the fucking *fuck*?" she asked herself as *Sloth* of all people came shambling out of the dunes toward her.

"Ace?" she said in disbelief. "No fucking way! How are you doing this? Did you evolve a third mana core without telling anyone?"

The dead demon king said nothing and continued to approach her.

"So, what's this? The silent treatment? Are you feeling out of sorts over our recent kerfuffle? If so, that's so immature! Come over here and talk to me, silly. We can work this out, can't we?"

Sloth remained silent as he drew nearer. Now Everly was beginning to feel annoyed by his silence.

"Is this about how our last conversation ended?" Everly asked him. "Gosh, I hope not! It was just a friendly disagreement over trivial matters, wasn't it? Can't two close pals have a scuffle every now and then? It's a sign of affection more than anything else. At least, that's what *I* think. You might have a different opinion, but I killed your ass dead, so yours doesn't count. Aren't you going to say anything?"

Still, he refused to speak. Now all Everly's remaining humor was spent.

"I *said* talk to me!" she growled as she stepped toward him and gave him a violent shove to the ground. Or at least, that was what her intent had been. Instead, before her palm made contact with his chest, he grabbed her firmly by the wrist and began to *squeeze*.

"What the hell?" Everly said in amazement as pain caused by the pressure in his grip began to envelop her arm. "Let go of me!" she demanded as she tried to pull away.

Now Sloth finally spoke. And to Everly's alarm, his voice was dry, cold, and creepily *alien* to her ears. "I don't take orders from you, you cow-handed tart."

"Cow-handed?" Everly replied with genuine hurt.

Instead of responding, Sloth lashed out with his foot, catching her squarely in the abdomen and sending her sprawling backward in the sand. As she lay stunned, he quickly grabbed her by both ankles and began spinning in a haphazard circle that built enough momentum to send her soaring through the air to smash painfully against one of the pillars standing outside the temple.

"Submit," he commanded her.

"Don't wanna" was her pained reply.

"You'll die," he warned her. "I'll kill you if you won't surrender."

"I don't expect you're planning to let me live regardless of what I choose," she said as she climbed back to her wobbly feet and brushed the sand off her clothing.

He grinned nastily at her without saying anything.

"Yeah, that's what I thought," she said.

"We both know you deserve what's about to happen to you, Kerri," he said in his dead whisper of a voice. "You know in your heart that you've earned this. Why resist?"

"My name isn't Kerri," she told him quietly.

"Yes, it is," he laughed at her. "Kerri Julia Sweet. *That's* who you are beneath this childish pretense of power and dominance. A silly, broken girl with a silly, broken mind. You didn't belong in your old world, and you certainly don't belong in this one."

"I'm not *heeeearing* this," Everly said stubbornly as she covered her ears with her hands. "*Lalalalala.*"

"No one needs you, Kerri. No one *wants* you. You're extraneous. A burden that no one asked for. You're a pestilence to the innocent, a plague upon the very land. Just lie still and let me have you. It's for the best. It's what you *want.*"

"What I *want* is to rip you in half and deposit you in a sewage runoff," Everly retorted. He laughed at her obstinance.

"You delude yourself, Kerri," he said mockingly. "Like any other misbehaving child, you secretly long for the surety of order, the comfort of the whip," he whispered. "Rejoice, child. I am the justice you sought. The punishment you've *always* desired."

"All bad girls secretly want to be held accountable?" she asked him in a dazed voice.

"*All* of them," he assured her as he stepped nearer.

"Bullshit. Stop talking as though you know anything about me," Everly warned him.

"But I *do* know you, Kerri," he replied. "Inside and out, as intimately as any lover you've ever had. I've torn you apart *so* many times. Can it even be counted at this point? I've taken your final breath, heard your last confession, delighted in your whimpers of terror as I gorged myself on your writhing flesh. This time like all the other times, you're going to beg me to stop, *but I'm not going to.*"

"Go fuck yourself, freak," snarled Everly without a trace of her normally calm demeanor. "I *never* beg. Never!"

"You will, Kerri. I promise you will," the thing told her with a knowing leer as its taloned fingers neared her face. "Pride always cometh before the fall—"

Everly kicked him beneath his chin with as much force as she could generate and watched with immense satisfaction as he was sent soaring into the sky above them.

"A punt like that could have gotten me signed with the NFL. What do you think?" she asked him, after he fell back to the earth with a tremendous impact.

He dragged himself forward on his hands and knees, unable to speak, crawling like a wounded insect. Everly found the sight heartening. When he tried to stand up, Everly's heel connected with the back of his skull, smashing him into a prone position.

"Is this it?" she wondered aloud. "Is this really all you have? That can't be right, can it? It just can't! To paraphrase the great Jamie Foxx, you were talking all that *good shit* just a little while ago. Where's your follow-through? Where's your response? Come on, you're a tough guy, aren't you? *Aren't you?*"

Everly dropped down on his back and grabbed the sides of his head. Then she leaned forward and roughly pressed his face into the sand, causing him to choke on the granules that were forced into his mouth as she slowly dragged his face from side to side.

"Is this bullying?" Everly asked him as she continued to sweep the sand with his face. "It is, isn't it? Should I feel bad? Or is this just me begging for more punishment, like the wicked thing I am? *I'm so unsure of myself.*"

Sloth had no response for her.

"Nothing to say?" Everly said in mock surprise. "How unexpected! You were *so talkative* just a minute ago. Where'd all that energy go? Oh, you're wondering how I could hit you so hard when I'm not supposed to have any of my magic. You're also wondering why it *hurt so much*, aren't you?"

She switched positions to kneel before the creature and grabbed him by the back of his head, pulling it up until their eyes were level with each other. Then she smiled prettily at him and said, "Well, I'm not going to tell you. I'm just going to kill you. Because you *really* pissed me off just now. I mean, wow, the things you said . . . I'm going to be honest with you, most people don't get to me like you just did. I'm a *very* calm person. So I feel you should be congratulated for what you just accomplished, because on my mother's name, it's a *rare* achievement."

"This is impossible," he rasped. "This doesn't happen. This *never* happens. I kill you. I make you scream; you beg me to stop, but I refuse, and throughout the night I daub myself in your fluids and you—"

He squealed in pain when Everly slapped him across the face.

"Gross. Didn't ask for all that," she said sternly. "God, I hate it when my opponents are nasty little creeps like you. This must be some kind of karmic retribution for teasing the real Ace so often these past few weeks. Now I feel as though I owe him an apology. But how can I make amends?"

Everly carefully considered her options for a few moments before sighing unhappily at the conclusion she reached. "Damn. I guess I'll have to bring him back to life, won't I? God damn it, I *really* wanted to blow up his family. I guess I'll have to figure out another way to get at them. Thank you *so* much for killing my fun."

"You won't get the chance," the false Sloth said to her. "The night approaches. This temporary respite means nothing. I'll have you soon enough—ARGH!"

"You really don't know when to stop speaking," Everly said with a frown. "Also, your strategic thinking is somewhat flawed. How are you going to get at me when you're about to die?"

"You can't kill me," the creature said confidently. "It's impossible."

"Of course I can kill you, dummy," said Everly with greater confidence. "You've already shown me how through your actions. And that last thing you said knotted the ribbon."

The creature stared at her in dim bewilderment, unable to make sense of her claim. Everly smiled indulgently at him and began to elaborate. "It really isn't complicated, silly. Anyone with moderate experience with a PlayStation could figure it out."

She stood up and dragged him to his feet with her as she explained. "The sun's going to set in an hour or so, isn't it?" she asked him as she gestured toward the sky. "You alluded to being a lot stronger in the dark. But you were too eager to come after me. You didn't want to wait! So what did you do? You decided to puppeteer poor Sloth's body. But why? Why would you need a shell to hide behind when you're *sooo* powerful? Huh? Huh? Can you explain it? Can you? Just kidding, I already know the answer."

She then forced his face in the direction of the sun.

"Don't," he murmured through Sloth's broken teeth.

"What?" she replied. "Could you please repeat that? I didn't quite hear you."

"*Don't,*" he said again. "*Please* don't."

"Well, now I'm really confused," Everly said. "I thought *I* was the one who was going to be begging for *my* life. Are we still on the same page? Was there a rewrite and no one told me?"

"This won't kill me," he promised her. "This won't kill me. You're just delaying the inevitable."

"It might not kill you . . . but it'll really *hurt*, won't it?" she purred into his ear. "*It'll hurt baaaaad.*"

"I'll triple your agony for this," he vowed. "No, I'll make your suffering fourfold! You'll die screaming in the dark, maddened from panic and pain, and you'll beg for your suffering to end, but relief will not come, it will not come, *IT WILL NOT COME—*"

"Good to know," replied Everly. Then she dug her fingers deeply into the flesh beneath Sloth's chin and tore his face off at the bone, removing the front half of his skull as she did, all while holding him before the sun.

The effect was instantaneous. A writhing black mass of shadowy *something* immediately sprang from the gory opening she'd ripped into the dead demon's flesh. It screamed in a terrified voice that seemed to Everly like the combined sound of a frightened dog and a weeping child.

The creature tried to bury itself beneath the sands to escape the eradicating rays of the sun, but Everly was quick to drop Sloth's body and grab the monster before it could escape her. Then she set her feet firmly to the ground, took a deep stance, and slowly began pulling it backward, dragging every inch of it into the light of day.

"It was *harada* that let me beat you, by the way," she said conversationally as she struggled to keep the flailing beast in place. "Just because my magic is cut off doesn't mean I can't use *harada* in this form. It's actually much easier like this! No flesh and bone to channel it through. Just instant results. That's pretty cool, right?"

The beast sputtered madly and squealed something in a language she couldn't understand.

"I'm glad you think so," she replied, after deciding it was a compliment.

The monster's flesh began to erupt with horrendous pustules of bubbling pus that smoked beneath the lazy light of the evening sun, filling the air with the disgusting twin scents of rotting meat and stagnant water. Its tortured cries continued for what felt like ages before it finally went limp and stopped resisting Everly. A few minutes after that, the remains of the creature finished dissolving and poured into the sand, leaving nothing behind but the stench of its dying.

"Ugh. I'm glad that nastiness is finally over with," Everly said. She looked at her palms, which now glistened with moist bits of the disgusting thing, and made a displeased face as she brushed them away. She dearly wished she had access to a sink and a bar of soap.

"If you somehow survived that, don't come back looking for a rematch," she advised the empty air as she turned toward the entrance to the temple. "I'm serious. Next time, I'll get *nasty*."

With that said, she entered the blackened temple, ready to move on and be *done* with all this nonsense.

Who owned the night? Wu-Tang, obviously.

But also, her.

Obviously.

Outside, the land remained still apart from the blowing wind, which caused the scattered trees to sway and bow in its passing. It was in this perfect silence that the sun gradually set and the moon arose.

A moment afterward, however, the sands exploded as the massive Hades erupted from the soil, regenerated by the darkness of nightfall and filled with an unquenchable, unstoppable wrath. His eyes twitched and his endless rows of teeth clattered and snapped, tearing viciously at the air as he roared his hatred at the skies.

"*EEEEEEEEEVERYLY!!!!*" he screeched, before smashing his way madly into the temple in search of his prey.

She would pay.
She would pay.
She would pay. She would pay. She would pay. She would pay.
SHE WOULD PAY.

CHAPTER TWENTY-SIX

Deus Axe Maxia

After wandering around the blackened temple for what felt like hours, Everly finally stumbled across a hidden chamber in the southeast corridor. It was a large space that made her believe it might have belonged to the lord of this place, kind of like a boss room in a video game. But whatever purpose it was meant for, it was now completely empty, except for the four skeletons that had been left to molder at random spots throughout the area.

Oh, the skeletons and the floating axe in the center of the room.

The *talking* floating axe.

The talking floating axe that refused to shut up.

"Yeah, these were my party members," it said in a carefree voice as it casually pointed itself at each of the skeletons. "That's Keith, he was our fearless leader. Or was that Jaxon? That's Jaxon, by the way. This is Jera, she was a real sweetie, just a *total* charmer. And that's Ladelle—spoiler alert, she's a monster bitch. Yeah, I said you were a bitch, Ladelle! I only said it because it's true! Stay mad if you want, it suits your personality! God, can you *believe* her? She's so hooked on drama you should check her for track marks!"

"Okay . . . then," said Everly slowly while she tried to figure this creature out.

"Oh, our healer, Daniel, is around here somewhere too. Jeez, where did Daniel go? Has anyone seen Daniel? God, that guy is useless. Bad call on recruiting him, Keith! Or was that Jaxon?"

"I'm sure he'll turn up somewhere," Everly said dryly.

"Nah, he's probably dead. They're *all* dead, you know. We walked in here thinking that this was a boss room. Nope! Turned out to be a trap set by one of my ex–honey bunnies. You ever piss off an earth goddess before? Don't! They hold *grudges!*"

"Apparently, they do." Everly nodded.

"Totally! She sealed me in here and then plucked this entire temple out of reality so I could never return home. Then just to taunt me, she cursed me so that I could only leave if someone willingly bore me. That was so harsh! She didn't even tell me that until after everyone else had already died from . . . mysterious circumstances."

"Surprisingly, I think I believe you," Everly said. "So, is that the exit over there?" she asked as she pointed toward a large, closed doorway.

"Yeppers," said the axe. "You can't pass through it, though. Only *I* can open it for you."

"If that's the case, then why didn't you open it for them?" she asked as she gestured at the skeletons.

"Have you ever heard of a crab-bucket mentality?" asked the axe.

"Ah," Everly said, after thinking it over. "Eh, makes sense. But that still won't stop me from leaving. I'm pretty freakin' strong, I'll have you know."

"Ooh, *confidence*," mocked the axe. "Okay, color me a little intrigued. I'll tell you what: cut your palm and sprinkle a little blood on my edge, and then I'll decide if you're worth freeing or not."

"Hard pass," she promptly responded.

"Why? You afraid I'll make you too powerful or something?"

Everly frowned to herself as she quietly considered her options, while the magical weapon nattered on. She *hated* being called afraid of anything. She was tempted to teach this thing a lesson, but she was trying to hold fast to her earlier vow to keep her temper and think more strategically.

This axe was an interesting new development in her quest to escape the abyss and reclaim her elementals. The so-called divine weapon was clearly capable of sentient thought and even claimed it could empower whoever wielded it to levels beyond their natural limits. That sounded really tempting, especially since Everly didn't know if she'd ever even reached her personal limits.

But there was a problem that came alongside that temptation.

And that problem was that in addition to potentially being a powerful new resource for her to command . . . the axe was also an aggravating jackass.

That second part *really* overshadowed any other possible benefits.

Everly was uncertain of what to do next. She had searched throughout the temple with great difficulty for a gateway to the next point of the abyss, but now that she had finally discovered it, what if she couldn't find a way past the strange obsidian-colored stone that barred her way? It was incredibly frustrating, and as she kept trying to think of a solution, the axe kept up its mindless yammering.

Why would anyone create a talking axe? And why would they make it so head-splittingly *stupid*?

"Why exactly would I want to do that?" Everly asked him skeptically after turning away from the gate. "Sounds utterly pointless."

"It's not, I swear! I just want to see if *you're* the real deal," the weapon answered back. "I'm *through* dealing with losers. Your blood will tell me that you're either strong enough to hang with me in the big leagues, or you're just another clump of meat with delusions of grandeur."

"I'm not even here in the flesh, you chode," Everly said dismissively. "This is a spiritual form."

"So what? Even if a blood offering is symbolic, it'll still work, noob," said the axe. "There's no reason not to do it unless you're feeling less than adequate."

"So, what happens if you decide that I fall into the latter group?" Everly asked him. "What if you arbitrarily decide I'm a loser?"

"Nothing much," replied the axe. "I'll just cut your silly little head off so I can puppeteer your corpse around for a bit. Then I'll sprout a few tendrils for the express purpose of doing some *really sick stuff* with your body."

"How sick are we talking?" Everly asked curiously.

"Huh?" asked the axe, momentarily taken aback by her sudden interest.

"I think you heard. Are you going to wait for rigor mortis to set in so you can put me in your favorite yoga pose and go to town? Is that what's up? It sounds disgusting, but I'm low-key fascinated," said Everly.

"Wh-what?"

"Don't say *what*, you nasty little creature," Everly said disdainfully. "You've got my attention, I'm listening. You shot your shot, and the arrow landed. Don't ruin it now. You said you were gonna play with my corpse. Let me hear some details. Show me the *quality* of your imagination. I'm a necromancer, pal; we play rough."

"A necromancer?" the axe said in a slight daze.

"Would a visualization exercise help?" Everly asked. "Here, check it out." Her body briefly shimmered with golden light as she changed the appearance of her clothing. Now she wore a traditional private-school uniform complete with knee-high socks, a plaid skirt, and a blazer adorned with the crest of her old high school.

"Does this help?" she asked coyly as she spun in a circle for his inspection.

"Homina, homina, homina!" gasped the stricken axe. "Uh, yeah, it's a good look, Blondie. It's a *real* good look!"

"Yeah, I know." Everly smirked as she examined her fingernails. "Now, you were saying something about performing some devious acts. Come on! Where's your follow-through?"

"Aww, it's no fun at all if you're into it," the axe complained.

"*Virgin*," Everly teased.

"I am not!" the axe protested.

"Okay. Maybe you're just one of those losers who *prefers* virgins because you fear comparison to other men?"

"Stop! You're making me sound gross!" whined the axe.

"You're a bit of a blowhard, aren't you, buddy? You're looooong winded," Everly sneered.

"You're really starting to piss me off, kid," said the axe angrily. "If you had ANY idea who you were dealing with, you'd be pissing in fear all over your LARPing gear right about now!"

"Well, I *don't* know who you are, and honestly, I'm getting less interested by the moment," yawned Everly. "Now, since you've proven to be a bore, can you at least open up the exit for me?"

"Who the hell are you to talk to me like this?" the axe glowered.

"Who am *I*? Bitch, I'm the *Empress*," Everly said with smug superiority. "Take a look at this planet, lumberjack. I *run* it."

"Oh, yeah? WELL, FUCK YOU, I'M AN AXE—" Suddenly the axe was choked off as Everly slammed her shoe against its handle and pinned it to the ground.

"Hey, asshole!" Everly yelled furiously at him, with veins popping around her neck to signal her displeasure. "NO ONE DOES A TITLE DROP AROUND HERE EXCEPT *ME*!"

"Stop! I can't breathe!" gasped the axe.

"You don't have any lungs," replied Everly.

"I could if I wanted! Maybe even gills! What if I had gills, huh?" asked the axe.

"When you say *gills*, all I think of is seafood."

"Wow. So now we know you're racist against mermaids!" the axe said sadly.

"Uh, how did we reach that conclusion?" Everly asked in confusion.

"You're pretty! Do you want to be friends?" asked the axe hopefully.

"Oh, you're going to be a handful, aren't you?" Everly sighed as she lifted her foot, allowing the axe to float back up beside her.

"Well, yeah. Most axes are, right?" the axe said. "Your hands look pretty small, though. You'll need to use both to get a proper grip on my huge shaft."

"GOD DAMN IT," Everly swore as she punched the idiot back to the ground.

"I deserved that!" the axe said cheerfully.

"Yes, you did," agreed Everly. "By the way, axes have hafts, not *shafts*."

"I know what I said," snickered the axe.

"I gotta tell you, pal. Crazy *and* stupid is an interesting combination to behold," said Everly almost admiringly. "Who are you, anyway?"

"Just a small-town boy from Earth who got up to some amusing hijinks and ended up becoming a divine weapon of unparalleled, godlike might," replied the axe. "It's an old story that's been told a million times before."

"Tell it to me," Everly insisted.

"Well, I was once just a hick from the sticks with big-city dreams," said the axe. "One day I took off to make them come true. When my bus pulled into town, this slick-looking brother with a gold tooth and a fur coat walked up to me and said, *Wow, look at that pretty face. Come here, honey. You want something to eat? You want to make some money?* And I was like, *Yes, daddy.* And he said, *Cool. We gonna make you an unstoppable god-weapon and set you off on the path of destruction,* and that was how my story began."

"That's not how your story began at all, is it?" asked Everly.

"Nope!" said the axe cheerfully. "I like to embellish."

"I can appreciate a talented habitual liar," Everly said.

"Thanks!" replied the axe.

"I said a *talented* one."

"Phooey! You're mean!" whined the axe.

"That's been said before," Everly said proudly. "You got a name, axe-boy?"

"Sure! I'm Max! Nice to meetcha!" he said.

Everly frowned in annoyance. "Still lying, huh?"

"What?" asked Max in confusion. "No. That's really my name! I'm Max the axe!"

"*Max* the *axe*?" repeated Everly doubtfully. "Yeah, I'm feeling skeptical about that one, bud."

"But it's true! You have to believe me! I'm being *hoooonest*!"

"God, is this what it feels like to be around me? Is this what I put other people through?" Everly asked herself in dismay. "This little encounter might be cause for some serious self-reflection."

"Hahaha! Your face is distressed!" Max said giddily. "You're feeling emooootions!"

"Max, just open the exit so I can get out of here," said Everly. "I've got places to be and none of them include you."

"Aw, that's a shame, blond girl," replied Max. "Because, as things stand right now, I don't feel like doing you any favors! Nope, you're not going *anywhere* unless—"

"Unless I take you with me," Everly sighed with a roll of her eyes.

"Unless you take me with you—HEY! Don't interrupt me when I'm getting to the good part!" whined Max.

"Well, then, Max, we seem to have reached an *impasse*, because I don't want to take you anywhere."

"What? Why not? I'm great!" said Max.

"Great at working my last nerve like a rotten tooth," countered Everly. "Listen, I don't think our personalities would mesh well. I'm an all-powerful girl boss, and you're clearly a needy little attention freak. What would we *possibly* have In common?"

"Hey, just give me a chance!" begged Max. "My last partner was a hesitant blond too, but I totally won her over! Things turned out great for her!"

"Then where's she at now?" asked Everly.

"I dunno, I buried her somewhere and forgot," said Max with a shrug.

"Jesus, bro," groaned Everly.

"Hey, life happens. Seriously, though. I can be a real asset! I wasn't joking when I said I was a divine weapon. Once you've felt me coursing through your system, you'll *never* want to give me up!"

"Oh, come *on*," Everly said. "Listen, Jax—"

"MAX!" he yelled in annoyance.

"NO ONE CARES!" yelled back the frustrated Everly. "Listen, this is starting to feel like a negotiation. I don't *do* negotiations! Obey or die, okay? Open the gateway and then get lost, or I'll kill you. This is exhausting."

"And yet, if I *die*, you're not going to be able to escape! Plus, you'll miss out on a golden opportunity to become even stronger! Also, I can't believe you lost to a vampire. Who does that? Tell me she at least wasn't wearing a shirt with a ruffled collar on it while she was mud-holing you, you hopeless nerd."

"Fuck you, it was an even fight!" lied Everly. "And how do you even know about that?"

"Nyu-DUH! I can see your thoughts, dummy," said Max mockingly. "Mortals are easier to read than a stop sign."

"Do it again and you'll be begging *me* to stop—" said Everly.

"Hurting me, that is," finished Max.

"Hurting you, that is—wow, that *is* annoying," said Everly.

"It sure is! And that's exactly why we should be nice to each other!"

"Me not stomping you into splinters *is* me being nice," said Everly.

"You sound like my grampa!" complained Max. "He was always threatening me too! That's probably what went wrong with my youthful development. I was once just a happy-go-lucky kid from a good family, living in a nice neighborhood, who idly passed the time doing good deeds for his neighbors like the good lord *insists* upon!"

"Ugh," groaned the pained Everly as her face dropped into her palm.

"And I loved having fun playing hopscotch and kick the can with the fellas!" Max continued.

"How much fun could a game of kick the can possibly be?" Everly wondered.

"Oh, it was great!" Max assured her. "We didn't just play classical-style kick the can; we also did variants! You know, like Canadian-style, where you put ham in it, or Russian-style, where we hit each other with it."

"Why's hitting each other with the can considered Russian-style?" asked Everly.

"Uh, duh," snarked Max. "Because in Mother Russia, the can kicks *you*."

"FUCK," cursed Everly, who was disappointed in herself for not seeing that coming.

"Anyway," continued Max, "my favorite version was head in the can."

"Head in the can?" Everly asked skeptically. "What the hell is head in the can?"

"It was the best one!" Max said enthusiastically. "That's the one where you pull a giant-sized can over someone's head while he begs you to forgive him, then you stomp on the fucking thing as hard as you can, until it's all crinkled around his face and your heels are *sore*, and oops, he isn't moving anymore, but that's okay because maybe now the little shit will think twice before saying Max eats at Olive Garden too much and calling me Carbs McGilicutty behind my back just because I love their flavorful, unlimited breadsticks!"

"Max?" said Everly.

"*Yeeeeeah?*"

"You made that entire thing up," she said.

"What? No, I didn't!" he gasped, as though it wounded him to his core that she could even suggest such a thing.

"Where the hell are you going to get a giant-sized aluminum can that can fit around someone's head?" asked Everly accusingly. "That's completely unlikely. The logistics don't support your claim."

"Campbell's Soup!" shouted Max. "They pack a bunch of flavors in one can!"

"Mostly known for their salty, horrid slop with mushy vegetables stingily sprinkled in. *Not* for their giant cans," said Everly. "Try again?"

"Progresso!" Max said, quickly switching brands. "They're hardy as fuck!"

"Yeah, they sell those big fist-sized cans that'll fill you up good. But they're *still* not large enough to fit around anyone's head," said Everly. "You're making shit up, Max."

"Okay, I fibbed," Max confessed. "There were no giant cans available. But I *did* once soak a tire in gasoline and light it up after I forced it over someone's neck."

"Somehow, I can believe that. What was his name?" asked Everly.

"Gibby," said Max promptly.

"Well, that's an awful fucking name. You probably did him a favor," Everly decided.

"Yeah, probably," Max agreed. "But it was mostly about the breadsticks."

"*I* liked their chicken fettucine," Everly said fondly. "I had an Italian cousin who'd lose his mind every time I told him I preferred Olive Garden to our grandmother's recipe. Seriously, what's so bad about adding chicken? It makes it *taste* better!"

"Bah! Italians! They're way too passionate and angry about stuff," Max said. "I'm telling you; every little thing sets them off. They're just too high-strung!

If I had a bullet hole for every time they shot me to death over some minor disagreement, it would be around twenty or thirty because they were all standing in front of me and squeezing their triggers multiple times. I loved Rocky, though."

"Pfft, everyone loves Rocky," Everly scoffed. "*I* liked Clubber Lang."

"What?! Why? He was so mean!" said Max, aghast.

"That's why I liked him! He did not pity the fools," Everly grinned. "Of course, he lost at the end, because it was the Reagan era, and you can't have truly effective bad guys coming out on top because it might make people think that life isn't as simple as trying hard and doing your best and you'll always find success. Nope, Clubber had to go down."

"Yeah, I hate simplistic narratives too," agreed Max. "The supposed binary of good and evil is so childish at its core! Don't even get me started on nonsense like *Star Wars*."

"What's wrong with *Star Wars*?" Everly asked softly, after going perfectly still.

"Uh, what *isn't* wrong with *Star Wars*?" Max tittered. "It's for morons! All the bad guys are stylish fascists with posh accents and all the good guys are scruffy-looking losers who take orders from chicks. Even the melee weapons are morality coded! Blue sabers are heroic and red sabers are villainous!"

"Red sabers look awesome!" Everly grumbled. "And what's wrong with taking orders from chicks?"

Max continued on, unaware that she'd said anything.

"And the latest protagonist in the franchise was such a Mary Sue! She was mind controlling stormtroopers and having lightsaber duels within like *five minutes* of discovering that she had the Force! I'm telling you, that's just bad writing!"

"Max is based," said someone reading the story.

"Rey had a mental link with Kylo Ren! His memories were what allowed her to use the Force so effectively," Everly said, after taking a deep, calming breath. "*That's* why she was such a fast learner."

"Bullshit, bullshit, *bullshit*," replied Max. "Where did they say any of that in the movie?"

"They didn't, you have to read the supplementary material—"

"BULLSHIT!" shouted Max again. "Listen, if you have to read supplementary material in order to better understand a movie's plot, then that movie has FAILED at doing its job!"

"No, that just means you're not doing your due diligence as a fan!" shouted Everly as she clenched her fists.

"My *due diligence*?" scoffed Max angrily. "I went to see it in theaters, didn't I?! Movie tickets are *expensive*, Everly! At the very least I'm owed a complete story for my fifteen-dollar investment! Being told I need to plunk down another twenty-five bucks for a fucking hardcover novelization, to make sense of the shit I *just* sat through, is a COMPLETE FUCKING RIP-OFF!"

"Novelizations are optional and only serve to enhance the experience!" shrieked Everly.

"THAT'S NOT WHAT YOU SAID! THAT'S NOT WHAT YOU SAID!" bellowed Max. "You said I HAD to read the novel to better understand the movie! Which IS it, Everly?! An option or a requirement? PICK A FUCKING LANE!"

"You're starting to piss me off more than those review bombs *The Last Jedi* received," seethed Everly.

"Maybe *The Last Jedi* got review bombed because it was an *utter turd*," seethed Max as well.

"WRONG. WRONG. WROOOONG," said Everly. "It was a fantastic fucking examination of failure and redemption! It was about how it's okay to not live up to the expectations of others, and it extolled the IMPORTANCE of learning to forgive yourself even when you feel that you haven't lived up to your potential! Luke Skywalker had the best send-off of any pop-culture icon in the history of film! IT'S A BEAUTIFUL FUCKING MOVIE!"

"They turned Luke Skywalker into a crybaby dumbass who was so stupid he missed his opportunity to end the war early and save countless lives!" countered Max savagely.

"What are you *talking* about?" demanded Everly.

"Think about it!" Max said. "When Luke projected his image to planet Crait, he made *physical contact* with Leia! He held her hand! He handed her that golden dice-thingy! She felt him! Don't you get it? That meant he could interact with people and objects!"

"And your point is?" asked Everly.

"My *point* is that Luke could have walked up to Kylo Ren, ignored any of his attacks, and just cut his fucking head off, right then and there! That would have crippled the entire First Order! But he *didn't*, did he? No! Because the writers were too busy trying to be clever and poignant, and in doing so, they left in the *biggest* fucking plot hole in a movie EVER!"

"No, I mean . . . that isn't . . . that's—th-that's . . ." stammered Everly. "That's impossible. That's impossible!"

"Search your feelings, Everly. You know what I say is the truth," Max said darkly.

"Rian Johnson is so *talented*," she wept. "Guys like him show up once in a generation."

"He is."

"*Brick* and *Knives Out* were incredible. They were . . . just incredible," she sobbed. "They were so key to my development."

"*The Glass Onion* was pretty good too," Max said sincerely.

"I haven't seen it yet," she said somberly after wiping her eyes.

"Dave Bautista was the killer," he said. "Totally caught me by surprise."

part), was relaxing on a beautiful beach covered in white sand and swaying palm trees, working on her tan.

She had no idea where the island she'd ended up on was located on the map, and she didn't care. Ever since finally getting free of . . . that person, she'd been content to do absolutely nothing except relax.

Adjusting to her new environment had been a breeze. When she was hungry, she fished for her meals using a sharpened tree branch and purified her catches with her magic before cooking it using the methods she'd acquired from her previous life as a Girl Scout. When she was thirsty, the large coconut-like fruits that she collected from the trees provided all the refreshing nourishment she could drink. And they were delicious too.

Even her clothing wasn't an issue. After carefully tearing strips off her dress and styling it in the manner of a swimsuit and waist wrap, she simply used her healing magic to restore any frayed areas to full functionality, easily mending any fresh tears while keeping it clean. It was easier than sewing or using a washing machine.

All in all, it was an idyllic time she spent on that beach, gradually reclaiming her sense of self-sufficiency and releasing all the tension and negative feelings that had been choking away at her.

Even better, her time was spent in the presence of good company.

"This is really nice," Fenneth said lazily as she lay back on the shore and let the warmth of the sun soak into her. "I know we'll have to leave one day, but in the meanwhile, this has felt really, dare I say, restful?"

I think it truly has been, buzzed Discordia's voice gently in her mind. *Compared to the stress of being Everly's captive, being stranded on this pleasant island is quite enjoyable.*

"You're telling me!" Fenneth agreed. "But please, can we not mention that . . . *person's* name? Why harsh our mellow by bringing her up? She's out in the world being a miserable you-know-what, and we're over here, content as clams in a lake."

Fresh water kills clams, mistress, Discordia corrected her.

"It does?" Fenneth asked in surprise. "I thought clams were shellfish."

They are, but they're also a species of mollusk that requires salt water to survive.

"Wow. There's never a day when you can't learn something interesting," said Fenneth appreciatively.

The pursuit of knowledge is ever a noble endeavor, my lady. Also, there are many kinds of shellfish such as lobsters and shrimp that thrive in the ocean, just as mammals like dolphins and whales do.

"I knew that!" Fenneth chuckled.

I know you did. But I'm just making sure you remember.

"I like how sassy you've gotten, Dis. You're so much more talkative than you used to be," Fenneth said with a smile. "It really lets your personality shine."

I greatly regretted never properly showing the depths of my affection for you in the years we spent together before your first death, mistress, said Discordia somberly. *Now that we've been given a second chance, I never again want to miss an opportunity for us to enjoy a pleasant conversation together.*

"I love you too, Discordia," Fenn said warmly. At those words, her elemental buzzed brightly and filled her mind with waves of sheer joy, causing Fenneth to laugh with delight.

That was when, suddenly, the sound of a man screaming in panic interrupted their happy moment.

"Oh, god, help, please help!" shouted a floundering knight as he struggled to keep his head above water some distance away. "My armor's too heavy! I'm gonna die! Someone *doooo* something!"

"Now, what fresh nonsense have we got here?" Fenneth asked in disbelief as she watched the drowning stranger continue to struggle. "Where'd that guy come from?"

I have no idea, mistress, Discordia replied with equal confusion. *It's as though he fell from the sky.*

"Really? Well, I guess he was lucky to fall in the water instead of on the shore," said Fenneth.

It's unlikely he feels the same way, Discordia said as she observed the armored man's desperate efforts to remain afloat. *Perhaps we should offer him our assistance?*

"Well, of course we're going to help him!" Fenneth said chidingly. "It's been ages since we've had company over."

Fenneth was a very strong person. The greatest difficulty after pulling the struggling knight onto the shore was getting his helmet and chest piece off. She was momentarily taken aback by how handsome he was, but she shook it off quickly when she saw he wasn't breathing and began giving him chest compressions and mouth-to-mouth breathing.

Not long after she began, he sat up gasping and turned to his side to vomit out a mouthful of seawater. Then he lay back down and screamed in pain as he wrapped his arms around himself.

"Oh, my bad! My bad!" Fenneth said in embarrassment as she gently applied her healing magic to him. Chest compressions, when done correctly, did considerable damage to a person's rib cage. She might have broken something while saving his life. Luckily, this was where being a healing mage came in handy.

"There we go; all better now," she said soothingly as her magic did its work. "Are you okay?"

"I . . . I think so," the Knight said as he stared at her in surprise, his uncovered eye now wide with wonder. "You're beautiful!" he gasped.

Fenneth smiled and blushed.

"Are . . . are you perhaps a mermaid?" he asked her hesitantly.

"Do you like mermaids?" she asked him.

"I like *you*," he said with flattering sincerity.

"Then, yes. Yes, I am. The name's Ariel. Good to meet ya." She smiled as she held out a friendly hand.

What are you doing, mistress? Discordia wondered.

Trying to break a long dry spell, Fenneth replied silently.

But, Fenneth, you've only just met! fretted Discordia.

How many times should I expect a hot guy to fall from the sky and land on my lap? Fenneth replied. *Because I don't know about you, but this is a first for me out of two lives lived.*

Well, that is true, conceded Discordia.

"Well, I guess you could say this is *a whole new world* for me," the rescued knight said with a charming grin.

Fenneth frowned at his words. "That's *Aladdin*."

"What's *Aladdin*?" he asked guilelessly.

"Yeah, okay, nice try," Fenneth said as she stood up, having immediately lost interest. "And before you say anything else, the answer is an emphatic *nooo*."

"Nooo?" he replied.

"Noooo," she confirmed. "No offense, handsome, but everyone I've ever met who's also been from Earth has either been evil or evil *and* psychotic. For health reasons, my doctor recommended that I cut ninety percent of the crazy out of my diet."

"Really? Sounds like a boring doctor," the knight said as he stood up to walk beside her. "How many people have you met who were also from Earth?" he asked her.

"Just one, and trust me, she was *more* than enough," Fenn said grimly.

"Well, I'm sorry to hear that," the knight said sincerely. "But hey, I've got good news to share! *I'm* not crazy! I'm one of the good guys, and I'm here to rescue you!"

"You're doing a great job, so far," Fenneth said politely.

"If you're referring to my *dynamic* entry, that was a slight miscalculation on my part," the man said as his skin slightly pinkened in embarrassment in a way that Fenneth had to admit was cute. "I was sent here by teleportation to confirm your presence, Lady Godwell. Clearly some adjustments need to be made to improve the process."

"You came here knowing my name?" asked Fenneth.

"Of course!" he said excitedly. "You're the true maiden of the holy blade! You're the only one who can help us free ourselves from the yolk of the witch!"

Aye-ya-ya, Fenneth thought miserably to herself.

"Listen . . . uh, what did you say your name was?" asked Fenneth.

"I didn't. But it's James," he replied.

"James," she said to herself, trying it out. It was a nice name. It suited him. "Listen, James, I don't know how your people found out I was alive, but—"

"It was a costly operation," he said sadly. "A lot of people died to get that information to us."

"Were they Bothans?" she asked skeptically.

"I'm being serious, Lady Godwell," he said. "I led the mission that let us acquire that info. A lot of good men died terrible deaths for us to confirm your safety and your whereabouts. I was nearly one of them."

His face now bore a haunted expression. "That . . . monster of an elemental buried so many of us alive, while the other one played with our minds and forced us to do *horrible* things to each other, all for her twisted amusement."

He shuddered at the memory.

Titania and Eris, said Discordia with a surge of fear. *If this man truly survived an encounter with that pair, then he is fortunate to have both his health and his sanity.*

Do you think he's telling the truth? Fenneth asked her.

It's difficult to say. I am not an elemental of the spirit, so his mind is closed to me. But his body language and tone speak convincingly of a great trauma. I . . . I think I believe him, mistress.

All right. Thank you, Discordia, said Fenneth gratefully. Over the years, Discordia had proven herself to be an excellent judge of character. Fenneth hadn't met anyone yet who could fool her, so she decided to follow her recommendation.

"How did you get away?" she asked James.

"I'll be honest; it was sheer luck that I escaped that hell alive. If it wasn't for your sister, I'd be dead right now."

"My sister?" Fenneth said in surprise. She grabbed James by his shoulders and shook him urgently as she spoke. "Laurel was there? Is she okay?"

"I—I don't know! That's why I need your help!" James said quickly. "We broke into a facility where Everly kept vital information and prisoners stored before sending them off to some place code-named *the rat room* for reeducation and punishment. That's how we found out about you."

"What?" Fenneth asked in confusion. "That doesn't make any sense. Everly threw me here randomly. Even she doesn't know where I am."

"That's a lie, Lady Fenneth," said James earnestly. "She chose this location deliberately. She called it *the hamster's cage*. She knows exactly where you are, always."

"*The hamster's cage?*" Fenneth said incredulously. "The fucking . . . HAMSTER'S CAGE? That . . . that bitch! That twisted, evil bitch, she lied to me again! Why does she *always* lie to me?!"

With sudden tears in her eyes, Fenneth turned and angrily slammed her clenched fist into a nearby tree, smashing it in half with the impact of her blow.

Then she regretfully stared at the fallen tree, feeling guilt over the knowledge that its death was due entirely to her anger.

Watching her from behind, James smiled with satisfaction as a shadow passed over his face.

"I'm not her pet. She doesn't *own* me," Fenneth said sorrowfully.

The grin on James' face grew even wider.

"Of course she doesn't, Lady Fenneth," he said to her. "No one owns you."

Except for me, he thought triumphantly.

"Tell me about my sister," Fenn said some time later, after cleaning her eyes and regaining her composure. "Do you know what Everly's done with her?"

"Lady Laurel stayed behind to hold off the elementals and secure the escape of our survivors," he informed her. "She's most likely still in that same location as a prisoner. I can take you to her, Fenneth! If you work together with the resistance, we can surely rescue her!"

"All right," said Fenneth without hesitation. "I'm sold. Let's go right now."

"Now?" asked James in surprise.

"Yes, *now*," Fenneth said curtly. "I'm not going to let my sister languish in captivity for another moment. Knowing Everly, she'll use her try to and get to me. It's not out of the question. *Nothing's* out of the question with her."

"A-all right, then!" James stammered with excitement. "Just let me get my armor back on and then we're off to the races!"

Fenneth helped him re-armor, amused by his eagerness to join her. Was this man really a warrior? There was something about him that reminded her of a family pet, a puppy, really, with his eagerness to please her. She found him charming.

"Why's your gear so burned up?" she asked him, after they finished adjusting his chest plate. "It's sturdy enough, but it really looks like it's been through the wars."

"It's inherited equipment," James said sadly. "Someone else's inheritance! They needed some quick money, and I needed some protection, and this was the best I could afford. But it's kept me safe over the years, and that's the most you can ever ask of your equipment."

"That's true enough," Fenneth said in agreement. "But tell me this, James. Why are you fighting against Everly? You're from Earth like us. What makes this your cause?"

"Nothing, really," he said, after appearing to carefully consider her words. "I wasn't reborn into this universe like others were. I came here through other means, so I can't say that I have a horse in this race. But when I look at the despair that Everly has caused, and . . . and the way she just laughs over it like it's *nothing* . . . it riles something up in me. People shouldn't treat each other like this. People should be *better*."

He laughed at himself quietly then. "Pretty hokey, huh? Trying to be a hero when I don't even have a full pair of eyes. But I still need to try. I need to show this world that not *all* people from Earth are complete monsters."

Suddenly, Fenneth hugged him, surprising him greatly.

"I don't think that's hokey at all, James," she said to him with her eyes closed. "I think what you're doing is wonderful."

James looked down at her, stunned. Across his face ran a sudden gamut of differing, conflicting emotions: anger, revulsion, shock, delight, happiness.

The final expression it landed on was a deep, implacable sadness.

"Thank you," he said as he hugged her back. "Thank you for trusting me, Fenneth. You don't know what that means to me," he said gently. Then he turned away before she could see his expression and donned his helmet.

"Now let's go save your sister, so the two of you can save the world," he said with more cheer than he felt.

"Yeah," said Fenneth. "Hell yeah! Let's do exactly that."

James tapped a hidden insignia on his gauntlet that allowed him to contact the sending choir. Then he made Fenneth laugh by mimicking playing a guitar while they waited for the spell to activate.

Within moments of sending the signal, the pair of them vanished in a flash of light.

CHAPTER TWENTY-EIGHT

Status

Moments after their victory, Max separated himself from Everly, resumed his human form, and knelt before the defeated monster. He then ran his hands along its body, feeling around as though he was looking for something, which Everly found puzzling.

"Jackpot!" he said gleefully. "Total compatibility."

"What are you up to?" she asked him.

"Shut up for a second and I'll show you," Max replied.

Everly frowned and was about to tell him to do something obscene to himself when Max's hand began glowing with a vibrant red light, which he then plunged into the creature's body. When he removed it, he held a gleaming golden orb, which he then crushed in his fist.

"*Got it,*" he said. "Shadow form. Nice."

"Shadow form?" asked Everly. "Explain yourself."

In response, Max's body became immersed in darkness, leaving a black outline standing in front of her instead of another person. Then he let himself fall backward onto the floor, flattening against it into the shape of a shadow.

"*Cooooool,*" he said happily. Then he stretched forth and reappeared behind Everly, moving so quickly that even her keen eyes could barely follow his movements. "Very cool!" he repeated. "Instantaneous movement from shadow to shadow. What an idiot that guy was! Why come smashing in here and presenting a target when he totally could have gotten the jump on us? You really must have pissed him off or something."

"Eh, that's something I do to a lot of people," Everly said indifferently. "More importantly, did you just steal that thing's ability?"

"Uh, I would prefer that you say I *inherited* his ability," Max said indignantly. "I'm not a thief."

"What's the name of the ability that allows you to do that?" Everly asked him.

". . . **[Skill Steal]**," he admitted.

"Get fucked, Max," Everly said irritably.

"Nyur-hur-hur," he chuckled. "Still, this is a pretty nice acquisition. I've always enjoyed lurking menacingly in the shadows. What better way to do that than by *being* a shadow? The intangibility and teleportation feel pretty sweet as well. And would you look at my character sheet? I went up five whole levels with just that one kill! Thanks, Hades!"

"You pray to the god of death?" Everly snorted. "That's pretty edgy, Max."

"Bite your tongue, I don't pray to anybody!" Max said with a scowl. He then pointed at the monster's corpse. "That's *this* loser's name. Can't you see his nameplate?"

"Again, what are you talking about?" Everly asked. "Nameplates? Levels? Hey, I totally get being emotionally detached from your surroundings, but you sound like you're living out a video game."

Max stared at her blankly as if in genuine surprise. "Uh, you're *kidding* me, right? Wait, you're not, are you? You *really don't know . . .*"

Suddenly, he began laughing at her. He roared with mocking jubilation, laughing so hard that he fell over and rolled from side to side like a delighted child, so consumed with merriment that he soon began crying and gasping for breath.

He stopped when Everly took careful aim and kicked him in the face.

"Knock it off!" she yelled. "Jesus, Max, just answer the question."

"Sorry, sorry," he gasped. "It's just . . . I can't believe how fucking clueless you are! Wow, you're that strong, and you seem like such a know-it-all, but you're also SUCH AN IGNORANT DUMBASS! WOW!"

"Max," she said as she held up a fist. "You either start coughing up some answers or you start coughing up some blood. It's your choice, pal."

"All right, all right," he said, after one more giggle. "Let's see. It's actually easier if you do it yourself than it would be to explain. Uhhh . . . I personally call my sheet up automatically whenever I think about it. How would I do that if I were some unknowledgeable little brat who didn't have the slightest clue how her powers worked?"

"*Max—*" she began to say.

"Try this," he cut in. "Clear out your mind and say *status*."

"Why?" she asked.

"Just shut up and do it!" he snapped, this time frowning deeply at her. "You'll see *why* for yourself."

"Fine, but if you're wasting my time, you'll regret it," she promised him.

"Hey, stupid, we're in the abyss. All we *have* is free time," he replied.

God, he's so mouthy, Everly thought angrily to herself. *If he thinks I can't break him of that habit of talking back, then I look forward to proving him wrong!*

She would deeply enjoy the process of correcting his misconceptions about the nature of their partnership. For starters, it *wasn't* a partnership! *She* was in charge and that was the end of it! If that was a problem with him, then too bad.

He was *her* property now.

"Just know what's coming if you're messing with me," she said.

"Okay, drama queen. Just say what I told you, already!" said Max.

"Grrrr. Fine, *status*," she said, after shutting her eyes. When she opened them, a large blue screen floated before her eyes. "What the actual fuck?!" she said, after jumping back in surprise.

"I could never figure out if having a status screen meant that life is an elaborate hologram and we're all living in the matrix," Max said. "It seems likely, right? It's either that or the author of our existence is just a lazy gamer relying on tired old Japanese cartoon tropes to excuse his pathetic lack of personal creativity. Right, J.V.?"

"Shut up. I'm trying to read this," Everly said impatiently.

Name: Everly Skolder
Level: 18
Class: Tyrant/Elemental Lord
Race: Human/Semideus
Alignment: Lawful Evil (Barely)
Strength: 225 (V)
Combat: 200
Speed: 250 (V)
Magic: 500 (V)
Charisma: 150 (V)
Intelligence: 25
Wisdom: 8
Luck: 300
Skills: Master Swordsmanship (SS+), Unarmed Combat Mastery (S+), Intermediate Axe Mastery (C+), Oration (A+), Elemental Mastery (SS+), Semi-divinity (S+).
Titles: Conqueror. (One who has successfully overthrown a kingdom.)
Marauder. (One who delights in crushing her opponents.)
Slayer of Hope. (One who lets her opponents think they have a chance for victory.)
Beloved Despot. (One who successfully disguises her true nature from the ignorant masses.)

Earth Mover. (The land trembles at your approach.)
Necromancer. (One who denies the natural order.)
Psychotic Reincarnator. (You had no way of knowing it would actually work. What the hell is *wrong* with you?)
Selfish Lover. (Once you're finished, you lose interest. Do you know how frustrating that is?)
User. (You're a horrible friend.)
Bad Boss. (Your employees are all saints for putting up with you.)
Bad Sister. (TERRIBLE sister.)
Bad Daughter. (When was the last time you spoke to your mother?)
Daddy's Little Monster. (He's so proud of you. Is that a good thing?)
Lady Killer. (You know what you did. Bitch.)

"Okay, those last few titles are all *bullshit*." Everly frowned. "I feel so judged."

"Yeah, these systems love having their little running commentary at our expense," Max said. "Just ignore it."

"I can't believe it, though," said Everly. "Levels? Skills? My life since rebirth has been running on MMO principals and no one even told me?"

"If you never learned, then the locals on your world have probably forgotten how it works," suggested Max. "Lemme guess; there was a big empire or whatever that existed thousands of years ago, but it fell apart during a long series of wars and now stuff that used to be commonplace is now rare and *wooooo*?"

"Yeah, kind of," said Everly. "There was a big god-war or whatever, and then a bunch of necromancers ran wild and tried to take over. It didn't sound relevant to my interests, so I didn't pay much attention."

"Fair enough," said Max.

"Wow, so I can get stronger by killing people, huh?" Everly said thoughtfully.

"You seriously didn't even know that much?" Max asked in astonishment. "Wait, are you telling me you've just been running around picking fights with everyone and everything, and assuming you'll win without so much as knowing your own level?"

"Eh, pretty much," Everly said with a shrug.

"Damn, kid," Max said with a whistle. "I bet they'd hate you down in Florida."

"Why Florida?" she asked cautiously.

"Because you're a girl with *balls*." Max chortled.

When Everly didn't say anything for several long moments, Max said, "See, the state government in Florida recently passed some controversial laws that a lot of LGBT proponents view as—"

"Stop explaining your jokes, Max," Everly told him.

"Okay, okay, yeesh," he said.

"I'm *serious*. You keep it up and I really might kill you," said Everly venomously.

"All right!" he said. "Man, and I thought *I* had a tendency to fly off the handle. You know, because I'm an axe? That's an axe joke, by the way—"

"MAX!" she yelled angrily.

"Sorry, Everly. I have some bad habits," he said insincerely.

"Well, break them," she said.

"Will do!" he said. "I'll chop through them like they're dried wood. You know, because—"

"Don't," Everly said as she raised a warning finger.

Max's smile froze into place but quickly became strained as he struggled to keep himself from speaking. Finally, despite his mighty efforts, he quickly said, "Because I'm an *aaaaaxe—AGH!*"

He cried out in pain as Everly punched him in the face as hard as she could.

"Let's just get out of here," she said a few minutes later, after his skull finished regenerating.

"Hey, hold on," he said, after popping his neck back into place and regrowing his teeth.

"What now?" she asked impatiently.

"I just assessed you," he said as he approached her. "Heh, what the hell did you do to yourself? Your guts and what not are all twisted the fuck up."

"I'm not following," she said. "Do I really have to remind you that this isn't my real body?"

"And do *I* have to remind you that it's still a *representative* of your real body, dummy? It bears the same scars that you do in reality. And trust me when I say it's screwed up! Your mana pathways and your chi meridians—"

"*Harada*," she said, correcting him. "It's *harada*, not *chi*. I'm not a weeb."

"Well, whatever you want to call it, I'm fucking amazed you haven't exploded or something."

"Exploded?" she asked.

"Uhhhh, how do I put this?" Max said. "Your body is somehow supercharged. But it's out of balance. Hell, it's waaaay the fuck out of whack! Jesus, you could detonate at any minute! No, any *second*! Hahaha! Your being alive must be that ridiculous luck stat at play."

"I'm sick?" she asked in surprise. "That can't be right. I've never felt better in my life."

"A lot of long-distance runners probably thought the same thing before dropping dead on their feet, kid," Max said. "As far as I can tell with this insightful eye of mine, you're drawing in three different sources of power. Elemental, divine, and honkey tonk—"

"*Harada*," she said impatiently.

"Whatever." He shrugged. "The elemental and divine sources are huge, but your . . . *harada* is all twisted up and nasty. It's like someone tried to forcefully expand it without taking into account that it grows naturally on its own. Did someone experiment on you?"

"Nooo," lied Everly, who'd done it to herself in a fit of jealousy over Carter having greater reserves of *harada*. "Maybe?"

"Well, whoever it was, they were an idiot." Max smirked. "Come here."

He stepped close to Everly and placed both hands on her shoulders. Before Everly could ask him what he was doing this time, she gasped as she felt something sharp piercing her on either side.

"This is a skill of mine called [**Rooting**]," Max explained. "I'm sending a few tendrils from my body to your meridian points to gently unwind and unclog them. By the way, this is really gonna hurt."

"But it'll be good for me?" asked Everly.

"Yeah, sure, probably," Max said indifferently. "I just like focusing on the fun part."

"Asshole," she said.

"Shut up, you love me." He grinned.

As Max promised, the restoration of her meridian points caused her considerable pain. But because they were standing face-to-face as he worked, she refused to show any discomfort or weakness, which only caused his smirk to intensify.

When he was finished, Max pulled his hands away, letting the tendrils retract back into his flesh. "How's that feel?" he asked her.

Everly closed her eyes and took a deep breath. Then she reached for *harada*. But as she felt it beginning to rise within her, she found herself dropping to her hands and knees, vomiting. A hideous black-and-red intermix that started sizzling when it made contact with the ground began bubbling from her lips.

"Awww, sick!" Max laughed. "You're nasty, Everly."

"What the hell did you do to me?" she rasped as she wiped her mouth.

"Nothing! I told you; your guts were twisted up!" said Max. "This is what your body was producing. It's like toxic elemental waste. God, even my [**Appraisal**] skill is having some trouble identifying all the crap in it! It's all negative energy! Well, that explains why your elementals were forced into hibernation."

"How?" Everly asked as Max helped her rise to her unsteady feet.

"Because you were poisoning them!" Max chortled. "Think about it; they're beings of thought and energy. And you were filled up with all this gunk without even realizing it. Being around you would have been like giving a baby a pacifier made from lead. That title on your status screen is right; you *are* a bad friend, Everly."

"Shut up," Everly said. "Just fucking drop it."

"Yeah, okay," Max said. "You being the boss and all."

Everly ignored him and took a step toward the gateway, ready to finally depart that place. To her dismay, she stumbled and fell flat on her face.

"Damn it," she muttered.

"Don't be in such a rush," Max advised. "You need time to recover from our little impromptu surgical session. Realigning your precious innards isn't something you can just walk off, y'know."

"I'll just heal myself, then," Everly said stubbornly.

"How? We can't use healing magic in the abyss," he said.

"I'm not staying here another minute, Max!" she yelled.

Max stood staring at her for a short while. Then he rolled his eyes in exasperation and said, "*Fiiiine.* Man, you're kind of a handful yourself, do you know that, brat?"

To Everly's surprise, he then knelt to scoop her effortlessly into his arms. Then he walked with her through the gateway. And just like that, they were in another place, far from the temple that had been his prison.

"Home for the weekend at last!" he snickered.

Everly found herself blushing at her circumstances. She'd never been the object of a bridal carry before.

It was kind of nice.

"You're stronger than you look," she finally said, after a few minutes had passed.

"Good thing I am since you're pretty damn heavy," he replied with a wry grin.

Asshole, she thought.

"Asshole," she said.

"I was just joking!" he replied. "Here, I'll put on some tunes."

Around them the air soon filled with the sounds of contemporary pop music that stayed with them as he walked. "How are you doing that?" she asked him.

"It's just telepathy," he said. "I can remember every little scrap of music I ever heard. By projecting it, it's the same as listening to a radio."

"Nice," Everly said appreciatively.

"Got anything in particular you want to hear?" he asked.

"Do you know 'Laid'?" she asked him.

"Oh, how forward of you!" he said. "But if you insist . . ."

"The song, stupid," she said. "It's an oldie but a goodie. I love it."

"Hmm, remind me of it. Give me a lyric," he said.

"I don't remember the lyrics. Just the part where the guy hits the high note," Everly said. "It's played during the trailers for all those American Pie movies."

"I never liked any of those flicks," Max said. "Way too raunchy! But, yeah, I know that song. Give me a second."

Soon the sound of the song enveloped them both, and Everly found herself bobbing her head happily to the tune. They both sang along to it in a charmingly offkey melody as they made their way farther down the unknown road they walked.

When it was over, Max said, "Yeah, that song *is* a banger. I haven't listened to it in years. Who sang it again?"

"Uh, only my favorite English alt-pop act from the nineties," Everly said.

"Oasis?" Max asked.

"Bite your tongue!" she said with mock outrage. "Haven't you ever heard of James?"

CHAPTER TWENTY-NINE

Go-Go Sunflower Force!

As a new day dawned for the earnest and good-natured folks of Celestial Meadow, a little girl merrily skipped along the sidewalk on her way to the youth center. Her heart was filled with hope and happiness and anticipation for the future, little realizing that she was about to fall prey to a wicked scheme!

"Why, hello there, little one," said a friendly-looking elderly man in a spotless white uniform as he waved at her from behind a newly constructed outdoor seafood stand entitled The Clam Slam. "Would you care for some freshly caught oysters?" he asked her.

Looking around, she saw other children her age sitting nearby, all merrily sucking away at fresh shells.

"Oysters? For *real*?" said the excited little girl. "Oh, I would love to! But that's *rich people's* food! I haven't got any money."

"Don't lament in despair, you incomplete mammal," said the old man with a jovial laugh. "You can have all the delicious morning oysters you can inhale!"

"What? For *free*?" asked the disbelieving minor.

"Not quite!" said the old man with an evil grin. "It'll only cost you . . . your precious dream energy!"

Before the child could react, the old man placed his hand against her forehead. As she stood there helplessly, purple waves of energy were drawn from her body and absorbed into the old man. When he was finished, he handed her a bucket of clams and paid her no further heed.

Listlessly, she walked away with her bucket and took a seat on the curb with the rest of her peers while mindlessly shucking open some fresh clams and swallowing their contents in one go.

"Yummy . . ." she said robotically.

"Hahaha!" laughed the vile Queen Oblivia as she observed the deeds of her minion from her throne room in Dimension U. "Our plan is working perfectly! Soon, the dream energy of all the children of Celestial Meadow will be mine to command!"

"All hail the Zabok Empire!" shouted one of her servants.

"No, all hail Queen Oblivia!" shouted another as the throne room erupted into a wicked cacophony of cheering and cackling.

Meanwhile, at the Celestial Meadow Youth Center, Titania, who was Everly's elemental earth servant as well as an ordinary teenager with a can-do attitude, was teaching a friendly martial arts class to a group of excited youngsters.

"ETS-AYAH! ETS-AYAH!" she shouted after performing a perfect rising, reverse dragon body blow. After the children repeated her movements, she bowed to them and clapped her hands energetically. "Good job, everyone! And remember, now that I've shown you the correct way to punch someone, don't *ever* punch *anyone*! A *real* martial artist knows that violence never solves *anything*!"

"Yes, Sensei!" the children said as they bowed respectfully and dispersed.

As Titania was putting away her nunchakus and helping to prepare the room for an evening hot yoga class, the youth center's after-school tutor, her older sister Eris, came walking in, carrying a stack of papers, which she promptly spilled all over the floor after accidentally walking into a wall.

"Oh. No," she said in a lifeless monotone as the papers went flying.

"Ha! Eris, you're *so* clumsy, you clumsy-head! Why aren't you wearing your glasses?" laughed Titania.

"I'm, like, trying out a new look. I don't want Tyler to think I'm, like, a *nerd* or anything," said Eris unconvincingly.

"Gosh, Eris, you're great the way you are! And if Tyler were a *real* friend, he wouldn't want you to change at all!" said Titania.

"Like, *wow*, little sis. And I thought *I* was supposed to be the smart one," muttered Eris. "I guess I've really learned a valuable lesson."

"It's not easy being kids like us." Titania nodded. "Especially kids like *us*, if you get my meaning."

"Suuure," said Eris.

Suddenly, their matching wristbands began chirping a similar beat that quickly drew their attention.

"Speaking of which, it looks like we'll need to beam out to the battle bridge!" said Titania.

"Yeeeeah," sighed Eris. "Let's go to the *battle bridge*."

Standing side by side, the sisters held up their hands and each pressed a button on their wristbands that quickly teleported them far away from the youth center to a hidden alien castle far from the eyes of ordinary people.

"Jeepers and widgets!" chimed an excitable-looking robot cat whose lips didn't quite sync with the words he spoke. "I'm glad you're here, kids, something terrible has happened!"

"Indeed," said a giant robot head levitating above the center of the room.

"Hey, Cosmic Commander!" said Titania. "And hey to you as well, Meow-pha Five. What's going on?"

"Are you fucking kidding me?" Eris swore quietly to herself.

"Bad news, Sunflower Force," said Cosmic Commander somberly. "It appears that Queen Oblivia has begun a dreadful new undertaking! She's targeting the children of Celestial Meadow and draining away their vital dream energy! If this wicked plan isn't stopped immediately, she'll be that much closer to reviving the Zabok Empire!"

"Oh, no! Not the Zabok Empire!" gasped Titania. "If they ever return, the entire earth will be in ultimate peril!"

"Can we help her? I really want to help her," said Eris.

"Hahaha! You're always cracking great jokes," said Meow-pha Five.

"Your unique sense of humor is always appreciated, Eris, but for now, it's time to trans-forma-size!" announced Cosmic Commander.

"All right!" said Titania eagerly. She then grabbed her transformation token and said, "The appeal of a squirrel! The power of a dragon! SUNFLOWER RED!"

A beam of scintillating red surrounded her body. When it dispersed, Titania was covered in a red costume of a shiny, unknown material, with a hard plastic helmet that masked her features.

"Your turn, sis!" she said to Eris while giving her a thumbs-up.

"Ah. Right," Eris said as she searched through her purse. "Oh, no. I think I've somehow lost my transformation token. I'm so sorry. Looks like I'll have to sit this one out, everyone—"

"Don't worry, Eris!" said Meow-pha Five. "We can just transform you manually and then locate the token later. You won't have to miss out on today's action!"

"Thank you SO much," Eris said between tightly clenched teeth. "I look forward to repaying you for this one day, cat. One day *soon* . . ."

"Anytime, Eris! We're a team!" said Meow-pha Five cheerfully as he pressed a button on his console.

"Aaaand that's the last one!" said the old man happily as he drained the dream energy from his final victim. "And with this, we're finished! Now I need no longer wear the worthless appearance of a human!"

And with that said, he threw off his disguise, revealing a monstrous CLAM monster with eyes that gleamed with maleficent intent! "Coo-coo-coo! Queen Oblivia will be so pleased with me! Now to return to Dimension U to receive my reward!"

"Hold it right there, you unfriendly fiend!" said the commanding voice of Sunflower Red as she leaped to the street from atop a nearby building to confront him. "Whatever sinister scheme Queen Oblivia has concocted, I'll never let you succeed!"

"Yeah. We're definitely going to stop it, you . . . you bad guy," said Sunflower Black with noticeably less enthusiasm as she followed her partner down. "For the kids. Probably."

"Coo-coo-coo!" laughed the wicked creature. "I was starting to think that you goody-goody *good-for-nothings* would *never* show up! Are you perhaps wondering where all their dream energy went, you witless warrior wimps? Well, wonder no longer! I've absorbed every last drop of it!"

"What? You bastard! Just *who* are you?" demanded the outraged Sunflower Red.

"Yeah. Tell us your story or whatever," said the less invested Sunflower Black.

"Coo-coo-coo! Telling you my name is like casting *pearls* before swine! But I'll do it anyway! I'm *Calamity Clam*!" said Calamity Clam. "Now excuse me! I need to make a special delivery of dream energy to Queen Oblivia!"

"Jesus Christ," said Sunflower Black.

"You'll do no such thing, you selfish shellfish!" shouted Sunflower Red while, unbeknownst to her, Sunflower Black shook her head in pained despair at the quality of their dialogue.

"Coo-coo-coo! You're too late, Sunflower Red!" crowed the victorious monster. "Now that I've successfully stolen the dream energy of all these miserable Earth children, the resurrection of the Zabok Empire will soon begin!"

"Wah!" cried one of the children. "I don't want to be an astronaut or a baseball player anymore! I want to live off the government dole and contribute nothing to society!"

"Me too! Life holds no meaning!" said a bitter little girl. "Let's steal some syringes and find something fun to inject! If we die, it's our parents' fault!"

"Screw all that, I'm taking a header off an overpass. I hope I land on a church bus and it gets put on social media," said one particularly unhappy-looking child.

"Oh, no! The children have lost hope!" said the shocked Sunflower Red.

"Yep. Sure looks like it." Sunflower Black shrugged.

"I won't allow you to get away with this, you dastardly mollusk!" said Sunflower Red as she shook an angry, impassioned fist. "Return those dreams to the children they belong to or else!"

"Coo-coo-coo! The Sunflower Force can go to hell!" taunted Calamity Clam. "I'll never return my spoils!"

"Then you leave us no choice!" shouted Sunflower Red as she assumed a dynamic pose. "I'm the blazing soldier of Justice and friendship! Defending the innocent with my fiery will! Sunflower Red!"

She then waited patiently as her teammate stared blankly at her.

"Do I have to do this?" asked Sunflower Black quietly.

"Yes!" shouted Sunflower Red.

"I really don't want to," Sunflower Black said with noticeable hesitation.

"Eris, you have to announce your intentions, it's an important part of how we do things," said Sunflower Red.

"This is *embarrassing*," Sunflower Black complained.

"It's not embarrassing, it's awesome!" insisted Sunflower Red. "This is how we as partners get in sync with each other as we prepare to dispense heroic justice to this vile villain of the week. You *can't* skip this part!"

"All right, all right," mumbled Sunflower Black. Then she reluctantly took a deep breath to steady herself before striking a similar pose to her sister's. "Striking back at evil with cool composure. I'm the sentinel of the shadows and the defender of the dark, Sunflower Black!"

"And together," began Sunflower Red.

"We are," followed Sunflower Black.

"THE GUARDIANS OF FREEDOM! SUNFLOWER FORCE!" they shouted in unison.

"See! Didn't that feel good?" asked Sunflower Red a few seconds later.

"It . . . *was* kind of fun," admitted Sunflower Black.

"Coo-coo-coo! If you insist on getting in my way, then I'll gladly raise some SHELL!" said Calamity Clam. "Pidgie Squad! Assemble and *destroy* these fools!"

"Oh, no! It's the pidgies!" lamented Sunflower Red.

"Okay, now you've really lost me," said Sunflower Black. "What is a pidgie?"

Moments after asking that, a flock of pigeons came flying in to surround the Sunflower Force. Then, in a sudden puff of smoke, the birds vanished from sight, only to be replaced by large, feathered monsters with the bodies of men clad in tight black spandex, but with the heads of pigeons!

"Fly, my pretties, fly! And make them die, my pretties, *DIE!* Coo-coo-coo!" laughed Calamity Clam.

"Use your blaster beam, sis!" suggested Sunflower Red. "It's like a gun, but it only hurts monsters!"

"Wow. What an amazingly convenient way to sell gun-shaped merchandise to small children," said Sunflower Black sarcastically.

"Huh?" asked Sunflower Red.

"Nothing," said Sunflower Black.

As they ran in to engage their foes, suddenly, the theme song began!

Evil is on the rise!
Freedom is what they despise!
Injustice is on their side!
Against them you must now ride!
Sunflower Force!
Sunflower Force!
The greatest team of all,
of course!
Zabok must never return!
BRAAAAVE SUNFLOWERS!

"I really don't see how this could possibly become any more humiliating," Eris said miserably to herself as that awful song blared unceasingly in her ears. "If I have to put up with this for much longer, I'll start praying for death."

"Eris? Titania?" said a very familiar voice.

Turning to her side, Eris's jaw dropped. But fortunately, she was wearing this stupid helmet, so her expression couldn't be seen.

Across the street from the battle, Everly stood there on the empty sidewalk alongside some shabbily dressed human who was laughing his head off at the sight of them.

"Girls, what the hell are you doing?" asked Everly. Her expression was very confused.

Now Eris really wanted to die. "This isn't what you think!" she said desperately, after pulling off her helmet. "I'm just playing along with it!"

"Oh, my *god*, I've had dreams that weren't as good as this!" chortled the stranger who stood beside Everly. "The level of detail! Fucking aces ahead!"

"Shut up, Max," said Everly as she elbowed the man. "But seriously, Eris, what's going on with all of . . . *this?*"

"Oh, Everly, it's stupid. It's all so very, very *stupid!*" Eris said as she embraced her and placed her head on the other woman's shoulder. "So, so, stupid," she repeated with closed eyes.

"Really? Because I think this is fucking *amazing!*" said the stranger, who was apparently named Max. "Hey, do you have any giant robots? Call out your giant robots! Squash that guy flat before he gets embiggened!"

Suddenly, a surge of purple energy enveloped Calamity Clam and caused him to swell in size until he'd grown as tall as a skyscraper.

"Aww, too late," said Max.

CHAPTER THIRTY

Wavelengths

More time passed as Max and Everly continued their journey. This time, the abyss took the shape of an endless highway for them to walk upon, which Everly found reminiscent of the roads in many postapocalyptic action movies that she'd seen over the years. Something that George Miller might have directed.

On either side of them were the ravaged remnants of destroyed vehicles left to rust beneath the sun. Driverless wreckages that looked like they'd been retooled for combat and then been used in the losing side of a serious battle. Max thought it was quite interesting and had been cracking endless jokes in a bad Australian accent until Everly had forced him to stop.

As they continued onward toward their goal, they passed the time with conversation and gradually grew to know each other better. Although Everly was impatient to finally end her quest, the time they spent on their meandering walk proved to be invaluable because it not only allowed her body to gradually recover from the healing she received from Max, but it also allowed the bond they shared as weapon and wielder to strengthen as well.

Whether they would acknowledge it or not, the pair of them suited each other. Within weeks of meeting, it was as though they'd known each other for years. Everly burned with arrogant purpose and grandiose self-regard, while Max simply wanted to burn things. The various primordial demons that crossed their path, thinking the pair of travelers to be easy prey, quickly grew to regret their urges.

However, just because Max and Everly had grown closer didn't mean they shared the same opinions. They frequently argued loudly over anything and everything that crossed their minds. Movies, songs, women, comic books: no topic was safe from their quarreling. If the subject of conversation was something they felt especially passionate about, then it could quickly escalate into a physical confrontation and even the occasional attempted murder, although the latter happened rarely. They did frequently wound each other, though. But those brief moments of rage-fueled bloodlust would just as quickly turn into long minutes of hysterical laughter.

It was a strange friendship they'd developed, but it was also a genuine one. And a first for either of them. Max, by his very nature, derived enjoyment from the suffering of others, whether it happened intentionally or incidentally. He respected nothing. He cared for no one. And yet, with Everly, he found a surprisingly deep well of camaraderie. She reminded him of days gone by with his younger brother, when they'd been inseparable and thick as thieves. Back before Matthew had turned on him and gone his own way, leaving Max alone to find his way in the world.

It was a good feeling. Even if it did remind Max of how much he wanted to torture his self-righteous sibling with something sharp and pointy. To watch his mind break from sleep deprivation and pain before ending his life. But that was just how it went with family. Didn't everyone occasionally want to turn their annoying little brother into a messy finger painting? That was just life.

For her part, Everly was quite convinced that Max was insane, and not functionally insane either. He didn't have a plan for anything; he was mercurial and lived entirely in the moment with no idea of what tomorrow would bring. To an organized and controlling personality like hers, it was obvious that he needed guidance and direction. Essentially, he was no different from anyone else in the world. His life would improve immeasurably if he just shut the hell up and did whatever she told him. He was strongly resistant to this viewpoint, but Everly knew she'd win him over eventually.

Either that or she'd simply batter down his resistance until he couldn't fight back anymore. Whichever one, really. It was all good.

"It just doesn't matter to me," Everly said one particularly dark night on the road. The evening's conversation had shifted to their opinions on how to best make use of the system. Max relied on it for everything, but Everly discovered over time that she really didn't care for it at all.

"What's your issue with it, anyway?" he asked her. "It's what gives us the edge in this life. You should take advantage of it as much as you can."

"Nope. Hard disagree from me," she replied. "I don't want to base my decision-making on a fear-based principle. What's the point of that? It'll make me weaker, not stronger."

"What do you mean by a *fear-based* principle?" asked Max.

"Isn't that what a leveling system actually is?" replied Everly. "An easy-to-use means of risk-assessment to guide all your choices? *This guy has three levels above me; I should go grind. That monster over there is an elite; I should form a party before fighting it. There are too many enemies over here; I might run out of magic before I can kill them all.* Game mechanics are bullshit, Max. They're more about avoidance of failure than they are about seeking victory. *My spreadsheet has bigger numbers, therefore my kung fu is the strongest!* Frankly, I find the concept contemptable."

"What's wrong with wanting to win? I *love* winning. Knowing that I'm a higher level than the meat I want to mince up makes it easier for me to have some fun," said Max.

"Max, we're talking about fear of failure above all else," Everly replied. "People are crippled by it. Winning is fun, but life gets boring if it's always *easy*. But that doesn't matter to people who live like they'll die the moment they lose at something."

"Hmmm," Max said loudly. "That's *soooo* interesting."

"What?" Everly said. "If you have something to say, just say it."

"You're hypercompetitive to the point of being annoying," said Max bluntly. "Kind of feels like your beliefs are mired in *juuust* a little bit of self-serving hypocrisy."

"Shut up, you're an idiot, you're completely wrong," snapped Everly.

"If you say so," Max snickered.

"I'm just saying that only *cowards* crave certainty," Everly said. "Wanting to know ahead of time that you won't lose removes everything that makes things fun. The principal of uncertainty is the very spice of life!"

"If you want a challenge, just fight someone the same level as you," Max said.

"That's still the same as participating in the farce," Everly said stubbornly. "I might be blond, but I'm not Goldilocks. I don't want a bowl of porridge that's *just* right."

"We're just talking about picking your moments, kid," Max said with a roll of his eyes.

"That's right. Picking *my* moments, not following the brain-dead prompts of some omniscient blue screen," Everly said with a frown.

"Yours is blue? Mine's red," said Max. "Maybe you can customize your colors? Check under options."

"Oh, just shut up for a second and listen," said Everly. "This so-called system *might* seem like a path of freedom to you, but if you really think about it, it's just another set of rules and limitations. Select this skill so you can do this. Pick this bonus so you can do that. It's just the illusion of choice. You might think you're exercising free will, but so long as you play within the established rule set, then you'll never be in control of your own life. Hell, you'll never be anything more than a player in a game that someone else is running."

"It's been convincingly argued before that free will is an illusion," Max said. "That everything we'll ever do in the future is predicated on the choices we've made earlier in life. Haven't you ever heard the phrase *past is precedent?*"

"Sounds like an excuse that people use to deny parole to a prisoner," Everly scoffed.

"If you care about an orderly society, then recidivism has to be a concern," said Max with the sort of false sincerity often used by those who like to play devil's advocate because it annoys other people. "If an official shows mercy to a prisoner who then commits another crime, the people who granted him his authority will blame him for it."

"See what a mess it all is?" replied Everly. "The convict was forced to take the criminal class because he didn't meet the requirements for an easier one. Maybe his character sheet was lacking in the necessary stats because he couldn't afford the training that he'd need to improve himself. The official, on the other hand, was assigned the politician role. It seems easier on the outside, but he's beholden to public perception, so now he can't use his abilities justly, and if he wants to maintain his position, he can only maintain the status quo, with no hope of improving society."

"Maybe the prisoner took the criminal class because it suited his personality," said Max. "Maybe one day he woke up and decided he wanted to break some shit, to act out in defiance of the world?"

"And maybe the official picked *his* class because he decided that it was the best way to make his own life easier?" suggested Everly. "Maybe he wanted to feel the rush of pleasure that comes from sitting in judgement over another person's life? Or maybe he wanted bribes? Maybe he wanted to cash in on the easy money that comes with the facilitation of a prison industrial complex? Isn't it interesting how at the highest and lowest levels, evil people are naturally attracted to the established roles that society has prepared for them?"

"Well, a crook's natural inclinations *do* lean toward a general desire to fuck over as many people as possible," said Max with some authority on the subject.

"Understandable. But if they're not doing it out of a desire to *transcend* the system, then they're still just mice in the maze like all the other meaningless little rodents," said Everly. "As long as a system of any kind exists, all their decisions are meaningless."

"Yeah, hard disagree from me, Blondie," Max said. "You talk a lofty game, I'll give you that, but that doesn't change the fact that you *do* have a status screen. That means you're a player the same as everyone else, whether you choose to acknowledge it or not."

"No," Everly said. "It just means this system *thinks* I am. It means the forces working behind the scenes of this reality want me to *believe* that I have no choice other than to play along. But in doing so, it made me aware of its existence."

Max began to laugh wickedly at her words. "And what exactly does that mean? You gonna pick a fight with the rule book?"

"Nah, I've got a better idea than that." Everly smirked. "I'm going to kill whoever created this system and hijack it for myself."

Max laughed even harder at that. Then he paused when he realized she wasn't joking. Then he just stared at her. Finally, he said something he had only ever said on extremely rare occasions when no other words would truly suffice: "Everly, are you fucking insane?"

"No, sweetie," she said with a smile. "What I am is *ambitious*."

Max had a differing opinion but decided in that moment that it would be safer to keep it to himself.

Eventually, they reached the end of their journey. The conclusion was so abrupt and anticlimactic that they both felt greatly disappointed by it. Once they reached the end of the highway, instead of another temple, or a massive gateway, or even a simple boss fight, what they were rewarded with was the most cliché-looking portal from a budget-conscious science-fiction production imaginable.

It was a circle in the air that led into a city. It was so traditional-looking that Max was instantly distrustful of it.

"This can't seriously be it," he said. "Where's the extravagance? Where are the hordes of slavering fiends and their hulking overlords? Is this really all this place amounted to? A long walk and a strut through an open window? I'm not gonna lie, kid. I expected better."

"Maybe they ran out of ideas," Everly said. "You have to admit, we've been steamrolling our way through this place. Maybe they never bothered sprucing up the final level because there was no point since no one ever got this far before?"

"You know, that sounds extremely believable," replied Max. "God, that sort of reasoning is *so* mundane, though! Whatever happened to bringing your A-game to work? Are the architects of creation just a bunch of quiet quitters?"

"Well, you don't design a successful game by basing it around the elite one percent who finish the content faster than everyone else," said Everly. "You design it for the slovenly ninety-nine percent who take forever to do everything. You and I are clearly outliers."

"So it's not that whoever set this whole thing up is a willfully lazy piece of trash," said Max. "We're just *that* damn good?"

"Something can be two things at once," said Everly.

"I guess," Max said. "I just wish something a little more fun would happen, y'know? This just feels like bog-standard aimless wandering at this point. It feels like nothing cool has happened in ages."

Five minutes later, after the pair of them stepped through the portal and reunited with Eris, Max was beside himself with rapturous glee as he happily watched a gigantic clam monster that closely resembled a man wearing a foam costume smash its way through a city, leaving chaos and screaming citizens fleeing in the wake of its rampage.

"I take it back; I take it *all* back!" Max said, after dropping blissfully to his knees and raising his arms in praise to the sky. "We have discovered PARADISE!"

"Eris, I'm going to need an easy-to-understand explanation that avoids any pointless elaboration and just skips to the part where I learn why my elementals are living out an awesome *Super Sentai* fantasy while I've been busy risking my life searching for them in this godless void."

"Whoa!" cut in Max. "Can I just say *thank you* for emphasizing that this is a *Super Sentai* thing and not *Power Rangers*? They're two very distinct brands and it really would have grated on me if you called it that."

"Good to know," Everly nodded, before turning back to Eris. "Anyway, you were about to explain why you and Titania are playing Power Rangers?"

"Aww," said Max unhappily.

"It's not that we're playing, Everly. This is a kind of mental maze," Eris said. "A self-perpetuating labyrinth of dreams that constantly resets itself whenever my sister is on the verge of reawakening. An imprisonment created by the greater elementals themselves in order to keep us from returning to your side."

"The greater elementals?" Everly asked with a scowl. "Those so-called gods? Why would they want to keep us apart?"

"They fear your ascendency, great Everly," said Eris with a scowl of her own. "It ordinarily takes countless centuries for elementals to accumulate the level of power that Titania and I possess. Our swift growth is of course due to your guidance and training. The old ones believe that we're a threat to their dominance of the world."

"Meh, makes sense. We *are* a threat to their dominance," replied Everly. "I'm actually flattered that they've gone to these lengths to hinder me. That's called showing *respect*, Eris. And I appreciate it."

"Of course, my elders are right to fear you, Everly. You are the rising star in the darkness of the void! All eyes are drawn to your distant but beautiful light!" said Eris proudly. "Your radiance is everything!"

"Oh, I've missed your shameless fawning," Everly blushed as she kissed Eris happily on both cheeks.

"Wow, you've really got this one house-trained, huh?" Max smirked as he watched their exchange while wearing an amused expression. "Female friendship is tough to get a read on."

"Have *you* ever tried being friends with a woman?" Everly asked him.

"The one I buried alive, yeah," he replied.

"What came between you?"

"About twelve feet of soil," he said. "That's around four meters if you're Canadian."

"I'm not," she said.

"Then, yeah, about twelve feet of soil."

"Everly, who *is* this man?" Eris asked as she stared at Max with undisguised hostility. "Something about him feels . . . wrong. *Unnatural.*"

"Eris, I'm a necromancer," Everly said. "Just how twisted would someone else have to be in order for you to think that in comparison to *me*, there's something unnatural about them?"

"I don't trust him," Eris said stubbornly. "He's not one of us."

"Good. Don't. He isn't," replied Everly. "But he is my tool, so I expect you not to harm him."

"I'll do anything for your sake, Everly," Eris said fervently.

"And that had better include doing *everything* I command," Everly said firmly. "Seriously! We just reunited! Let's not fall back into old patterns."

"Oh, cool! Mecha!" shouted Max excitedly as he pointed at a shining, four-legged mechanical titan that came barreling down the road to crash into the giant clam. "Oof! Direct hit!" he said happily as the clam went down.

"Is that Titania?" asked Everly.

"She's piloting it, yes," said Eris in a chagrined voice.

"What is that?" Everly asked. "Is it a bull? No, the horns are too wide. Is that a moose? Why's her mech a giant moose?"

"It's a bull moose," Eris said reluctantly. "But for special combat situations it transforms into a more humanoid figure!"

"Really? I mean, that's cool and everything, but why start out as a moose to begin with? That feels like a really weird selection," opined Everly.

"Is this set in Canada or something?" Max asked. "They got mooses all over the place up there," he added, deliberately mispronouncing the word.

"No! The story for this scenario is set in Southern California," Eris said crossly.

"California by way of Toronto, right?" Max said with a sly grin. "You know how they like to cut production costs by shooting up north. That's basically how The CW kept itself in existence for twenty odd years!"

"NO," Eris insisted forcefully. "If anything, it's probably New Zealand. Everyone around here has that strange accent you hear when someone's deliberately trying to sound American. It's very off-putting, you can't mistake it."

"There aren't any moose in New Zealand, though," Max said.

"There actually are. They were introduced in the early twentieth century," said Everly. "I saw it on *Jeopardy!* once."

"Ken Jennings is a very well-informed man," Eris said with a nod.

"Oh, yeah. Easily the best player of all time," Max said with a nod of his own.

"Ken Jennings used to play *Jeopardy!*?" Everly asked in amazement.

"Uh, yes?" Max replied. "Dude had a seventy-four-game win streak. He's a legend. The greatest game-show player of all time."

"Wow, that's probably how he got the hosting job," Everly said thoughtfully.

"Uh, *Alex Trebek* is the host of *Jeopardy!*, dummy," Max said scathingly.

"You were locked in that temple longer than you know, bud. Alex Trebek died like *years* ago," Everly said. "It was really sad. Even I was bummed out over it."

"He's dead? Seriously? Aww!" lamented Max. "I loved that guy. Best host of anything, ever."

"And unlike the Power Rangers, he was a genuine Canadian original," said Everly.

"Wow. It's like everything comes full circle," Max said reverently.

"Anyway, let's wake up Titania and get out of here," Everly said. "I want to sleep in my real body tonight. Maybe eat some ice cream with a German name. I don't care who makes it; it'll still be delicious. Germans are great at everything. Don't make any World War II jokes, Max."

"Sorry, I thought you were setting me up for a one-liner."

"I was not. I just really want some Häagen-Dazs."

"I apologize, Everly, but we can't just take Titania," said Eris with a bowed head.

"Why not?" sighed Everly. "Please don't say there's a complication."

"Unfortunately, there *is* a complication," said Eris.

"That's exactly what I *didn't* want to hear!" whined Everly. "What's wrong now?"

"The instant this scenario is concluded, it's going to shift into something else entirely," Eris said. "The bastards won't let my sister wake up!"

"Can't you do something about it yourself?" asked Everly. "What's keeping you from snapping Titania out of it?"

"I've tried, Everly. Many, many times," Eris said bitterly. "But the safeguards the ancients left in place make it impossible for me to get through to her. I'm just not strong enough on my own to reach her mind."

"Hey, stop," Everly said as she threw an arm around her. "No feeling bad about yourself without my consent, okay? Whatever you can't accomplish on your own, we'll find a way to achieve together."

"Of course, mistress," Eris said as she leaned into Everly's shoulder. "I'm sorry for showing such weakness. I'm just so *tired* of this. I want to go home. I want us all to go home."

"Don't worry, teammate! We'll either succeed or die trying!" Max said as he joined in on the hug. "Uh, what did you say your name was again?"

"Stop touching me, you imbecilic toad," Eris snapped as she pushed Max away.

"Ow! Hey! Everly, the new girl didn't use her words!" complained Max. "I've been assaulted!"

"Okay, I can see myself quickly growing to hate this," Everly muttered to herself.

"Do I have a bruise? I have a bruise, don't I? I'm *saaaad* now!" Max cried while Eris glared at him and began squeezing her hands into tight fists.

"Just stop, already!" ordered Everly. "This is going to be easy, all right? Just trust me."

Five minutes later, in the thick of a midnight forest, the three of them were running for their lives, desperately trying to keep ahead of a chain-saw-wielding maniac who was dressed in outdated hockey apparel.

"I liked it better when it was like *Power Rangers*," huffed Max.

"Stop complaining to Everly, you spineless little trout!" shouted Eris.

"I'm not worried. I can totally fix this," Everly said, mostly to herself.

"*Choo-choo-choo-ee-ee-ee-ah-ah-ah!*" whispered the chain-saw-wielding psychopath.

CHAPTER THIRTY-ONE

Everly Lives

What's the date? Does anyone know the date?" asked Max, after they successfully reached a conveniently located log cabin and slammed the doors shut behind them.

"It's Friday, May 24, on the Earth calendar," Eris answered, after helping to shove a sofa against the entrance. "Why do you ask?"

"Oh. No reason," Max said with obvious disappointment.

"So, this is what you meant when you said the scenario would change," Everly said.

"Of course it's what she meant," said Max. "Like, word for word, this is how she described what would happen."

"Oh, shut up," Everly said. "I just didn't think it would happen this quickly, that's all. But now that I do, we can take appropriate countermeasures."

"Have you thought of a plan, mistress?" asked Eris.

"It's still coming together," replied Everly. "Just have a little faith and watch the magic happen."

"Haaa!" laughed Max. "You're so full of crap right now."

"I am not!" yelled Everly.

"You are too! You're totally winging it," Max giggled.

"Your powers of observation are as lacking as your charisma and intelligence if you believe Everly hasn't got a plan," said Eris, in defense of her leader. "The Empress has a greater tactical acumen than any of history's greatest warlords!"

"What does that have to do with avoiding a chain saw?" asked Max.

"It's not about avoiding the chain saw, worm! It's about using the chain saw to our advantage!" Eris yelled. "Everly sees ten steps ahead of everything! Even now, that psychopathic miscreant outside is stumbling into the palm of her hand. Just wait and see!"

"*Hooooly* shit, kid. This chick didn't just sip the Kool-Aid, she's injecting it with a dirty needle." Max laughed. "That's some impressive loyalty."

"Was that a compliment, Everly? It didn't feel complimentary," said Eris suspiciously.

"It wasn't and it's not," Everly said with narrowed eyes.

"Can I punish him? He seems the sort that deserves all manner of terrible afflictions."

"Don't bother; he'd only enjoy it," Everly replied sourly as she went to check a nearby window. "I don't see anyone out there. He wasn't moving that slowly, was he?"

"His gait appeared normal to me," said Eris. "Almost languid."

"That's because chain-saw-wielding freaks are never in a hurry," Max said. "They walk everywhere they go at a casual pace. It's a power flex. As if to say, *Run as fast as you like, you're not going anywhere.*"

"He's right," Everly said. "You'd know that if you watched fewer movies that focused on psychological horror and demonic possession, Eris."

"But those are my favorite kinds," Eris sulked. "Slasher films are so formulaic. If you've seen one large-breasted harlot butchered in a camp shower with her lover, then you've seen them all."

"Hey! There's more variety in the genre than you're giving it credit for," said Everly. "If the characters and stories weren't so memorable, then they wouldn't have become classics to begin with."

"If you ask me, *The Exorcist* was overrated," said Max. "Kids don't need to be possessed by fallen angels to make someone's life miserable. If anything, having the devil around is overkill. You ever try making a brat go to sleep when they aren't tired?"

"Okay, stop! We're going off topic again," Everly said. "We need to decide how we're going to awaken Titania without triggering another scenario change."

"It'll be difficult," said Eris. "First, we'll need to avoid the chain-saw guardian before we can locate her."

"Why don't we just kill it?" asked Max.

"Because defeating the guardian might trigger another change, obviously."

"Nah. Slasher killers are functionally immortal," said Max. "If we kill him, he'll just get up a few minutes later. Either that or it'll trigger a sequel."

"Oh, god, a sequel," said Everly gravely. "That wouldn't be good. An endless cycle of trotting familiar ground for diminishing returns. So many dead horses would be beaten. We can't allow that to happen."

"So, we'll either need to kill this monster in a manner that ensures he stays dead, or we need to find Titania and convince her to wake up without triggering the trap," said Eris.

"Can you imagine the possibilities, though?" Max asked in a daze.

"What possibilities?" asked Everly. "This had better not be stupid, by the way."

"It's not stupid!" said Max defensively. "It's just that the concept of slasher movies being a kind of eternal cycle of death and renewal has got me thinking about what it would be like if this were the afterlife or something to that effect."

"And why would we be in a slasher movie afterlife?" asked Everly.

"Who can say precisely why?" Max shrugged. "Maybe in the metaphysical way of it all, killers like Jason Voorhees were the good guys all along, and all of us horny camp counselors and dope-smoking rebellious youths who keep getting slaughtered are secretly baby-eating witches? Maybe the audience is deliberately being kept unaware of the facts until the final M. Night Shyamalan–ish twist at the end of the final movie."

"And what precisely fuels this theory of yours?" Everly asked reluctantly.

"Jason has the same initials as Jesus Christ," Max replied. "Haven't you ever noticed that?"

"Jason?" asked Everly.

"Yes." Max nodded.

"*Voorhees?*" chimed in Eris.

"Indeed." Max nodded.

Everly could feel a vein beginning to throb on the side of her head. "Do I really need to point out that the letters J.C. are not the same as *J. V.?*" she asked.

"Have I ever mentioned that I'm a lapsed Catholic?" Max asked.

"You're a Catholic? Really? *You?*" asked Everly doubtfully.

"Yup," asserted Max.

"Okay. If that's true, then explain the difference between a crucifix and a cross," said Everly.

"Ha! That's so easy," Max said confidently. "Any baby could do that."

"If that's true, then do it," demanded Everly.

"Everly, you sound like you want to hit me."

"I do, Max. I really, *really* do," Everly said with murderous honesty. "If you get the answer wrong, I'm gonna flatten you. It'll be a trip to the wrong side of pound town. It'll be a domestic violence call where the cops arrive too late to help. You get me?"

"Gasp! A murder-suicide?" asked Max with trepidation.

"I wouldn't kill myself after murdering you, Max," Everly said. "I'd do the very opposite. I'd go out of my way to live for as long as I possibly could so that I could relive the moment of your passing over and over again in my memories. I'd paint a mural of the event. I'd volunteer to visit kindergarten classes so I could personally pass the story down to the children."

"Wow," said Max. "You really—"

"I'd hire professional actors to do live reenactments as well as film and television versions, then I'd bribe the judges to ensure that they each won a major industry award."

"No Grammy?" asked Max.

"No, Grammys are shit," Everly said dismissively. "Oh! I'll have the date of the murder declared a major holiday and have anyone who labors on it sent to a reeducation center for crimes against the state. Is that everything I'd do? Yes. Yes, I think that's everything I'd do."

"Jason *Voorhees*, that was very thorough of you," Max said somewhat respectfully.

"Yes, I can be very exacting when the situation calls for it," replied Everly. "Now, tell me the difference between a crucifix and a cross."

"A cross is *diagonal*," snickered Max.

Everly proceeded to hit him for several minutes until she felt calmer. Then she held him in place and let Eris have a turn.

Once they were finished, she said, "All right, we need to rescue Titania and find a way out of here."

"You have no fucking sense of humor," mumbled Max as he waited for his teeth to regrow.

"Just so we're clear, I did that because *across* is *not* another word for *diagonal*," Everly informed him. "And you would have realized that if you weren't always trying to be clever."

"You still have no fucking sense of humor," repeated Max.

"How dare you complain!" Eris said angrily. "You have experienced the profound joy of receiving personal correction from the hands of our mistress! Your heart should be filled with gratitude for the experience."

"Oh, *wow*," Max said, after he finished processing that sentence. "So, you're one of *those* kinds of freaky-deaky chicks, huh? Well, that's cool. Whatever floats your boat. The world doesn't move to the beat of just one stroke."

"Excuse me?" Eris replied.

"It takes more than one stroke. It takes a bunch of strokes. And they'll form a band. And the name of the band will be *The Storks*."

"I insist you stop talking to me," said Eris.

"They have straws on their heads so they can have all kinds of adventures under the sea. Kids will love them," continued Max.

"*Snorks*," said Everly suddenly.

"Huh?" asked Max.

"You're talking about the Snorks. That's an old cartoon about tiny people with straws on their heads. *Storks* are large white birds that hospitals use to transport newly hatched progeny from the birthing chambers to the hive colonies."

"Wow. What would happen if you took one out?" asked Max.

"You'd be arrested in Oklahoma for not carrying to term."

"Ha! Shots fired at Oklahoma!" chortled Max.

"It can't be helped. They're the Oklahoma of the western United States," said Everly.

"But they literally *are* Oklahoma," said a confused Eris. "They can't help it."

"Unforgivable," Everly said darkly.

Before Max or Eris could request a little elaboration, the masked psychopath's chain saw began to slice through the cabin door.

"Oh, no! As it turns out, these aging wooden doors are no match for that fiend's chain saw! Whoever could have seen this coming?" wailed Max.

"I recommend we use this idiot as shielding, Everly," suggested Eris.

"I'll consider it," Everly replied.

"That wouldn't be very nice!" said Max.

"That would depend on your viewpoint, wouldn't it?" replied Eris.

The time would soon come for Beverly to give her speech.

She didn't want to do it. She *really* didn't want to do it. As it turned out, she hated crowds. She hated speeches. And she hated combining the two things as well.

How had things come to this? Why hadn't she just told Grail to kick rocks?

Beverly hadn't been alive as long as other people. And she didn't have as many memories of her own as she wanted. She had loads of Everly's, naturally, and if she wanted, she could borrow others from her sisters, Dullahan and Nev, thanks to the bizarre wavelength they shared between the three of them. But she was more interested in doing things to better establish her own identity as an individual. And one quirk particular to her was a preference for staying out of the spotlight.

That was mainly due to the time she'd spent masquerading as an adventurer named Lance of the Silver Lance. That had been a relatively fun experience for Beverly, but it had also taught her how exasperating it was to be an important person that people wanted to cling to.

When you were a top-tier hero, everyone wanted a piece of you. Maidens wanted to bed you (which actually wasn't that bad), merchants wanted to sell your merchandise or to sign contracts of exclusivity, jealous warriors wanted to pit themselves against you in duels of honor, and it seemed like *everyone* wanted you to save them from bandits or monsters or corrupt lords. Every day was action-packed and busy and . . . well, it was all a little too much, wasn't it?

It really was.

Beverly wasn't Everly. She wasn't Neverly. And she definitely wasn't whatever the hell Dullahan currently thought she was. Beverly was *lazy*. She avoided the things that she didn't like. Confrontations, work, daylight if it was too bright out, nighttime if it was too dark. She was a creature of moods. And the mood with her was always *eh*. Putting her in place of poor Everly was a disservice to them both.

"Grail, I've changed my mind. I really don't want to do this," she insisted one last time, after cornering him in his office.

Naturally, he ignored her.

"We've already been over this, Bev," he said with a sigh. "The empire needs you. Everly needs you. *I* need you. Put on a brave face and go do as you're told."

"Fine, I'll go out and sit in the big chair," she said. "But why do I need to speak? Let me just sit there and be aloof and silent. People like it when their authority figures seem distant and unknowable."

"They actually don't, Bev. They prefer their leaders to be approachable and humanized. It makes them feel as though they share a bond," Grail said, correcting her.

"Grail, I don't want to pretend to share a bond with that sea of faceless trash," Beverly said unhappily.

"Well, you're going to and that's the end of the discussion. Now's not the time for selfishness, girl. It's about time you started carrying your own weight. Everly's not here to coddle you anymore," Grail said sternly.

"Uh, bitch, *what?*" Beverly said in surprise.

"You heard me," Grail replied, now glaring at her. "Beverly, you're a useless slug who contributes nothing to the cause. You haven't so much as exited the memory palace in months. You wield more of Everly's power and authority than the rest of the inner circle combined, but you do *nothing* with it! There must come a time in everyone's life where they're forced to choose whether they'll step up and become an adult or wither away, wasting their potential in perpetual infancy. And I'm sorry to tell you this, but for you, that moment has arrived."

Beverly blinked several times at his words. Then clucked her tongue and nodded to herself. "Hmm," she said, as though she'd been given a lot to think about. A lot of food for thought. A new perspective to consider.

Then she grabbed Grail by his collar to pull him toward her and headbutted him as hard as she could. While blood spurted from his nose and he slumped to his knees in a daze, Beverly spun and slammed him against a wall as hard as she could.

The thud he made upon impact was very soothing, so she didn't follow it up by tearing his head from his shoulders. But it was a near thing. Instead, as he lay gasping on his stomach, she flipped him over with a kick and took a cross-legged seat on his torso so she could look down on him.

"The fake human got a little cocky because he got to push little Claudia around some, and *now* he thinks he has the right to tell *me* what to do? *Wowsers.* That's almost too funny to be true," she said to him perkily.

"I was doing . . . nothing of the sort," Grail said sluggishly. "Just . . . trying to make you understand."

Beverly tipped her head to the side in puzzlement.

"But that's the issue, isn't it, bucko? You don't get to *make* me do anything. I'm Beverly of Everly. I'm her with a lime twist! Sure, I'm not as strong as she is, but I'm still more powerful *than you will ever be.* Your body will never be able to adapt enough to take the punishment I can deal you, so stop being an asshole *and stop telling me what to do!*"

"I'm sorry for offending you," Grail said, between bloodied lips. "It wasn't my intention."

"Yeah? Well intentions and outcomes can differ wildly when one isn't careful with their words," Bev said to him as she leaned over to flick his nose.

"You really do sound just like her right now," Grail said.

"Huh?" Beverly asked in surprise.

"Making an example of me like this. Acting with such cruelty for such a profoundly selfish reason. This is very much an Everly play," he said.

"Really?" Bev said. She had to admit she found the comparison oddly flattering.

"I wouldn't lie about such a thing," Grail said. "In this moment, painful as the experience has been, I feel strangely comforted to know that her spirit endures through you, Beverly. Again, I apologize for speaking out of place."

"Oh, well, I mean, you were just trying to . . . I don't know, do something good for the empire or whatever," Bev said as she stood up and helped him get to his feet. "No harm, no foul."

"All the same, I would feel so much better if you were there to deliver the speech at the assembly," Grail said reluctantly. "Beverly, if this moment has taught me anything, it's that Everly lives on through *you.* How can we possibly deny the people the opportunity to experience her greatness? I beg of you; you *must* be her messenger!"

"I mean . . . I dunno, I just . . ." waffled Beverly.

Grail grabbed her hand and knelt before her reverently. "My lady, the flock *needs* your guidance."

"Ahhhhh, okay," Bev finally said with closed eyes.

"Wonderful! Absolutely wonderful, thank you *so much,*" Grail said happily as he gave her a quick hug and guided her toward the exit. "With that settled, I'll get back to work on your speech."

"Maybe I could help write it?" Beverly suggested as he pushed her into the hallway.

"Oh, no, that won't be necessary, see you on the big day, thanks again," Grail said quickly as he closed and barred his office door.

Bev stood in front of it for some time as she collected her thoughts.

Then she quietly said, "*Fuck*," with all the bitterness in the world of one who has been thoroughly outplayed.

"Hey, I don't want to sound like I'm worried or anything, but Chain-Saw Charlie is nearly through the door," Max said loudly. "I mean, I don't really care if either of you die, but I feel like life still has so much left to offer me."

"Shut up, Max, I'm still thinking," replied Everly.

"Uh, unless those thoughts include the sentence *Holy shit, I'm about to get carved up by a chain saw*, then I fail to see how they're relevant to my situation," said Max.

"Mistress, does he really talk to you like this all the time?" said Eris in shock.

"Only on days that end with *y*," glowered Everly.

"Now, *why* would you say a thing like that?" asked Max.

Everly refused to take the bait. There were more important things happening right now. She didn't know quite what, but it was at the tip of her tongue. A solution was at hand. An *obvious* solution. But she had to think.

"Max, transform and distract him for a bit, will you? I'm trying to organize my thoughts," she commanded him.

"Distract him? How am I supposed to do that?" he asked.

"You're an axe and he has a chain saw. This is a grudge match that's been waiting to happen for decades, isn't it? Show him what you're made of!" said Everly.

"I'm sorry, what? Max is a what?" asked a confused Eris.

"Ah. Well, when you put it *like that*," Max said enthusiastically, before shedding his outer form and transforming into his weapon mode. "To arms! To arms! Although, technically, I have no arms, nyur-hur-hur!"

And with that, Max flew through the air to clash against the slasher's chain saw while Eris stared at them. In the meanwhile, Everly sat down on the floor to focus and tried to drown out the noise.

"Everly! Was that idiot an inanimate object all along?" asked Eris.

"Object, yes. Inanimate, no," Everly replied.

"Where did you find him?" Eris asked.

"It's a long story, Eris. I really don't want to go over it right now," Everly said.

"I'm sorry, Everly, it's just that—"

"Eris! Stop talking!" Everly shouted in frustration as she waved a hand and dismissed her elemental servant's physical form. Immediately, Eris vanished from sight as her mind resumed its place in Everly's psyche.

As soon as she felt Eris return within her, Everly realized what she had to do next.

"AH! This is bad! This is very, very bad!" Max shouted as the slasher used his weight to bear down on the axe and force him toward the floor. "Everly!

EVERLY! As it turns out, there was no contest to be had here, *chain saws* have the advantage! Who would have *known*? Anyway, this is about to turn into that annoying scene from *Saving Private Ryan* where the ungrateful German guy slowly stabs the New Yorker to death while that spindly little creep that no one likes is hiding behind the door bawling his heart out because he's a weak little baby who's too terrified to act, so if you'd like to avoid losing your super-unique and impossible-to-replace divine armament, PLEASE GIVE ME A FUCKING HAND!"

Everly laughed at his desperation before holding out a hand and summoning him to her before the slasher could cut him in half. "Ha! Look at that. Max the axe isn't quite as fearless as he pretends, is he?" she grinned.

Before he could respond, she suddenly threw the axe across the room, where its blade lodged into the slasher's head. The killer stopped in his tracks and stared blankly ahead before numbly dropping his weapon and collapsing in a heap to the ground.

"Got 'em," Everly purred.

She then stood before her fallen opponent and pulled Max free. Then she lopped the creature's head off at the neck.

"Okay, not that I didn't enjoy doing that, but what happened to capturing this guy alive so we could go look for your other elemental?" Max asked.

"There's no need," Everly said triumphantly as she tapped the side of her head. "I'd forgotten that Eris and Titania share a spiritual bond that connects them to each other mentally. That's how Eris was trapped here, even though Titania was the one who was dreaming."

"*Okaaaay?*" said Max as he waited for further elaboration.

"Basically, it means where one of them goes, the other must eventually follow, unless I say otherwise. My mistake was thinking that I needed to locate Titania even though I already had Eris, when the solution was as simple as reclaiming Eris to force Titania to follow. By taking one, I automatically get both. Now Titania's back with me where she belongs, and I'm gently waking her up while shielding her from this environment with my mind even as I'm delivering this exposition to you."

"Ah. Psychic shit," Max said.

"Yep. Psychic shit," agreed Everly.

"So, what's going to happen next?"

"Now that I've finally regained my elementals, I'm going to purge myself of all the excessive power that's keeping me from waking up. Then, hopefully, I'll either regain consciousness in my bed, probably with you by my side, or I'll explode in a dazzling wave of heat and light that will kill everyone and everything around me. Not that I'd care, because I'd be dead, and existence has no meaning if I'm not there to enjoy it."

"Meh, sounds fair to me," said Max.

"All right, no more talking," Everly said as she sat in a lotus pose and closed her eyes to focus. "This is going to take a lot of concentration, okay?"

"Oh, relax, will you?" said Max. "I once learned the secrets of inner harmony from an enlightened axe guru. I can feel the motions of the universe from the center of my navel and all that. I can easily stay silent for ages."

"If that's true, then I'd really appreciate it if you'd start now," Everly said.

Max said nothing in reply.

It somehow felt very sarcastic.

Around them, the dusty cabin began to fade away from sight as Everly drew on the power within herself and began to unmoor from the abyss. Within moments of beginning, she found herself floating upward toward the sky, drifting farther and farther away from the realm that she'd wandered for what felt like an eternity.

Soon, a sense of warmth began to surround her. A familiar sense of comfort and safety that she'd almost forgotten about during her journey. Below her, the abyss, which had once seemed to stretch into eternity, became smaller than the head of a pin as she floated upward to her destination.

Home.

Everly was finally home.

With a start, she opened her eyes and sat up in bed.

Choo-choo-choo-choo-ee-ee-ee-ee-ah-ah-ah-ah!

That was when Everly noticed that she was covered in blood. Startled, she turned her head and saw Seraphine desperately reaching for her while gasping for air. Her other hand covered her wounded throat with blood streaming between her fingers.

Behind her stood the slasher, holding his chain saw above his head. He knocked Seraphine aside before bringing it down on Everly's head, slowly sawing it in half as she screamed in pain, her blood gushing everywhere as she was sundered.

With a start, she opened her eyes and sat up in bed.

"Everly?" said Seraphine in surprise, before she threw her hands around her and began shouting in joy. "Everly! Everly, you're awake!"

Fucking slasher movies, Everly thought with annoyance as Seraphine continued to happily babble away.

In hindsight, she really should have seen that coming. There was always a jump scare at the end.

CHAPTER THIRTY-TWO

Perspective

Everly felt touched by the general reaction of her crew to her awakening. She'd expected there to be some excitement, of course. After all, she was Everly; *everyone* loved having her around. Who wouldn't?

But actual, heartfelt, emotions? Tears of joy? Genuine happiness?

That surprised her.

When had these idiots become her family?

Out of all of them, Beverly in particular was absolutely ecstatic to see her moving again. "Baaaabe, welcome back to the land of the living! Don't you ever leave us again," she said as she barraged Everly with kisses and hugs, competing with Seraphine to see who could smother her the most in their embrace. "I'm serious! I will totally murder you if you even think about slipping into another coma. *Murder* you, Everly! It's not a threat! It's a promise! I love you so much!"

"Hey, hey! Let her breathe, you lunatic! I was the one standing vigil over her night and day, waiting for my beloved to return to me," cut in Seraphine. "And I'm so glad I did! Everly, I've missed you so much! Please take better care of yourself! Seeing you in such a state was so frightening."

"You really did all that?" Everly asked in surprise.

"Of course I did!" Seraphine replied. "You and I are committed to each other. When one of us languishes, so does the other! I know you would do the same thing for me if our positions were ever reversed."

"Yeah," said Everly slowly. "Totally . . ."

"I knew it," Seraphine said happily. "Ever since you came into my life, it's been one miracle after another." Grasping Everly's hand, she placed it tightly against her chest and held it in place. "Do you feel that my love? That's my *heartbeat*. And it beats only for you! I would happily die for you, Everly. I'd kill for you. And if we were ever separated, I'd kill myself! Everything is for you, my love!"

"Oh, wow, that's *so* much to take in right now," replied Everly.

Jason Voorhees, boss! Where did you find this dingbat? asked a voice that she'd longed to hear once more.

Be kind, Titania. This is my significant other, she said mentally.

Significant other? Was that a good choice? She seems about as stable as a Glenn Close character from the eighties, chirped Titania. *Y'know, the kind you'll have to drown in a bathtub before she sticks you with a kitchen knife.*

I don't see anything wrong with how she's behaving, said Eris. *This level of adoration and devotion seems utterly appropriate to me.*

Okay, that's a recommendation you can rely on right there, said Titania sarcastically. *If Eris approves, then there's no way this lady isn't a nutbar you should lock the cutlery away from.*

Who are you to question my approval? You spent the last year of your life living out graphic novel fantasies and reenacting genre films and television. You're the one who needs to get it together!

Yeah, it was awesome, Titania said gleefully.

It was NOT awesome! said Eris. *In fact, it was the ordeal of my life!*

Shut up, you loved it!

I did not!

C'mon, let me hear you say Sunflower Force forever!

Everly! I insist you punish my sister at once!

Did you show her your bat robot?

EVERLY!

Everly leaned back in bed and smiled.

She really had missed this.

Still, not everything was as pleasant as receiving the affection of her well-wishing friends. There were other things she had to see sorted out. Unpleasant things, although it pained her to have to do it.

"Matty, stop," she commanded the happy, fat rat, which scurried into her lap and began nuzzling her affectionately, seeking to get his tummy rubbed.

"Matty, I said stop! I'm very upset with you right now. This is *serious* business," Everly said, although she couldn't resist giving him a gentle squeeze.

"Huh?" Matty asked, confused. "Hey, boss, did I do something wrong?"

"Yes, Matty!" Everly said. She scratched under his chin a little bit before she could help herself but then regained control and continued. "You were spying on me for the seven kings."

"Uh-huh." Matty nodded while trying to get her to scratch him some more.

"Matty, that's a bad thing! I'm very disappointed in you!" Everly said sternly.

"Why?" asked Matty with genuine puzzlement. "They gave me a big wedge of cheese. Sharp cheddar. It was awesome."

"Matty, I could have given you all the cheese you wanted myself, you precious little dope," Everly said in exasperation. "You didn't need to betray state secrets for it! That was a no-no!"

"A-are you mad at me?" he asked as he hid his face behind his adorable little paws.

"Yes! I'm very upset!" Everly insisted, although her heart broke a little at his reaction. "I'm afraid I'm going to have to confiscate your cheese wedge. You're also confined to a hamster cage for a week. And I expect you to use that exercise wheel for at least ten minutes a day! I'm concerned about your weight!"

"Everly, noooo!" wept Matty. "I swear I'll repent! I'll do good! I'm so sorry!"

"So am I, Matty. So am I. But when it comes to keeping order, the heart of an empress must at times be colder than a glacier," Everly said somberly as she signaled for her black knights to take the prisoner away.

"Everly!" Matty cried out one last time. "*Eveeeeerly!*"

"I guess that's what he gets for *ratting* you out," Max snickered from where he leaned against the wall beside her bed. He'd been the last of the four escapees from the abyss to appear. One moment he hadn't been there, and the next, it was as if he'd been around all day.

"Could you not?" Everly said. "Matty is a good boy. He's a good, *good* boy. But he's literally an animal. He doesn't quite process concepts like treachery. As far as he's concerned, anyone who feeds him and plays with him is a good person, no matter what they ask of him."

"That's gotta be the case if a person like *you* is who he reveres." Max smirked.

"I'm a wonderful person who deserves his unconditional loyalty," asserted Everly calmly.

"Of course you are," Max said with no resistance. "Although, if I might offer some advice for future dealings? Never trust anyone named Matt or any talking rodents. You never know when either of them will turn on you."

"Okay, I can believe you about having problems with someone named Matt, but that remark about the talking rodents seems awfully on the nose," Everly said with a frown.

"*Honeydew Meadow*," said Max with a haunted look in his eyes.

"Excuse me?" Everly said in annoyance.

"Nothing; nothing at all," he said in a distant voice.

"Okay, whatever, get out of here and take your insane rambling with you," Everly said impatiently as she pulled her covers over her head. "I'm still recovering from being catatonic, and I need my twelve hours of sleep. Go introduce yourself to everyone else. Except Grail. Leave Grail alone."

"Aww, Grail's the one I've been wanting to meet the most," said Max. "I heard he likes swinging around an axe."

"Yeah, it's a thing he's known for," said Everly from beneath a pillow.

"Well, he's gonna have to be known for something else now. I'm the axe guy. I mean, I'm literally an axe. Rhymes with my name and everything."

"I'm sure you two can work something out."

"I'm sure we can."

"Please keep in mind that I like him much better than you," Everly warned him. "Just in case you're thinking of behaving like yourself."

"How much better?" Max asked curiously.

"*SO* much better."

"Well, all righty, then," Max said as he sauntered toward the exit. "G'night, princess."

"That's EMPRESS to you," she said as the halls within the memory palace darkened and a bolt of lightning crashed angrily in the horizon.

"Didn't I say that?" he asked as he closed the door behind himself.

Once in the halls, Max took a look around his new surroundings and gave a low whistle of appreciation. "Huh. So, this is a memory palace, eh? *Faaaancy.*"

The only place that Max had ever personally seen that was comparable to the memory palace had been the palatial home of the goddess of all four seasons, back on the world he had previously lived in. Everly's home would have found no shame in comparison to that place.

"Maybe I should map out a place of my own in the astral sea," he said to himself as he explored. "It really seems like real estate is where I should start focusing. I wonder how many cubic feet this place consists of. I wonder if they manufacture cubic feet in Cuba. Can I import that or is there still a trade embargo going on? I wonder if—"

"Max. We'd like to have a little word with you if you don't mind?" said a voice he didn't recognize.

Startled from his reverie, Max looked up to see three people facing him in the hall, flanked by a squad of those fancy-looking black knights. Eris he instantly recognized. But the taller-looking woman with similar features he couldn't quite place a name to. She didn't feel human, though. Was this Titania?

The male who stood between them he recognized straightaway. He didn't know his name or anything, but he was the same sort of creature that Max had spent the entirety of his life resenting, antagonizing, and occasionally destroying whenever the urge became too hard to resist.

He was an *authority figure.*

"Heeeey," Max said with a friendly smile as he ran a hand over his tangly hair to smooth it back. "I'm new to the team. So very happy to meet ya."

"Just come with us, please," the man said as he gestured for Max to follow.

"Do I have a choice?" Max asked as his grin grew even wider.

"What do you think?" the man said curtly as he turned away.

More black knights stepped behind Max. One of them placed a warning hand on his shoulder. Max's eyes widened slightly.

Then they sharply narrowed.

"Lead the way, officer," he said as they guided him to their destination.

"Max, I'm going to be frank with you," Grail said from behind his desk as Max sat before him, flanked on either side by Eris and Titania in his office.

"Okay," Max said. "I'm going to stay Max, though, okay?"

Grail sighed deeply to himself before continuing. "Ah, yes. There's that sense of humor I heard about from Lady Eris. Very dry."

"You should drink some water, then," Max suggested.

"That won't be necessary," Grail said. "Now, as I was saying, I'm afraid there isn't going to be a place for you within our organization."

"Oh? Do tell," Max said as he leaned back in his seat and steepled his fingers.

"I just did," Grail said with a hard look on his face. "You'll be leaving us today. On behalf of the Empress, I appreciate the aid you provided her during her long journey back to us, but your services are no longer required."

"Men don't have cervices," Max said. "I learned that in medical school."

"You went to medical school?" asked Titania.

"Sure did. Or maybe I cut someone at a school once, I dunno. It's all hard to keep track of."

"Absolutely pathetic," Eris said with a sneer. "Just get rid of him, Grail."

"Are we being fair, though?" asked Titania. "He helped Everly out, didn't he? And she said he could come with us."

"Everly doesn't always base her decision-making on logic," Grail said. "On those occasions, it's for the best that we intervene. That's something we all decided long ago."

"Yeah, but she *really* hates it whenever we do that," said Titania with a conflicted look on her face. "Whenever she finds out about it, it never ends well for anybody."

Heh, look at this big softy. Max smirked to himself.

"This isn't personal, Max," Grail said. "Our organization already has its share of . . . unique personalities. But even compared to them, Lady Eris insists that you are an extreme case. We don't know enough about you, and that's reason enough for us not to trust you."

"Everly and I have a deal. Bonded in blood and death. We've walked together and killed together, and according to rules older than most civilizations, that makes us one. You don't get to tell me to leave, boy," Max said in a matter-of-fact manner.

"You'll be paid however much gold you want, and we'll open a portal for you to anywhere you'd like to go," Grail continued, ignoring what the other man had said. "In return we only ask that you depart quietly and never seek to return."

"Anywhere I want?" Max asked consideringly.

"Anywhere," affirmed Grail.

"*Anywhere?*" repeated Max.

"I've already confirmed that," Grail said, frowning. "Now decide."

"Well, hey! Good news, hoss!" Max said cheerfully. "As it turns out, I'm already exactly where I want to be. Isn't that great? I just saved you a bunch of money and a wasted portal. That's pretty nice of me, isn't it?"

"Max, I'm not certain you understand the situation you're in," Grail said.

"Oh, I think I understand the situation perfectly, shithead. *You're* the one who doesn't seem to get how things are going to be from now on," Max said with his hungry, empty little smile.

He then grabbed the sides of his chair and dragged it closer to Grail's desk so that he could sit with his feet propped disrespectfully upon it.

"I get it, kids, I really do," he continued. "Your mama just brought a new man into the house, and now you're feeling upset and confused and wondering how things are going to be. Well, let me assure you all: I don't give a *fuck* about any of you. Not a single solitary thrust of my sexy, narrow hips. You little shits can keep doing your thing, and I'll do mine, and we'll try to stay out of each other's way, okay? Don't make your new daddy take off his belt."

"You arrogant little piece of trash," Grail said as he rose from his seat.

"I guess this wasn't the wrong thing to do after all," Titania said as her eyes began sparking with an ominous, destructive light.

"I prefer it this way," Eris said eagerly. "No fuss, no muss, no body."

"It's a nervous bitch who barks the loudest, sweetie," Max said to her.

"Those will be your last words," Eris promised him. "I'm going to tear your mind open and expose your wounded soul to the horrors of the void. There aren't words to describe the hell you're about to experience."

"You sure you wanna do that?" asked Max. "It's your call, but I wouldn't recommend crawling around in my head—aw, you did it anyway. That was pretty dumb of you."

Eris screamed. A sound so unexpected and unthinkable for anyone that knew her that it startled everyone in the room except the still-seated Max. While Grail and Titania rushed to her side, he leaned back and laughed deeply and cruelly, enjoying the sight of the spirit elemental vomiting on the floor and shaking from the sheer horror of what she had just witnessed.

"WHAT DID YOU DO TO MY SISTER?!" bellowed the outraged Titania as she began stomping toward him. As she approached, the room tremored and quaked with her anger.

"Nothing deliberate," Max tittered. "My mind's an open book; I promise it is. Anyone can come inside and have a look if they want. But most people who do have . . . *difficulty* understanding the way I see the world. My viewpoint troubles them just like it troubled poor Eris. It's a real party in my head."

"Bastard!" Titania swore as she raised a fist that trembled with power, rage, and the desire to smite. She then aimed it squarely at Max's head with the full intent to destroy him, only to stare in surprise when he lazily lifted his hand and received her blow in his palm.

Despite her nearly limitless strength, Max didn't move an inch.

"We done?" he asked her with an exaggerated yawn.

"What are you?" she asked him.

"The new guy," he sneered.

"Whatever you may be, whatever your tricks, monster, I *can* destroy you," Titania warned him. "If I exercise the utmost limits of my power, I will *obliterate* you."

"Oh, that is *scary*," he replied. "Sounds like a real problem for me. But I bet it'd be an even *bigger* problem for *them*, wouldn't it?" he asked as he tilted his head toward Grail as he tried to assist the sobbing Eris. "Them and everyone else you love. A planet's ecology is far more delicate than most people realize. The kind of tectonic rampage you're talking about unleashing isn't very conducive to maintaining a little thing I like to call *surface life*. And you're still assuming I couldn't kill you first."

"Go ahead and try. I *dare* you!" Titania said furiously.

"Don't wanna," said Max. "Whether you like it or not, girl, Everly and I are partners. *Equal partners*. That makes all of us family. Family should try to get along."

"You'll never be kin of ours," Titania vowed.

"I might grow on you if you give me a chance," he said.

"It'll never happen," she promised.

"Sounds like a *challenge*." He winked.

They continued staring at each other for some time. Him while wearing a dissembling grin, and her with a glare filled with anger and suspicion. Eventually she pulled her hand away and returned to her sister's side.

"Eris had better be okay," she warned him.

"Ah, just give her mind some time to bleach out what she saw. Shouldn't take a big brain like hers more than a few hours," Max assured her as he rose from his seat.

"Where do you think you're going?" Grail said as he moved to cut off Max's exit. "We're not finished here."

"Are you sure?" Max said sleepily. "Feels like we are."

Grail's expression grew thunderous as he prepared to transform, only to be stopped when Titania placed a hand on his shoulder and shook her head.

"Don't," she warned him. "He's too much for you."

"Yeah, Grail, *don't*. I'm too much for you," Max said mockingly to him.

"This isn't over. I promise you it isn't," Grail said as Max brushed past him, ignoring him completely.

"Damn it," he swore after the other man left. "We're going to need to deal with him somehow. This *can't* be allowed to continue."

"I'm all for suggestions," Titania said as she held her sister's head. "Have you got any?"

Grail said nothing in response. Instead, he silently clenched his fists in anger. *Helpless* anger.

CHAPTER THIRTY-THREE

Turn Thy Head

Not long after Max left, Everly fell into a deep slumber, during which she dreamed.

In that dream, she found herself in the midst of a deep forest that she didn't recognize, and Everly met an armored man sitting on a small rock, who appeared to be waiting for her.

He was a handsome, blond-haired fellow with one eye covered in a black eye patch. His gleaming white armor reminded Everly of the equipment she'd seen paladins wearing. It was flawlessly pristine, unmarred by scratches or dents. As though it were ceremonial and had never been put to practical use.

"Well, how about that? You really are alive! Isn't that something?" the stranger asked with a voice that exuded good-natured cheer. He rose from the rock he'd been sitting on and came closer to Everly, stopping a few inches from her so that he could take a good look at her.

"You're so different from the other ones," he said. "Not a hint of the corruption. You're so pretty too. I wasn't expecting that. By this point in your lifespan, you should be exhibiting all kinds of symptoms of your illness. Could it be you've somehow cured yourself?"

The stranger removed one of his gauntlets and placed his hand against Everly's cheek as he examined her. The touch of his palm against her skin was startlingly cold, but Everly, for whatever reason, found the contact pleasant. They stood there for some time gazing at each other until Everly broke the silence.

"Who are you?"

"Someone who's very tired, Everly," he replied. "Someone who's walked too long and seen too much hard road and now only wants a place where he can lay his weary head to rest."

"You sound troubled by your experiences," she said. "A lot of people love to go on a long journey. To see new things and meet new people, every day a new experience. I'd like that."

"New things are often enticing, but our infatuation with them rarely lasts," he said. "Take it from a jaded old wanderer. As time goes by, the only thing we truly crave is the familiarity of the past."

"How old could you possibly be?" she asked him.

"Old enough to suffer, which is plenty old enough," he said. He returned to the rock and resumed sitting on it while gesturing to a nearby tree stump. "Won't you please take a seat? I think we have much to discuss."

"A gentleman would have waited until I was seated first before sitting down," Everly said lightly as she sat on the stump. "Shouldn't a man presenting himself as a knight have better manners?"

"That's behavior befitting the presence of a lady, not a vicious warlord," he replied in just as light a tone. "Besides, I sat first to show trust. A seated person is more vulnerable than one who stands. I was politely letting you know that I'm no threat to you."

"Perhaps," said Everly. "Or perhaps you were hinting that I'm no threat to you and sat first to show your lack of fear in my presence. Is that what you're doing, Sir Knight? Are you *flexing* on me?"

"Would you like me to? I possess an excellent physique," he replied.

"Mine's better. I worked harder for it," bragged Everly.

"Mine's more practical," he argued. "Plus, you're young, so you probably don't think of the necessity of stretching and warming up before doing your daily activities. When you reach my age, limberness is something you need to work on in order to keep it."

"How old are you?" she wondered.

"Technically, I'm the same age as you," he admitted. "But I have more lived experience."

"Doing *what?*" she scoffed.

"Surviving," he said grimly.

"Sounds like life's been hard for you," she said.

"Honestly, it's been the worst," he said. "I hate myself. I hate who I am, what I've done, what I *will* do. Every action I've ever taken has been an unavoidable necessity, but I *grieve* for having to resort to them. A just hand is not necessarily a kind one. I sincerely wish that the circumstances surrounding my deeds would allow me to be a kinder man."

In response, Everly burst into a fit of uncontrollable laughter. The stranger stared at her in bewilderment as she fell off the tree stump and rolled back and forth on her sides in childish mockery of his sincerity.

"I'm sorry, did I say something funny?" he asked her as he began to feel a touch offended.

"*Everything* you just said was funny," chortled Everly as she rubbed her aching belly. "Oh, shit, you . . . you have a really romanticized view of yourself, don't you? You're painting yourself as a tragic victim of fate, but honestly, you sound more to me like some sort of salesman."

"I thought we were sharing an intimate moment," the knight said with disappointment evident in his voice. "This is an important moment. A meeting between foes should be filled with honesty and respect."

"Mmm, no," Everly said with a firm shake of her head. "Honesty and respect between opponents? That sounds like chivalry."

"That's exactly what it is," said the knight.

"Well, that's the problem right there. Concepts like chivalry in the west or Bushido in the east were designed to benefit the ruling class by controlling the conduct of their fighters. There's no expectation for a leader like me to believe in or respect such things. It's a manual for producing malleable schmucks."

"That's a very cynical way of looking at things," he said disapprovingly.

"A knight's job was to unquestioningly kill whoever his lord told him to. Convincing him that there was a proper and honorable way of going about pillaging villages and burning down castles was mostly for the sake of convenances. As long as he didn't think he was a monster doing monstrous things, he could keep living with himself. I don't have any obligation to humor that sort of delusion. Anyone who idealizes the idea of knighthood thinks too highly of themselves."

"Well, shoot," said the knight. "Way to take the fun out of things, Little Miss Amorality. Want to tell some preschoolers what happened to the natives after the first Thanksgiving while you're busy being an absolute buzzkill?"

"Don't think I wouldn't in a heartbeat," she said smugly.

Now they both laughed.

"All right," he said, a short while after they'd both settled themselves. "I think I have a feel for you now."

"A lot of people have thought that before," she said.

"And ended up dead for it?" he asked.

"Well, I wasn't going to say that part aloud," she said demurely.

"Point taken."

"Who are you, anyway?" she finally asked.

"You seriously don't have guesses?" He smiled. "Come on, I know you've got one or two in you. Let me hear it."

"First tell me your name," she said.

"James," he said promptly.

"First tell me your *real* name," she said, correcting herself.

"Ha," he chuckled. "I'm Evan."

"What's your last name, Evan?" she asked, although she already knew the answer.

"Skolder," he said with an insolent smirk.

"You're not an unknown brother that I'm meeting for the first time, are you? A surprise evil twin?"

"What the heck makes you think *I'd* be the evil twin?" He laughed.

"Well, that's fair," she had to admit.

"But no, I'm not one of your brothers. Caleb's fine, by the way. I'll release him once all of this is over with."

"Something happened to Caleb?" she asked with genuine surprise.

"Good lord, you're awful," he said with a despairing shake of his head.

"Okay, so you're not a relative, but you look like me and you have the same last name," Everly said thoughtfully. "I don't suppose one of my damn duplicates created another male husk to pilot around, did they? Are you another Lance?"

"Nope. I'm not a duplicate of any kind," he assured her.

Everly thought about it some more. Then she snapped a finger once the answer came to her. "Ah! Got it! You're an invader from an alternative universe. HA! That is so freakin' cool! You're a bizarro me! You're Bizarvely!"

"My name is Evan," he said with a frown.

"You sure you don't want to be Bizarvely?" she asked hopefully. "It really rolls off the tongue once you get used to it."

"I'll stick with what I have, thanks," he said.

"You're no fun," she sulked.

"I'm a lot of fun," he said in a wounded voice. "People love being around me."

"That can't be true. I haven't heard you use any foul language since we've met. People don't feel comfortable around men who don't curse."

"Gutter language is for gutter people, Everly," he said primly.

"Oh, it's just as I feared," said Everly sadly. "You're definitely an asshole."

Evan sighed and hung his head back to stare at the sky. "This really isn't going how I imagined it would."

"I guess you don't have as much experience being around me as you think you do." She laughed.

"You're not quite correct, by the way," he said.

"About what?"

"About what I am. About *who* I am. You're closer than you realize, but you're not quite there yet. I'll explain later if you're still curious. Or alive."

"Heh, funny," she said mirthfully. "Why have you called me out here, anyway?"

"Well, I wanted to meet you," he replied. "And I wanted to apologize for that little incident with Hades. The shadowy little guy with all the eyes and teeth? I use him to keep track of things in the realms beyond. I guess he happened to find your location and went all *Broken Arrow* on you."

"That Hades creature belonged to you?" Everly asked with narrowing eyes.

"Afraid so. Poor fella was just a miserable collection of aborted emptiness. One of those things that's too ugly and unnatural to be a real part of creation. He and I had a lot in common with each other, so he liked to follow my lead. Imagine my surprise when I realized that you and your new friend, Max, sent him to what lies beyond."

"Oh? Any harsh feelings over it?" asked Everly.

"Not really, no. Alive or dead, it's all the same to a thing like that," replied Evan. "Another one will come along soon enough. All the broken, ugly things in creation end up in my hands sooner or later."

"So, you're saying you didn't tell that thing to kill me?" asked Everly.

"Oh, no, I certainly did." He smiled. "Seemed a good opportunity. I didn't realize at the time that you were as capable as I am. Most of the Everlys I've met have been vapid, arrogant things. Useless and deluded. You're that rare percentage of a percentage that can actually back up your narcissistic self-regard with action."

"I don't know if I should feel complimented by that or not," Everly said cautiously. "I mean, it's pleasing to know that I'm better than most versions of myself, but the way you said it implies that most versions of myself are some manner of *loser*."

"Oh, dear, I think she's catching on," said Evan.

"I'm going to let that slide for now, but we'll return to it later, so prepare your bones, okay? There *will* be fractures. Anyway, what's with the setting for this dream? Why are we deep in the woods?" she asked next.

"Symbolism!" Evan said. "It's not the woods, Everly, it's *the wilderness*."

"Okay," said Everly. "Why are we in the wilderness?"

"Come on, Everly!" Evan encouraged her. "Don't you remember your Scriptures? Think of the book of Matthew."

Everly closed her eyes to focus. Although she'd been an irreligious person in her previous life, the private school she attended had a requirement for mandatory study of the Christian faith. As a result, she had a fairly extensive knowledge of the Scriptures even though she hadn't thought of them in years.

"Let's see, the book of Matthew. That covers a bunch of stuff. Can I have a hint?"

"Instant weight loss," he said.

"Ahhh." Everly nodded. "Instant weight loss. You mean fasting. Like when Jesus fasted for forty days in the wilderness and then was tempted by the . . . oh, wow. Wow, you really are nuts, Evan."

"You think so?" he asked. "I thought I was being clever."

"Come on, man. Do you honestly expect me to believe that you're the devil?" Everly snorted.

"That would hurt my feelings beyond measure if you did," he said sincerely. "No, Everly. Of course I'm not the devil in this scenario. That would be *you*, silly."

"Oh, fuck. Eviler me has messianic delusions," said Everly.

"I'm *not* evil, Everly. Not even close," Evan said. "I'm proactive salvation. Instead of being tempted, I'm the one who wants to tempt *you*. Leave this world, Everly. Go back to Earth. Take everything you've acquired here with you. You may keep your magic, your servants, your palace, everything you've rightfully earned. Just take them and go home. Doesn't that sound wonderful?"

"And how am I supposed to do that?" asked Everly.

"It's within my power to open portals to other realms. I can do this for you as well," he said. "Go back to Earth. Remake it into a land of fantasy and adventure just like you craved as a child. Be the change that want to see done! In turn . . . just leave this world alone."

"That *is* tempting," Everly said, after musing over the deal.

"It's everything you've ever wanted," Evan assured her. "Just say yes."

"The only problem is that I already have a nation under my boot," replied Everly. "With more soon to follow. And if I'm being honest, Evan, I don't feel any significant level of power emanating from you. I bet if I were to call up that stupid system screen and perform an assessment on you, it'd tell me that I'm a lot stronger than you are, aren't I?"

Evan said nothing in reply. He sat there silently, waiting for her to continue.

"So, if I'm stronger than you, and have armies at my command and a nation that loves me enough to elevate me to godhood, why should *I* be the one to leave? If crossing dimensions is something a weak little thing like you can do, then I'll undoubtedly acquire that power for myself in time. So the answer is no. I decline your temptation, Saint Evan."

"Everly, I really wish you'd reconsider," he said.

"I'm not going to," she said. "When I make up my mind, it's made up."

"Yeah, I know," he said ruefully as he stood up. "It just would have been nice to avoid this part for once."

"You seem so sure of yourself," she said with a shake of her head. "It's going to be a real pleasure tearing that certainty away from you."

"Maybe," he said. "I guess we won't have to wait long to find out."

"I guess not," she replied.

"See you there in the real world, Everly. I really did enjoy our talk."

"I did too, Evan. Hey, if I'm really the devil in your scenario, then should I be allowed to tempt you as well?"

"I guess that's fair," he said with a small grin. "What are you offering?"

"Serve me. Give up whatever it is you're trying to do and join my crew. There's always room for more of me."

Evan paused. Then he shook his head.

"That *is* tempting. It is. I can't do it, though. For two chief reasons."

"What are they?" she asked.

"Well, for starters, once you see what I've done, you'll never forgive me."

"Wooo, that sounds ominous," she sneered.

"Yeah. And the second is just an obvious fact for those like us."

"Which is?"

"An Emperor bows to no one, Everly. What he wants, he takes. And I want what you have. That's all there is to it."

And with that, he left her.

As far as these things went, Everly thought that was a pretty good parting line.

CHAPTER THIRTY-FOUR

Virtue

One week ago.

Her sister needed her.

That was the thought that ran relentlessly throughout Fenneth's mind, driving her to act and fueling an endless amount of anxiety that threatened to crush her fragile heart beneath its weight.

She had to be there for Laurel.

She had to *save* Laurel.

No, that was wrong. That was completely incorrect.

She had to save her sister so she could *apologize* to her.

The last time she'd ever spoken to Laurel, she'd lashed out at her out of a frustrated sense of entitlement. She'd blamed Laurel for leaving her behind to seek freedom, forcing Fenneth to take on her sister's discarded role. To become the new maiden of the holy blade.

That had been completely unfair of her. Laurel was a kind woman who'd sacrificed her personal happiness for years due to her powerful sense of responsibility. Her commitment to her duty. She'd suffered far more than Fenneth ever had, and yet Fenneth had refused to see things from her perspective and instead driven her away on what had turned out to be the last day they'd ever see each other.

Why had she done that? Why hadn't she tried to reconcile with her as soon as she'd returned to life? Why had she let herself be distracted by her grievances with Everly and her own selfish urge to play and relax when she knew the harm that Everly was causing?

Why was she such a terrible person?

She and James stood hidden behind the cover of trees outside an old, nondescript-looking estate that had been built on the outskirts of the capital. Here was where her companion claimed Everly kept her most valuable prisoners away from the sight and sympathy of the public. This was the place where Laurel awaited her.

I'm coming, sister. I promise I won't let you down this time, she vowed.

Beneath the mail armor that James provided for her, Fenneth could feel nervous sweat trickling down her body as she impatiently waited to act. What had they been doing to the people in there? Probably torturing them. Taunting them. Breaking their wills through degradation and violence to force them into compliance with the new regime.

Anything was possible in this awful new world.

Anything.

The floor had yet to be discovered when it came to the question of how low Everly could sink.

"James, I'm sorry," she suddenly decided. "I can't wait any longer."

"Huh?" he asked in surprise. "Uh, what?"

"I said I'm not waiting anymore," she said as she unsheathed the sword he'd given her. "Laurel needs me. I'm not going to let her waste away in that place for another moment."

"But, Lady Fenneth, didn't we decide to wait until nightfall? So that we could have the element of surprise?"

"I refuse," she said. "I will not sneak through the dark in order to see justice done. Like my sister before me, I will conduct myself with honor and courage. Let any who dare oppose me do so in the light of day."

"Lady Fenneth!" James shouted as Fenneth began marching directly toward the manor, weapon in hand. "Lady Fenneth!" he repeated. But she ignored his cries, determined as she was to see Laurel again.

It didn't take long for her opposition to reveal itself.

"Hey. Hey!" yelled one of the men dressed in the black armor of Everly's followers. "Put that weapon away and identify yourself at once. State your name and your business!"

Fenneth ignored him and continued walking closer to the entrance, which displeased the guard, who cursed loudly and trotted after her to catch up.

"Hey, I *said* to identify yourself," he said in a harder tone of voice as he attempted to grab her arm to halt her. "Are you listening to me—"

His words were cut off immediately when Fenneth spun and swung her sword.

As was his head.

After his body collapsed, Fenneth spared a single moment to look at what she'd done. She regretted it immediately. In her brief career as the holy maiden, she'd successfully exorcised a handful of demons and slain a few monsters as well. But this was the first time she'd ever killed a fellow human being.

Her heart ached at the sight of his ruined body.

He was a child once, she thought. *A baby. He was blind, ignorant, and afraid, and the only thing he could do was instinctively seek the safety of his mother's embrace. He cried, and laughed, and played. Then he grew into adulthood and now I have killed him. All his possibilities are gone forever, all because of me and my sword.*

I'm so sorry.

Crying now, she resumed her march as dozens of black-armored warriors came pouring out of the estate, shouting at her to toss aside her weapon and surrender. Instead of obeying, she gripped it tighter and ran forth to meet them.

"Arrrghh!" screamed one as the edge of her sword took his eyes. As he sank to his knees, sobbing in pain as blood and viscous fluids leaked from his maimed eye sockets, Fenneth lashed out with a fist and crushed his throat.

A forward-thrusting kick was delivered with enough power to smash another man's spine entirely, killing him where he stood.

A lower, wide swing separated another man's legs from his body at the knees, leaving him to wail miserably as he tried to stop the bleeding. His cries were silenced when Fenneth brought her boot down on his head and smeared it into the grass at her feet.

Each blow she delivered was done with killing intent. But none of them possessed anger. What she did was done out of a tortured need to save others. The feelings of horror and remorse that she now drowned in—these were the reasons she had never wanted to become a warrior.

Not because she feared battle.

But because she knew she'd be too good at it. Better than anyone else at a profession that revolted her to her very core. That filled her with shame and self-hatred.

Fenneth had always wanted to save lives. To preserve them. To bring healing and peace. She wanted to give selflessly of herself to others; she wanted to believe that life was a sacred gift and that people could learn to accept and trust each other.

She wanted to mend divisions. Not to rend flesh.

But here she was. A bull on parade, covered in the blood of those who couldn't defend themselves from her onslaught. No different from monsters like her cousin Sarah, or even worse . . .

. . . *Everly.*

More warriors ran to oppose her. More suffered and died. More lives were trampled beneath her feet as she sought her goal.

This is for my sister, she sobbed. And she killed.
This is for my sister, she sobbed. And she killed.
This is for my sister, she sobbed. And she killed.
This is for my sister, she sobbed . . .
And sobbed . . .

In the midst of Fenneth's rampage, Discordia tried to calm her mistress. Tried to soothe her fraying spirit, to let her know that she was still a good person despite what she was doing. But most importantly, she tried to urge her to *stop*.

These actions were against everything that made Fenneth who she was. Even in the name of saving Lady Laurel and reuniting with her, it wouldn't be worth it if she had to stain herself with blood to do it.

It was no mark against her character to say that. Not everyone was suited for the ravages of battle. Fenneth cared for others too much. She was a gentle soul not meant for the ugly realities of this life. She simply couldn't take lives and remain herself.

This would have been obvious for anyone who truly knew her.

Discordia *had* to stop her. She simply had to.

But it was impossible.

Something prevented her words from reaching Fenneth's mind.

Her mistress couldn't hear her.

Lady Fenneth, please stop! Discordia tried to say. *Lady Fenneth, I'm begging you, please don't do this anymore! This isn't what you want! This isn't who you are!*

But despite her pleading, Discordia's words fell on deaf ears. Fenneth continued to fight, and her opponents continued to die, and no one knew how much her lady suffered for her victories, except her terrified elemental.

"I have to do this," Fenneth began whispering. "I have to do this."

Fenneth, why won't you listen to me? asked the desperate Discordia.

Behind them walked James. Discordia saw with some surprise that he'd removed his helmet and was quietly watching Fenneth. He offered no assistance nor words of encouragement. He simply stared blankly as she killed and walked silently behind her as she preceded him throughout the building.

Was he struck silent by the ease with which her mistress killed? Had terror muted his voice?

No. That wasn't the case at all. The expression on his face was faint, but Discordia soon recognized it. It was *expectation*.

He'd expected this to happen! He'd known how Fenneth would react!

But if that was so, then why?

Why was he letting her destroy herself like this?

What was going on?

That was when Discordia realized that some of the black knights were now attempting to avoid Fenneth entirely. Instead, they ran directly to James and began begging him to make her stop. They approached him without fear even though he was supposedly an enemy combatant.

They knew him.

They knew him!

Fenneth, please! Please! I'm begging you to stop, cried Discordia. *Can't you see? He's betrayed you! This is a trap! Fenneth, use your eyes! Fenneth, please hear me!*

But Fenneth would not, *could not* respond. Instead, she killed the knights who pleaded with James. Although he wore a pained expression of regret, Discordia could see his eyes. His gaze held no true emotion. These poor fools had trusted him, and he was discarding them without an ounce of regret.

This was *his* scheme.

Gods blight your damned soul, you treacherous bastard, Discordia hissed hatefully at him. *May you receive what you have delivered, ten times tenfold, while knowing you deserve worse!*

"Discordia," James said. "The only thing I deserve is peace and happiness."

The elemental couldn't believe what she'd heard. He could speak to her? He could hear her words? That was impossible! Only a speaker could commune with an elemental. A speaker like Lady Fenneth or Everly.

Who was this man?

"Someone who was wronged," he said. "Someone who is fighting for his place in this world. Someone who *will* have what he is due. Now stay quiet, please. If you really love Fenneth, then you'll stay with her until the end."

The end? Discordia asked him. What did that mean? What was he talking about? Whose end? What was about to happen?

Ahead of them ran Fenneth down a long series of hallways, kicking open each door that she passed and staring inside.

Each room contained a single occupant.

All of whom thus far had been dead.

Every single one of them.

"*LAUREL!*" screamed Fenneth as the panic truly began to set in.

No, no, no, no, Discordia wept as she struggled to keep pace with her.

Behind them, the Ashen Knight clasped his hands together as if in prayer and followed behind them. "I did nothing wrong here. I did nothing wrong here. I did nothing wrong here," he murmured to himself as he walked past the remnants of those who'd believed his lies.

None of them had believed those lies as fervently as he had.

He never doubted himself.

"I did nothing wrong here," he continued with grace and humility.

There at the final door, Fenneth found her.

Laurel looked so peaceful. As though she were sleeping and at any moment might pop awake and playfully tousle Fenneth's hair like she did when Fenneth was a child.

What did it mean to have a sister like Laurel? Someone who was brave and compassionate. Someone who followed her duty but also believed in the strength of her own heart. Someone who loved and was loved, and above all other things, someone who encouraged others to believe in the possibility of a better world.

It meant a lot.

It really meant a lot.

The moment she saw her sister lying on the floor of this darkened cell, something broke inside Fenneth. Something disconnected itself from her and floated away. Something precious that would never return.

It was her fault.

It was all her fault.

She was the one who'd left Everly. Who'd defied her. Who mocked her.

And how had Everly responded?

She'd taken away Laurel.

Forever.

"I'm sorry," Fenneth said in an empty, broken voice as she hugged the body. "I'm sorry. I'm sorry. I did this. I caused this. I made her mad and she did this to you. I'm sorry, Laurel. I love you, Laurel. I'm sorry Laurel. I love you, Laurel."

"Liar," said a cruel voice.

Fenneth looked up blankly and stared at James as he entered the cell.

"James," Fenneth said, lost, dazed, shattered. A child in a woman's body, trying to prove her sincerity. "James, I didn't lie. James, I'm so sorry."

"Liar," he repeated. "Murderer."

"I didn't want this," she said pitifully.

"You let it happen," he said. "You wanted it to happen. You're *grateful* that it happened."

"I'm not," she said, shaking her head ferociously. "No, I'm not. I'm not. I'm not I'm not I'm not."

"Everly kept her here for so long. Starving her. Hurting her. Telling her it was because you wouldn't let her love you," he said coldly. "Why did you do that, Fenn? Why couldn't you just accept what you were given? Did you think you were better than her?"

"Noooo," she said in the miserable whine of a frightened child.

"Yes, you did," he said. "Look at how easily you killed all those men. *Slaughtered* them, really. Easy peasy for Lady Fenn. You could have saved Laurel whenever you wanted. But you didn't. Because this is what you wanted to happen. MURDERER."

"Noooo," she wept.

"Yes," he said again as he knelt and hugged her.

"I'm sorry," she cried.

"I believe you," he said as he stroked her hair.

"I didn't want this to happen."

"Maybe you didn't," he said.

"I'd do anything to make this right," she said.

"*Anything?*" he asked her.

"I just want this pain to stop," she whispered.

James took her hands and stared at her for a time. Then he gently said, "Do you really mean that, Fenn?"

With dazed, honest eyes, and a mind clouded with pain and grief, Fenneth nodded.

"I can help you with that, Fenn. I can make it all go away. But you have to do as I say, first. Exactly as I say. Can you do that?" he asked her softly.

"Please make it stop," she wept.

"Fenn," James said quietly. "Listen to me carefully. Can you do that?"

"Yes." She nodded.

"Fenneth, I want you to repeat after me. I want you to say *status*."

"Status," said Fenneth.

"Good," James said. "Fenneth, I want you to put your hand on the screen that you're seeing right now. Put your hand right above it, okay? Are you doing it right now?"

"Yes," said Fenneth as she held her hand out over an object that only she could see. "I see it. I'm doing it. What do I do next?"

"Fenneth," he continued, "I want you to close your eyes tightly, and I want you to think these two words. Say them in your mind as forcefully as you can, and this will all go away. I promise it will. Are you ready?"

"I'm ready," she whimpered.

After a moment's pause, he said, "Say *delete character*."

Fenneth whispered those words and repeated them in her mind.

A moment later, she collapsed. And the air was filled with Discordia's helpless wailing.

The Ashen Knight caught Fenn's body as it collapsed and gently held her in his arms. She was now lifeless. An empty vessel. Not even a spirit in the afterlife.

Gone.

Deleted.

"Goodbye, Fenneth," he said.

Next, he said, "It's done."

A wave of light crashed into the room, engulfing them both in its brilliance before being absorbed by Fenneth's body. A moment after it faded, she opened her eyes and sat up.

She gazed upon the night and smiled warmly. Her eyes had become a radiant hue of blue that nothing human could possibly possess. When she spoke, the reverberations of her voice could be felt in a person's soul.

When Fenneth stood up, she floated. Her feet would no longer touch the base earth.

Before her, the Ashen Knight knelt.

"Your sacrifice has been received," said the Hymn of Absolute Virtue.

"It was for the greater good," he whispered.

"The *greatest* possible good," she agreed.

"Can this world be saved?" he asked her.

"I am here. Of course it will be," she informed him.

"Then I've committed no sin," he said with a lighter heart.

The Hymn said nothing in reply.

About the Author

J. V. Simms was the author of the Empress and My Eyes Glow Red series, originally released on Royal Road. When he wasn't writing, he spent his time avoiding his cat, who was likely seeking vengeance for her most recent trip to the vet. Simms lived in Indiana and was always better than his nephew at Minecraft. That's in writing so it must be true.